Readers love the Marshals series by MARY CALMES

All Kinds of Tied Down

"This book is classic Mary Calmes, from the characters that are easily lovable down to the quick and witty banter."

—Joyfully Jay

"…a lot of laughs, some serious hotness, wrapped around action/adventure and an incredible story."

—Rainbow Book Reviews

"I want to dive right in and read it again, immediately!"

—Hearts on Fire Reviews

Fit to Be Tied

"Mary Calmes takes us on a fast-paced, action-packed ride that will have you holding onto to the edge of your seat. You will be so wrapped up in the drama you will forget to breathe."

—MM Good Book Reviews

"All in all, this book was better than the first and possibly one of the best layered stories written by Queen Calmes."

—Boys in Our Books

"True to Mary Calmes' style, she takes you on an adventure, ensuring plenty of laughs along the way."

—Under the Cover Book Blog

By MARY CALMES

Acrobat
Again
Any Closer
With Cardeno C.: Control
With Poppy Dennison: Creature
Feature
Floodgates
Frog
Grand Adventures (Dreamspinner
Anthology)
The Guardian
Heart of the Race
Ice Around the Edges
Judgment
Just Desserts
Lay It Down
Mine
Romanus • Chevalier
Romanus & Chevalier (Author
Anthology, Paperback Only)
The Servant
Steamroller
Still
Tales of the Curious Cookbook
(Multiple Author Anthology)
Three Fates (Multiple Author
Anthology)
Timing • After the Sunset
What Can Be
Where You Lead
Wishing on a Blue Star
(Dreamspinner Anthology)

CHANGE OF HEART
Change of Heart

Trusted Bond
Honored Vow
Crucible of Fate
Forging the Future
L'ANGE
Old Loyalty, New Love
Fighting Instinct

MANGROVE STORIES
Blue Days
Quiet Nights
Sultry Sunset
Easy Evenings
Sleeping 'til Sunrise

MARSHALS
All Kinds of Tied Down
Fit to Be Tied
Tied Up in Knots

A MATTER OF TIME
A Matter of Time: Vol. 1
A Matter of Time: Vol. 2
Bulletproof
But For You
Parting Shot
Piece of Cake

THE WARDER SERIES
His Hearth
Tooth & Nail
Heart in Hand
Sinnerman • Nexus
Cherish Your Name
Warders Vol. 1 & 2

Published by
DREAMSPINNER PRESS
www.dreamspinnerpress.com

TIED UP IN KNOTS

Mary Calmes

DREAMSPINNER
PRESS

Published by

DREAMSPINNER PRESS

5032 Capital Circle SW, Suite 2, PMB# 279, Tallahassee, FL 32305-7886 USA
www.dreamspinnerpress.com

Tied Up in Knots
© 2016 Mary Calmes.

Cover Art
© 2016 Reese Dante.
http://www.reesedante.com
Cover content is for illustrative purposes only and any person depicted on the cover is a model.

ISBN: 978-1-63477-754-4
Digital ISBN: 978-1-63477-755-1
Library of Congress Control Number: 2016911387
Published September 2016
v. 1.0

Printed in the United States of America

This paper meets the requirements of
ANSI/NISO Z39.48-1992 (Permanence of Paper).

My sincerest thanks to:
Lynn West, who makes everything I do so much better.
Rhys Ford, I always know you're on my side.
Lisa Horan, without the safety net you keep ready, I'd be in real trouble.
And Captain West, without your expertise,
I'd be a lost ball in the tall grass.

CHAPTER 1

IF I lived, I was going to make sure by whatever means necessary that I'd never be loaned out to the DEA again.

If this were a normal assignment, I'd have been following my partner, Ian Doyle, as he ran like a madman after our suspect. But this time, I was hotly pursuing a police officer I met a week ago who was a few feet in front of me, careening around corners after a fleeing DEA agent. If we didn't catch him before he locked himself into a bolt-hole, the cop and I were probably dead men. We didn't know how far his dirty fingers reached or which member of his team he'd gotten to smear their badge.

I hated those prima donna DEA assholes to begin with, and normally it wouldn't even be an issue, but my boss, Chief Deputy US Marshal Sam Kage, was on vacation, and the nozzle covering for him disregarded Kage's golden rule on interdepartmental sharing. Basically, unless we, the marshals, were running the op, his team didn't come out to play. It first went into effect when I was almost killed on a bust run by the bureau. I had no idea how he got away with it, but his word was law, and he didn't want any of us put into danger by members of a team we were working with. The "no sharing clause" was ironclad.

The problem was that Phillip "Call me Phil, there, buddy" Tull was all about grandstanding and kudos from the mayor and public relations wet dreams. Since the highest-profile cases involved drugs… he loaned us out almost immediately. I was the only one who ended up having to fly to the West Coast; everyone else got assigned much closer to home.

"I fuckin' hate Wisconsin," Becker had griped as he grabbed PowerBars out of his desk before he left with Ching to drive to Green Bay.

"At least you're not going to Maine!" Ryan yelled, and Dorsey gave me a grimace of agreement as they left together.

I was the only one going alone because Ian, my partner slash lover slash best friend and maybe fiancé—hard to say how he felt about that word—was deployed, along with the rest of his Special Forces team, and not running for his life with me. If I died on this job, Phillip "Call me Phil, there, buddy" Tull, who also made finger guns whenever he said that, would be fed to our dog, balls first. Nobody wanted to mess with Ian Doyle, especially not where I was concerned. He was slightly possessive.

IT WAS funny, really. I'd been loaned out to the DEA to dig up their dirt, but the op had changed when a guy with hard blue eyes and an even harder handsome face walked into Broken Record on Geneva as I was having an after-hours snack of lobster mac 'n' cheese at the bar. I had a lot of late nights when Ian wasn't around because when he wasn't, I didn't sleep. I could have taken something, but that was a slippery slope I never wanted to start down. So I was there, and the cop came close—he was obviously on the job, no mistaking the strut—and took a seat beside me. I was all set to make some small talk in greeting to a fellow badge when he picked up a fork from the place setting in front of him on the counter and helped himself to a mouthful of my food.

I turned my chin and looked at him, and he said the magic words through a mouthful of cheesy goodness. "Eli Kohn says I can trust you."

Since the guy he just mentioned was a fellow marshal in Chicago who transferred from the San Francisco office, and since I trusted said man with my life, I waited to see what else the stranger had to say. Using Kohn's name to parley with was smart. It held a lot of weight with me. I needed to hear him out.

"I'm listening."

"Senior Inspector Kane Morgan, SFPD." He showed me a gold badge that'd taken a few hits in its lifetime, but he looked like the kind of guy who'd wear those dings and scratches proudly.

I didn't have to flash my badge. He'd come looking for me, and oddly enough, in a city of millions, found me easily, but I did him the courtesy of introducing myself. "Deputy US Marshal Miro Jones."

"Oh, I know. See, I have a problem, boyo, and you're right in the middle of it." There was Irish in his words, a roiling reminder of dark beer and black-hearted men.

It was never good to hear you were at the center of someone else's shitstorm, and what the hell was it with me and Irishmen, anyway? Couldn't get away from them.

"And what's your problem?" I asked, because there was no way I couldn't after we bonded over Kohn and mac 'n' cheese.

"A DEA agent you're working with is moving more drugs than a Colombian cartel."

It was an overstatement, of course, but it made his intention clear. "No," I groaned.

"Yes," Morgan said almost cheerfully. "Goes by the name Sandell."

"No, no." It was getting worse, not better.

He gave me a quick nod with an accompanying grin.

Godfuckingdammit.

No one wanted to hear a DEA guy was dirty—even though in my experience most of them were—but I especially didn't want to hear that it was the one guy I was in town to work with. When Sandell had met me at the airport with a couple of his men, I'd thought he was okay, ordinary, not a thing remotely interesting about the man. Nothing he'd done or said had tripped any alarms in me or put me on edge. But apparently my instincts were for shit if Morgan was to be believed, and really, it was obvious I should.

"And the worst part is," he continued, still eating my food. Clearly the man had skipped dinner. "I have a string of dead girls his men used as mules, but I just need a bit more evidence to connect the dots so we can take him down."

He was already saying "we."

Jesus.

I turned my head to appraise the man sitting beside me. With the glossy jet-black hair and blue eyes, I bet he had lots of men and women doing whatever he needed or wanted. But I was both very taken and very much by the book.

"Sounds like you need my help."

"What do you think I'm doing here? I mean, the mac 'n' cheese is good and your company is charming, but come on."

I ignored the last bit. "Is there someone local here you can tag? In the DEA? Do you know anyone besides him?"

No response, but it was hard to tell if he was hungry or thinking.

"I'm just in for a quick op," I explained. "So unfortunately I don't know all the players. I mean, his whole team could be dirty, and I couldn't tell you a damned thing unless they were holding a kilo of coke in their hands."

He cleared his throat. "Let me tell you about my local DEA contact, Alex, and the shit he's been handed."

Clearly he'd been thinking about a response and was hungry to boot.

I listened as he told me about a buddy of his, Alex Brandt, laid up in a nearby hospital and fighting for his life because he'd been hit enough times to actually be classified as a piñata.

Brandt had been tracking product while Morgan was looking into a string of drug mule murders when their investigations crossed paths. Already friends, they shared information instead of doing the usual posturing and figured out someone in Brandt's office was ten kinds of dirty.

Once Brandt turned up tenderized nearly to death, Morgan was pretty sure he knew who it was. At that point he didn't have jurisdiction or clout, and once his unofficial partner went to the hospital, he was left swinging in the wind, not knowing who he could trust. So Morgan reached out to Kohn, whom he knew from before he transferred, who in turn handed him my name.

That was seven days ago.

After lots of skulking around the office, some easy hacking, and help from Brandt's best friend, Cord Nolan—a private investigator—to break into Sandell's house, Morgan and I found the go-to guy. So we started Thursday there, traipsing up six flights of stairs to an office where we hoped we could convince Tommy Hein, money launderer, that turning on Sandell was in his best interests. Halfway up Morgan passed me an earpiece.

"What is this for?"

"What do you think?"

He was a smartass just like Ian—that's what I thought.

"Stop for a second and I'll pair it to your phone. We'll keep a line open between us for in case we get separated, I can guide you back in. Especially since you've no idea where you're going and this part of town is like a damned maze."

He was right; I knew nothing about San Francisco. I took it and hooked it over my ear. "I feel like a real douche with this on." I hated being in line for coffee somewhere and thinking people were talking to me, only to turn around and get a look like I was a leper—that sneer of contempt—because they were talking to the person in their ear.

His inelegant snort made me smile. "Yeah, well, you'll be thanking me if you end up standing in a back alley smelling of piss and cabbage and can't find your way out."

There was that.

He got us connected as we closed on the office. Once at the door, I went to knock, but Morgan raised a hand to stop me.

"Better way of doing this, Jones." And he kicked it down.

"Really?" I said drolly. Why? When had subtlety become *not* a thing in police work?

"It's called element of surprise," he assured me.

Jesus, could he be any more like Ian?

Morgan flashed his badge and had his hand on his gun. "SFPD, Hein. Put your hands where we can see them."

"You can't come in here!" Hein bellowed from behind his desk. He was shoving papers into drawers. "You can't—"

"He can, he's with me. Federal marshal," I announced, following Morgan's badge with my star and watching as Morgan's grin in all its wicked glory spread across his chiseled features. That was what shit-eating looked like.

"Fuck," Hein groaned.

"Hands away from the computer," Morgan ordered.

According to what Hein was trying to hide, Sandell had offshore accounts, some in the Caymans and even some Swiss. Everything about Sandell and his operations, including a conversation about taking out Brandt and Morgan, was right there in front of us on files small enough to fit on my phone.

Just as the final file hit my memory card, Sandell came through the doorway of the office with a duffel bag. "I've got some cash you need to drop, Hein," he said, stepping through the broken door, apparently just noticing its appearance. "What the hell hap—"

He stopped short, his eyes frozen on Hein sitting on the floor with PlastiCuffs on his ankles and his hands zipped behind his back. One blink and Sandell bolted back out into the hallway, lugging the duffel with him.

I got that he didn't want to ditch whatever was in there, and when I reached the sidewalk, I understood why.

Money was flying everywhere, drawing a small crowd of people between us and a fleeing Sandell. He had cash in the bag—quite a bit, by the look of it—and now he was letting the bills loose on the breeze, and having them flutter all over the street was a great diversionary tactic that would slow us down considerably.

"Jones, I'm going to switch over to dispatch," Morgan said, breaking past the crowd. "Try to keep up. Dispatch, do you read me?"

And we started to run.

We had to leave the sidewalk, which became too clogged with people trying to get ahold of the cash floating in the sunshine. It was a madhouse.

"Fuck," Morgan swore, a resigned tone to his growl. "Dispatch, do you have my position? Need backup. Tenderloin. Suspect is on foot. Heading towards Taylor. Carrying a black duffel and—"

I knew we'd hoped to keep things quiet, but it had just blown up. There was no way Sandell was going to simply stop running and turn himself in, and he was probably calling for reinforcements himself. So Morgan was making sure we weren't alone, waiting to get picked off.

"—going to intercept," he continued, because that told dispatch we were moving, not waiting on anyone to breach or take a suspect, instead already engaged. He was hearing the whole unit's advised talk-track, and he was answering questions about where we were, giving them coordinates as he ran so that everyone was in sync. Because neither he nor I was in uniform, and we didn't want to get shot by accident.

"Suspect is armed," Morgan confirmed.

More money lay scattered on the concrete, a trail of green crumbs for us to follow, and Morgan took the corner in a sharp leap.

As we charged across Eddy Street in the Tenderloin, I had a moment to appreciate the ridiculousness of my situation as Morgan slid over the hood of a car *Dukes of Hazzard*–style and kept running, never slowing, never losing concentration, nothing. Ian was fond of that maneuver; I, on the other hand, had never been a fan.

"We could go around!" I yelled, swerving to miss the parked Lexus. "There's no problem with missing the goddamn car!"

Morgan ran on, which was impressive considering how long we'd been at it—at least ten minutes running flat out at full speed—and he'd gone down six flights of fire escapes while I took the stairwell inside Hein's building. Normally Ian and I switched it up, but clearly Morgan was used to being the alpha doing all the high-wire work.

A bullet hit a car window, shattering it, and he shouted, "Watch your back." I ran by, and another made a divot in the brick wall in front of me.

"Somebody's shooting at us," I cautioned.

"No shit," he thundered. "Keep moving. Harder to hit."

Even though I was grateful for the laws of physics, we couldn't keep hoping our luck would hold.

I wove as I ran, yelling, "We need to get off the main street."

"Tell him, not me."

Barreling around the corner onto Taylor heading north toward Ellis—I only knew that because Morgan was giving a running commentary on our location to dispatch—Sandell darted through the intersection, only to be cut off by a cherry-red Trans Am. He couldn't stop—he was running too fast, flat out, and he ended up sprawled halfway across the hood. Morgan pulled up, allowing me to finally catch up with him, and I stood there at his side, panting, then bent over and trying not to hurl as I heard other cars come to screeching halts close to us.

"We might be a bit screwed here," Morgan confessed under his breath.

"Follow my lead," I ordered as I straightened.

"Freeze!" The guy in the Trans Am came out with a gun, yelling at me and Morgan. Clearly Sandell's backup had arrived.

Lifting my head, I saw Sandell leaning on the car, trying to catch his breath while two SUVs emptied. Using their vehicles as barricades, they drew down on us.

"Federal marshals," I roared in response, including Morgan, pulling my gun and aiming it at Sandell, letting all his men know, in case they didn't, that they were messing with people above their pay grade. A lot of corrupt cops never let their underlings in on who they were actually shooting at. I was hoping the shock factor would work in our favor. "You need to drop your weapons and get on the ground!"

Doing as I asked and backing me up, Morgan had already pulled his Glock and aimed it at the dirty DEA agent we'd been trailing. It was impressive, really, that he was standing with me. It was his clusterfuck to begin with, but still, the man had some big-ass balls. Surrounded, outmanned, outgunned, he refused to back down and hadn't left me hanging. Hopefully we'd both live long enough so I could return the favor.

"You need to stand down, marshal," Sandell roared, having pulled his gun to join all the others.

"It's you who needs to stand the fuck down," Morgan retorted. The boom of his voice must have startled Sandell because his trigger finger was shaking. Morgan's, on the other hand, held steady. He reminded me a lot of Ian—he was a rock under pressure as well—and at the moment, that was so very comforting.

No one moved. It was like time held its breath, but after several long moments, I glanced at Sandell and saw his smirk.

"You're making career-altering decisions here, gentlemen," Sandell insisted, and I realized fast there would be no time for us to be screwed over, demoted, or whatever else because he was going to murder us right there in the street and take any evidence off us and no one but his team would be the wiser.

"On the ground, all of you!" Morgan insisted, not backing down an iota. We were in the right, and it appeared that no matter what the consequence, he would follow through.

I felt like I should have been scared, but I was more worried about Morgan.

"They're dirty cops! Take them down!" Sandell shouted. "I've got the evidence right—"

I tensed for a bullet's impact, but a foghorn siren blast caught everyone's attention at the same time. It was not the normal one from a police car, but instead came as a low *brrp-brrp* from a massive black ARV with a golden eagle emblem on its sides and windows so black they ate the light. After rolling to a shuddering stop, the ARV's back doors exploded and a SWAT team deployed in a solid stream of enormous, angry-looking men. Even as happy as I was to be rescued, something about the men in full-body armor pointing their automatic weapons in my direction was disquieting.

"Drop your weapons and get down," barked a mountain with lieutenant bars on his black vest. "Now."

It was funny how fast a SWAT team could make a dirty cop and his crew toss aside their guns and kiss the asphalt. No one on the ground moved or even breathed. I sure as hell wasn't going to go facedown, and from the looks of it, neither was Morgan. He simply holstered his gun, put his hands on his hips, and sighed with clear disgust.

The SWAT team moved in to take custody, everyone except for the lieutenant. He approached and the team parted like the sea did for Moses. There was no question of moving. His rank was in every rippling muscle, the swagger of his walk, and simply the sheer size of him. His shoulders alone were enough to get me to back down from a challenge.

After reaching us, he took off his helmet and aviators, then flashed me an improbable grin before he put his hand on Morgan's shoulder.

"So," the lieutenant said with a snort of warm laughter. "You called for backup."

I was reeling. We'd just been saved by the Terminator, who was very obviously giving Morgan shit. What the hell was going on?

"What the fuck are you doing here?" Morgan groused, gesturing around at all the armor-clad men. "I called for backup, not the Mongol horde."

"We were the closest to your twenty, and hell, you nearly gave dispatch a heart attack with you needing help," the lieutenant said with an eyebrow waggle. "You never call for backup; they thought there was a riot."

Morgan shook his head, seemingly annoyed even with what I thought to be a reasonable explanation. I'd have seen it then, even if I'd missed the similar black hair, shorter but the same jet color, and the sinful glint in the deep-blue eyes, and the name Morgan stitched on the TAC vest.

"You should introduce me. You were raised better than that."

Morgan growled in response, the irritation rolling off him as he gestured at me with a tip of his head. "This is Deputy US Marshal Miro Jones, who's been my new partner for the week. Jones, this asshole is my older brother, Lieutenant Connor Morgan."

"SWAT, huh?" I said, holstering my Glock.

"Con's always had to be the one with the biggest dick. Or *be* the biggest dick. I get that all confused," Morgan replied sarcastically. "Because getting a gun and a badge wasn't good enough, he wanted a tank and a battering ram too."

"I know the type." I had a Green Beret of my own who was of a similar disposition.

Connor's guys were bagging up the guns on the asphalt and zip-tying everyone. People just didn't fuck around with SWAT. If they were on-site, no questions asked, they could just kill somebody. Everybody knew that, even dirty-as-hell pieces of crap who worked for the DEA. The clean ones knew they'd be shaken loose, but the ones on the take knew they didn't have a chance in hell of walking away.

"Hey," Morgan said, taking hold of Connor's bicep. "Let's not mention this to Miki, okay?"

Connor guffawed. "Then I suggest you and the marshal get the hell out of here because dispatch just told us Dad's on his way."

"Shit, that'll bring the vultures and their cameras," Morgan grumbled, glancing around. "I'll meet you at the precinct." Connor nodded and Morgan reached out for his hand, and Connor clasped it tight for a second.

"Thanks, Con."

"Always," his brother murmured, and I heard the depth of the feeling in the singular word.

As I followed Morgan, walking briskly down the street, dodging the people rushing toward the action we were trying to ditch, I had a question.

"Your dad?"

He grunted.

"Speak."

Heavy sigh. "He's a captain, and we're about on the edge of this territory."

Okay, two questions. "Lots of cops in your family?"

"You have no idea. We're up to five at last count. We've got one who's a fireman because, well, he's shite with a gun, and one who's a professor. History and whatnot at the college. Baby sister hasn't decided yet. She'd do it if she could wear heels with her rookie uniform."

"Who's Mickey? Like the mouse? Wife? Girlfriend?"

"It's Miki, no E or Y, and he's my boyfriend."

"Got it."

I must have sounded odd after my near-death experience, because even though he snorted out a laugh, there was an edge to his voice when he spoke. "Problem?"

"Oh fuck no," I assured him. "I was just being nosy."

His laugh turned warm.

"Thank you for saving my life."

"That was my brother that did that."

"No, it was you."

He shrugged. "Thank you for believing me. It would have been just as easy to trust Sandell."

"I have a good track record with Irishmen," I teased.

"Do you, now?"

I shot him a grin.

ONCE AT the precinct, Morgan downloaded the files from my phone while we watched through the glass windows as Koegle, Sandell's superior, screamed at Morgan's boss, Lieutenant Casey.

Koegle was turning red. Casey looked bored.

"Your boss is cool under pressure, huh?"

Morgan just scoffed. Clearly this kind of thing happened to Casey a lot. When we'd first walked into the area right outside his office, the DEA head was apparently lying in wait because he came roaring out and right up to us.

"You had no warrant, Morgan! How the hell did you even—"

"Sir," I said softly.

"You think you can just—"

"Sir." I got louder, even adding a cough.

"—barge into a—"

"Sir," I barked, and when he turned in a huff, clearly irritated, I lifted my badge for him to see. "Deputy US Marshal Miro Jones out of the Chicago office," I explained. "I was here on temporary assignment with the Northern District here, and—"

"I don't give a damn who you think—"

"Step back," a voice had called out.

Fun was everyone swiveling around to see the very tall, very elegantly dressed man in a topcoat and dark navy pinstripe suit with brown buttons and a red pocket square come striding into the bullpen, flanked by four other men. He was handsome—as I'd thought when I first met him when I got into town— imposing like my boss, his skin a deep rich umber, his teak-colored eyes taking in the room in one glance just like Kage always did. It wasn't protocol to meet the higher-ups when one got to town, but Vance and Kage were friends, so I'd been directed to pay my respects.

"Who the hell are—"

"Supervisory Deputy Xavier Vance," he announced, stepping around Sandell's boss to reach me.

I took the offered hand and he clapped me on the shoulder.

"You good, Jones?"

"Yessir."

"Excellent," he said in a low baritone. "Kage wants you on a plane tonight."

"Yessir," I said, smiling. "He must be back."

"It's why I got a call."

"Yessir."

He turned to Morgan and extended his hand. "I need to see your boss."

After shaking, Morgan said, "He's right over there," gesturing toward the glass-walled office at his lieutenant with the same tip of his head from earlier. "Name's Casey."

They all went in the office—Vance and the other marshals—and I had seen the DEA guy lose his fucking mind once the door closed. Casey and Vance looked bored as Koegle screamed on.

Now, back in the present, there was still yelling going on but both the only one raising his voice was Vance. I also noted that all his ire was directed at the DEA supervisor.

"It's not bad, you know," I said, turning from the scene inside the office back to Morgan.

"What's that?" he asked.

"Having a supervisory deputy for a friend," I told him. "Vance is a good guy, and now he owes you."

"Owes me?"

"For saving my life."

"Well, you helped me and Brandt."

"How's he doing, anyway?"

"He's good. If I ever get out of here, I'll go see him on my way home."

"To your Miki."

"Yeah, to my Miki."

"Who'll kill you if he finds out you almost died today, right?"

"Ye have no idea. He'd have my balls, he would."

The accent was a surprise, but I was guessing it came out when the man was agitated or when he was emotional, which he was at the moment. "Maybe he won't find out."

"He had a session today, so hopefully not."

"Session?"

"Recording."

"Oh, he's a what—a musician?"

Morgan nodded.

"Is he famous around here?"

"And other places as well."

"Oh yeah? Think I've heard of him?"

"Maybe." Morgan's grin was sly. "Miki St. John."

I knew that name. "He fronts a rock band, yeah?"

Morgan gave me the full wattage of his smile, clearly pleased.

I winced. "I'm more a blues guy, Ian's the rocker."

"Ian?"

We hadn't discussed much beyond the case during our short time together, which was why I was just learning about his rock star and he was only now hearing Ian's name. "My"—the label was still a weird thing—"partner," I went with. It wasn't completely correct, but it wasn't wrong, either. "You'd like him; he's a lot like you. I'm sure you guys'd get into all kinds of trouble together."

"What you call trouble I call good police work."

"I have no doubt," I patronized.

I heard a commotion in the hall then, and I saw Connor coming in, several of his men in tow. He sauntered over to us—I would move like that, too, if I were him—and explained that all the DEA agents were downstairs, waiting to be processed.

"They're all gonna walk," I told them.

Connor nodded. "But *when* is the question."

"I see the evil runs fast in this family."

Morgan grinned widely. "If you were staying, I'd take you to see my mum so you could see the truth of that."

"You made the news," Connor informed Morgan with a twinkle in his eye.

"Fuck," Morgan whined before turning to me. "I think you better put me in protective custody."

"Why? Your guy's a rock star. How scary could he be?"

Connor's cackle was a little bit unnerving.

IT TOOK hours to sort everything out, collect all the evidence, book Sandell, get Hein from his office where we'd left him and then book him as well. It was going to take time to figure out who was dirty and who was clean among the DEA agents, so everyone got processed before they were put on administrative leave. I was pretty sure Brandt was going to get a promotion when he got out of the hospital, as he would be one of the only good guys left standing.

Since Morgan had been running the undercover op with Casey's full backing, in the end, all that was left for the SFPD to do was have the marshals' office take Sandell and Hein into federal custody. They also told the DEA to kiss their ass and basically stomped all over Koegle. I was worried Morgan had made an enemy of him, but he'd also made a friend in Vance, so I figured it would balance out. He didn't seem worried.

That night he drove me to the airport where we parted ways, and I got a hug as I tried to extract a promise for him to visit Chicago.

He winced. "It's cold there, yeah? I mean, we get cold here, but you guys, that's glacial."

I shook my head and he chuckled, and I was inside before he pulled away.

On the way to the terminal, I stopped at one of the last open stores to grab water for the plane and spotted the cover of *Rolling Stone*.

"No shit," I said, staring at Miki St. John with the rest of the band before grabbing it off the rack. Kane Morgan was a lucky man, as were whomever, men or women, the rest of the boys belonged to. They were almost blindingly gorgeous all clustered together.

"Is this it?" the clerk asked.

"I know this guy's boyfriend," I told her.

She gave me a patronizing nod before ringing me up.

I was surprised when my phone rang while I sat in the boarding area, even more so when I read the caller ID.

"Hey," I said hoarsely.

"You had to be rescued by SWAT?" he growled.

His voice sounded really good. Tense, but good. "It wasn't as bad as it looked on TV," I assured Ian, wondering if Morgan's balls were in a vise at this exact moment. The news crew—all of them—made the entire situation, even without benefit of our names, sound a lot more dire than it was.

"You better be on your way home."

"I am." I swallowed hard. "Are you?"

"Yep."

A two-week Special Forces op had turned into a just-over-four-months marathon, so him telling me he was coming home to our overpriced Greystone sent a shiver of anticipation through me. I'd missed him bad. "I'm just waiting to board, so I'll be home in the morning. You?"

"Saturday night."

My stomach, which had not reacted to imminent death earlier today, flipped over in response to those words. I sighed deeply. "I can't wait to see you."

"Me too," he croaked.

"Ian?"

"Goddammit, Miro, you're supposed to stay home when I'm not with you!"

"It wasn't my fault," I said with a smile he couldn't see. "It was Phil."

"Who?"

I explained about the nozzle who was in charge while our boss took a much-deserved vacation with his family.

"Yeah, well, I bet Kage had him killed already."

"I seriously would not put it past him. Kage left orders and Tull disregarded them. We both know how well that goes over."

He grunted.

"So you're all in one piece?" I asked, trying to keep the worry out of my voice.

"I am."

"Any new scars you want to tell me about?"

"No," he said hesitantly, and I finally heard it, the pain in his voice. "But Sunday... I need you to go to a funeral with me."

"Of course," I breathed, waiting to hear who'd died.

"Buddy of mine."

I'd been worried that maybe it was his father. Ian and his dad weren't close, and the last time they saw each other had been a disaster, but.... "So your friend—"

"Laird. Eddie Laird."

That was really fast. "He wasn't there with you on the op?"

"No."

It wasn't the time to ask for specifics, but I was curious, I couldn't help it. "Okay, so I'll see you at home on Saturday. Call me from the—"

He coughed. "No, uhm, why don't you pick me up."

I was ridiculously touched. Never had I been allowed. Most of the time he didn't know exactly when he'd show up, but also, Ian liked our homecoming scenes private. He was not a PDA kind of guy at all, and the reception of men returning home from deployment was loud. Artillery barrage, explosions, boots on the ground, all that big-ticket noise, Ian could do. Squealing high-pitched joy was beyond him.

"Miro?"

"Sorry. You just never want me at the airport."

"Yeah, well, now I do."

I was excited and nervous at the same time because if I went, it was possible I might meet other men from his unit. I had only ever met one in the past, and he transferred out not long after that, so this would be a first time for me with the group. But maybe I had it all wrong. Maybe it would just be Ian, and that was the reason for the invite. "Will it be just you or—"

"No, we're all on the same flight."

Interesting. "What's the flight number?"

He gave it to me, and I heard his sharply indrawn breath, which told me it hurt for him to move. "Are you sure you're all in one piece?"

"Yeah."

A short answer was not good.

"So, M," he began softly. "You been sleeping okay?"

Ian was a Green Beret who'd seen and done things that would have given me night terrors for years. I knew he'd been on secret missions to countries the US wasn't supposed to be in, that there was blood on his hands and his horrors were legion, while mine amounted to one man, one time that showed me how futile struggle could be and how truly powerless I was. It made me feel ridiculously whiny and weak to ever complain to Ian about the PTSD I experienced after being kidnapped by Dr. Craig Hartley. Our department shrink diagnosed me while Ian was gone. Ian was actually the one who made me see the doctor, but really, confessing to the man I loved—who had real ghosts that haunted him—would not be something I ever did.

"Miro?"

"I sleep better when you're here." And that was not a lie. Between sex or cuddling, I slept like a rock when I had him plastered to my back.

"Same," he sighed.

My voice was going to go if we kept talking. I missed him too much to keep the emotion out of it. "All right, well, I'll see you soon."

"Yes, you will," he murmured.

There was a silence.

"Ian?"

He coughed softly. "I really... missed you."

There were no better words.

CHAPTER 2

I WALKED through O'Hare at seven Friday morning, and I was surprised when I came through the security area and had Kohn and Kowalski there to meet me.

"The fuck?" I said by way of greeting.

"Nice work in San Francisco," Kohn said, smiling wide. "My city is the shit, huh?"

"It's hilly" was all I gave him. "I didn't get to appreciate much of it running through alleys and chasing down dirty DEA agents."

He shrugged.

"So what's with the reception?" I asked him and his partner.

"Well," Kowalski began, smiling smugly. "We're here to take you to breakfast and then officially give you back custody of your children."

I was confused, and it must have shown on my face.

"Those fuckheads, Cabot and Drake," Kohn snarled. "Jesus Christ, Miro, that shit is a full-time job!"

I chuckled, even though I knew he was right. Drake Ford, now Drake Palmer, and Cabot Kincaid, who used to be Cabot Jenner, were two witnesses Ian and I not only took custody of, but took under our wing. A lot of it had to do with the fact that they were young, both eighteen when they entered WITSEC, and we were the ones they bonded with.

"First you ask us to watch them last year when you and Doyle were in Phoenix, and then after when you were gettin' better from the whole kidnapping, and—"

I called him on his bullshit. "That's crap, man. Ian and I took them back from you as soon as I was off desk duty."

"Yeah, but then you left the boys with us when Doyle was deployed and you were sent to San Fran, and we're here to officially give them back."

"What'd they do?"

Kohn threw up his hands. "Drake saved a little girl who fell in the water at Navy Pier."

I scowled. "Why is that a bad thing?"

Kowalski shook his head. "The saving was good, the forgetting to call us before he talked to a reporter… was not."

"Oh shit," I groaned.

"Yeah, so we're all set to ship him and his boyfriend off to New Mexico or wherever, but they're crying about school and jobs and mostly—I shit you not—you and Doyle."

"Fuck."

"I told you before, those guys are way too attached, and Kage says you have to ship them out or they're out of the program."

"Out of WITSEC?"

"Apparently the shit they were in for is over. They're not considered targets at this stage."

"You checked with the Feds?"

"Yep."

"And the investigation is closed?"

"He and the boyfriend are cleared, but because of the threat from Cabot's father to both he and Drake that you noted in his file, the call can be made to keep them in the program, but just not in Chicago."

I understood. "So they can be out of WITSEC altogether and stay in Chicago, or remain in WITSEC and move."

"You got it," Kohn told me.

"Fuck."

"Kage is giving you today and the weekend to get it all sorted out. Come Monday morning he wants a status report."

"And why's he sending that message with you guys and not telling me himself?"

"He sent you a memo," Kohn clarified. "And us. Do you need him to yell at you too?"

I did not, no.

"I mean, he can. We both know he'll be fuckin' happy to do it. I think he was just cutting you some slack until Doyle got back."

"Which'll be tomorrow," I informed them.

"Good," Kohn said, grinning at me. "So what, you ready to eat?"

Kohn wanted to take us to Jam over on Logan, but Kowalski wanted mounds of food and something closer, so we hit a diner on our way from the airport, some greasy spoon where a short stack of pancakes was six high. Just watching Kowalski eat was terrifying.

I cleared my throat. "That doesn't frighten you?" I asked Kohn, tipping my head at Kowalski's shovel of a fork.

"I make sure to keep my hands away from his mouth and we're good."

It was fun to watch sleek, metrosexual, model-handsome and manscaped Eli Kohn partnered with the belching mountain of muscle that was Jer—short for God knew what because he'd never tell me—Kowalski. Their banter was always fun to listen to, especially about fashion, but heaven help you if you threw out a dig about the other in his presence. I'd seen Kowalski put an FBI agent on the wall—like, several feet off the ground up *on* the wall—for quietly insinuating Kohn was more interested in his hair than in taking down a fugitive. The guy was lucky to keep his lungs.

"Hey."

I looked back at Kohn from my plate.

"You sleeping okay?"

I was really sick of people asking me if I was or wasn't. I could see the dark circles under my eyes as well as anyone else—I just didn't want to talk about it. There was nothing to say. The dreams would stop when they stopped. "Why, don't I look all right?" I teased.

"You look like shit," Kowalski apprised me, his raised eyebrow daring me to contradict him.

"I'm fine," I muttered, going back to eating even though I wasn't that hungry.

"Oh fuck," Kowalski groaned after the bell on the door jingled, bumping Kohn with his elbow. "It's this shit again."

Turning in my seat, I was surprised to see Norris Cochran, along with another guy I'd never met, walking toward me.

"He can't eat in peace?" Kohn barked at Cochran as he closed in on us.

Cochran gave him his arrogant cop grimace that didn't hit his hazel eyes, and when he reached us, grabbed the chair beside me, turned it around, and flopped down. The man I assumed was his new partner took the seat on the other side of me so I had to lean back to keep an eye on both of them.

"The fuck do you want?" I asked my ex-partner.

"Nice," Cochran said, forcing a chuckle. "Didn't I tell you he loved me, Dor?"

The guy to my right nodded.

"Miro, this is Dorran Barreto. Barreto, my first love, Miro Jones."

We didn't shake hands. I didn't offer and Barreto didn't either.

"What do you want?" I asked Cochran again.

"You ain't even gonna ask after my kids?"

"Your wife and I are friends on Facebook," I informed him. "I know how the kids are."

That surprised him. I could tell from the flicker of annoyance and the trace of something else crossing his face. But it had been a long time since I'd been around him, so I was out of practice reading him. Not that it mattered. We weren't friends.

"So what, detectives stalk marshals now," Kohn baited.

Cochran glanced over at him. "If you had just told me when he was coming back instead of giving me the runaround, I wouldn't've had to do that."

"And I told you," Kohn replied fiercely, leaning forward, pointing at Cochran, "that we are not in the habit of giving out personal information to people who are not family or friends of members of our team."

"I'm his ex-partner and I'm a cop."

"And cops in the city are, of course, to be trusted," Kohn scoffed.

"Yeah, maybe not, huh?" Kowalski rubbed salt in the open angry wound that was the ongoing Justice Department investigation of the Chicago PD. "I'm not sure any of you fuckers know what procedure is."

Before things escalated, I got up and headed for the door. Cochran was no more than a half a step behind me.

Outside, I rounded on him, already annoyed that my food was getting cold, and he took a step back so he wouldn't run into me.

"What do you want?" I growled, venting every bit of irritation, not caring, not bothering to filter as I would with practically everyone else.

"A gun," he answered flatly, crossing his arms, his gaze locked with mine.

"Explain." A demand, clipped and cold.

"It's about Oscar Darra."

Everyone knew the story. "The ex-mob enforcer?"

"Yeah."

I had to think. "I thought he was dead."

"Yeah, so did a lot of people, but he turned up last week in a routine sweep of a Turkish bath down on Cicero."

"No shit."

He shrugged.

"Where the hell's he been all this time?"

"He's been laying low down in Springfield with some cousin."

I grunted, leaning back against the wall of the diner. November in Chicago right before Thanksgiving wasn't arctic yet, but it was cool. I was glad I had on a hoodie under my leather jacket. The wind would have blown right through me. "What does any of this have to do with you being here?"

"I—"

"Is this gonna be a long-ass story?"

He didn't answer, just coughed and put his shoulder against the wall so he was facing me. To anyone walking by, we looked like two buddies out shootin' the shit.

"Fine," I sighed. "Talk."

"Okay, so after we pick him up and get Darra back to the station, he starts telling us that if we agree to cut a deal with him, he'll tell us where the gun is that was used to kill Joey Romelli."

I shook my head. "You lost me."

"You don't remember Romelli?"

"I remember *Vincent* Romelli, who was in charge of the Cilione crime family, but he's been dead awhile. Who's Joey?"

"His son."

"He had a son?"

"'Had' being the operative word, yeah."

"And how'd he die?"

"Well, according to Darra, he was shot by one Andreo Fiore."

"Who?" I could feel myself getting annoyed all over again. I hated playing name the thug and I especially didn't want to do it with Cochran.

"He was Vincent Romelli's muscle back in the day."

"Okay, so lemme get this straight," I began, turning to face him. "You guys pick up Darra because he's in town for whatever reason, and when you grab him, he wants to give up this Fiore to cut a deal."

"Yeah."

"And you care about this why?"

"Well, we don't at first. Barreto and I figure it's bullshit, right? But we go to where he says he's stashed the gun and—"

"This is already fucked up, Nor," I said, slipping back into calling him by a nickname like we'd never been apart. It just came out. Shit. "I mean—"

"Just stop." We stood there in silence, him staring at me and me finally looking away because I had no idea what the hell to say.

"It was good you caught Hartley."

My eyes were back on him.

"I'm sorry we—"

"It's not—"

"It is," he croaked, stopping me, hand slipping around my bicep, squeezing tight. "We—I didn't know what to do with how that went down. It would've been better off if you let me shoot him."

I cleared my throat. "I know."

"More people died because you let him live that night."

I yanked free of his hold and took a step back. "I know that too," I retorted, angry but quiet, feeling my body wash hot, then cold with regret and shame.

He moved forward into my space, grabbing hold of my jacket. "But it was right, what you did."

I searched his face for clarity because he was making no sense.

"If I'd shot him, I would've been guilty because I had him."

I understood like no one else could because I was there. Hartley had me in his hands, a knife shoved into my side, and Cochran was looming above us, gun in both hands, and he could have shot Hartley, killed him if I hadn't used my body to cover the psychopath and keep my partner from becoming a murderer.

"You—" His voice bottomed out. "—did it to protect me, not him."

That revelation had only taken close to four years. "Fuck you," I raged, the hurt and anger over his betrayal—he'd never even visited me once when I was in the hospital—boiling over like it always did whenever I revisited that time in my life.

He had been my family, his wife and kids, his parents, his siblings, and in one moment he was gone and so were all the rest of them. His wife had come around, finally, but no one else did, and it still hurt. Mostly it was that helplessness that came from things being taken away while I'd had no control. I hated that. I was a foster kid, so I'd never had a say about any part of my life, and to have that happen again when I was older had made me gun-shy of partnership and putting my faith in anyone. Ian was the one who changed that, the only one strong enough to break through the wall I'd put up.

From the beginning, Ian had simply assumed I belonged to him, his backup, his friend, his shadow, and because he took me for granted, I had uncoiled, relented, and finally trusted. Anyone but Ian, anyone who wasn't a battering ram, all prickly vulnerability, dangerous temper, and raw, primal heat—constantly in my space, close, leaning, bumping, touching—I would have kept at a distance. But there was no saying no to Ian Doyle. The ache that welled up in me made it hard to breathe.

"Fuck me?" Cochran yelled.

I couldn't even be bothered to have my head in a fight. That was how much I didn't care about Norris Cochran. After shoving him back, I strode to the edge of the parking lot. He was there fast, walking around in front of me.

"So," I demanded shortly, meeting his gaze. "If Fiore killed Romelli, where did your guy get the gun?"

He took a breath. "Well, so Fiore shot Romelli, Darra's sure of it. He was in the bedroom when he heard the shot, and when he came out, he saw somebody run out the front door."

"So he followed him out to the street?"

"No, Romelli was killed in his penthouse."

"Oh, so your guy follows this Fiore down however many stairs."

"Yeah," he confirmed. "And when he gets there, he follows him into an alley and watches him stash the gun in a drain."

"Why would he do that? Why not just take the gun with him?"

"Well, I don't know if you remember, but at that time, with his father having just been murdered—everybody was watching Joey. They found him that night like a half an hour after the shooting."

"And this Fiore, he was a mob enforcer like Darra?"

"No, not at all. Like I said, he was just one of Vincent Romelli's goons."

"Then why kill his son?"

"We don't know."

"Does he still work for Strada?"

"No, I ran him through the system and he's clean. He's always been clean. He was a known associate of Vincent Romelli and he was questioned when Vincent Romelli was gunned down, but he and his buddy Sal something were the only ones who got out."

"But—"

"Oh, and Joey Romelli."

"The son was there when his father died?"

"Yeah. Fiore was the one who got him out of the massacre."

I needed a second. "I'm sorry, what?"

"I know!" he snapped at me. "It makes no sense."

"So Fiore saves him and then turns round and kills him?" I was incredulous. "This is what Darra would have you believe?"

"Yeah."

"Tell him to go fuck himself and charge his lying ass." I was done and turned to go.

He grabbed hold of my shoulder to keep me there, and I rolled it, out of habit, instinctively, because someone I didn't like was touching me. "Wait," he barked. "The gun he gave us, the ballistics matched."

"What gun? The gun he turned over to you?" I said, exasperated that I was having to stand there and listen to his bullshit.

"Yeah."

"Well of course the ballistics match. He killed Romelli, probably on orders from Tony Strada. The last thing you fuckin' want around when you're the new boss is the old boss's kid."

"Yeah, that's what we thought, but when we ran the DNA on the gun—there was Romelli's on the muzzle, like the gun was shoved down his throat—and someone other than Darra's on the grip."

"So?" I was so aggravated. Cochran had always taken forever to get to the point.

"So Romelli was killed execution-style with a bullet in the back of his head. That's why everyone figured it was a mob hit."

"Then what?"

"Well, now we think whoever did it shoved his gun in Romelli's mouth first—probably so he'd know who was pulling the trigger—and then shot him like he did to make it look like everyone would expect."

"Okay, so lemme wrap my head around this. You have the gun, the ballistics match, so it's for sure the one used to kill Romelli, but Darra's DNA isn't on it, and he says it was Fiore."

"Yeah, plus we have Fiore's prints."

"You have Fiore's prints on the weapon?"

He nodded.

"So bring his ass in." I almost growled. "The fuck does this have to do with me?"

"We can't."

"Why not?" I retorted, done, at the end of my rope. I wanted to eat and go home and pass out. "You've got prints, DNA—get a court order and test Fiore's DNA."

"Yeah, we can't get an order."

"Why the *hell* not?!"

"Because we don't have the gun."

"What do you mean you don't have the gun?" He was making no sense and I was a second away from walking—hoping he'd try and grab me again. I *really* wanted to hit him. Some of it was his fault because of our past and because he'd always been fucking irritating. But a lot of it was Ian and how much I missed him and how stretched thin with yearning I was. I needed my man home, and this close to getting it—a mere day—I was in that headspace where anticipation became panic racing around in my head like a cat scrambling after a mouse. I was scared something was going to happen and Ian would be gone again. I was taking it out on Cochran, but he was taking for-fucking-ever to get to the point. "You just said you got prints and DNA and—"

"We don't have the gun 'cause it was transferred to the marshals by mistake," he explained almost sheepishly.

"Come again?" I asked, incredulous, beside myself.

He cleared this throat. "My lieutenant—"

"Who's that now?"

"Cortez."

"Okay, sorry, g'head."

"Yeah, so Cortez transferred three guns to your office because, like your guy said in the diner, lots of cases are being looked at by Justice right now, and lots of evidence is being reexamined. So our gun went back to evidence after ballistics and prints and DNA was run, but from there it was accidentally transferred to you."

"What does it matter? It was tested for prints, which you got, and you've got the sample of whoever's DNA was on it, so just get Fiore's sample and match it… or not. It's done either way."

"It's not that simple."

"Of course it is. The prints will compel the DNA sample."

He shook his head. "No."

"No? How the hell you figure no?"

"The ASA assigned to the case—Sutter—she says that without the gun, it's our word against Fiore's that the prints were from the gun. She says they could've come off anything, and it could look like we're trying to set him up. Fiore could make a case for tampering."

"Are you serious?" I asked, overwhelmed with the stupidity of all of this.

"Yeah, I'm serious!" Cochran flared. "Without the goddamn gun, we can't make Fiore give us a DNA sample."

If I thought about it logically, that made sense. No judge in their right mind would issue a court order to compel Fiore to give them a DNA sample if the item his DNA was supposed to be on was, in fact, missing. What if it was always missing? Never found? What did that say about the police department that they'd had the weapon in their possession but didn't anymore? What if the prints in question had come from somewhere or something completely different, and Andreo Fiore had, in fact, never even been in the room where Joey Romelli was killed? It was a mess.

"I get it," I admitted. "You need the gun."

"Fuck, yeah, I need the gun, and that's where you come in."

"How?" I could hear how icy and stilted I sounded, so no way Cochran was missing it.

"Chain of custody says it's in your property room."

"But?"

"But your boss says the gun's not there."

Now I was really lost. "Okay, wait. You're telling me that you already questioned the chief deputy about the gun?"

"Barreto and I did, yeah."

This finally felt like the gist of it. "And?"

"And like I said, he told us that it's not there."

"Then what the fuck, Norris? If he says it's not there, it's not there."

"But I think it is, and I think he's lying."

"*What*?" My brain was ready to explode. "How dare you fucking—"

"Calm the fuck down!"

"Don't tell me to calm down!" I roared, drilling two fingers into his collarbone. "You don't know shit about Sam Kage because if you did you'd never—"

"I think your boss is purposely hiding the whereabouts of that gun," he yelled over me.

"For *what reason*?" I shouted.

"I have no idea."

"Does Sam Kage even know Andreo Fiore?"

"Not that we can tell. There's nothing at all that links them."

"Then why the hell would you think he would lose the gun?"

Cochran cleared his throat. "You know, back in the day, his partner was dirty, and guess where that guy went—into WITSEC," he said offhandedly.

"What are you insinuating?" I asked, feeling my skin heat under my clothes, afraid of what I would do if the words actually came out of his mouth. Irritation, annoyance, all of it was gone, replaced solely by anger. How fucking *dare* he.

"Dirty partner… you understand."

"I don't think I do," I said flatly, my vision tunneling down to him, lost on the edges, going black, my throat dry, my heart beating so fast I wondered how he couldn't hear it.

"C'mon, Miro, don't be stupid."

"That was a long time before my boss was even a marshal," I ground out.

"Whatever. It's not right and you know it."

"*What* isn't?" He had to be clear. I couldn't bury his career if he wasn't.

"Your boss is fuckin' dirty."

It was worse than I thought it would be, hearing his words, having them out there, the accusation making my stomach churn.

"Did you hear me?"

The rage filled me up, made me see red, and fisted my hands at my sides. Only the thought of Kage, his disappointment if I surrendered to my base instincts, kept me still. "You don't know him at all." I bit off each word.

"Like I said, I know *of* him. I know his partner was dirty and he—"

"Well, I know him," I spat out, my voice hoarse. "And he would never, ever, tamper with evidence, any evidence! If anyone is screwing with you, it's your boss. Who the *fuck* transfers the *wrong* guns to the Justice Department?"

"Cortez signed a piece of paper to transfer a crapton of evidence, not just one gun! Do you have any idea how many cases and reports and everything else Justice is going through? It'll take years for them to get through it all."

"And then they can start looking into Homan Square," I blasted.

"Fuck you, Miro!" he yelled, shoving at me hard but barely moving me, as I was prepared for his reaction. I knew Norris Cochran; his fuse was far shorter than mine. "You know I never—"

"I don't give a shit that you never," I roared, knocking him back several feet. "But don't you dare come at me with some bullshit accusation about my boss covering up a crime by tampering with evidence. For all we know, the goddamn gun was never even there in the first place!"

He threw a wild roundhouse punch that I ducked easily, and I would have tagged him right in the jaw, but someone grabbed me from behind and got my arms pinned behind me.

As I struggled to free myself, Cochran caught me in the right eye, but I managed to twist hard enough to take the next one in the right shoulder instead of the side of the face, and the last one in the gut. He was ready to hit me again; I saw the fury all over him, knew he'd been waiting years, ever since we arrested Hartley the first time, to kick the shit out of me.

Then we both heard a bellow of outrage. I was released instantly, and before I hit the gravel, I was in Kowalski's arms.

"You better fuckin' run!" he thundered after them. "I'll have both of your motherfucking badges for this!"

"For crissakes, Jones," Kohn grumbled as he reached us. "We can't leave you alone for a second? Why didn't you yell for us?"

"I didn't know he had backup. How is this my fault?" I railed.

"Jesus," he moaned, "lookit your face, man. I think we're gonna have to get you to the hospital."

"Fuck that," I groused, spitting out a mouthful of blood. "Nothing's broken. Just take me home."

"We'll call Kage on the way."

I couldn't argue with that.

CHAPTER 3

KOHN EXPLAINED to our boss what had happened as I lay on my couch at home with an ice pack on my face. I got to hear it all and add in a few details of my own since he had Kage on speaker. The part about Cochran accusing him of being dirty he didn't react to at all, but me getting hit while his partner held me—that he took issue with.

"I'll have them both brought up on charges."

I was not innocent in the whole exchange. "I shoved him."

"You defended yourself," Kohn argued. "I saw the whole thing, so did Jer. We just missed his fuckin' partner going out the back."

"Yeah, it would've been a fair fight," I explained, trying to sit up, but Kowalski snapped his fingers, shook his head, and went back to flipping channels on my TV. He had the volume down for the time being, but once the call was done, ESPN would be loud in my Greystone. Not that either of them would stay once my friend Aruna got there with her one-year-old and Ian's dog—technically my dog now too—Chickie Baby.

"Jones?"

"Yessir," I answered.

"You realize," he growled in that way he had where there was no confusion—even on the phone—that he was a great big scary man, "that you don't have to defend my honor, right?"

"Begging your pardon, sir," I said, taking a breath and thinking of all the things my boss had personally done for me that no one else ever had. "No one is allowed to say anything derogatory about you in my presence."

It was quiet in my living room then.

"That's true," Kohn concurred, his voice sounding loud in the silence.

"Agreed," Kowalski chimed in.

After a moment Kage exhaled sharply. "They'll be brought up on charges, Jones. Your old partner isn't allowed to kick the shit out of you just because he's frustrated over missing evidence."

"Kicking the shit out of me would imply it was one on one," I pointed out defensively, certain that I could have defended myself if it had been just him. "That was not the case."

"I'll be sure to put that in my report."

"Just me and Cochran, I would've killed him," I added, wanting that on the record.

"Duly noted," he said, and I recognized the patronizing tone. "And by the way, do they actually have any evidence that the gun they're looking for is even with us?"

"I dunno."

"Do they have a signature of whoever it was that signed the gun into our property room?"

"Cochran didn't say."

"Well," Kage sighed, "according to what I'm seeing here in the log, the only firearms that were signed into evidence within the last month are all Glocks from the Chicago PD that ballistics are being redone on for their open officer complaints."

"So the gun he's looking for isn't even with us."

"Not that I can tell."

"Well, that goes along with his story. He said that the gun is there, but we're saying it's not."

"He needs to realize that we're saying it's not, because it's not."

"Of course."

"I almost wish we could let him and his partner into our property room so they could see that the gun's not there," Kohn snapped. "Almost."

"Never happen," Kage said flatly. "So I need an official statement from start to finish of the incident, Jones. Don't leave anything out, and I want it e-mailed within a couple of hours, tops."

"Yessir."

"Be ready to give your report to the department liaison, Chicago PD IAD, and OPR."

Office of Professional Responsibility. I so loved talking to those guys. They would go over everything with a fine-tooth comb. "Or we could just not report it at all."

"I'm sorry, Jones. They're not allowed to think that hitting you is okay."

"Doesn't Chicago PD have enough problems without me adding to the mix?"

"Two hours, Jones, start typing."

Fuck. "Yessir."

"Kohn, Kowalski, you too, whatever you saw."

"I'm on it," Kohn assured him.

"Working on it now, sir," Kowalski echoed.

"Good," he said, and I thought he was going to hang up, so I was surprised when he didn't.

"Sir?"

"Are you sleeping, Jones?"

Shit. "I will now that I'm home, sir."

"See that you do," he commanded and then hung up.

How did he get away with ordering me around in my personal life? "This is not how I saw my homecoming going," I griped.

"What homecoming?" Kohn asked as he got up to go to my kitchen to get me more ice. "Doyle's not even here?"

But his question was answered a moment later by a knock on the door, a jingle of a key in the lock, and one of my oldest friends, Aruna Duffy, coming through the door with her one-year-old daughter, Sajani, my dog, and her husband.

"Ohmygod, Miro, who hit you?" she shrieked right before 150 pounds of werewolf came barreling across the room and landed on me.

Chickie was very happy to see me, as evidenced by the whining and whimpering, the rolling on his back on top of me, and the tongue bath my face got, which hurt like hell.

"Aruna!" I groused, trying to get Chickie off.

"Jesus, it looks like he's getting ready to eat you," Kowalski said, clearly enjoying the show. "That hurts, huh?"

I growled at him.

"That's disgusting," Kohn choked out, the revulsion thick in his voice. "Dog slobber."

"Eat him, Chick," I ordered, pointing at Kohn.

"The hell, man," Aruna's husband, big and burly and blond built-like-a-tank Liam Duffy said as he strode over to the couch. One-handed, he moved Chickie and then sat me up to study my face. He was a fireman, not an EMT, but he knew first aid.

"I think we need to get you to a hospital," he concluded as he studied me, even as Chickie thunked his head down in my lap. "That's a lot of bruising on your cheek and eye, buddy. You may have some broken bones."

I scratched the mutant dog's ears, under his chin, and then stroked his head over and over, telling him what a good boy he was. His tail thumping the floor sounded like an outboard motor, as fast as it was going. "Nothing's broken," I promised. "Seriously. It might look bad because everything shows up on my skin, but I'm good."

"Miro Jones!" Aruna yelled. "Do not tell me you're not hurt and blame it on your beautiful milky complexion with the fabulous rose undertones."

Silence. Both Kohn and Kowalski were staring at me like I'd grown another head.

"She's a journalist," Liam explained. "Her business is specific words."

"Huh," Kohn said.

"I'm fine," I assured her, smiling to try to get her to stop biting her bottom lip and not look at me like I was dying. "I promise. I just need more ice."

"Your lip's split, your right eye's black and blue, and—"

"I swear to you I'm perfectly fine."

She caught her breath, shoved her daughter at her husband, and flung herself down into my arms. We both grunted seconds later as Chickie climbed on top of us, and Sajani clapped her hands from Liam's arms.

He was going to crush us.

"Get the monster dog off me," I begged Liam.

After passing Sajani to Kohn, he hauled Chickie off and took him into the kitchen to find him a treat.

I was going to reiterate that everything was okay when my phone rang. "Lookit," I told Aruna. "It's Janet."

Snatching the phone from me, turning so she was now in my lap, she answered it after putting it on speaker. "Dammit, Janet."

It was always the same, even after so many years. It was all our friend Min's fault, since she was the one who dragged us all to the *Rocky Horror Picture Show* a hundred years ago when we were all still in college.

"Why are you answering pretty boy's phone?" Janet Powell asked, snickering as she said it.

"You're rude and mean," I informed one of my oldest and dearest friends. "So what the hell do you want?"

"Hold on," she ordered, and then we heard buttons being pressed.

"I just got in bed," Min Kwon groused from the other end of the line. "Do you know what time it is here in LA? Why are you calling me so early in the goddamn morning?"

"Hi, Min," I singsonged to her, cackling.

"Minnie, honey," Aruna cooed. "Howya doin'?"

"Miro?" She sounded exasperated and surprised at the same time. "Aruna?"

"Why're you just gettin' to bed?" I grilled her. "Been in poundtown with some guy all night?"

"Shut. Up," she snarled. "I've been going through discovery on a case since—"

"Janet, what the *hell*?" Catherine Benton almost shrieked over what was now a party line. "How dare you lie and call me out of surgery to—"

"I'm going to have a baby," she announced breathlessly.

Silence.

"Oh my God." Min was the first to speak, or cry, as it was, and I knew she was because I could hear the wobble in her voice, the unmistakable sound of brimming-over happiness.

"You've been trying so hard," I said, my voice cracking with the same emotion Min was feeling. "Awww, honey, you did it. You got yourself knocked up."

The dam broke then, and we were all talking at the same time, all congratulating her, sending love to her husband, and Catherine hit her with medical questions since she was a doctor and needed to know.

Janet and her hubby had been trying for a couple of years with no success. We all teased her—because that was better than the sympathy her husband's family doled out—and told her he was a sex maniac. But the truth was they had done all the things you had to do when chasing the dream of children through miscarriages and specialists. I had no idea how she stayed so strong and optimistic in the face of that kind of pain, but now, finally, she was being rewarded.

"I'm so happy for you," Aruna sighed. "Now we just need Catherine to have one."

There was coughing, like Catherine swallowed a bug or something, and then the click of disconnect.

Tired and giddy, the rest of us couldn't stop laughing.

ARUNA AND Liam were gone an hour later, right after Aruna explained that she'd cooked to stock my refrigerator, and I got to hear Chickie's latest tale of valor. Apparently Aruna was at the park with some other mothers, and a man came asking for money. He had a friend with him, and they inadvertently put themselves between the mothers and the children. Aruna got scared and called Chickie.

Just fuckin' called him.

He was lying beside the small jungle gym Sajani was climbing on, and when he came… fast… the guys ran even more so. Everyone cheered, and Chickie was the belle of the ball for the rest of the day. None of the other mothers were afraid of him, even those with infants.

"He's a hero," Aruna sighed, kissing and hugging the monster dog who had feet as big as a bear's. I watched the animal that could have eaten her preen under the attention.

The vet thought perhaps he was malamute and mastiff, with maybe some Caucasian Ovcharka thrown in along with some husky, and maybe— he confided in me the last time I was there—even some wolf. But since hybrids were illegal in Chicago and he couldn't prove it, he was keeping his suspicion on the down low and had not recorded it in any official paperwork.

Whatever Chickie was, he'd been making my two fellow marshals nervous, but once he lay down beside the couch with his head on my lap, making the grunting noises he made when he was happy, even they warmed to him and took turns scratching his ears.

"I guess you never have to worry about burglars," Kohn offered.

"Yeah, neither do the neighbors on both sides," I yawned. "That's one of the reasons this Greystone cost a bit more. We're in a cluster of four, and all the backyards are gated and butt up against each other."

"Oh, I thought you had, like, a small park behind you."

"No, four lots are connected so we can walk from my back door to the neighbor's and come out one street over."

"I wondered what made your mortgage payment so high," Kohn replied.

Kowalski and I both looked at him.

"What? You left your computer screen open last week. I was supposed to not look?"

"Yeah," Kowalski chided. "You don't look, ya animal. What the hell? I've met your mother; I know you weren't raised in a barn."

Kohn made a dismissive noise and tipped his head at Chickie. "So you said the neighbors don't worry about burglars either?"

"Yeah, no," I said, snickering. "Some guy came through our neighbors' backyard across from us, and I hear Mrs. Sasaki yelling at him that 'that's not allowed,' and then out goes Chickie and the guy turned and ran."

"I'd run too," Kowalski confessed.

"Yeah, so after the guy gets out the gate, Chickie ran the length of the fence and snarled and barked, and Mrs. Sasaki, who I swear to God has never said two words to me, is smiling and waving before she comes down her back steps and is all over him, telling him what a good boy he is," I said with an eye roll. "After that, all three neighbors are happy to have Chickie out whenever he wants and they all give him treats when he goes up to their back doors."

"So he guards the whole place." Kowalski seemed really interested.

"Yeah, he's a little too vigilant. That's why Ian put in the doggie door leading to the backyard, so we don't have to get up and let him out anymore whenever he hears something weird in the middle of the night."

"This is still Chicago, though. You're not worried some guy'll get in here through the monster dog door?" Kohn sounded concerned.

I arched an eyebrow. "And run the risk of being face-to-face with Chick?"

"No, I mean during the day when he's not here."

I snorted. "Ian made the door. When it's closed, it's like Fort Knox; no one's coming in through that."

"Speaking of, when's he getting in?" Kowalski chimed in.

"Not until tomorrow around seven."

"I'll call the guys, then, we'll have poker night over here tonight."

"What? Why?" I just wanted to sleep. Didn't I look tired?

"Maybe he wants to sleep?" Kohn threw out.

Kowalski scoffed. "Fuck that, he owes us all money from last time."

I did, it was true.

"Ain't no rest for the wicked, everybody knows that."

I flipped him off, and then Kohn as well because he started laughing.

CHAPTER 4

MY FRIENDS—AND I used the word loosely since they had no problem taking my money and not giving me the opportunity to win it back—stayed until the early morning hours. They'd all come, except Sharpe, who had a hot date with an Eastern European ballerina he'd met on a DEA bust. He showed up at nine the following morning, pounding on my front door because I was close to where he was when he woke up and got the hell out of her apartment. Since he'd become single again, the term manwhore could officially be applied.

I took him to breakfast at Firecakes, my favorite donut place over on Clark, because the idea of eggs and bacon made him a bit green around the gills. But warm sugary goodness worked and he looked a bit more human when we left. I loaned him my sunglasses so he wouldn't go blind, and then he walked back home with Chickie and me.

"This is nice." He sighed as he kept pace with me and my werewolf in the chilled morning air while we navigated the tree-lined streets. "I think I need a place out of the city."

I didn't want to correct him and say that Lincoln Park wasn't really a sleepy little 'burb because his head and stomach were still a bit dicey.

"But then I'd be far from all the clubs."

There was that to consider.

"If I try and pet the dog, will he eat my hand off?"

I snorted out a laugh and moved around Chickie so he was walking between us. It was nice that Sharpe didn't even have to bend to reach Chickie's head. There is something so soothing about petting a dog.

I watched the last of the night drain out of Sharpe. "You know, if going out and getting laid makes you so miserable that you drink and feel like crap and are totally stressed, maybe you might wanna rethink it, huh?"

"Are you kidding? I love getting laid."

I was not going to inspire him into some cathartic moment. "Why don't you come sit on my couch and watch football while I clean the house."

"Yeah, all right. You got clothes for me?"

I did. I gave him sweats and a T-shirt and heavy socks, which worked out fine after he took a shower so he didn't smell like cigarette smoke and alcohol anymore. He passed out on the couch watching not football, but Netflix. I cleaned around him and Chickie, the dog only opening one eye when I bumped him with the vacuum.

I woke Sharpe up around four and made him an omelet and toast, and between that and the ice tea, he looked better when he left. I got a hug that we normally didn't engage in, on his way to the curb to get into the cab I'd called for him.

I hadn't eaten because I wanted to wait for Ian, and with how excited I was, there was no way food was happening.

A bit later I got a call from Min, who was upset after making her weekly pilgrimage to see her mother.

"You guys get it," she vented. "Why doesn't she?"

I sighed. "She's worried if you don't get married and have kids that you won't ever truly be happy in life."

Her exhale was full of exasperation and sadness in equal measure. "But you guys know that's not true. I love my job, I love dating, I love my life. I'm happy except for when I have to deal with her."

It hit me. "You told her about Janet, you dumb broad."

She giggled. "That was stupid, huh?"

"No," I soothed. "You were happy for your friend, so you shared the news with your mother. You didn't think it was going to boomerang back and hit you in the face."

I got a real laugh then. "No, I certainly didn't."

"Think before you speak, Min," I teased. "You're a lawyer, after all. I shouldn't have to tell you these things."

That was it; she dissolved as I did a really good impression of her mother, Soon-Bok Kwon, who had never warmed up to me or Catherine but loved Aruna and Janet dearly.

"Your mother hates me," I said for the eight billionth time.

She didn't argue.

"You suck."

"Not on the first date," she corrected.

"Oh God," I groaned. All my friends were disgusting, men and women both.

"Are you sleeping?"

I hustled her off the phone after that, and she said we'd talk about it next time. And while I didn't want to talk about how much rest I wasn't getting, it was nice that I talked to her and Janet and Catherine at least once a week, if not more, even after so many years out of college. I was always so thankful that, when they'd left Chicago, I hadn't lost them.

I was still thinking about her and the others, about friendship and the family I'd made, as I drove to the airport that evening. But by the time I got there, the girls were out of my head and I was back to worrying. The thing was, I'd thought of something earlier, and as I stood outside the security point, leaning against a wall close to the benches in the waiting area, I realized my stomach had gone from gentle butterfly-wing fluttering to full gale-force wind tornado. What kept running through my brain was that sometimes Ian said things in the heat of the moment that he regretted once the ache of need passed. I hoped he still wanted me there when he emerged with the rest of his unit into the terminal from the concourse.

"You don't think this is a bit like an ambush?" a woman behind me said.

"What're you talking about?" another replied.

"He's coming home from a mission that took four months longer than it was supposed to, and as soon as he gets here, the wife of one of his buddies springs a blind date on him?"

"You could've skipped it, if that's how you really feel."

"And I probably would have, but then you had to go and show me his picture."

An amused chuckle followed. "I told you Ian Doyle was gorgeous."

It felt like someone punched me in the gut.

"And you're sure there's no one special?"

"Not that I've ever seen when I come pick up Paul."

"Yeah, but Paulie's brand new to the unit. This is only his second time out with these guys, and the last time he came home at like six in the morning, didn't he? Was there even anyone else here but you?"

"No," the second woman snapped. Clearly it was a sore subject. "All the other guys actually think about their wives and girlfriends and don't make them pick them up before dawn."

"Well, then Ian could be married and how would you even know?"

"It's true, Paul doesn't know either. He said Ian's not a real talkie guy, but I understand he's not only a reservist but also a US marshal. How hot is that?"

"Hot," the first woman purred. "Really hot."

"Yeah, so that's why we're here, dressed better than usual for the airport—to catch you a man." She giggled.

I had to know what she was wearing to snag the love of my life, so I did a pivot, pretending to look behind me, and caught four-inch heels, black tights, a long cream-colored angora sweater with a chunky cowl, and beige cashmere overcoat. Not slutty, not skanky, elegant, with immaculate makeup and jewelry. She was lovely.

Her friend, Paul's wife, was just as fashionable in her asymmetrical sweater with the shawl collar, jeans, and knee-high platform brown leather boots, all under a black swing coat. Both women looked classy, ready for a night on the town.

I got a quick, easy smile from each of them, which I returned before I was facing front once more.

I felt a shiver of dread because occasionally, I still worried whether I was enough for Ian Doyle. After all, the world was full of men and women more attractive than me who had way less baggage.

"Miro?"

I turned sharply to see a pretty blond woman dressed more like me, very casual, ready not to go out, but just to go back home after this.

We were both in old jeans and T-shirts, but whereas mine was under a white wool knit button-up cardigan, hers was under a hoodie and a motorcycle jacket. Her over-the-knee distressed black leather boots were as flat as my white Converse sneakers. Neither of us had dressed up at all.

"Yes," I answered as she closed on me, hand out in greeting.

"I'm Stacy Qureshi. I'm Mo's wife."

I smiled at her even as I shook her hand. "I'm sorry, I haven't met—Mo?"

"Mohammed," she said kindly, looking at me askance.

"Yeah, I'm a bit out of the loop."

"Don't worry about it. It's just great to finally put a face to the name, or, you know, part of a face, at least," she teased. "Lights too bright in here for you, marshal? Gotta wear shades in the terminal?"

I pointed at my eyes under the aviators I had on. "I got hit on the job. It looks worse than it is, but still. I don't wanna scare people."

She waved a hand dismissively. "Sweetheart, I'm here to pick up a Green Beret. You think he comes home abrasion-free?"

I chuckled and took off my glasses, hanging them on the collar of my T-shirt.

"Oh, see," she sighed. "He's gorgeous."

"You're very nice."

"No," she said impishly. "Really not. Kind of a bitch, actually, but you'll learn that and find it charming down the road."

I grinned at her.

"Oh yes, definitely pretty. I can totally see you and Ian together. That must be something when you guys are out together, stopping traffic and all."

The chatter behind us ceased instantly.

"It's Ian. Everybody looks at him."

She nodded. "Yes, I'm aware. The first time I met him, my husband said 'You're drooling.'"

She was fun, I liked her already. "It's really nice to meet you," I said sincerely.

"Oh, you too," she said, slipping her arm though mine, closing the distance between us. "I kept meaning to pick Mo up at least once so I could check you out after my husband told me you and Ian were together."

"Ian told Mo about me?"

"He told all the guys, and frankly, I was thrilled."

"You were?"

She nodded, waving to another woman wearing a sweater dress, leggings, and boots who came darting over to us. "I was. I always worried about Ian because there was never anyone he talked about or who came here to grab him after an op, and that was so sad."

"Hey, girl," a beautiful woman said as she reached Stacy, leaning in to give her a hug. "How are you?"

She was the kind of woman you watched walk by on the street: brilliant smile that made her dimples pop, big sepia eyes framed in long thick lashes, and gorgeous smooth brown skin with golden bronze undertones. I would bet the reason for the size of the rock on her finger was her husband wanting to send a clear, concise message to any would-be suitors before he was forced to kill them with his pinky. The man was a Green Beret, after all.

"I'm good," Stacy replied before squeezing my bicep tight. "Zahra, this is Miro, Ian's guy."

Zahra's whole face lit up. "Oh, it's so good to finally meet you," she said warmly, like she meant every word, walking around Stacy to give me a hug. It was nice. She wasn't one of those hover huggers where you barely felt it. Instead, she grabbed and squeezed. I was a fan already.

When she pulled back, she was beaming at me. "It's so great to put a face to the name. I'm Danny O'Reilly's wife."

"Ian hasn't introduced him to any of the guys, so he has no idea who our hubbies are," Stacy explained.

"Ah, sounds like them," Zahra said, and then she noticed the two women behind us. "Hi there, can I help you?"

"Oh" came a gasp, and I finally had a reason to turn when Stacy did as well. "I'm sorry for staring. I'm Paul's wife, Chloe Jermaine."

Zahra's scowl was instant. "I don't understand."

"I'm sorry?"

"I mean," Zahra began, her voice going cold, "why are you here?"

"To pick up Paul."

"And why would Paul be here?" Zahra clipped the words, and the change from how sweet she'd been with me, how warm, to frigid ice queen, was odd.

"Because he's a member of the team, of course."

"Did your husband tell you to pick him up here?"

"No, but I checked his e-mail, and the time and date were in there," she told Zahra, who made a tsking noise.

"That's probably Danny's bad. He didn't take you off the list, and I bet you didn't get put on it, did you, Miro?"

"No," I answered, even though she didn't turn and look at me, too focused on Chloe and her friend.

"Well, I'll make sure he fixes that," Zahra promised as she pointed at Chloe. "And I'll make sure he takes you off immediately."

"I don't understand what's going—"

"What's going on," Stacy began coolly, "is that your husband, Paul, is no longer a member of this unit. How do you not know that? We all know that."

And when she said "we all," she gestured at the ten or so other women now milling close to us.

"I think you're mistak—"

"Listen," Zahra said acidly, "if your husband told you he was going on a mission, he lied, so you best sort that out when you find him. But I can assure you that he will *not* be coming though that security point with the rest of our boys."

"I... he—"

Zahra advanced on Chloe. "As you know, my husband commands this unit, and he told me he transferred yours out after the last time he nearly got him and the others killed. Not only did Ian Doyle have to save *my* husband in a firefight that *your* husband caused, Danny was hurt enough that Ian had to carry him out," she said, then taking a deep breath. "So don't tell me that he's still a part of this team, because the hell he is!"

As certain as I was that none of that should have been shared, I was just as sure that Zahra O'Reilly was overwrought. Her husband had confided to her that because of the actions of one man, he was nearly killed, and because of the actions of another, he was still alive. All of that information was there, in her head, in her heart, running around, and seeing the wife of the guy responsible for her husband's brush with death tipped her over the edge.

She broke down then, the tears simmering right there below the surface.

Stacy was quick; I was quicker. Before she reached her, I had Zahra in my arms, wrapped up and held tight.

She cried into my chest as Stacy rubbed her back, and then Stacy turned to Chloe.

"It's not your fault. She knows it, I know it. No one's blaming you, but you're here, and that's reminding us all that our husbands and fathers and sons and boyfriends could be coming home in body bags if it weren't for the quick action of certain members of the team when your husband's actions put them all in jeopardy."

Chloe stood there, not sure what to do, but her friend, the one who was after my man, grabbed her arm and pulled her away from us.

"I'm so sorry, Miro, I cried all over you," Zahra lamented.

"Any time," I assured her.

"Oh, he's a keeper," Stacy said, putting an arm around Zahra's shoulders. "And look, there they are."

The first guy came out, wearing his Army combat uniform—ACUs—and hefting a huge duffel, but he was still able to drop it and easily catch the woman who flew up to him and vaulted into his waiting arms. She hit him hard, but he absorbed the impact and wrapped his arms around her.

All the women there were greeting men who, like Ian, left for two weeks and were gone four months more.

They all came through then, all in the same color fatigues, all with caps on, all with duffels. Zahra's husband was big, and when he took off his hat to greet his wife, I saw a lot of red-orange hair before she wrapped her arms around his neck and delivered a scorching kiss that he returned until neither of them could possibly breathe.

Stacy ran and jumped, too, and her husband took hold of her thighs to make sure her legs, coiled around his hips, wouldn't get dislodged. Clearly he didn't want to be parted from her for even a second.

Even if I hadn't seen Ian's face, I would have known it was him just from his swaggering, fluid stride. Before we were friends, I used to wish I could be intimidating just by moving. People never got out of *my* way, but I'd seen people scatter for Ian as they did now, making room for him to get through.

The dogtags with black silencers contrasted sharply on the tan of the T-shirt he was wearing under his open field jacket. His cap was pulled down low, but I still saw the bright blue I was looking for and marveled at the beauty of the man, the innate power, and I felt instant joy in seeing him strong and whole.

It was like walking in the front door after being away, that overwhelming feeling of rightness, of belonging, of peace. He was my home, and I had to grit my teeth with the surge of emotion and the sting behind my eyes.

Ian was my home.

I didn't wave. I didn't have to because he saw me and immediately scowled. His reaction caused the reverse in me. I smiled big, huge, relief and happiness, lust and love all swirling together in a tempest of gratitude that I was sure every other wife, girlfriend, partner, and significant other felt as well. I was probably glowing. The closer he got, the madder he looked until he reached me, dropped his duffel, and took my face in his hard, callused hands.

"What the hell happened to you?" he growled.

One of his eyes had blood in it. I saw purple-and-yellow bruises from fingers that had been around his throat, fresher bruises along the right side of his jaw and he had a splint on the pinky and ring fingers of his left hand. Not his shooting hand, so it would not impact his ability to do his job, or be with me on said job. Because any more time spent away from him, for any reason, would be too much.

"I could ask the same question," I teased, so happy to see him I could actually feel my skin heat. I wanted his hands all over me as fast as they could be.

"I'm fine," he said, stepping closer, bumping against me, scrutinizing the bruises.

"Yeah? You're fine?"

"I—"

I dropped my voice to a whisper even though no one was sparing us even a glance and the closest couple was several feet away. "Good enough to fuck me into the mattress at home?"

I saw my words wash over him. His pupils dilated, he parted his lips and caught his breath. Taken all together, it was a thoroughly satisfying reaction.

"Can you?" I asked, closing my eyes, bumping my forehead gently against his, inhaling his scent and slipping my hands around his hips. "Ian?"

We stood there, silent, breathing each other's air, and his sigh, like he could finally relax, made me smile.

"You have no idea how much thinking about you I've done," he confessed, swallowing hard. "I dreamed about holding you down."

The jolt of arousal slammed through me.

"I just—I need you so bad it feels like I've got ants crawling around under my skin."

It was good to hear I was not alone in my desire. Normally I did the fucking, but sometimes I wanted to be on the bottom, and at the moment, I was ready to be, excited to be. All I could imagine was his weight on me and being under him, begging.

"You miss me?" My words came out rushed and aching.

"More than you could possibly imagine," he rumbled, nuzzling a kiss against the side of my neck.

Opening my eyes, I looked at his good one and his hurt one. "Then let's go home."

"Yes," he said before he slipped a hand around the back of my head, tangled his fingers in my hair, and brought me in for a kiss.

I had no idea he'd do that in front of people, in front of men he fought with, their wives, and any strangers who might pass by. I was amazed for a moment before I forgot everything else and kissed him back, wrapping my arms around his waist and bringing our bodies flush together.

Already it was the best homecoming ever.

CHAPTER 5

IAN INTRODUCED me to all the members of his unit from the guy in charge on down. I shook all their hands, and it seemed to me they were all genuinely pleased to meet me. I could have been wrong, it could have been an elaborate act, but it was doubtful, as tired and wrung out as they all looked. Obviously, whatever they'd all been through had been an ordeal.

Thinking about how long they'd been gone was not a good idea, because instead of being happy Ian was home, I started thinking about how long he'd been gone, and that only led to resentment. So it wasn't a surprise when the question popped out, even inadvertently, and neither was Ian's standard reply.

"I dunno when I'll have to go back," he said, looking out the window of my Toyota Tacoma at the rain-washed streets. What started out as a drizzle was now looking like the fifth day of Noah's journey. "They could call us back up tomorrow, you know that."

I concentrated on the road, even though the drive was easy. The Lincoln Expressway was not going underwater anytime soon.

"So you're gonna be pissed now?" he snapped after a few minutes of silence.

"No," I assured him, trying to keep my voice calm and steady, without any bite. "I shouldn't have asked. I just—like you here, is all."

"You don't think I wanna be home?"

I cleared my throat. "I do and I don't want to fight with you. That was not my intention."

"Then what'd you bring it up for?"

"It just came out, I'm sorry."

He was quiet, I was quiet, so we could both hear the tires on the wet pavement and the rain on the roof of the car.

"You don't get it because you've never served."

"I know," I acceded quickly, careful not to get tripped up there.

"And I can't tell you where I was or what I did."

I knew that too. The few times I'd asked, all he said was, "We were in the woods." Sometimes I'd see things on the news about a firefight in some village halfway around the world and wonder if Ian was there. It had become—much like the marriage issue—a question of what Ian would do. What could he do and still be him.

We'd answered the question of us getting married with an absolute, rock solid… someday. It was on the table for sure, but the when was the issue. Yes, he loved me; yes, he wanted to be married—or could see it now instead of not at all—but there was still no definitive plan. What loomed even bigger lately was the military service.

As an Army reservist officer, Ian served at the pleasure of the president, which meant anytime they needed him, he went. I was proud of him for his service as a Green Beret, but I also felt like he'd done enough, given enough of his time, and watching it erode his mind and body got more and more painful to witness.

His dreams made him cry out in his sleep, the injuries he came home with were a horror, and the fact that he had as of late started sleeping with his spare gun, his SIG Sauer P228, under the bed was cause for concern. We didn't say PTSD because Ian said he knew guys who had it "for real" and a few nightmares were not that big a deal. But I knew better. It was eating him up, things he did, things he saw, and at some point he was going to have to deal with all that, just as I had to deal with being kidnapped by a psychopath a year ago. The difference was that my horror was over except for the fallout, and Ian's was a constant in his life.

"So," I said, clearing my throat, "what time is the funeral tomorrow?"

"Eleven."

"I'm really sorry about your friend."

"We weren't friends," he corrected me, finally turning from the window. "But he was in my old unit, so I gotta go."

"Of course."

"Is this gonna be a thing?"

"What?"

"Me going?"

"No."

"You're lying."

I had to think. "Not—it's both, right?"

"Explain."

I shrugged. "It's your service, and I get that it's what you feel you need to do, but I think, why are you still doing this? When will it be enough?"

He exhaled sharply. "You don't understand."

"Because I've never been in the military, I know. You say that all the time. But seriously, why do you have to go? Why does it have to be you?"

"What if something happens to my unit because I'm not there?"

"You're saying you're the only person who can do your job?"

"I'm saying I do my job really well, and there aren't a lot of guys with my training or my experience, so yeah, I'm the most qualified."

"So there's nobody else with your skill set."

"That's not what I'm saying. I'm saying, of the guys out there, I'm one of the best."

"Which I don't doubt in the least, but this is something you choose to do."

"Yeah."

"So I'm asking, when will it be enough? When will you stop?"

He was silent a moment. "I'll stop when they don't need me anymore."

"Which is never," I mumbled. "Okay."

"Okay what?"

"Okay, I have my answer."

"Which means what?"

"It means I know what I'm in for then."

We were silent until I pulled up on our street in Lincoln Park and slid in behind a sleek little silver Saab.

Getting out, I grabbed the umbrella behind the seat and went to dart around the side to cover Ian, but he threw open the door, yanked his now soggy duffel from the bed of the truck, and started charging down the sidewalk toward home.

Locking the vehicle with the remote, I jogged after him, but when I tried to cover his head, he batted the umbrella away.

"Why're you being an ass now?" I shouted over the sound of the driving rain.

He rounded on me. "If it's not worth it, we should just call it quits already," he barked.

I was stunned… for a second. And then I felt the anger wash through me, over me, spread to my tightening gut and up into my throat I could barely get sound out of.

"If you want out, be out," he said flippantly. "But the bitching about me serving my country is killing me."

The serving his country part was a nice dig.

"Did you hear me?" he asked curtly.

"I did," I replied, meeting his gaze. "And yeah, I'm out."

His eyes went wide as I pivoted and stalked down the street.

Chickie met me at the front door, but instead of petting him, I wrenched him outside by his collar and pointed him down the street.

"Look, it's Daddy," I choked out and watched as the werewolf flew down the stoop, heading for Ian.

Slamming the door shut behind me, I turned on the lights, hurled the umbrella into the stand, kicked off my sneakers, and headed upstairs. I had my coat hung up and everything that was wet off my body when I heard the front door bang shut.

"The fuck are you doing?" he roared up at me.

Standing beside the railing on the loft, staring down into the living room at him, I realized he was shaking. Hard to tell if he was cold or mad, but I was guessing a little of both.

"You—" I started but stopped, unable, even in the midst of a crisis, not to smile.

"The hell are... you... oh, for fuck's sake."

Chickie.

He was so happy to see Ian, he was jumping up and down beside him. He wasn't touching Ian, but he was obviously so excited, so over the moon, that he could barely stand it, and as a result, he was doing a really good kangaroo impersonation. The height he was reaching was impressive.

Up and down, over and over, the epitome of joyful delight.

Stupid dog.

Ian did a slow turn, and Chickie whimpered and whined, stopped hopping for a second and made a circle, singing to his master in a sweet low howl he normally saved for serenading Sajani before he put his front paws on Ian's shoulders and licked his face all over.

The chuckle that came out of me was involuntary, but watching Chickie bounce around, there was no way to keep a straight face.

"Get down," Ian grumbled as he petted his wet dog and tried to wipe rain and dog slobber off his face with his own dripping sleeve.

"You should take a shower," I told him. "I'll come down and dry off Chick."

His head snapped up. "How could you just say—"

"How could you," I fired back, leaning over the railing. "That was bullshit and you know it, but you said it anyway because you're mad at the situation and taking that crap out on me."

His glare was dark.

"I've never once said I didn't want you, not ever. Do I get the whole putting yourself in danger all the time? No, I don't. Do I get you signing up to be away from me? No, I don't get that either," I growled. "What I *do* get is that you feel like you have to because you're the only one who can. And even though I think that's a helluva lot of ego there—because I'm betting there are others just as trained up as you—I get that if something ever were to happen and you weren't there, you'd feel guilty for the rest of your life."

"Ego?"

I made a noise in the back of my throat and turned to go to the bathroom. "Fine, if that's your only takeaway, I—"

"Don't you dare move!"

"Then listen to me, for fuck's sake!" I yelled at him as I turned.

He threw up his hands in reply.

"Where the combat is concerned, yeah, I think that's your ego at work," I retorted, not backing down. "Because the only place you're not replaceable, where no one else will do, is right here with me. Here, at home—you're it, and if you're too stupid to—"

"Shut up," he rasped, his jaw clenching as he inhaled a breath through his nose.

I crossed my arms and waited.

"I'm a soldier."

I was going to tell him I knew that already, but he lifted a hand to keep me quiet.

"First before anything, that's what I am," he ground out, flicking his gaze up to meet mine. "It's not going to change."

"But that doesn't mean that's all you are because you yourself have told me it's not."

It took him a moment before he gave me a nod. "Yeah, that's true."

"And I know you're not going to change being a soldier." That hurt. It did. I felt in my heart that he wouldn't stop doing it for me on the chance his commitment could mean his death. I was certainly taking a backseat to his military career, if I chose to think of it that way. But the other way to see Ian's choice was through his eyes. Being a Green Beret was part of who he was, long before he met me. It was what made Ian, Ian. His promise to his country meant the world to him, and who was I to make him give that up? And if he didn't do it, would he still be the man I loved?

"Miro?"

I refocused on him.

"Do you still want me if this is your life?"

I scowled at him and I saw him swallow, watched his throat work, from where I was.

"Yes, Ian," I replied soberly, feeling the tightening in my jaw, the burn behind my eyes. "I want you, and that's never gonna change."

He stood below me, not moving, simply giving me his patented blank stare.

"But let's not pretend I don't care and that I'm happy about it. You're the one who's gotta think, is this going to be too hard for me to know that; yes, he supports me, but he hates it when I'm gone?"

"I—"

"No, you have to really think about it."

He shook his head. "I don't."

I shivered because I was in underwear and a T-shirt and nothing else.

"You being upset 'cause I'm leaving you and missing me and waiting for me to come back—I'm thinking there are worse things."

I grunted and then gestured at the dog. "You get to dry him now; I'ma take a shower and then I'll make some dinner."

He nodded and left for the laundry room where Chickie's towel was hanging from a peg by the back door.

I was freezing, so instead of putting on clothes, I took a really hot, really fast shower. I was drying off when the bathroom door opened and Ian came through.

"It's all yours," I said, stepping aside.

He barred my path.

I stopped towel drying my hair and looked at him.

Ian had beautiful eyes that were this clear, vivid blue, creased in the corners by the greatest laugh lines anyone had ever seen. At the moment, though, they were marked with worry and pain. I felt like crap knowing I was some of the reason.

"I hate that you're a reservist," I blurted.

"I know."

"But don't ever confuse that with how I feel about you."

He nodded.

"Are we clear?"

Second nod.

I went to move around him, but again, he stepped into my path. When I smiled, I heard his sigh of relief. "I wanna feed you so you'll still think it's a good thing to have me pick you up at the airport."

He closed the slight distance between us and put his hands on my hips. "It'll always be a good idea. I'm sorry I didn't do it before."

The silky rasp of his voice made my pulse jump, and I moved that quickly from how sweet the man was, to how sexy, to how long it had been since he was in my bed.

When he touched me, the groan that came out of me was needy and desperate. The dirty grin I got from Ian, all heat and lust, sent blood rushing to my cock.

"Oh yeah, I had different plans," he husked, leaning in and taking my mouth in a hungry kiss that left no question of what those were.

But my brain was playing the conversation over and over and my heart was hurting, so just because he got what he wanted didn't mean I was ready to go all warm and willing on him.

Easing him off me, I tried to smile and left the bathroom, promising him food as I went.

"What was that?" he asked, stalking around in front of me as I reached our closet. An armoire that held underwear, briefs, and T-shirts, as well as socks, stood inside of it because we'd needed more space. Well, I had. Ian's wardrobe was minimalist to say the least.

"What was what?"

He studied me a moment before crossing his arms over his chest. "What're you gonna make?"

I sighed, thankful that he wasn't pushing. "Aruna made roasted jerk chicken with carrots and potatoes for us. All I have to do is warm it up."

"When did she bring that over?"

"Yesterday," I said, shucking the towel and pulling on a pair of briefs. "And oh, I gotta tell you something."

He listened as I told him about Janet being pregnant and then smiled as I gently patted his cheek before ducking out of the room.

I darted back into the bathroom just to use the requisite items so I didn't smell and my hair didn't stick straight up. Down in the kitchen a few minutes later, I was going to open a bottle of wine, but thought better of it because Ian wasn't a fan.

"Hey."

I walked into the living room so I could look up at him in the loft. I was surprised he was standing there naked, and it hurt to see so many new bruises. There were also stiches beneath his collarbone on the right side.

"That looks bad," I said, pointing.

"That's what you're looking at?" he teased, the grin absolutely lethal.

I gave him a shrug.

"Tough room."

"You could have been killed."

He shook his head. "It's nothing."

"It needed a needle and thread."

"A long time ago," he informed me.

"Couldn't have been that long."

"Can you just drop it?"

I turned to go back in the kitchen.

"Hello."

Stopping, I gave him my attention again.

"Are you going to lighten up?"

I remained silent.

"Maybe I shouldn't have come home at all."

Any word out of my mouth I would instantly regret, so I swallowed down the attack and kept my eyes locked on him as I crossed my arms. It was a low blow, and childish, and I wanted to climb the stairs and both beat him and hug him as hard as I could.

He cleared his throat. "Okay, so that was a shitty thing to say."

I lifted one eyebrow in complete agreement.

"Yeah," he sighed. "Really shitty."

I felt like I was standing in the middle of a minefield. Any way I turned, there could be another explosion, so I kept quiet, jaw clenched, focusing on that, on being still, instead of blowing up and venting my frustration all over him.

"So, uhm, do we have anything to drink?"

It took a second for me to speak, and when I did, my voice sounded strained and filled with gravel. "I have all kinds of beer for you."

"Do we have any of the KBS left?" he asked hopefully.

"We do."

"That's what I want," he almost whimpered.

"You got it. Shower," I commanded before returning to the kitchen.

Things felt odd, unbalanced, like we were off somehow, and I wanted to fix it but I wasn't exactly sure how to do that. How did you restore normalcy after that talk?

I WAS tossing a salad when the doorbell rang. It was Saturday night, a little after nine, so it was a strange to have someone there, but since Chickie got up and rambled to the door, taking his sweet time, not barking, I figured whoever it was, he knew.

Checking the peephole, I found Barrett Van Allen. He had a bottle of wine in one hand and a bag of what looked like Chinese food in the other.

"Aww shit," I said as I opened the door. "Did we have plans that I spaced on?"

"Nice greeting," he teased, smacking my abdomen as he chuckled and walked by me into the house. He didn't wait for an invite. We'd already established on a number of occasions that he didn't need one, and he petted Chickie as he passed. "And no, man, how could we? You just got back. But I saw your light on when I got home from work, figured there was nothing in your fridge, and thought I'd help you out."

It was thoughtful of him and one of the many reasons I'd grown to like him since he'd moved in next door a little more than three months ago.

"But it smells great in here already," he said, passing me the bottle of the Trimbach Gewurztraminer he knew I liked. "And since I don't hear any jazz and you're cooking—is your guy back?"

"Yeah, Ian's home."

"Oh, then I'll go," he said, trying to give me the bag of food as well. "I didn't mean to intrude."

I shook my head, holding the bottle out to him. "Don't worry about it, but take this with you so you—"

"Hello."

We turned to see Ian in a white T-shirt and jeans, standing at the top of the stairs.

"Hey." Barrett smiled at him. "Sorry to intrude. Just dropping off some alcohol and takeout."

Ian smiled back, but it didn't reach his eyes as he descended. He glanced at Chickie, who was standing beside Barrett, letting him scratch behind his ears, and then padded across the floor in his bare feet to join us.

He reached out, and he and Barrett shook hands.

"Ian, this is Barrett Van Allen. He bought the house on the left," I explained. "And Barrett, this is Ian Doyle, who you've heard all about."

"I have," he replied affably. "It's good to meet you, marshal."

Ian nodded and withdrew his hand, taking the bottle of wine Barrett had brought over from me. "I heard what you said, and you're right, there's no jazz on. Miro thinks I don't like it, but I just like my music better."

Barrett chuckled. "Well, I have to tell you, Miro had the windows open the day I moved in, and the music was coming out of here along with the smell of—what was it?" he asked, turning to me, hand on my bicep.

"Pot roast," I supplied, remembering.

"That's right," he sighed, and I heard the regard in his voice, the warmth and contentment. "And the mix of the two of them, and then Miro out back throwing the ball for your werewolf—I felt better than I had in months."

"Werewolf," Ian repeated, using my word for Chickie just as Barrett had.

"He took pity on me and fed me, and—well, when you're new to a city, it's really nice to make a friend."

"It is," Ian granted with a nod.

"And even though I've met a ton of new people now—Miro was the first, so I've got kind of a soft spot for him."

"Sure," Ian mumbled. "So where'd you move from?"

"Manhattan," Barrett sighed, giving Ian a lopsided grin. "But it was time for a change, and when Mayhew and Burgess came calling, I had to say yes."

"I don't know what that is."

"It's one of the biggest law firms here in Chicago along with Jenner Knox and Pembroke, Talbot and Leeds."

Ian looked sideways at me.

I shrugged. "I had no idea either."

His smile made my pulse race; he had that effect on me. "We don't know any lawyers here that's why, only in LA."

I was ridiculously touched that he remembered where my friend Min practiced law, and slipped my hand into his.

"You do now," Barrett interrupted, giving Ian's shoulder a gentle pat.

"Barrett's now one of the top defense lawyers in the city," I told Ian.

"Well, lucky we're marshals, so we don't need him," he said, lifting my hand and kissing my knuckles before he let me go.

"But friends we can use," I said, flashing him a smile before I went into the kitchen to check on the food and finish making the salad. "Especially ones who bring good wine."

"Aww, gee, thanks, I feel so loved," Barrett volleyed before walking by Ian to follow after me, putting the takeout on the counter. "And I got your favorite, the spicy eggplant, so you've got to keep it."

"How 'bout this. I'll keep that, and you take your weenie-ass mild kung pao chicken."

His snort of laughter made me smile.

"Not all of us can handle hot," he said, walking around behind me and putting a hand on my back. "But I've got to ask, what did you make? Because it smells fantastic in here."

"Aruna cooked, not me."

"Really?" His voice cracked.

"Do you know Aruna?" Ian asked as he joined us in the kitchen.

"Yes, I met her when Miro took me with him to her house on Labor Day. We had this amazing meal, her husband made smoked lamb—which I thought would be disgusting—but it didn't taste like anything I'd ever had, and the sides she made were just phenomenal."

"You sound a little starved for home cooking," Ian observed. "How long's it been since you had any?"

"Two weeks ago I took Miro to a Blackhawks game and he fed me before that."

Ian nodded.

"It was just meatloaf and mashed potatoes and green beans," I commented, because he didn't need to make a big deal out of such a small thing.

"No," Barrett said with a long exhale. "It was fantastic and I owe you a good dinner out in return. Next time Ian's deployed, it's a date."

I groaned. "Don't say deployed. I just got him back."

"I'm sure it will be a long time from now," Barrett soothed.

"God, I hope so," I sighed, checking on the food.

"You should stay and eat," Ian said, passing the wine bottle back to Barrett. "And open that up for you and Miro. I'ma get a beer."

"No, man, it's your homecoming. I don't want to be a third wheel."

"It's just food," Ian assured him, opening our Philco refrigerator and hunting for the beer he wanted. "There's no floor show."

Barrett laughed, clearly liking Ian already.

"Just stay and eat," I insisted. "Put the bag in the fridge unless you wanna run it back to your place."

"No, I want to get the wine open because I'm dying to hear what happened to your face there, gorgeous."

"My fuckin' asshat ex-partner tagged me."

"I'm sure there's more to the story than that."

"There is, but you're not hearin' it," I teased.

"I need to, though," Ian reminded me.

"Well, you're allowed," I quipped. "But not the lawyer."

"No? Are you sure?" Barrett prodded, finding his way around the kitchen easily, rummaging in the junk drawer for the corkscrew and going to work on the bottle. "Because I think I need to sue someone."

I made a face.

"Seriously, the two of you together look like you beat the crap out of each other."

My scoff was loud. "Please, it'd be no contest. Ian could kill me if he wanted."

"I don't know, Special Forces or not, I think you could hold your own, M."

"You're hysterical," I said sarcastically. "You need to go look up Green Berets and what they actually do."

"He doesn't have to research shit," Ian said, having found the bottle of KBS he was looking for and getting the opener out of the same junk drawer Barrett had just been in. "'Cause, yanno, we're never gonna have to find out who could kick the crap outta who."

"No, of course not," Barrett allowed as Ian flipped the bottle cap into the sink before taking a long pull on his beer.

"And I'd only hurt Miro if he begged me," he said seductively, the look he shot Barrett not altogether friendly.

"Kinky," Barrett said before turning back to me. "You sure you can't share?"

"Yeah. Sorry. It's interdepartmental shenanigans."

"Well, listen, if anything gets weird between you guys—like if your ex-partner gets representation, you call me."

"I don't need a lawyer to talk to IAD and OPR and everyone else. It's just procedure," I explained. "Part of the job."

Barrett shrugged. "Things change fast, I've seen it. If they do, you let me know."

I bumped his shoulder when I passed him his plate. "Thanks."

The dinner conversation was nice, with Barrett telling Ian about him and his friends finding me and mine at a pub close by.

"All my friends except Miro are all lawyers, right," he said, laughing. "So he's playing pool with his guys and we get there and start to do some trash talking, and all of a sudden, there's some damn serious pool happening."

Ian was grinning.

"And this is where it gets sad," I explained dramatically.

Barrett pointed at me. "He doesn't need to know that part."

"Aww, I think he does," I baited, leaning into Ian as I drained my third glass of wine.

Ian bumped his knee with mine under the table and then wrapped his hand around the inside of my thigh. "Tell me," he pried.

Barrett cleared his throat. "I met Ethan."

Ian squinted at him. "Sharpe?"

He shifted in his seat and drained his second glass.

I watched Ian lean forward, studying Barrett, his eyes brightening as they hadn't since he came down the stairs in that sinful pair of ass hugging jeans he had on. "What happened with you and Sharpe?"

Barrett groaned.

Ian's smile was incorrigible. "Did Miro not tell you that Sharpe hustles pool?"

"He did," Barrett grumbled. "But I thought, you know, how good could he really be?"

Ian's snort of laughter sounded good.

"He takes his pool very, very seriously," Barrett almost whined.

"He does," Ian agreed, still with the merciless cat-that-swallowed-the-canary-grin on his face. "And he never lets anyone out of a bet."

"Shit."

"How much are you into him for?"

"It's not money," I informed Ian. "Sharpe needs a new wingman."

"Oh no," Ian said, cackling. "That's terrible."

"Did you know Sharpe frequents dance clubs?"

"I did, yes." Ian was enjoying Barrett's distress quite a bit. "He has an entire wing of his closet devoted to club clothes."

"Oh God," he moaned.

I started laughing.

"Miro has a fuckton of fashion himself, but Sharpe—and Kohn too—that's some scary shit."

"I don't dance."

"I'm thinking you do now," Ian said, waggling his eyebrows.

"It's like high school all over again."

Ian's laughter was such a good sound. When he reached out and patted Barrett's shoulder, I saw my new friend flip him off.

The rest of dinner was nice, and Barrett told Ian some of his better court appearance stories and found out what everyone who knew Ian had discovered at some point—that having his full and undivided attention was more addictive than any drug. The way he leaned in; how animated his face got as he sat and held eye contact; and the evil, conspiratorial smile at the end—like it was just the two of you in on some big juicy secret—was all its own reward. I heard Barrett's catch of breath, and when he glanced at me, I gave him the nod.

Later, in the kitchen as he was grabbing the takeout that only he would eat—Ian didn't like mild anything either—from the fridge, he said "Yeah, I get it."

"What do you get?" I asked innocently.

He made a conciliatory noise, sort of a grunt and acknowledgment together. "He's the whole package: pretty and funny and dangerous. I see why you're so devoted."

"I totally dare you to tell him he's pretty."

His laughter was warm as he leaned in for a hug. When he pulled back after the tight embrace, he told me he wanted us both to come to his place for Thanksgiving.

"We'll definitely stop by," I promised as I started rinsing dishes.

"Good," he said, giving my arm a pat before he turned to leave.

"You don't have to go," I assured him. "I promise I'm not trying to get rid of you."

"I know, and that's awfully nice of you, but Miro, come on, you're awfully easy on the eyes there yourself, and if I was Ian and I just got back from four months away—I'd want the new guy from next door to get the hell out so I could make with the homecoming already."

I shook my head. "We're fine."

"Listen," Barrett said, leaning in close. "If Ian was looking at me the same way he's been looking at you all night, I'd have put you on the sidewalk with a plate of hot food in your hand."

"Uh-huh," I placated, watching as he crossed the living room to the front door.

"You're an idiot," he called over, stopping in the doorway he'd opened, half-in, half-out of our Greystone.

But I was really good at reading Ian's signals, and he'd had a relaxing evening just eating and having a few beers. "Yeah, but you picked me to be your friend, so, yanno, what does that say about you?"

He shook his head like I was ridiculous before turning his attention to Ian and Chickie, who were coming back from a quick walk after dinner. He and Ian did the guy clench, and I watched, pleased they'd hit it off.

Turning back to the cleanup, I heard the door shut and the lock slide. "Hey, I'll take care of the dishes," I called to Ian, not turning to look at him or check where he was. "You go veg and watch TV or whatever."

There wasn't a lot to do. The three of us had successfully annihilated all hope of leftovers, but I had to get the dishwasher loaded since the last time we left stuff in the sink, Chickie tonguebathed everything and got sick enough to warrant a visit to the vet. That had been fun to explain to Dr. Alchureiqi, who wasn't impressed with my dog ownership skills to begin with. To him Ian was the more responsible pet parent.

"I don't wanna watch TV," Ian said as he came into the kitchen.

"All right, but I saved all the episodes of *The Walking Dead* for you."

"I appreciate that."

And we were back to being awkward. I had to figure out what to do to fix things. "Sorry if Barrett embarrassed you."

"Why the hell would I be embarrassed?" he asked, coming up behind me and pressing a kiss to my nape.

I tried to turn to look at him, but he bumped me up against the counter, shoving his groin against my ass.

"Why're you being so weird?"

"Me?"

"Yeah, you," he growled, kissing down the side of my neck, curling his right arm around my chest, taking firm hold of my left pectoral, groping me savagely with the other hand, showing me what he wanted. "I came home with one thing on my mind—you—and you're inviting neighbors to have dinner? The fuck is that?"

"We—fuck!" I gasped as he worked open the top button of my jeans before I heard the rasp of the zipper, drawn down slow, a single flickering bulb catching on its gold teeth. I felt it, like a heartbeat, each fraction it moved.

"We what?" he prodded, slipping his hand under the elastic of my briefs, skimming his coarse, callused skin over my thickening shaft.

"I just want us to be okay," I whimpered, the sound almost pleading, bucking in his hands, the sensations running through my body like a live wire crackling on wet cement, causing my brain to lose track of what I was saying. "And we keep fighting."

"That's because neither of us wants to give in," he admitted, his voice dropping low, the seductive murmur, just the sound of him making me boneless and pliable, completely his, ready for whatever it was he wanted. "Both of us want the other guy to say, 'Yeah, fuck, you're right.'"

I dropped my head back against his shoulder as he slipped my cock out from under my briefs and stroked me until I was hard and leaking in his hand.

"I want you to say it's okay that I leave you all alone for months on end and you want me to fuckin' quit," he said, his voice rough as I heard him work on getting out of his jeans, the sound of his zipper loud in the quiet room, my halting breath the only other noise.

"Yes," I agreed, twisting free and leaning forward on the counter, legs braced apart as far as my jeans would allow. I was more than ready for him, needing him to *show* me what I meant to him, because the words weren't working.

"But it's not gonna happen," he said, forcing me to turn around and face him, manhandling me so there was no choice, we were that close. "We want two different things 'cause we're two different people." It was difficult to focus on his words when his jeans were shoved half way down his muscular thighs. "But you knew the job was dangerous when you took it."

"Job?"

"Loving me," he explained, his lip curling into a rakish grin.

I searched his eyes, the blown pupils letting me know—as if his own erect, dripping cock bumping mine didn't—that he was very much aroused.

He stepped into me, wrapping his big, strong hand around us both as he first traced the seam of my lips with his tongue before taking my mouth in a hard, plundering kiss.

I moaned deep, no way not to, and the answering rough chuckle made me smile.

"Concentrate," he ground out before he shoved his tongue inside, pushing and rubbing, hungry and urgent, his teeth bumping my lips as he began stroking us both, the languid movement in direct contrast to the raw possessiveness of the violent, ravenous kiss.

Ian had a way—this dizzying, breathless way—of getting me to melt into him, wrap my arms around his neck and simply hold on as he became the epicenter of all my yearning, of all my devouring, ravenous need.

I was his, I belonged to him, there was no end to that, and he knew it. Knew he could take until there was nothing left. I loved all the way; I held nothing back. I was lucky he was the same.

"Ian," I gasped because I had to have more. More friction, more pressure, more slide. When I tried to add my hand over his, I was surprised when he shoved me off.

Bumping me back against the counter, he dropped quickly to his knees.

His eyes were like a slice of midnight, and I could only watch, not trusting myself to speak or move, as he leaned forward and took me down the back of his throat.

"Jesus," I whispered hoarsely, grabbing the counter behind me, gripping tight as my knees nearly buckled with the force of the suction on my dick.

Ian, who had never given head before he was with me, knew what he liked when I did it, and so did the same. Sucking and laving, his nose buried in my pubes one second, pulling back a moment later, he was in constant motion that threatened to have me spilling down his throat if he didn't stop and let me breathe.

I clutched his head, tipping his face back so I could stare down into his gorgeous eyes. Being swallowed in all that deep dark blue made my heart clench.

"I don't wanna... come."

The smile he gave me, wicked and hot, made me shiver. "But I want you to," he rumbled, closing his hand around my length, slippery with spit. "I want you to come, and then I wanna swallow it all, and then you're gonna go upstairs and get on your hands and knees in our bed."

The sound of his voice, deep and husky, working up from the back of his throat, almost set me off right there.

"All I've thought about this whole time," he murmured, scraping his teeth gently over the head of my cock, "was you."

"Same," I promised.

"Then give the fuck in."

No question. "Yes," I garbled out as he followed his teeth with his tongue.

"Now, Miro," he commanded as I slid my hand over the top of his head, brushing my fingers over the short military buzz-cut that would take time to grow out, and yanked him forward so I could fuck his mouth.

Between the heat and pressure, the easy slide and constant rhythm, I was there in seconds, spurting, releasing, giving myself over to him as I had to no one else since he said yes to me the first time.

He swallowed fast but didn't lick me clean, instead leaving me messy and dripping as he rose and kissed me sloppily, almost drunkenly, mauling my mouth so I could taste myself on his tongue, smell myself on his breath, and know I'd been at his mercy.

When he stepped back, giving me room to gulp air, I got my legs to work, stepped out of my jeans and underwear pooled around my ankles, and moved past him on my way to the stairs.

I didn't stop. I reached the second floor, stumbled around the railing, and walked to the bed, collapsing down on top of it before pushing myself to my hands and knees.

My heart hammered in my ears, all I could hear, so I jolted when he slid a hand down the middle of my back.

"There's something about seeing you like this that really fuckin' does it for me."

"Why's that?" I rasped as he got on the bed beside me, smoothing his hands down my sides, tracing over my ribs, my hips, and finally reaching the curve of my ass.

"I think it's knowing how strong you are, that you could stop me if you wanted," he said, turning my head sideways so he could reclaim my mouth, biting gently, kissing, sucking until I had to pull back to breathe.

"You never kiss me this much."

"I will from now on."

"How come?" I couldn't keep from asking.

"'Cause I dreamed about it every night," Ian confessed, and his grin wasn't predatory, but sheepish, sweet. "I dreamed about your mouth and kissing you and touching your skin… hearing you scream when I fuck you."

The glint in his eyes made my dick throb.

"Look at you," he said reverently, sliding his hands over my hips before he closed them on my ass and spread my cheeks.

"Ian," I barely got out, my voice deserting me as he licked over my hole.

"You're gonna have to do better'n that," he said before he speared his tongue inside me. A whine I wasn't proud of tumbled up from my gut. "Say my name, love."

The endless rimming, deep inside to my core and then out, circling, loosening my muscles, sent me again and again to the verge of a splintering orgasm, only to lessen and keep me from slipping over the edge. I was helpless to do anything but fist my hands in the comforter and let Ian explore and devour me, unable to manage more than a mewling plea for him to not stop.

"Who do you want?"

I yelled his name a second time.

"Better," he agreed, holding me open as he continued the ravishing onslaught for almost longer than I could bear.

When my arms gave out, I went facedown on the mattress, loose and ready, and I was surprised when Ian rolled me to my back and got off the bed. My confusion must have shown on my face because he smiled wide as he went to the nightstand.

"I thought you wanted to fuck me," I said, admiring the wide, thickly muscled chest, his sculpted arms and long legs and perfect taut ass, marveling as I always did at the carved lines of the man, all of him built strong and powerful.

"Oh, I do," he assured me, coming back around the end of the bed with the lube. "But I'm gonna be holding those beautiful thighs of yours when we do it."

I grinned. "You've been thinking about holding on to me while you fuck me."

He exhaled sharply and I saw the muscles cord in his neck as his left hand fisted tight. He was keeping a tight leash on himself. "Yeah."

"Then come on."

He pounced on me, not careful; opened the lube and spread it fast, the coldness of his slick fingers pressing inside me a perfect counterbalance to the wet heat there.

"You okay?" he asked, checking on me, his voice gravelly and low.

"Yes," I answered softly. "Please… now."

Even with all the prep, Ian was careful, moving slowly, screwing himself inside inch by inch, allowing me to get used to him before he sank in any deeper, until finally his impressive length was buried to the hilt in my ass.

"Jesus, that thing is fuckin' huge," I sighed, loving the feeling of fullness with the stretch and burn, all the sensations together running the razor's edge between pleasure and pain.

"You feel so good," he crooned, taking my cock in hand, squeezing and pulling, working my flesh in his palm, easing out, then back in so when he pressed down into me the second time, his dick grazed all the places I needed.

"Oh fuck, Ian," I cried out as he gripped my thighs, spreading and lifting as he slid within me, back and forth, his motion small at first but slowly increasing, faster and faster. He was watching me, absorbing the sight of me coming apart in his hands.

"You're with me," he snarled, his voice thick and dark as he lifted my legs and draped them over his shoulders. "Everybody knows that, right?"

"Of course," I promised as he thrust hard, driving deep, each snap of his hips punishing and exquisite at the same time.

"You need to tell people when I'm not here," he said as his hot skin, slick with sweat, slipped over mine while he pistoned inside me, everywhere feeling electric and connected.

"I do," I reminded him gently, moving my legs from his shoulders and wrapping them around his hips, bringing him closer. "Now stop."

"You want me to stop?"

"Not with your body, with your head," I clarified. "Stop thinking and worrying, baby, we're good."

He searched my face, stilling as he studied me. "Yeah?"

"I swear. We're okay. We're gonna be okay."

Deep heaving breath out of him as he nodded quickly.

"Do me a favor?"

"Anything."

"Either fuck my brains out or lemme have you."

"Hold on, love, I've got you."

The pounding he delivered was brutal and perfect, and when he pegged my gland, I came in a shuddering rush that was overwhelming, fast and unexpected.

"Fuck, you're loud," he crowed as my muscles clamped down around him, and he came in a roaring climax that nearly deafened me.

We collapsed together in a sweaty, sated, panting heap, Ian still buried in me as we tried to pull air into our lungs.

"I missed you," I told him.

"Yeah," Ian replied as he slid gently, tenderly from my body, rolling me to my side so he could plaster himself to my back. "I can tell."

My eyes fluttered shut as he tipped my head back and began to place languorous kisses up the side of my throat.

"I missed the hell outta you too."

I knew that as well.

CHAPTER 6

THAT SUNDAY morning, I walked into the refrigerator, bumping it hard, no idea what it was doing there. Ian's snort of laughter didn't help, and I turned away, facing the cupboard as he walked up behind me.

"Lemme see."

"You're an ass," I grouched, lifting my head, turning it to the side so he couldn't touch me.

"Come on, I'm sorry." He snickered, grabbing my bicep, forcing me to face him. "I wanna make sure you're all right. Did you hurt your nose?"

I shoved him off me and his head fell back and he laughed hard and loud, *at* me, not *with* me, as I told him to go straight to hell.

The laughing did not subside. Apparently the tension relief was a welcome diversion. Charging over to the couch where my black cashmere overcoat lay, I pulled it on over my black Hugo Boss suit and began buttoning it up. The cab was coming to pick us up momentarily.

"You've got a uniform kink," Ian teased, crossing the floor to reach me and put his hands gently on my hips to hold me still.

He was stunning.

Between the Army dress uniform, the blue pants and navy jacket, along with the green beret, Ian was mouthwatering. I would certainly not be the only one who noticed.

"What are these, again?" I asked, sliding my fingertips over the multicolored pins attached to the left side of his uniform.

"Service ribbons," he answered, stepping in close.

"But you have medals too."

He nodded.

"One of these is a Bronze Star."

"Yes," he agreed, but he didn't point it out.

"And you have a Silver Star, too, don't you?"

"I have a Valorous Unit Award, as do all the guys in my unit from that time."

"When was that?"

"A while ago," he murmured, cupping my chin and dragging his thumb gently across my bottom lip. "You look terrible."

We both did, which was why each of us needed to hide behind sunglasses. Between Cochran's sucker punch and Ian's ravishing kisses, my lips looked just as bruised as my face. Likewise someone had taken a lot of rage out on Ian, as evidenced by the discolored patches—everything from black and blue to crimson—everywhere under his clothes. His body was battered and scarred from combat.

"You don't look so good yourself."

He shrugged. "You're still hot for me, so what do I care?"

I put my hands on his chest and thought for the millionth time how beautiful he was. The blue-blue of his eyes, the crow's feet that showed how much he laughed, the sculpted cheekbones, the lines on his face that also denoted how often he squinted and scowled, and his irresistible lips and the way they curled when he smiled, hinting at all manner of decadent pleasures. I loved to trace the thinner top lip with my tongue or bite the puffy lower one when he was trying to break a kiss. His currently freckled and sunbaked skin told me he'd been in the desert, no matter where he tried to tell me he'd been.

"Hey," I began, my gaze meeting his. "Did you go more than one place this last time out?"

"Yeah. How'd you know that?"

"You wore your ACUs home, but you're all brown from baking in the sun."

"You're not supposed to notice that kinda stuff." He winked at me.

Ian being playful was as seductive as him holding me down in bed. It was all I could do not to jump him. "I notice everything about you," I said before I leaned in and kissed him.

It was sweet, loving, and when I heard a horn from outside, I eased back. I was surprised when he followed, keeping contact.

"Get off me," I whispered. "You're gonna get me all wrinkled, and what will your friends think?"

I was surprised how fast he scowled. "These are not my friends."

"How come?"

He turned, grabbed his military-issue black trench coat with belt and slipped it on as he headed for the door. "I'll tell you in the cab, come on."

Ian gave the driver the name of St. Paul Catholic Church over on West Twenty-Second, and we settled in for a ride that shouldn't take more than fifteen minutes, but in Chicago, who knew.

He sat close to me, knee against mine, and I noted the hard clench of his jaw.

"So?" I prodded. "Not your friends. Speak."

"They, uhm—these are guys from my old unit before I went into Special Forces."

"When you were a Ranger?"

"I'm still a Ranger," he corrected me. "My military occupational specialty is scout and I'm a Ranger on top of that, but I'm in a Green Beret unit now."

"Okay."

"I asked to be transferred, and then I was assigned to the one I'm with now."

"How long ago was this?"

"Before I met you, so—" He was thinking. "—four years ago."

I was surprised. "You haven't seen these people since before you were a marshal?"

"No, I haven't."

"Then how did you even hear that Eddie died?"

"I got an e-mail from Eddie's wife's sister."

The fuck was going on? "Start from the beginning and tell me why you left the unit."

His head shake was so slight I would have missed it if I hadn't been looking closely.

"Talk to me."

He made a noise of disgust. "I'm not proud of it, and they're not either. I wouldn't even go, but—Eddie... he's the one who insisted they go back, even though he didn't want to."

"Go back?"

"For me," he sighed. "Yeah."

"Where did they leave you?"

"In Musa Qal'ah."

"Where the hell is that?"

"It's in Afghanistan, in the Helmand Province."

I twisted in the seat, angling my body so I could see his face. "Look at me."

He turned his head.

"Explain from the beginning."

"I can't right now," he said, indicating the driver with a tip of his head. "But I will."

"I really need you to."

All I got was another nod of agreement.

AT THE church we took our seats toward the back, and since we were the only ones in the row, we didn't end up speaking to anyone. There weren't a lot of people there, which made the space—even though beautiful inside— seem cavernous and cold. I was betting normal Mass on any given Sunday was a much warmer affair.

After the service we waited as the pallbearers carried the coffin outside to the hearse before following the other mourners. On the steps both of us shook hands with the priest, and then Ian was faced with his fallen comrade's wife. Whatever he was expecting, from the stricken look on his face when she lunged at him, wrapping her arms around his neck and hugging him tight wasn't it.

"Ohmygod, Ian, you came!" she wailed, crying all over him. "Sherri said she e-mailed you, but I wasn't sure you would come."

He was stiff; he didn't enfold her like he did Aruna when he hugged her or even like the last girlfriend he had. He gave her a pat before he put his hands on her forearms and gently but firmly uncoiled her from him.

When she stepped back, another woman was there, in his space, hugging him.

"I knew you'd come. You were always better than all the rest of them."

He didn't have to peel the second woman off him. She moved back quickly and looked around him to me.

"This is my partner, Miro Jones. We're both marshals," he explained to the women, hand on my shoulder, drawing me forward. "M, this is Rose Laird, Eddie's wife, and her sister, Sherri Arbolita."

Each of them smiled for me as best they could with puffy red eyes. I shook both their hands, and then a woman introduced as Rose's mother, Janice, appeared, happy to meet me and Ian and insistent that we follow them to the cemetery and on to the house.

Ian cleared his throat as soon as she walked away, heading toward the limousine that would follow first behind the hearse. "I don't think so, huh, Rosie," he said gently, his hand on the small of my back. "I just wanted to pay my respects to Eddie, but they don't want me here, and I don't wanna make a scene."

He glanced toward the hearse as he spoke, and when I turned, I saw ten men standing around, all in the same uniform as he was, down to the dress coats. The only noticeable difference was the color of the beret: Ian's green, everybody else's black.

"You know he talked about you all the time, Ian," Rose said, stepping in close, taking his hand. "And he was so sorry that he hadn't done more."

"It was a long time ago," he assured her, slipping his hand up over my shoulder. "And I wasn't blameless. I fucked up bad."

"Yes, but it was a personal thing that they made business—or what that amounted to," she said with a catch in her voice, glancing at me. "At least that's what Eddie told me."

"Yeah, well—" Ian took a breath. "—still. I don't think it's a good idea."

"But—"

"I just wanted to say good-bye to Eddie and tell you how sorry I am." Her eyes welled up with tears.

"Listen," Sherri began, taking hold of Ian's bicep. "Rose really wants you to—"

"Doyle."

We turned to see a man standing there, one step down, smoking a cigarette and looking up at him. He was tall—six three, I was guessing—all muscle, no neck, with a blond buzz-cut and small dishwater-blue eyes. I could only imagine how many times a nose had to be broken to have that many bumps.

"Odell," Ian replied, and I heard the bite in his tone.

He turned his head, blew the smoke away before crushing the butt on the step. His gaze locked with Ian's a moment before he offered his hand.

Ian shook quickly, and the grip wasn't warm, not like when he met Barrett the night before and held on and gripped his shoulder.

"Come by the house after the cemetery. Greta and her mom are cooking, so you know that's gonna be good."

Ian squinted at him.

Odell cleared his throat. "And the major needs a word."

"What does Delaney need with me?"

"The fuck do I know. He just said whoever saw you first needed to make sure you showed up at Eddie's place."

Shifting on his feet, Ian bumped me with his shoulder. "We'll have to call a cab and—"

"Nah, man, you can ride with me and Bates. We've got room for you and"—he tipped his head at me—"your friend."

"Miro." Ian breathed out my name. "This is Sergeant First Class Pete Odell. Odell, this is my partner, Deputy United States Marshal Miro Jones."

We shook fast, his gloved hand in mine, and then it was done and he was back to dissecting Ian.

"Nice flash," he said in an odd, strangely menacing way, like a dare and a put-down all together.

"Some of our forces are more special than others."

Odell tipped his head at the beret on Ian's head. "The beret says it all, right?"

"I would hope so."

I hated the modulated flat tone Ian was using because it was so alien, so not the passionate man I knew and loved.

"You followed through on the other, too, huh." Odell smirked, the condescension crystal clear in his tone when he spoke. "Did the whole marshal thing."

Ian nodded.

"You in the Reserve now?"

"I am."

It was not the most stimulating conversation I'd ever heard, but when you were talking around the elephant, it was difficult to think of what to say.

"All right," Odell wrapped up, leaning in to kiss Rose's cheek. "We'll see you at the cemetery, and then we'll all follow you home."

Rose nodded and then she and her sister rejoined the priest, who was glaring at Odell.

"What's with him?" he snapped.

"You put a cigarette out on the steps of his church," Ian responded dryly. "He probably thinks you were raised by wolves."

The glare Odell gave Ian should have been scary, but he grinned after a moment to take away some of the obvious hatred.

Bending down, Ian picked up the crushed butt and told the priest he'd take care of it.

"Thank you, my son."

"You always were a suck-up, Doyle."

"You're just mad 'cause you're going to hell," Ian responded, his voice flat, emotionless.

"Just come on," he muttered and turned to walk down the front steps.

Ian grabbed my arm and yanked, so I didn't even have time to say anything before we were following him.

Odell had mentioned a Bates, so I assumed that was who was driving the white Chevy Tahoe he led us to.

"He's a marshal now, and this is his partner," Odell said, disgust in his voice as he got into the SUV.

"Oh, Doyle," the man said, and he, unlike Odell, seemed happy to see Ian. "You look good. Special Forces agrees with you, I see."

He was handsome himself, probably my own almost six feet, with dark-brown eyes with lines that said he laughed often.

"Hello, partner," he said, offering me his hand over his shoulder. "Tyler Bates."

With his name now confirmed, I shook quickly. "Miro Jones."

"Good to meet you."

And that was it until we got to Graceland Cemetery and Arboretum at the intersection of Clark Street and Irving Park.

The drive was oppressive, the day outside gray and cold and wet, inside only the sound of the heater running. I wanted to touch Ian, to comfort and reassure him, but he was leaning against the door, looking out the window, and didn't seem to need the closeness.

"How the hell is Rose affording this?" Odell asked Bates, looking around and giving a low whistle.

"The family has plots here," Ian answered, and Odell turned in the seat to look at him.

"How the hell you know that?"

Ian shrugged. "He told me a long time ago. His mother wanted him here with the family, but there was no place for Rose."

"That's shitty," Bates chimed in.

"I'm betting Rose didn't have a say," Ian concluded.

"Man, I knew we should've skipped this and gone right to the house," Odell groused.

"We're pallbearers, man," Bates reminded him. "We ain't goin' nowhere."

Of course, since this was the Sunday before Thanksgiving, we got five inches the night before. It was cold, trudging to the graveside, and the crunch of the packed snow was loud as everyone moved off the shoveled and salted paths to the white-covered grass. Outdoor carpet had been laid down and a canopy put up along with chairs, but there were only so many and the rest of us ended up fanning out.

I watched the soldiers take the flag off the coffin, fold it, and present it to Rose before an older woman I assumed to be Eddie's mother, as I hadn't seen her before, took it from her. Rose's face crumpled and she leaned sideways against Janice, who shot the other woman a murderous glance as her daughter fell apart in her arms.

"Aww, man," Bates groaned, his gaze meeting mine.

"Gonna be a long day for Rose," I sympathized, the whole scene almost more than I could bear. It was a graphic reminder of my greatest fear—Ian lying in a coffin while I clutched a folded flag to my chest.

"Amen," he returned as the priest began addressing the crowd.

FUNERALS WERE exhausting. I had no idea until I went to my first one when I was twenty-two. One of the guys I was in the police academy with was hit by a drunk driver while crossing the street and died instantly. I barely knew him, but the entire class went to the funeral. When I got home, I'd passed out on my couch and only woke up when Aruna arrived a full ten hours later with food.

She was a good friend, always thinking of me, and as I stood in the cold in the cemetery it hit me that I should call and tell her. I tried to always reach out when I thought of telling someone something, instead of waiting and letting the surge of whatever kind of feeling it was, good or bad, go to waste. Sometimes that wasn't so great when I was pissed. I vomited out things I should have never said, but when I was feeling grateful, it normally worked out well.

"What?" Aruna greeted after answering on the fourth ring.

Except, of course, when I was calling one of my snarky as hell friends. "Thanks for always bringing me food. You're a nice person."

There was a pause. "Why're you drinking so early in the afternoon?"

"I'm not drinking, you witch. I'm at a funeral and I'm feeling sentimental."

"Well, knock it off. I got custody of you when everyone else moved away, so I'm contractually obligated to take care of you, and by proxy, Ian. The others send me support payments every month."

"Jesus, the mouth on you."

"That's what Liam says," she said suggestively.

I hung up because, Christ, that was TMI, and she texted me lips and a heart and the poop emoji. She seriously needed medication.

After I got off the phone with Aruna, I was surprised to get a text message from Mike Ryan, one of the members of my and Ian's team. The picture I got was of a huge fruit basket taking up most of the space on my desk.

"They're getting bigger," Ryan said when he answered his phone on the first ring.

"I told her to stop sending them," I sighed, smiling as I thought of Oscar Guzman's mother. "But she won't."

"You and Doyle saved her kids from a sex trafficking ring. How're you not drowning in kiwi for the rest of your fuckin' life?"

"Is there really kiwi in there?" I asked.

"Oh hell yeah. There's mango and papaya and—what the fuck is this?"

"Lychee," I heard his partner, Jack Dorsey, answer in his booming baritone.

"Lychee," Ryan repeated. "Whatever the fuck that is."

"Tell him there's starfruit in there, too, and Valencia oranges that came straight from Spain without stopping at the local farmer's market."

"I'll send her another e-mail," I told Ryan. "I bet it costs a mint to send that to us every month. Maybe I can get her to go to once every three or six."

"I'm taking the peaches for my mother so she can make pie. She's gonna lose her shit when she sees these in the middle of fall."

"I want some. They're my peaches," I said, pulling my cashmere scarf tighter around my neck as I stood on the sidewalk watching Ian shake the hands of more and more people. Rose had wanted to introduce Ian around, so when she slipped her arm into the crook of his, I mouthed that I'd wait for him and got out of the way.

"You realize this is gonna be something else that we'll have to explain to the new guys we get in here," Ryan said offhandedly.

"What're you talking about?"

"You heard Kage a while back, we need a couple more teams of guys."

"And you're worried about what, filling 'em in?"

"Yeah man, it's a pain in the ass having to tell the new guys about all the inside jokes and the way we do things and everything else. He needs to just leave it alone."

"Because you fear change," I scoffed. "That's a great reason not to work at full capacity."

"You hate it too," he accused me. "Remember Littlefield and Posner? They didn't work out and they were supposed to be good."

"That's not fair."

"The hell it's not."

"Littlefield got shot and decided he never wanted to be shot again. You can't fault him for that. At least he was honest."

"And Posner?" He said snidely.

"Oh come on," I said like it was obvious.

"What? It wasn't even that big of a jump. I went and looked at it."

Of course he had. "Not big to you."

"Not big to anybody!"

Poor guy.

Douglas Posner had transferred out of Investigative Operations—where we were—to Judicial Support after spending just one day backing up Ian. I'd still been riding a desk and so Kage had the new guy sub in. I was never convinced that he didn't have reservations about Doug Posner and so had used Ian as sort of a trial by fire.

"I don't care if it was the Grand fuckin' Canyon," Ryan went on. "You follow your partner no matter what."

The reports were spotty at best and when asked, Ian couldn't say for certain if the space between the buildings was five feet or eight. What was clear was that Ian had been chasing a fugitive and made the leap to follow the guy and Posner had stopped, looked around, and gone back down the five flights to the ground. By that time, he couldn't provide Ian with any backup as he had no clue where his partner, or the fugitive, was. After that, he'd been lucky to get two words out of the love of my life for the rest of the day.

The fallout was that between the leap he didn't make, the DEA agent he listened to over Ian, and the background check he didn't run, he had an infuriated Ian Doyle all over him in the middle of the office at the end of their shift. It was funny because there was Ian, thundering on about standard operating procedure—which coming from the king of "just kick it in" was hysterical—and Posner yelling back that Ian was a menace and a maniac. It might have been okay, possibly, except that I'd come out of the back office then and Posner pointed at me and said that Ian was probably the one who got me hurt in the first place. It took Becker and Kowalski, together, to grab him and hold him.

Kage sent Ian on home—with me—and invited Posner into his office. He was gone the following day, which was good because Ian got worked up all over again on our way in. Four other guys had come through since then with no one gelling with the rest of us.

"I just don't like new guys," Ryan concluded.

"Ian and I were both new once."

"I don't remember," he said dismissively, clearing his throat. "Hey, me and Jack are done in a couple hours. You and Doyle wanna meet at Portillo's for food, and then we can go to The Befuddled Owl?"

It took me a second. "I'm sorry, what?"

"Just say no, Jones!" Dorsey yelled in the background.

"The fuck is the Befuddled Owl?"

Ryan cleared his throat. "It's a coffeehouse close to the university."

"And why're you going there?"

"I just thought it sounded like fun," he replied cheerfully.

Oh, there was fuckery afoot. "I'm calling bullshit on that."

"Listen—"

"Do they happen to have live music at the Bewildered Owl?"

"Befuddled," he corrected.

"Well, do they?"

He coughed.

"Oh, screw you, Ryan," I snapped. "I refuse to listen to your sister's band again."

"Come on," he begged.

"Once in a lifetime is good enough for The Crimson Wave."

"They're not that bad."

"Not that bad," I moaned. "Are you kidding me right now?"

"And besides, they changed their name. The drummer was worried that they might get sued by the University of Alabama for copyright infringement."

"Alabama is the tide, not the wave."

"Yeah, I know, but I didn't wanna argue with him 'cause, yanno, the name was gross."

"The name of the band is not the glaring issue," I said, unable to keep a straight face. "Jesus, Mike, their music is so bad."

"So bad!" Dorsey echoed me in the background. "Just say no, Jones. Save yourself!"

I heard a bump and a crash and Dorsey laughing, so I figured nothing was broken.

"Listen," I told him. "If me and Ian get done with this funeral business at a reasonable time, I'll call ya and see where you guys are."

"Good man," Ryan replied. "I'll save ya some pie."

I grunted and hung up and saw Ian scanning the crowd for me. Lifting my hand to get his attention, I saw his face sort of unclench—his jaw, the tight smile, and the furrowed brows as he started toward me. He hadn't taken more than three steps when a beautiful woman with gorgeous long thick blonde hair stepped out from a crowd of five other women and into his path.

He stopped short or he would have plowed into her, and to keep his balance, he had to take hold of her arms. Her hands went immediately to his chest.

They stood there, staring for a long moment, and then he let her go and she backpedaled at the same exact time. Even from where I was, I could see the awkwardness. She looked at her feet, checking on the black patent T-strap pumps and then up at him, curling her hair around both ears, smiling like she wasn't sure if she should. He swallowed, took a breath, and shoved his hands down in the pockets of his coat. Together they made a nice picture, him in his masculine military alpha resplendence and her in the ivory turndown collar coat that made her seem delicate and alluringly feminine. They should have been on posters for why opposites attract, as good as they looked together.

"That would be funny," Odell said, like whatever it was wouldn't be at all.

I turned and looked at Odell and Bates, who had joined me, one on either side.

"What's that?" I asked, turning to Bates because I liked him better.

"Doyle with Danita Stanley," Odell answered, moving so he was on Bates's left, facing me now. "He did tell you why he transferred out of our unit, right?"

I shook my head.

Bates made a noise.

"What?" Odell snapped at him.

He shrugged. "Maybe Doyle doesn't want his new partner knowing all that shit. I mean, no offense, Jones, but, I mean, are you guys even close when you're not working?"

"We're close," I said, holding my breath.

"See," Odell said with a cackle, thumping Bates in the chest. "They're tight, so Doyle wouldn't mind us telling Jones here that the reason he left our unit was because he fucked the wife of one of the guys who was supposed to be his brother."

I stayed quiet because, from the menacing look on his face, I could tell there was more.

"And so in return, we accidentally left him behind after a raid went south."

Not at all what I was expecting.

"Oh shit, Jones, look at your face!" Odell crowed. "Were you under the impression that Ian Doyle wasn't a total fuckin' piece of shit?"

Bates winced and put his hand on my shoulder. "We only meant to leave him for a couple hours, just to scare him, yanno?"

The urge to smash my fist into his face and then turn my rage on Odell was almost overwhelming. It was like I was drowning. I could barely breathe around my desire to hurt him, to hear him cry out.

"But things changed so fast, and before we knew it, his position was compromised and he was taken into custody," Bates continued.

It sounded so benign when he said it, not at all like the life-and-death struggle I was sure it had been.

"Thing was, even before we *had* to go back, Laird begged us to. He was the only one who refused to get on the bird when we left him. We had to pick him up and carry him."

And that was why Ian and I were here paying our respects to Edward Laird.

Bates rambled on. "It was stupid, but—you get it, Jones. I mean, it's the same thing with cops or marshals like you, it don't matter. The guys you serve with—they're your brothers. You don't fuck your brother's wife, no matter what."

No matter what.

"And it's not like we planned for things to get as bad as they did. Part of this was just dumb luck," Bates said, his voice rising. I guessed me not responding was starting to freak him out just a little. "We never planned for him to be there that long."

Everything was too tight: my clothes, my coat, but mostly my skin. I needed to peel everything away, flesh, muscle, bone, and unleash the furious hatred I could feel burning me up from the inside out, starting with the hole it was eating through the wall of my stomach.

"We got him back," Bates choked out, sounding more like he was pleading with me than telling me. "Obviously."

"How—" My voice splintered, hoarse with pain. "—long did you leave him?"

"We didn't *leave* him. He got stuck. We left his ass for a couple hours, tops. He's the one who got captured," Odell answered snidely, the dare all over his smug, angry face. He hated Ian; I could almost smell it on him, like tainted meat rotting from the inside out. "And they had him for three days in all."

My eyes met his and held.

"But don't you go spreadin' that around now, Jones, 'cause no one knows about that but us. That didn't go in no report."

Plus it was a long time ago.

Slowly, calmly, I drew cold, wet air into my lungs and then exhaled. "You guys should go on ahead to the house. Ian and I will catch up to you."

"Aww, now, don't be like that," Odell cajoled, his words thick with rancid honey he was trying to spread around. "Don't get mad on his behalf. That's water under the bridge, that is."

"Is that what you tell yourself?"

"Don't say something you'll regret there, Jones."

I shrugged. "I'm just wondering why you really left him."

"I just told you why."

"Nah," I taunted, grinning like I did when I was being a dick. "I'm not buying that your buddy was the only guy whose wife was fuckin' Ian."

He flushed red. Just whoosh, scarlet. It was awesome. "You son of a—"

"I heard you talk about your wife." I put the leer in my voice easily, suggestively. "Greta, was it?"

"You better shut your filthy fuckin' mouth!" he roared, pointing at me.

"Miro?" I heard Ian call out behind me.

"Did he fuck all the wives, or just yours and the other poor sonofabitch?"

He shuddered with rage, and I saw his eyes go dead just as I imagined a shark's did before they took a big, fat bite out of a seal.

"You don't have any kids, do you? Around five years old?"

Apparently he did, the way he came at me.

The thing was, if I hit him, I could be suspended, or worse. If I didn't, how could I ever look Ian in the face again, knowing what I knew now?

There was only one viable alternative. I had to get Odell so enraged that he came at me like a charging bull. He had to throw the first punch. But how in the world did one bait a trained soldier? What did one say to get a man with nerves of steel to crack?

It was a crappy thing to do to the guy, but abandoning Ian to certain torture and possible execution was higher on the scale of fucked-up shit. So when he threw the roundhouse punch and missed, I countered with an elbow in Pete Odell's conceited, self-righteous prick face. After that the only smug asshole brawling at the funeral was me.

CHAPTER 7

YOU CAN tell when you break someone's nose. There's really never a question. The wet crunch, like a soggier version of stepping on freeze-hardened ice over snow, is unmistakable. And of course the gush of blood and that high-pitched animal wail most people who weren't boxers or hit men let out. In the movies everyone takes it like a man, even the women, but in real life, knees buckle and down they go.

Odell was impressive. He took a knee, but that was as low to the ground as he got.

Bates shoved me back, and I understood. He and Odell were buddies, brothers-in-arms, so he'd do his best to get me off him.

"Leave him alone," Odell ordered, rising from his kneel, facing me. "I've got this."

I pivoted when he swung again, so he caught my shoulder instead of my face just as Cochran had the day before. I would have to e-mail my combat instructor from the police academy; her moves were serving me well in the field. Sergeant Garza loved throwing all of us candidates around. She said it was her sworn duty.

"I'm gonna have your ass for this, Jones," Odell vowed as he spit out a mouthful of blood. "You can kiss your career good-bye."

"I'm just defending myself, dickhead," I taunted. "You can't touch me."

His eyes narrowed and I took another step back as he came at me fast with moves that might have incapacitated me, or even really hurt me, if any of them connected. When he stopped, and I saw him weave a little, I finally understood why I wasn't dead already—he was a Ranger after all—and why he'd been letting his buddy handle the driving all day when he had so much to say about how it was being handled.

"He's fuckin' hammered," I announced to Bates.

All things converged at that moment.

Odell stopped midcharge, blood running from both nostrils as he stared dumbly at me, seemingly unsure of what was going on.

"The fuck, M?" Ian must have run because he was there at my side.

"Your partner's a dead man, Doyle!"

"Are you all right?" he asked hurriedly, ignoring the blustering Odell, checking me over, hands on my arms, shoulders, lifting my chin, finally stilling gently, reverently, on both sides of my neck as he stared into my eyes. "Did he hurt you?"

"Did I hurt him?" Odell was indignant and fuming from the few feet away Bates had dragged him. "Fuck you, Doyle!"

"Don't you fuckin' touch him!" Ian rounded on him, and I had to scramble to grab ahold of him before he lunged at Odell.

"He called my wife a whore!"

A surge of bodies enveloped us, men coming from everywhere, and we were surrounded. Ian and I were pushed back, buffered by the crowd. Odell and Bates were mobbed and lost from view. I let Ian go so I could walk beside him and texted Ryan, who was waiting to hear from me.

No lights.

It would make no sense to anyone who wasn't on our team. "No lights" was one of our boss's things, a Kage-ism that meant danger wasn't imminent, but hurry the fuck up and find me and get to wherever the hell I was.

"The hell were you thinking?" Ian demanded, refocusing my attention on him and off my phone as he wrenched me around to face him.

I couldn't speak; I hurt for him too much. Instead I walked backward a few feet and then turned fast, needing to put distance between us and the others, knowing he'd follow without me having to tell him.

"Where the hell are you going?"

Seeing what I was looking for, I slipped behind what looked like a family crypt. Ian was seconds behind me, shoving me back against the marble, pinning me there.

"And why in the world would you go after Odell?" he yelled.

The look on my face must have answered his question, which was good since I still couldn't speak around the enormous, jagged lump in my throat.

He sucked in a breath and I saw his face register what I now knew. "Fuck," he groaned, shaking his head, angry and hurt at the same time. "I didn't want—goddamnit."

I concentrated on keeping my voice level. "Were you ever going to tell me?"

"No," he murmured, hands fisted on the lapels of my overcoat.

"Why?"

"You don't—I don't—" He stopped, inhaled sharply, looked at my chin a second, and then lifted his gaze and locked it with mine. "I can't ever have you thinking I'm weak."

It took a second for his words to register because they were so alien. "What?" That made zero sense. "You're the strongest person I know!" I shouted. How could he think something so ridiculous at all, let alone think it about me? "Jesus, Ian, don't you know me at all?" I gasped and I could hear my heart breaking in my words.

"Yes, I know you!"

"Then what the hell?"

He let go of me but didn't move. "Yeah, but already you're thinking I did something wrong and—"

"Who am I to criticize you for who you slept with before we got together?"

"I wasn't a good guy."

"I was a slut, and you've never once been judgmental about that."

"I hate it," he confessed. "And when we run into guys you've been with... I don't like it."

"But you don't think bad of me."

"No."

"So how could I do that to you?"

He nodded.

"You're a very good man, Ian Doyle."

I watched the emotions chase across his features: fear, relief, anger, hurt, happiness, all of them tightening his jaw, creasing his brows, and making him swallow hard and breathe deeply through his nose.

"This isn't just about you and a married woman."

"No," he agreed, moving away from me, pacing, stopping a few feet away.

"Contrary to popular belief, I am not a mind reader."

He scoffed. "Please, no one ever accused you of being a—"

"Ian!" I barked.

"Fine! I don't want you to feel sorry for me about what happened in the desert!"

"I can't help that."

"But if you think I'm weak or—"

"We covered that already," I said, closing the distance between us, moving into his space, taking hold of his elbow so he couldn't move away and bringing us flush together so we were breathing the same air. "I know you're strong."

He closed his eyes.

"Just tell me."

He made a noise, not quite a cough, but enough. "There's this way you look at me, and it's only for me and I can't—if you stopped feeling that way and then looked at me different because of it"—his voice cracked—"I couldn't... I'm afraid you're gonna stop."

"Stop what?"

"Loving me."

Ah.

The truth. Finally. It was always good when it came out.

"Yeah, no," I said, sighing and smiling, rubbing my clean-shaven cheek over his stubbly one, the sound as well as the sensation sexy and soothing. "Never happen."

He trembled against me.

"We fight, we make up, but I know you're never gonna say when. You're never gonna say stop and go away. We both say shit like it could, but it can't."

"No, it really can't," he assented, wrapping his arms around my neck and hugging me tight. "I was afraid it would change things if you knew."

"It doesn't," I vowed. "But I need to hear it all."

He let me go slowly, and when there was space between us, I saw a glint in the depths of his eyes, the blue at the center of the flame. "It could never make you less, idiot. How could you even think that?"

"I think stupid shit sometimes."

"Yes."

"They left me, and I didn't want you to know 'cause I thought you'd care about the why."

"I don't."

"Okay."

"And we really should stop that." I sighed, so tired, zapped of my strength because it took so much just to get Ian to hear me sometimes. It was worth it, always, but that didn't mean it wasn't hard.

"Stop what?" he asked, trace of alarm in his tone.

"Stop saying that either one of us could go. It's like when people bring up divorce all the time when they're married. One of those times it'll stick."

"Yeah, okay."

"I mean, it's stupid, right? I can't imagine me without you."

His grin was warm. "Me neither."

"So then—"

"That's why I was so pissed last night."

"We were both mad."

He shook his head, closing on me again. "No, I mean when I came downstairs and the lawyer was there talkin' to you, putting his hands on you and pettin' Chick."

This was a surprise.

"What?" He was surly.

"You were not jealous of Barrett."

"The hell I wasn't!" he flared.

"Are you serious? You're being serious right now?" I didn't believe him; there was no way Ian Doyle was jealous of any man, but it was something I could fix, instantly and without question. The normalcy of that made me smile. And that was how it was with Ian and me. Big reveals followed by whatever the thing was simply being absorbed and becoming part of our shared history. It was one of my favorite parts about us, and how I knew, beyond a shadow of a doubt, he was the one for me.

"I am," he growled, and I saw the uncertainty, pain and self-recrimination was gone from those gorgeous blue eyes, replaced by a healthy amount of irritation.

"What the hell would you be jealous for?"

"Oh, I dunno, a rich, handsome lawyer who's crazy about you moves in next door, likes Chick, and has already met your friends without me…. I think jealous about sums it up."

"Oh, come on."

"If the roles were reversed, you wouldn't be worried?"

I thought about it a second. "No."

"Why the hell not?" He was indignant now, and it took a lot of concentration not to smile at how adorable that was.

"Well, for one, you're not as charming as me," I replied, loving the fact that even though he had nothing to worry about with me, ever, that he was still rattled. There was a vulnerability there that touched me deeply. Scary-ass Ian Doyle worried that anyone could turn my head was terribly endearing. "And we both know you don't make friends as easy, and—"

"Go to hell, M," he groused, whacking me in the belly. "I'm plenty fuckin' charming."

"—I know you'd never cheat on me."

He froze. "Now, wait, I never said you did somethin' with him."

"No?"

"Fuck no!" he yelled, getting more worked up by the second. "You'd never."

"That's right, I would never."

"It doesn't make me any less jealous," he husked, leaning in and kissing my cheek. "But that's on me. I'm the one who leaves you all alone."

I was not getting into his military service at a funeral for his fallen team member. "Well, I'll always be right here, waiting."

"That's good," he said, letting out a deep breath and hugging me tight again. "That's all I need."

I hugged him back so he'd know, of course, I felt the same.

"Okay, so we better go back," he said, and I heard the hesitance in his voice even as he nuzzled a kiss against my cheek before slowly easing free. We moved like honey, savoring the contact, hesitant to break it but knowing our quiet moment of respite was done.

Walking around the crypt, we moved out onto the cemetery drive that ran the length of the property and made our way back toward the others.

"Goddamnit, Doyle!"

There was Odell, Bates, and two other guys I didn't know, and really, my plan was to be good. I was going to just shut up until it was time to leave, but then I got a clear look at the man I'd punched and the laughter rolled right out of me.

"Fuck you, Jones!"

It was hard to look menacing with tampons shoved up your nose, Ranger or not, and Odell—the picture he made, all puffy-faced and outraged—was hysterical. Even when I tried to stop laughing, the staccato snickering couldn't be helped.

"You proud of this shit?" one of the guys I didn't know flared, the hostility thick in his voice and in his hands fisted at his sides.

I shrugged. "He came at me first, man."

"It's a funeral, you fuck!"

"Yeah, I know," I replied, gesturing at Odell. "Tell your boy."

Two other men joined them, and I saw Ian's eyes dart around. We were away from other people and we were outnumbered, and probably it was just going to be a lot of back and forth, but I wasn't taking any chances. All of these men were trained soldiers who could hurt me—Odell notwithstanding, with him being three sheets to the wind—and I wasn't about to let any of them harm Ian again. Once was more than enough.

"Hey, what's goin' on?"

Everyone turned to see smiling Deputy US Marshal Chris Becker. At six three, built like the linebacker he was in college, he was one of the nicest guys anyone could ever hope to meet—until he wasn't.

"What's up, ladies?" he asked Ian and me, snorting out a laugh.

"Sorry to bug you at a funeral and all," his partner and best friend, Wes Ching, said as he bumped through the men surrounding us and walked up on me. "But if we're going to the Befuddled Owl for torture, we're making sure you and Doyle are too."

At five ten and the smallest member of our team, people made the mistake of thinking he was not the scariest of us all. That was *so* not the case. I'd seen Ching with three bullets in him taking down a fugitive, seen him run down the middle of the Eisenhower Expressway dodging cars and trucks, and I'd seen him sprint over scaffolding twelve stories up at a construction site. His balls were so big it was a wonder he could walk, so when he moved through a crowd, people got out of the way, even the clustered military elite. They made a hole for him. He, like our boss, had been a Marine. Apparently that chip stayed on the shoulder even when you left the Corps.

"Attention!" came a yell from behind the men.

Everyone froze where they were and saluted the man who also moved easily through the crowd. Ian showed the same respect, saluting as well, and held the rigid posture as the man stepped directly in front of him. The uniform's black nametag read "DELANEY."

"At ease," he said to Ian, but everyone else relaxed too. "Doyle."

"Sir," Ian answered, and the icy tone was not lost on me.

"I need you to come to Laird's house so we can discuss an issue of a highly sensitive nature that impacts all of us."

"Pardon the question, sir, but I haven't been a part of this unit in quite some time."

"But you were when Lochlyn was, and therein lies the problem."

"Sir?"

"I believe he's trying to kill a few of us."

CHAPTER 8

BEFORE WE got to Eddie Laird's house in Canaryville on the 700 block of West Forty-Eighth Street, I made Becker stop at a Dunkin' Donuts we passed on the way so we'd walk in with something. Three dozen glazed seemed the least we could do. When we got to the house, I was surprised by how much Janice appreciated the gesture.

"Come in, have something to eat," she urged us.

"Ma'am," Ian said, introducing her to Becker and Ching, who were there with us now, as well as Ryan and Dorsey, who'd gotten held up at the office, but since Ryan knew I needed backup, he'd sent the others on ahead.

The house was built around the 1800s, I could tell from the neighborhood. As I looked around, I realized it was two stories of small box rooms with an asphalt roof and a basement covered in wood paneling Eddie and Rose never got around to renovating. A scrolling metal railing—brown with rust instead of black—wrapped around the front porch, the front door had a tiny window that looked like a porthole in it, and inside shag carpeting patterned in green, white, and black became beige Travertine linoleum in the kitchen. I had no idea what was in the bathroom because I had no reason to go in there. An oppressive damp coldness inside the cluttered home felt real, but could have just as well been my imagination. I didn't ask anyone else if they felt it too. I just needed to bide my time so I could take Ian home.

As we stood in the living room, all of us still in our coats with plates and drinks Janice insisted on, Ian finally got around to asking our fellow marshals what they were doing there. He'd been so busy in the car, catching up from being away for four months, happy to see them, that he didn't notice the timing was odd.

"You needed backup," Becker explained, smiling at Janice as she came by to check on us. "Ma'am, may I say that this chicken tetrazzini is marvelous."

Her smile was instant and flushed her cheeks a very becoming shade of pink. "Thank you, it's my mother's recipe."

"Well, she must be a great cook."

She patted his arm. "Yes, she was."

"Oh, I'm sorry."

"No, no, it was years ago. It's just so lovely to see you eat. I always wanted to cook for Eddie, but he was never home, and now I won't have grandbabies to cook for either."

"My condolences," Becker said gently.

She squeezed his bulging bicep and then turned to Ian. "I know you're not in their unit anymore—Rose just told me—but are you still on active duty?"

"Reserves," he told her.

"Oh good, that's good," she sighed, smiling at him through welling tears. I suspected she'd be weeping on and off all day. "Stay home and settle down, Ian. There's more to life than being a soldier."

"Yes, ma'am," Ian replied automatically.

Of course my heart was lodged in my throat, so I could not have said one word. Amazing that people just spoke your wildest dream out loud.

When she left, we were all quiet until Rose joined us.

"The meal is wonderful," Ching offered.

She nodded. "Yeah, Greta, Odell's wife, she's a great cook, and my mom made the chicken dish 'cause it was Eddie's favorite."

We fell silent again, not sure what else to say to her. She wasn't my friend. I had no shared memories to offer up in the moment.

"Where are Eddie's folks?" Ian finally asked. I'd watched him scan the room.

She scoffed. "Oh, Ian, come on. You know they never thought I was good enough for their son. They buried him in the family plot and took the flag right outta my arms—did you see her do that at the grave?"

He nodded.

She leaned into him, against his chest. "That's the last I'll see them, just you watch."

"No," he said because it was expected.

She held up her hand with the diamond engagement ring and matching band. "If she comes for this ring he gave me—just 'cause it's been in their family for however long—I tell you what, she can kiss my ass."

He squeezed her tight, and after she gave him a gentle pat, she left us to visit the next group of people.

"Doyle."

It was his former CO, the same man who'd made sure we came to the house, Major Delaney, and he gestured for Ian to follow him outside.

I moved to go with them, but Delaney shook his head.

"Then no one else goes out there with you guys either," I insisted.

"And why's that?" He dared me to speak, clipping the words.

"His safety would be in question," I retorted.

"Is that right? What precisely do you think I'm going to do to him?"

"I dunno, could be anything," I shot back. "But at least I know you can't leave him anywhere again."

Ian lifted his hand to quiet me as Delaney, fuming, threw open the door as well as the screen and pounded down the steps that led to the yard. Ian shot me a look—which I gave him right back—and then went after him, closing the door behind him.

"Don't worry about your boyfriend," Odell called over to me from where he was on the couch. "The major won't touch his faggoty ass."

"We saw you two duck out of sight at the cemetery," Bates said, adding his two cents. "That's disgusting, and if I'd known Doyle was like that, I wouldn't've ever gone back for him."

"Is that right?"

"Yeah, that's right," Bates jeered, standing up. "Better dead than gay."

I lunged toward them but Becker caught me, holding tight as Ryan walked over to the men seated on the huge sectional.

"Ya best quit runnin' your mouths there, boys, or I'll take you in for threatening the life of a federal officer."

Bates scoffed up at Ryan, who was looming over him. "Go to—"

"We can hold you for seventy-two hours just for the threat alone."

"I'm a soldier, you prick."

"Me too," Ryan assured him. "But we're not talking about soldiering. We're talking about right here, right now. And right now… you keep jawin', and you're going downtown."

All eyes were on him.

"So," he said with a sigh, the epitome of boredom. "What's it gonna be?"

None of them said a word. Apparently federal marshals trumped Rangers when said Rangers were not on active duty. They all got up to leave, and they gave Ryan a wide berth.

Becker let me go with a straightening of my coat and a pat on the back, and I went to the window to look out at Ian and his old CO.

"Excuse me."

Turning, I found Danita Stanley in front of me. Up close she was flawless, perfect, like a 1940s Hollywood starlet standing luminous in a spotlight. I got why Ian had done it, why he'd reached for her. If girls did it for me, I would have too. "Yes?"

She cleared her throat. "Did I hear Odell say..." She trailed off because it hadn't been a nice word the asshole had used and she must not have wanted to repeat it. "Is Ian gay?"

"Ian's bi," I corrected, giving her a look. "Obviously."

"No, we— He must've told you about us because you're his... his... you're with him."

"I am."

"So you know that we didn't...."

"Didn't what?"

She exhaled sharply. "When we, that time, it was—"

"Actually I really don't need to know any of this. It's none of my business."

She was quiet, thinking. "Yes, you're right. It's not, except that you should know that Ian was the only one who *saw* me."

I waited for her to say more, but she couldn't, as evidenced by her reddening eyes and trembling chin. I took her hand and I saw her relax, sort of cave in, before she gave me a trace of a smile.

"My husband," she began. "He was into being a soldier, and he left me alone even when he was home, and Ian.... Well, he saw me."

I nodded.

"He would talk to me and flirt, of course, but they all did with all of us—all the wives. It's fun and friendly and sweet in a way, so that we all know we're loved by the group, a family, and it was great. But I was so lonely. And when Jace came home, he still wanted to be with those guys, going out, raising hell, drinking. Most of them have families, so they couldn't, but a few of them did, and then he had friends who weren't those guys, too, and... then there was Ian."

She'd been waiting a while to tell this story, I could tell.

"How was I supposed to turn down attention from that man?"

I understood. Ian's attention, once given, was something one developed a taste for. Just his eyes on you was enough to illicit surrender.

"I've never been kissed like that in my life."

I smiled at her because, yes, I agreed. Ian had a wicked mouth, and he knew how to use it.

"But when it was time to...." She looked uncomfortable.

"Pull the trigger?" I offered.

"Yes," she breathed. "When it came time to do the thing… he couldn't."

I caught her wandering gaze and held it. "Couldn't, or wouldn't?"

"Wouldn't," she amended. "He said he didn't want to compromise me, and he couldn't do it to Jace and still look him in the eye."

"But?" I heard the "but" in her voice.

The tears came fast. "I was mad, right? I wanted to be compromised. I wanted to be Ian Doyle's conquest."

"So you lied," I concluded, releasing her hand.

"I lied."

"And your husband told his buddies and everything that happened, happened, and then Ian came back and left, and today's the first time you've seen him."

Quick nod of her head.

"Does anybody else know?"

"I told Jace when the divorce became final two years ago."

"How did he take that?"

"Not well," she said quickly, so I was guessing that was an understatement. "We're no longer speaking."

"And where is Jason now?" I asked formally, using what I assumed was the long form of his name.

"He moved to Florida."

"Not a soldier anymore?"

"Oh no," she said hotly, and I could hear the lingering anger. "He got out and married some teacher he met there. They've got a couple of kids already."

"And you?"

"I have a type," she replied, her voice crackly. "But most men my age who serve are married or have someone."

"Sure."

"And everyone talks a good game about cheating, but once it's there, on the table, you'd be surprised how many men chicken out."

Or were just good guys who were caught up in the moment but came to their senses before it was too late.

She crossed her arms. "I saw Ian and I didn't see a ring."

"Right."

"He looks better now than he did six years ago."

There was no doubt Ian would get better looking with age. He'd have people propositioning him right and left when he was seventy.

"I thought I'd been given a gift, a second shot at what I'd missed out on the first time around."

"Makes sense."

"But now he's gay."

I wasn't about to correct her a second time.

"Or bi," she added. "Right?"

"He was always bi."

"What about latent homosexuality and all that?"

"I dunno," I answered, because having been gay all my life; I had no idea how anything else worked and honestly never cared to learn. Since Ian liked both women and men, and now liked me best of all—that was really the extent of my interest in any discussion of his sexuality.

"But he's bi, you said, so that means he likes women too."

Was she asking me or telling me?

She tipped her head, studying my face. "That doesn't scare you? That it's not just one or the other, but both?"

I didn't need to let her in on my thoughts, on the fears that sometimes still plagued me because, just as I'd thought the night before, even though Ian was equally attracted to both genders, I was the one who had his heart.

"That would scare me to death."

I would have answered her, but Ian was striding in from the middle of the backyard where he'd been talking to Delaney, and was now closing in on the door. Slipping around her, I was there when he reached it and opened it for him.

"So?" I asked him.

"I need to go to the office before we hit Portillo's," he said, grabbing my bicep and yanking me after him.

"Wait," I argued, pulling free so he had to turn and face me.

"What?"

"Is there actually someone out there that you think is trying to kill you and whoever else?"

"Not me, but Delaney's spooked, because of the six of us who went out with Lochlyn the night he freaked out, Laird and Regan have both died in hit-and-run accidents over the past five months."

"Okay, but who's this Lochlyn guy?"

"I'll explain at the office, I swear."

"Then let's go now."

He smirked at me. "You saw that I was trying to get us out of here, right?"

I glared at him and he opened his mouth to defend himself.

"Ian," Danita called out to him.

He turned from me and waited as she moved around in front of him.

"Before you go, could I get your number? I'd love to get a drink and catch up."

His squint would have made me smile, but I bit the inside of my cheek so I wouldn't. "What for? We don't have anything to catch up on."

"I would—" Her breath hitched like she was nervous. "—love to see you."

It took him a second to get that she was hitting on him. Normally he was quicker, but he had a ton of stuff on his mind. "Oh, I can't do that," he informed her. "I'm basically engaged."

"You are?" she asked, her gaze flicking to me and then back to him.

"Yeah. I asked, it was a yes. We've just gotta pick a time to get it done."

"You're getting married?" She was flabbergasted, if her tone and how wide her eyes got were any indication.

"Yeah," he said, looking from her back to me. "Stay here while I go say bye to Rose and her mom."

"'Course."

He left quickly and I was alone with Danita.

"Is he marrying you?" she asked cautiously.

Normally I would have remained silent, but I was too proud of calling Ian mine. "At some point, yeah."

I watched her absorb the news, saw her brow furrow, lips press tightly together, eyes going vacant in that empty expression people had when they were completely lost in thought and aware of nothing else. In moments she was back, her gaze laser focused on me.

She cleared her throat. "I'm sorry. I'm just surprised yeah?"

I nodded.

"I didn't know he was—and Ian's not—I mean, I've always had a stereotype in my head about what gay men look like and act like," she confessed, clearly flustered, going by the flush of pink on her cheeks and her fluttering hands as she spoke.

"Sure."

She gestured at me. "You don't look gay."

I shrugged. "Gay isn't just one kind of person."

"No, I know," she said, sounding almost irritated, but I was guessing more with herself than with the situation. "I—but you know what I mean— what I'm trying to say."

I coughed softly. "I think we're back to those stereotypes you were talking about."

"Yes," she agreed, inhaling fast. "Yes."

Some people wouldn't have taken the moment, wouldn't have done any self-examination at all, so it was sad, really, that I wouldn't get to know her better because of the choice she'd made with Ian that inadvertently nearly cost him his life.

"He loves you?"

"Yes."

"He likes being with you, then," she said, and it was more rhetorical than anything else. "So that could be why… I mean, maybe that's why he didn't want me. Maybe that's why he never did anything but kiss me."

She must not have realized a lot of people were clustered closer than she thought—the living room was only so big—or she'd never have let loose with that confession. As soon as the words were out and she saw me lift my eyebrows—even before I glanced right and then left—in that exact second, she got it, what she'd said, and she lifted her hand to her mouth, covering it, as though that could possibly help.

Odell gasped from behind me. "Wait. What?"

I turned to look at him, and him at me. I saw new anguish there, along with betrayal and so much anger.

"He fuckin' should've said."

But Ian felt like the thought itself was enough to be punished for. He'd planned on seducing his brother's wife, and the guilt over that, to him, was the same as carrying out the act. I knew him, knew how his mind worked, and that was the reason for his silence and the acceptance of the judgment passed.

At the same time, though, when he got back, he was purged of the sin and left their company without a backward glance. That too was Ian. Once you were square, he was vapor, and there was no more talking after that. Had Eddie Laird not died, he would have never seen these men again. They were all still carrying him with them, still burdened with their guilt. But to Ian the debt was settled, and he never gave any of them a second thought. As I took in the faces of the men around me, all looking shell-shocked and pained, knowing what they were party to—especially Delaney, who sank into the closest chair to him—I had a moment of peace. I loved closure, and I was thinking Eddie Laird did too.

"Let's go," Ian called from the front door, refocusing my attention on him and off the stunned crowd around me before he slipped out.

The four other marshals and I went and hugged and kissed Rose and Janice before we left and were standing outside together on the front porch moments later. Ian was there, taking deep breaths, smiling.

"You all right?" I asked, joining him a few steps away from the others.

"Yeah."

"Feeling vindicated?"

He shook his head. "No. I did a shitty thing, but I paid for it."

I moved closer to him. "We're gonna need to talk about everything."

His grunt was more of a groan.

"I know how much you love that, but I need to know."

"Fine. I'll talk, then you."

"Me?"

He motioned with his finger to include all of my face. "Cochran."

"Right. It's a deal," I said hoarsely, because listening to Ian recount horrors perpetrated on him always turned me inside out.

"It was years ago," he whispered, kissing the side of my neck. It was a favorite spot because he liked the feel of my skin and the scent. "Keep it in mind."

"It won't help," I said, putting a hand on the side of his face, holding him there.

Turning his head, he kissed my palm and then leaned back. "I love you too, M," he muttered as the guys crowded around us. "Okay, so, I've got to go to the office before we go listen to crappy music."

"Yes!" Ryan cheered.

"Shit," Dorsey groaned, letting his head fall forward.

"I'm gonna drink a lot," Ching announced as he thumped down the front steps. "Not even kidding, just so you guys are prepared."

"He's kind of an ass when he drinks," Becker chimed in.

"We know!" I yelled out along with everyone else.

Ching flipping us all off was the best thing that had happened all day.

CHAPTER 9

SHARPE AND White, two other members of our team, were on duty when the six of us made it downtown to our office in the Dirksen Federal Building. Becker and Ching went to check on a warrant they'd put out on a drug trafficker, Dorsey and Ryan got on the phone with Homeland Security on a terrorism task force inquiry, and Ian and I sat at his desk and logged in to look for Kerry Lochlyn, a guy Ian served with four years ago when he was on active duty in Afghanistan.

"So what's the deal with this guy?" I asked as the computer hunted for the guy through every database we had access to.

"I dunno," Ian said as he typed and read what came up on the screen to prompt him for more information. "I thought he came home and got help."

"But you didn't know. You didn't follow up."

"We weren't friends."

"How long was he with you?"

"Six months, I think."

"Do you remember what happened with him?"

"Not exactly," he said, still typing. "We were out on patrol one night and—"

"Who was?"

"Me, Delaney, Odell, Bates, Regan, Laird, and Lochlyn."

"Okay, and?"

"He freaked out."

"About what?"

Ian had to think a second. "I remember me and the other guys were talking to some locals and he just lost his shit."

"Why?"

He shrugged. "It gets scary, right? Day after day you never know who to trust, can't tell who wants to kill you and who just wants to mind their own business."

It was second nature, a reality of life for him and a terrifying possibility for me.

"I remember he was yelling at this guy and his wife—or his mother, I don't remember—but a little kid went over to him, and she came up behind Lochlyn, and he started screaming."

"Did he hurt anyone?"

"No, because we got him outta there. Delaney took him back to base with Regan, and the rest of us stayed and finished up the patrol."

"So you don't know what went on from when they left you to when Lochlyn got put on a plane for home."

"No, I don't."

"Could he have been given a second chance?"

"I think that might've been it already. I seem to recall him freaking out before, and Delaney let it slide."

"But Delaney had a choice."

"Sure. Keep him there with us or send him home."

"And so he went home."

"Yeah. I mean, he had a meltdown; it wasn't something he was going to get over so Delaney made the call."

"Did he have to?"

He turned in his chair to look at me. "These are people's lives at stake, M. Lochlyn's carrying a big-ass gun and walking through towns with kids and old people. What if his paranoia got the better of him and he killed someone?"

"But what if all he needed was a little help?"

"No, it was more than that. You get to a place where you can tell the guys who are gonna make it. He wasn't, and Delaney knew it too."

"Did you ever see him again after that night?"

Ian was quiet a second. "No. I never did."

"So it's very possible that if this guy, Lochlyn, had a hard time when he got home and blames Delaney for sending him, that he also blames you for not sticking up for him."

"Yeah, I guess," he agreed with a grimace.

"What?"

He glanced at me. "That's kind of a stretch, isn't it?"

"How?"

"Delaney sent Lochlyn home, and now he's out to get us?"

"You said he was unstable."

"Yeah, but once he got back here to the world, maybe everything righted itself."

"Or not," I said, playing devil's advocate. "And if he never saw you again, he would assume that you're still in that unit."

"Probably."

"You're not buying it."

"Not really, no."

"Why not?"

"Lots of guys have a hard time over there, and I'd say most of them come home and get help."

"But you don't know what he came home to."

"No, I don't, and—shit," he growled before leaning back in the chair and gesturing at the screen. "This certainly isn't helping."

I checked the screen myself and saw that according to our database—not only the same one the bureau and Homeland Security used, but also our own warrant information network—Kerry Lochlyn was nowhere to be found.

"He refused treatment and was discharged, and that's the last record we have."

"Look, though," I said, pointing at the address. "His folks live in Trenton." Turning in my chair, I yelled for Sharpe.

"Jesus, I'm right here," he snapped.

I ignored his tone. "Hey, remember when you went to Jersey to pick up what's-his-name—the cat burglar who saw the mob hit...." I had to think. "Tommy something?"

"Timmy," he corrected me. "Timmy Halligan. Yeah, why? What about him?"

"You worked with a couple guys you said would fit right in with us, remember?"

"Yeah, I remember the guys, but"—he turned to White—"what were their names?"

"Kramer and Greenberg," White supplied.

"Yeah," he said and then looked back at me. "Why?"

"Ian needs them to make a home visit."

"Send it over here and I'll call 'em."

Swiveling around, I was faced with a glower. "What?"

"I don't think it's such a good idea to mix military business and marshal business."

"If this guy is gonna try and hurt you, then it's all the same," I assured him.

"I don't think so, and Kage probably wouldn't want us wasting company resources on—"

"Let's see," I said, standing up.

"Miro," Ian snapped irritably, trying to grab me and pull me back down into my chair. "Just shut—"

"Men," I called out to the room. "Listen up."

I had everyone's attention.

"Who thinks Ian and I should check out a guy who may or may not have a vendetta against Ian's old team from when he was a Ranger and who might then want to kill him?"

It took a few moments for my words to sink in.

"Is this a trick question?" Becker asked.

I arched an eyebrow for Ian.

"I'm calling now," Sharpe let me know.

"Sit the fuck down," Ian grumbled.

It was fun being right.

CHING WANTED Greek food, so the six of us headed over to The Parthenon on Halstead to get our *saganaki* on. We all ate a bit at the house after the funeral, but not big full plates, so eating so soon was not a problem. We were caravanning to Hyde Park. Becker and Ching were leading in their car, and Ian, Ryan, Dorsey, and I were following in the tricked-out Hummer they had been assigned. It was one of the things we did, driving cars seized in drug raids and awaiting auction.

"This is nice," I said, wiggling in my leather seat. "We should carpool somewhere else before this baby gets sold."

"We could seriously help SWAT out in this thing." Ryan snickered. "I feel like people should get the fuck out of my way… in… traffic…."

"What's wrong?" Dorsey asked, able to read Ryan's voice just as I could Ian's.

"The fuck is going on up there?"

Ian and I leaned forward, and the four of us watched as, on the other side of the street, through the light we were now stuck at, Becker and Ching were stopped.

A police cruiser was sitting behind them, and as we waited for the red to change to green, another cruiser roared up and parked behind the first one while still another slid into the spot in front of Becker and Ching.

"What the hell?" Dorsey asked as we saw the four uniformed officers all draw their weapons and aim them at the interior of the car.

"Oh fuck, no," Ian roared as the light changed colors.

Things happened fast.

Ryan gunned the motor, and we were there behind the last cruiser, coming to a screeching halt that couldn't be helped with how close we were and how fast we moved. We all got out at the same time and jogged toward the scene.

The shouting was immediate as I heard sirens in the distance.

"Stop where you are!"

"Those are federal marshals!" Dorsey shouted back. "The hell are you doing?!"

There were more cops in minutes, but by then, the four of us were around Becker and Ching's car, all with our hands up but not giving up our weapons—if we in fact had them, which we did, but they couldn't see under our coats—and certainly not getting on our knees. The cops hadn't shot at us, luckily, and we hadn't stopped, stubbornly, but that was as good as it was going to get. Already, that fast, things had escalated. It was scary and really, it had to look odd, four men standing around a car while six officers held guns on us and no one backed down or away, everyone just static. As the first news helicopter flew over us, I thought it was time for the officers to rethink their position.

"You're drawing down on *six* federal marshals," Ryan informed the cops even as others joined them. "Do you want to maybe look at some ID at this point?"

"The man in the car refused to get out," one of the officers responded in a near shout.

"No, I said I would get out and I agreed to comply, but I also wanted to show you my badge." Becker corrected from inside the car. "I was taking off my seatbelt and pulling my ID when the first officer drew his weapon instead of waiting."

"Why the hell would he need to get out?" I asked, moving to the driver's side window so he no longer had a clear shot at Becker.

"Don't move!" the cop warned me.

"Miro, stop!" Ian ordered, and I heard the edge of fear in his voice.

"You need to put down your weapons," Dorsey bellowed at the cops. "We're federal marshals, you asshole!"

But the cops weren't buying it—as they shouldn't have, without ID—but wouldn't let any of us reach into our coats. Since we weren't about to let them take Becker or Ching out of the car, we were at a standstill.

It felt like we stood there for hours, with more helicopters and more policemen, and of course the crowd that formed. And it didn't need to be any of those things, but as far as I could tell, Becker and Ching had gotten pulled over for no other reason than Becker being black.

Ching was livid. I could hear him swearing. Both he and Becker still had their hands on the dashboard, but with the four of us around the car, the cops couldn't even see inside anymore.

"I'm still convinced that not all of these guys are racist or stupid," Becker said from beside me as I was standing at his window. "I just think that a few of them who perform these stop-and-frisk searches are, and they're the ones who end up looking like fuckups on the nightly news."

"Or do worse than look stupid," I said angrily.

"Yes," he agreed solemnly.

"And if they weren't racist, they wouldn't be targeting African-Americans," I griped, squatting down beside the window so I could look him in the eye.

"Shit, stop moving," he cautioned as there was a barrage of yelling behind me.

"Miro, freeze!" Ian demanded from the other side of the car.

"They're not gonna shoot me," I assured him before refocusing on Becker. "Tell him they're not gonna shoot me."

"I can't say that with any real conviction," Becker replied. "The only reason they didn't shoot me and Wes was because four white men surrounded the car."

"I don't believe that."

"Because you're white," he said pointedly and then grunted.

"What?"

"You said African-American before," he replied.

"Yeah? And?"

"It's very proper, very PC, very careful of you to say."

"What do you mean careful?"

"It's just, that's how I can tell whose report I'm reading—yours or Doyle's—when I see them even without looking at your names."

"You lost me."

He chuckled. "He'll put race down as black or white or Hispanic, you're all fancy and you say African-American, Mexican-American, Italian-American… it's fuckin' exhausting."

"It's correct."

"It's *careful*, and I get why you do it, but Doyle's in the military so it's different for him. The rank is important but not much else."

I thought about that. "I just never want to be disrespectful to anyone. I think because I don't know what I am exactly, I'm always careful with what other people are."

"Which makes sense," he agreed. "But you can say black and I promise you no one's going to lose their mind."

"So endeth the lesson?" I teased.

"Yeah."

I groaned. "I wish whatever the fuck this is could end too."

He snickered. "At least The Befuddled Owl is out."

"You didn't want to go either?"

His scowl made me smile in spite of everything else. "Nobody wanted to go, especially not Ryan."

I looked around, taking in the deadlocked scene. "Man, I had other plans for tonight, I swear to God."

"Well, just don't reach for anything like your phone, all right? I don't wanna get shot because they're aiming for you."

"No, come on, it's gone on too long already. They're just posturing now. They're committed to this, and now they can't back down until someone with power shows up."

"I hate to be the one to break it to you, Jones, but lots of people have been killed who were much less threatening than the six of us are at the moment."

I knew that too. I watched the news just like everybody else.

"And I don't mean just here, but all over."

"Yes," I agreed. "And now, these cops, they could be scared too, right?"

"True."

"For all they know we're mob enforcers packing Micro-Uzis."

"In the giant red Hummer you guys all came in and this piece of shit Olds we're driving?"

"It's the suits and trench coats," I teased.

He scoffed. "How does Ian's uniform fit in?"

"Oh God," I groaned. "I don't think anyone noticed his beret."

"I'm going with no."

"If he takes off his coat—Christ."

"Yeah. That'd be brilliant on the front pages of the *Sun-Times* and the *Trib* tomorrow."

"It'd be on the home page of MSN and Yahoo and all those too."

"Make sure he keeps his coat on," Becker instructed. "Neither one of us, CPD, or our office needs any of that."

"They started it," I flared.

"They did," he agreed. "But sometimes you gotta rise above."

"Kage is gonna have an aneurysm," Ching commented from his side of the car, letting his head roll forward and back and side to side.

"What're you doing?"

"This displaces tension," he explained. "And I need to pee."

"You should have gone at the restaurant," Becker told him. "What do I always say?"

He grunted.

"Why aren't you pissed?" I asked Becker, because I would have been livid.

"Are you kidding? This has been happening my whole life, man. I've been pulled over a hundred times more than you have, just because of the color of my skin."

"I'm sorry."

"I know you are, buddy, and I appreciate that, and I will say now that the badge normally makes this shit stop before it escalates, but that guy right there, holding the gun on us, he just wanted me out of the car. He didn't want to let me get my ID out of my coat or the car's registration out of the glove box. This could have been over before it started, but now he's *done*, and he doesn't even know it yet simply because he saw a black man and nothing else."

"So you *are* mad."

"Yeah. This is me mad."

I snorted and he smiled back, and then we all heard the command from above from one of the helicopters. "Show us ID."

All of us together, carefully, slowly, pulled out our badges. I had no doubt that the stars were very visible, as evidenced by the collective groan from the law enforcement clustered around us.

"Motherfucker," the cop holding the gun on Becker and me swore under his breath before he holstered his weapon.

Oh yeah, he was *so* done.

WE WERE all sitting in a conference room in the main police headquarters at Thirty-Fifth and Michigan, looking out our window and across the hall into another room, where our boss was sitting with the interim superintendent of police, Matthew Kenton; Alderman Robert Dias from one of the south-side wards; Chicago police chief of support services, Edward Strohm; and too many others I didn't know.

All these people coming in on a Sunday confirmed how serious a mess this was.

One of the mayor's aides showed up an hour later—and I only knew because she popped her head in on us first to make sure we were all okay, did a double-take as she saw Ian's uniform—and then went into the other room with everyone else.

"You see?" Ryan said into the silence. "This is why we don't want any new guys."

I turned to look at him, as did Becker and Ching.

"What?" Ian asked irritably.

"We're bonding here, right? How're new guys ever gonna be able to top this?"

"Oh dear God," Dorsey groaned. "I really don't think this is anything but a clusterfuck of biblical proportions."

"And you guys are gonna be in trouble," Becker made known.

"Not us," Ching clarified, "only you guys."

Ian grunted.

"We didn't draw our weapons," Dorsey reminded them. "We didn't escalate anything."

And he was right... kind of.

An argument could be made—and was by the police—that the four of us could have walked away, or even better, remained inside our vehicle for the duration of the stop. For our part, with the track record of the Chicago PD, it was reasonable to assume that we were in fear for Deputy US Marshal Christopher Becker's life, as well as that of his partner, Wesley Ching.

Clusterfuck was going to be an understatement, I was guessing.

While I was there, since Kage was a multitasker, he got the cops' Internal Affairs Department guy in to talk to me about the incident with Cochran with the marshals' service's Office of Professional Responsibility liaison, Shepard McAllister. He was a nice enough guy, but as far as I could tell, his mouth was broken, as he was incapable of smiling. Ever. There was a lot of squinting, so much legalese, and too many interruptions to count. The IAD guy—Trey Covington—got really annoyed, but McAllister kept banging away at the same stuff over and over.

"So Norris Cochran accused Chief Deputy US Marshal Sam Kage of lying to him," McAllister clarified for like the seventh time.

"Yessir," I answered.

And McAllister shot the IAD guy a look that clearly said *Are you getting the seriousness of this?* Covington's groan said he wasn't missing a thing.

"Are there records that support the chief deputy's claim?" Covington asked.

I was going to answer in the affirmative, but McAllister raised his hand to shut me up. "We are not here to debate the issue of whether or not the firearm does in fact exist, or whether or not it was ever in the custody of the marshals' service." He had a ferocious clipping tone that made every word seem like it was bitten off. It was really annoying, and if I were Covington, I'd want to pop him. "What we *are* here to determine is whether *your* detective attacked *my* marshal without provocation, and the glaringly obvious answer is an emphatic yes."

"I don't think we can conclude that at all."

"Oh, I think we can," McAllister snarled, levying his self-righteous tone at Covington. "I've already talked to the waitress and the manager on duty at the diner where the incident took place, and I have the sworn statements of two of Marshal Jones's colleagues."

"Well, I'm sure I'll have a signed affidavit from Norris Cochran's partner, who will claim that the incident did not occur how the marshal remembers it at all."

"That's fine. If you take away all the conflicting testimony, then we're left with what the waitress saw and what the manager saw, and those eyewitness accounts will corroborate what my marshal has gone on the record as stating."

We were all quiet.

"What is it that your office is looking for here?"

"Are you admitting fault?"

"I'm asking a question."

"For starters the detective will be suspended for no less than a month without pay and—"

"Not without pay," I interrupted, and both men turned to me. "He has kids."

"And how in the world would you know that?" McAllister asked.

"He's my old partner from when I was on the force."

"Oh, that's interesting," Covington almost crowed. "I imagine that old partners have a lot of reasons to beat the hell out of each other."

McAllister scoffed. "It doesn't matter. Again I have testimony, as well as tonight's incident, that shows a pattern of animosity from your department toward our office. I will have this conversation in the forum of your choosing, but know that all of them will be public."

"Your stance is that tonight's incident has to do with some sort of animosity between the marshals' office and Chicago PD?"

"Are you saying it's not?"

There was no right answer. Whatever Covington said, he was fucked.

McAllister waited, looking bored.

"You mentioning public anything sounds like a threat."

"No, but *again*, it's obvious that your officers are in the habit of physically attacking marshals, as evidenced by yesterday's confrontation and tonight's show of force. These facts can't possibly be in dispute."

"You're making a lot of assumptions," Covington insisted. "You can't in any way paint the entire department with the same brush."

"Oh no? Because I think the climate we find ourselves in presently lends itself to one of absolute mistrust of your department. I'll bet you if you took a poll of a thousand random Chicagoans, that across the board, they would rather be taken into custody by a federal marshal than a Chicago policeman."

"I think that's shortsighted of you and a rash statement to make."

"Perhaps. Shall we test it?"

Silence for the second time.

"I'll talk to Cochran's captain," Covington finally muttered.

McAllister's smirk was douchey, but it took a big man not to gloat, and I didn't think he had it in him to not lord it over Covington. Once we were in the hall, while holding his phone, he told me he was already sending Kage an e-mail for them to talk. It made sense that McAllister was chomping at the bit to report his probable success. Everybody wanted to be on the Chief Deputy US Marshal's good list. McAllister was no exception.

Back in the room, Ian asked how it went, and so I told him in the same detail I told McAllister, exactly what crap Cochran had pulled on me. Ian came to the same conclusion I had when I was done.

"So Cochran thinks this gun is in our evidence locker?"

"Yeah."

"I was just in there earlier," Ching told me. "I transferred the last of the guns out for processing. They're all on their way to Quantico."

"No, I know there was nothing in there," I said, fidgeting in my chair, tired of sitting, tired of the same topic, and mostly just wanting to leave. "This is Kage we're talking about. If there's a more by-the-book guy, I've yet to meet him."

"Oh thank God, here we go," Ian murmured, sitting up in his chair as we all saw our boss point at all the people in the room—except the alderman, who got a handshake—before hurling open the door.

In real life, Sam Kage was not eight feet tall. I knew that. *Logically* I knew. It just *felt* like it whenever he came into a room. I knew men who were bigger: Becker, for instance, and Kowalski, but Kage was scarier. Not because of the hard, heavy muscle he carried on his frame, but because he was a protector. He truly cared about what was his, and that included all of us. We were his men, and because of that, if you questioned us, you were questioning him.

You really didn't want to do that.

From the expressions of dread on the faces of the people still in the other room—except the alderman's, who appeared a bit smug at the moment—the others looked wholly traumatized. It made sense. Kage intimidated everyone, and I saw the collective breath the people in the room took when he left. Not only was he scary, but he had the power to back it up. When Kage reached out to his boss and he in turn reached out to his, there would be a whole new storm of shit falling on the Chicago PD.

Before he could open the door to the room where we were waiting, we all got to our feet. He moved immediately to Becker and offered him his hand.

Becker took it fast, looking almost shell-shocked as he stared at our boss.

"I'm so sorry about all this and very relieved that you weren't physically harmed."

Because Kage knew Becker'd been hurt in other ways, he added the physical part. People said a lot of things about Sam Kage, and people speculated about the kind of man he really was. But I knew. He was a *good* man.

"Thank you, sir," Becker replied, releasing a deep breath.

"I'm insisting on a formal public apology," Kage told him. "You can be there to make a statement yourself or not. That's up to you. I myself hate public anything, but I never assume anyone else's preferences."

"Yessir."

"You, of course, can sue the department as well, and based on the apology, I'm sure there would be compensation involved."

He shook his head. "No, sir."

Kage patted his shoulder before turning to Ching and offering him his hand, making sure he, too, was all right before rounding on the rest of us. "What the hell was wrong with taking out your badges *before* you walked up on the car? *Why* would that have been *hard*?"

The yelling surprised me.

"Were you intentionally trying to make the officers on-site look worse than they already did?"

He was waiting between questions, but I had the feeling that answering would be bad, from the way his gaze was boring into each of us, one at a time. The undercurrent of murder was there in his face. He was furious and, even worse, disappointed.

"We're all in this together, gentlemen. Us, CPD, the FBI, CIA, Homeland, State, all of us."

I noticed he didn't say DEA, and I made the mistake of smiling.

"Jones?" he said, his gaze zeroing in on me. "Something you'd like to add?"

I cleared my throat. "No, sir, except to say I didn't think of pulling my badge before we walked up on them."

The whole room around me groaned.

"But that's protocol, isn't it?"

Was it?

Ian swore, Dorsey rolled his eyes, Ryan shook his head, Ching looked disgusted, and Becker nodded, silently saying that yes, dumbass, that was protocol.

Kage's grunt was not a good one, full of judgment and recrimination.

Ian tried to defend me. "It was the heat of the moment, sir."

"I see," Kage said darkly, his tone menacing. "Well, because you didn't think of it and none of you followed protocol, but because what you did was actually in support of members of your team, I'm going to educate you instead of suspending you."

Oh God. My eyes might have fluttered as I imagined the horror.

He'd once sent me to Asset Forfeiture, where they managed and sold assets that were seized and forfeited by criminals, the proceeds doled out to victims and innocent people caught in the crossfire. Funds were also used for community programs and different initiatives that... God... I couldn't remember. I knew they did good work. Compensating people hurt by crime was a noble pursuit, but the day-to-day accounting of it was a snorefest. They were, in fact, heroes, but they didn't look cool doing it. I was vain enough to know that following Ian through the door, being the one on the ground, was something I got off on. I was as susceptible to praise as the next guy. So spreadsheets and endless reporting were not things I had the heart for. I was only there a week, but it had felt like a year. It was a huge responsibility. Huge. The marshal service managed assets in the billions, and I never, ever wanted to know anything about that. I was happy being in the field. I would die sitting behind a desk doing what others enjoyed because it wasn't me. Sam Kage knew it, and just the idea that he'd send me back was terrifying. I prayed he wasn't that mad.

Please God, don't let him be that pissed off.

"So you two," he said, pointing at Dorsey and Ryan, "will enjoy being on WITSEC intake this week, and you two," he continued—Ian and I were up—"will enjoy flying to Las Vegas to bring back a witness who is not presently in custody, but that the office there has under surveillance. Maybe then you'll all remember to pull your badges."

"Paperwork," Dorsey whined.

"Witness transfer," Ian groused.

There was nothing on Kage's face at all to indicate even a sliver of caring.

"You should get going, gentlemen," Kage told Ian and me. "That plane leaves at seven a.m. from O'Hare, I believe, and Monday morning traffic in Chicago means you better be there a helluva lot earlier than that."

I opened my mouth to protest.

"And before you go, you need to settle that business with Cabot and Drake. I want to know their status before the plane takes off in the morning since you won't be here."

I turned to Ian.

"Please just don't even look at him anymore," he begged. "And don't talk either."

That at least got a half a grin from our boss.

CHAPTER 10

"THIS IS why you're supposed to wear a mask," Ian said when we got to their door and Drake greeted us.

His smile instantly fell as Ian walked by him, but I reached out, grabbed him, and hugged him tight. He relaxed in my arms; he was still a kid, after all, and needed the support.

"You did a great thing. Everybody knows it. I know it, Ian knows it. But we have to make some decisions now."

He nodded into my shoulder, and when I tried to let go, he held on. After a few more moments, Cabot appeared beside him, the blond golden cherub he'd always been, beautiful and delicate boned in sharp contrast to the taller, broader, tightly muscled specimen his boyfriend was.

"Drake, let go," Cabot ordered. "I want to see Miro too."

Drake gave me a last squeeze and then Cabot was there, hugging me tight, shivering like something was wrong and he needed the comfort. I would have to find out what that was about.

"You all right?" I whispered just in case the problem was Drake.

"This got long," he said into my throat, ignoring the question, his fingers in my hair that needed to be cut, kicked out over my ears, got in my eyes, and would soon cover my nape.

"Enough of that," Ian muttered, walking up beside us and peeling Cabot away from me before standing in front of both of them, arms crossed, glaring. "So?"

I realized they were both looking at Ian the way I probably looked at Kage, with the same trace of wariness and respect. I liked Kage, but he terrified me at the same time. I suspected it was the same for them with Ian, especially when the man I loved was in his dress uniform, looking particularly breathtaking.

Drake nearly choked taking a breath. "You look awesome."

"Listen," Ian began. "You—"

"Were you getting a medal or something?"

"I was at a funeral," he answered harshly.

"Awww, man, I'm sorry," Drake said, moving forward to put a hand on Ian's shoulder.

The growl he got for his trouble was not surprising. "You need to shut up so Miro and me can figure out—"

"If we stay here, will we still see you guys?" Cabot blurted.

Christ.

Cabot and Drake were special to Ian and me. We brought them into witness protection when our relationship was brand new. Cabot's father was rich and crazy. Now he was cooling his heels in federal prison for the next eight years at least, and the word was the boys—both twenty now—no longer required protection. Originally Drake was witness to a murder he told Cabot all about, which began the whole spiral leading to them being on our radar, and Cabot's father took that opportunity to try to kill Drake. It was a mess, but we got it sorted out. But because Cabot's father was well connected even in prison, he still posed a potential threat to the boys.

However: Drake had saved a little girl—a great, wonderful thing—and his face got splashed all over the news. He was being called the Sexy Samaritan, and the shot of him coming out of the water, dripping wet with his shirt plastered to his carved chest and abdomen, went viral. Good heart and great body were the buzzwords. So, no more witness protection.

"Yes," Ian said quickly, and I was so stunned I turned to look at him. "We'll probably see more of each other, actually, and of course, if either of you gets the feeling like something just isn't right—you need to tell us right away."

"You can come have turkey with us," I told them, throwing that in since my man was being so accommodating.

"Really?" Cabot asked, his eyes lighting up.

"Yes, really," Ian grumbled irritably. "Now are you going back to Ford and Jenner, or keeping the new last names?"

They were keeping the new ones; those were what they'd used to build their new lives and what they'd use when they got married in the spring.

I envied them the wedding part.

"Miro, come look at this still life I did," Cabot pleaded, grabbing my hand and tugging me after him toward the bedroom.

It was a cute little apartment they'd moved into after they decided the one we initially put them in didn't fit the kind of people they were. This one was in Hyde Park close to the university Drake attended and had all the charm of a first place a couple got together: exposed red brick, a fire escape to sit on, wooden floors, radiators in every room, an ugly tiled kitchen, and the requisite black tabby alley cat turned house cat that had gotten huge from nonstop eating and sleeping. His name was Boozer, and I didn't want to know why.

It was a stunning picture, the cut fruit, bread, and flowers done in a sort of Gothic style that verged on being eerie but didn't go quite that far.

"Oh, it's beautiful," I assured him, turning with a smile.

"If I want to sleep with someone else before I get married, is that bad?"

It took me a second, because I was in "admire the art mode" and he dropped me into "camp counselor mode," and it was a jump.

"Miro?"

I knew why this question was being leveled at me instead of Ian. If he'd asked Ian, Ian would have just called for me. My partner took care of shooting people and saving them. I did the talking.

"Is this a rhetorical question or do you have someone in mind?"

He coughed. "I have someone in mind."

I nodded. "Okay. Well, if you do it and don't tell Drake first, then yeah, that's bad. If you tell him and he's okay with it, then you're good."

"But what if he thinks I don't love him because I just want to see?"

"Then you explain it to him over and over until he gets it, and if he doesn't, then you break up."

"But what if I don't want to break up?"

"It doesn't matter what you want if you also want to sleep with other people. Or, just one, as it seems like."

"Yeah, just one."

"Even one, though, it's better that you guys part ways than you cheat on him."

He didn't look convinced.

I shrugged. "He might wanna sleep with someone else too." His eyes got huge. "It goes both ways, right?" I continued. "He may be curious as well."

"But I don't want him to sleep with anybody else."

"You're both really young, Cab. Neither one of you has ever been with anyone else. It's natural to wonder, but you can't be naïve and think you're the only one."

He swallowed hard, I heard the gulp, and he looked like he was going to barf.

"Cab?"

"I don't think I've thought this all the way through," he rasped, his breathing rough.

"Sure," I said gently, hand on his shoulder. "Because right now you're thinking about some other guy's hands all over Drake, but you also have to realize that, that thought can't be what keeps you in this thing with him. Best thing to do is talk to him about everything and see where his head's at. For all you know, his headspace could be the same."

"That he wants to sleep with other people?"

I shrugged. "I know talking's hard." I really did. It was a horror at times. "But you have to do it."

He cleared his throat. "So what time should we come over on Thursday?"

Apparently we were tabling the sex-with-strangers discussion.

"Whenever you want, just not like seven in the morning."

He smiled wide.

I heard a loud thump and, in the living room, found Drake on the floor looking up at Ian, who was standing over him, arms crossed, looking bored.

"What happened?" I asked, chuckling.

Drake heaved out the words. "I've been taking tae kwon do lessons. I wanted to see if I could, you know, take him down."

Ian's arched eyebrow was diabolical. "He's not quite ready yet."

"To take on a Green Beret," I teased. "No, probably not."

"Bring rolls for dinner," Ian commanded the prone man beneath him.

"Yessir," Drake agreed, exhaling deeply as Cabot started giggling.

Ian offered his hand and Drake reached for him without hesitation.

Outside on the sidewalk, after reiterating to the boys to *not* show up at the crack of dawn on Thanksgiving, I smiled at Ian.

"What?"

"You were very good with them."

"I have my moments," he said, throwing an arm around my neck and pulling me close to him. "And now I just wanna go home."

"I should call Aruna and ask her to keep Chickie until we get back from Vegas. No reason to bring him back and forth."

"I agree and that way, you know, we can just go home."

Home would be good. It was all I wanted, to be there with him alone.

THE HOME part was not to be. We ended up having to go back to the office for Ian's laptop that we'd both forgotten to have him grab when we were there the first time. It was procedure to leave it at the office whenever he deployed, and it was also required it be in his possession as soon as he returned.

Once we were there, I saw Kage was in his office, which was weird since it was late on a Sunday, and he normally kept his weekends free for his family—except for the times his marshals found themselves in a life-threatening clusterfuck.

Like today.

While Ian checked his e-mail, Kage called me in to talk to him.

"Sir?"

"Jones, I'm flying out to Raleigh in the morning to speak to the family of Carrington Adams."

This was news. I'd had no idea he'd be the one going. I was surprised that the chief deputy would be involved.

I knew undercover police detective Carrington Adams, but only in a roundabout way. Last year I was kidnapped by Dr. Craig Hartley, who had escaped from jail where I helped put him, despite the bureau team watching him, and had learned of the detective's fate. It turned out that Special Agent Cillian Wojno worked for Hartley—unbeknownst to anyone—for several years and Hartley had been blackmailing him. Years earlier, Wojno had been an eyewitness to Adams's death, and Hartley had used that knowledge to keep the agent under his thumb. When Wojno confessed that to me, I'd had no clue he had any connection to Kage. But it turned out my boss had known Adams. When I was debriefed after my kidnapping and related what I knew of Adams's fate, Kage was quick to alert Chicago PD.

Kage was still talking. "I just wanted to thank you again for agreeing to speak to them if they have any further questions of a personal nature."

"I don't know what other information I'll be able to give them," I said, uncomfortable with the idea that because I'd been the one to find out what had happened to Adams, that I was now responsible for talking to his family. I didn't know anything about the man besides how he'd died, and I couldn't imagine that could be comforting in the least. I didn't want to talk to them, but I would do anything Kage asked of me. That was a given.

"I know, but the fact that you offered will give them comfort."

"It was you who offered," I reminded him. "I agreed because you asked."

He nodded. "Still."

And that was enough, I knew what he meant. I'd still said okay, and he apparently appreciated that. "May I ask a question?"

"Of course."

"Why are you the one going, sir?"

"To deliver the news of what happened to him to his family and give them his police star for his actions."

"No, I understand the reason for the trip. I just don't understand why it's you specifically."

"There's a department liaison going with me as well."

"No, that's not what I'm asking."

"Then I'm not getting your question."

"I mean why are *you* going at all?"

"Oh, because I was the last one to speak to Adams before he died." This was also news. "You were?"

"From what I can figure now with the timeline, I think so, yeah."

"Would you tell me what you two last spoke about?"

"Why is that important?"

"I think it's important to you," I replied, because it felt like it was. Ever since I'd first said the name Carrington Adams, it was like he was carrying around a weight on his shoulders. Just something extra, some strain that showed in the squint of his eyes, in a shadow on his face, in a catch of breath. "Can I be frank?"

"'Course."

"Is it guilt?" I asked. That was the only thing I knew of that gnawed at a person like that, that made even quiet moments anxious.

He took a breath. "He called to tell me that the man he'd been building a case against—Rego James—was going to prison. At the time I remember thinking that he must have been on his way with a warrant and backup to the club that James ran all his businesses out of, and that he was going to arrest him."

"But that's not what happened."

"No. You know what happened. Wojno gave James the heads-up that Adams was a cop, and James killed Adams and Billy Donovan that night in front of Hartley, who used that to blackmail Wojno down the road."

I saw the sadness on his face and spoke before thinking. "You don't blame yourself, do you, sir?"

It took a long moment before his gaze met mine. "I never followed up with him."

"With Adams."

"Yes."

"Was it your case?"

"No."

"Were you friends?"

"No, but he knew my husband."

"Oh, so, were they friends?"

"Not friends, no. My husband knew Rego James as well."

"So you're connected to both Adams and James through your husband?"

"In a way, I guess."

I squinted at him. "Why did Adams call you that night?"

"To tell me that my husband had acted very bravely in the face of danger," he sighed.

"Then the update on James was more a courtesy just to let you know how things had worked out, or how he thought they would."

"Yes."

"I'm sorry, sir, but why in the world would you have followed up with Carrington Adams? The case had nothing to do with you, and the man himself was not your friend."

"Are you thinking I'm looking for absolution, Jones?"

"No, sir, but I do think you've been blaming yourself since you heard what happened to him, and why in the world would you?" I was feeling again how I did about myself and Adams. Like, why the hell did I need to feel bad or answer questions? It had nothing to do with me beyond being the catalyst for Wojno's betrayal. I almost resented Carrington Adams because both my boss and I were responsible for his legacy when neither of us had known him at all.

"You blame yourself for the people Hartley killed when he escaped from prison because you put him in prison and not in a grave when you had the chance," he said flatly. "Don't you?"

"I do," I admitted.

"I think we all take responsibility for things that aren't logical."

Yes. "Perhaps," I allowed.

"Go home, Jones. You've got to be on a plane very early in the morning."

"Yessir," I said, turning and leaving his office.

Ian was in the hall, and when I got close, he grabbed my hand and tugged me after him to the elevators. Inside, he shoved me up against the wall and sucked on my tongue. He would have never done it in the elevator in the middle of the day—too many people to witness a PDA—but it was late on a Sunday night and we were alone.

He kissed me breathless, grabbing my ass, pulling me close, and my hands were on his face, holding him there, making sure he couldn't pull away. When he finally had to break the kiss for air, he held me there pinned to the wall.

"Enjoy this," I told him, "because when we get home, you're gonna be the one doing what I want, how I want."

I heard his sharp exhale, and his hooded eyes never left my face.

"Now let's go get a cab. I don't wanna wait for the El."

He nodded. "We should just go to impound and pick a car," he suggested.

My wince as we got off the elevator made him stop walking. "What's with the look?"

"There's a Cabriolet," I offered cheerfully before I bolted toward the front doors and out onto the street to flag down a cab.

He jogged to catch up with me. "The fuck is that?"

From the expression on his face, I couldn't even bear to tell him.

REALLY, I was in no way surprised when we got home and Delaney was there, waiting outside our door with several men in the same military trench coats like Ian had on.

When we got closer, two other men got out of the passenger and driver's sides of one of the parked SUVs, and they were in dress coats as well.

I paid the cab driver, got out on the street, not waiting for Ian to get out first onto the curb, and hustled around the back of the car so I could stand at his side.

"What's going on?" Ian asked from where we were.

"Marshals Doyle and Jones?"

"Yes," he answered coolly to one of the men who had gotten out of the SUV.

"We're going to need you to come with us, Doyle."

"Then I'm going to need to see a lot of ID," Ian parroted, because, well, Ian. He was a smartass of the first order.

One of the men came forward, and from his stride and the way he flipped open his badge, I figured he was in charge. "Special Agent Corbin Bukowski, Criminal Investigative Division."

"What the hell is this?" Ian groused.

I was about to say something else when another car pulled up alongside the curb, and this time the guy who got out of the passenger side immediately went to the door behind him and opened it, then held it open for the gentleman who got out. He was dressed exactly as Ian was, except his beret was black. When he was close enough, Ian stood at attention and saluted.

"At ease, Captain," the man said, and then turned toward me, walked forward, and offered me his hand. I took it quickly, and since I'd forgotten to put on my gloves, noted his handshake was warm and dry. "You must be Marshal Jones."

"Yessir."

His smile was kind, and I noted the lines on his face, the glint in his pale-blue eyes, the strong line of his jaw, and the long, straight nose. He looked like he should have been on recruitment posters.

"I'm Colonel Chandler Harney, CID, and I'm here to escort Captain Doyle and the rest of the patrol that served with Kerry Lochlyn to Washington, DC. We are investigating said individual."

"May I ask why, sir?"

"The deaths of Second Lieutenant Taylor Regan and First Lieutenant Edward Laird—who was, as you know, laid to rest earlier today—have officially been ruled homicides," he concluded.

The ice that ran through my veins chilled me from the inside out.

"The Criminal Investigative Division is in charge of the inquiry until we can determine if the individual in question is a terrorist threat or a nonmilitary one."

"Would it be possible to ask another question?"

"Of course."

"You're taking the whole team, including Marshal Doyle, to Washington, DC, right now?"

"I am."

"And are you looking for Kerry Lochlyn, sir?"

"We are. Yes."

"So you're convinced that he's murdering members of the patrol he was with the night that he had a breakdown."

"We're not convinced of anything, marshal. We're merely gathering facts at this juncture," he explained crisply. "As far as what happened on that patrol—that's classified." He looked sideways at Ian because clearly, he had no idea what had or hadn't been explained to me. "These are two separate issues."

Glancing at Ian, I saw his lips drawn into a hard line. Apparently he didn't like me questioning the colonel in the least.

"Can you tell me what the process will be, sir?"

"CID, the JAG corps, and finally," he sighed, "if it's not deemed to be a military matter, then the FBI, as I've said."

"And why is the bureau involved?"

"Because if Lochlyn is responsible, then these killings across state lines constitute a federal crime," he informed me.

"How long will the men be questioned, sir? Marshal Doyle and I are supposed to fly to Las Vegas in the morning to transfer a witness."

"We've contacted your supervisor, Jones, and marshals from the office in Las Vegas will meet you at the airport there when you land tomorrow to assist you in acquiring your witness. Then you'll be able to return him or her to Chicago."

I cleared my throat. "After the questioning, will Marshal Doyle be returning here, sir?"

"If he is not implicated or needed in the field," Harney said coolly, "then of course."

Which basically meant Ian could be gone, just like that, and this was the last time I'd see him for God knew how long... again.

"His unit just returned home, sir," I said breathlessly, trying not to let the raw, pained, aching sadness bleed into my voice.

"Do you presume that Special Forces units take time-outs, marshal?" he asked me, his tone biting and clipped. Clearly he was not enjoying me questioning him. "That the enemies of our country ever rest?"

It was probably meant to shame me, being a civilian, but I didn't care. The only thing I cared about was how Ian was perceived, and so I answered respectfully. "No, sir."

"And are you prepared to do your duty, Captain?" he asked, turning to Ian.

"Yessir," Ian almost shouted.

The duty part was meant for me, and I got it. I did. What Ian did was important, and I'd tied myself to a soldier. I knew that from the beginning and was so very proud of him. But... his job as a deputy US marshal was of paramount importance as well. Even if we were nothing else but partners at work, didn't his current job matter just as much as being a soldier? The answer was a clear and resounding no.

"Grab your gear," Harney ordered.

Ian had two bags packed at all times so that the second he got home, if he was called back to service that same night, he'd be prepared to leave. In the time he was gone, my job was to unload the pack he brought home, wash everything, and repack it so it would be ready. I knew most units came home from active duty and were off for months at a time. The difference for Ian's twelve-man team was that they were Special Forces, deployed for retrieval or to subdue a target by any means necessary. It was guerilla warfare on the ground in a foreign country, and it was his duty, and he could… easily could… be going immediately out on an active mission after he was questioned about Lochlyn.

Again.

I was having trouble moving air through my lungs.

Again.

Just got home and could be leaving again.

Ian moved quickly to the house, opened the front door, and moments later, Chickie ran outside to me. He came fast and stopped at my side, eyeing all the men but not moving, keeping vigil over me, protecting my flank.

"This is the life," Harney said to me.

My gaze met his, and I checked for any trace of disgust or judgment. Ian had told me that no matter how things changed on the outside—the death of Don't Ask, Don't Tell; the intolerance of slurs or prejudice—the Army still cultivated a mindset of non-acceptance. You just never knew when you were going to run into it. But as I scanned the colonel's face, I saw him only making a statement of fact that he would to any spouse or partner of a soldier.

"Yessir," I agreed.

It took Ian only moments and he was back. He didn't say a word to me, didn't even look at me, and I realized he was embarrassed. My questions, my obvious distress had shamed him in front of his superior.

"Marshal," the colonel said to me before he walked away.

Ian's eyes met mine only for an instant, but after he got into the car with the others and was gone, what surprised me and left me speechless on the sidewalk was how wrong I was. In that instant when he left me, I hadn't seen anger or humiliation. He wasn't judging what I'd said or done. I saw only longing.

He wanted to stay. I saw it clear as day. The yearning had been there, all over him, on his face, in the catch of his breath, the parting of his lips, the fist he made with his right hand, and the way he almost stumbled when he turned to follow the man who was taking him away. I was home for him, I knew I was, and leaving me was gutting him.

There was some small comfort in the knowing.

CHAPTER 11

I WALKED right by them, mostly because I expected them to meet me in the terminal at McCarran International, not on the concourse.

"Are you Jones?"

Pivoting, I faced… I wasn't sure. I would have guessed surfer, maybe some sort of instructor—paddle board, scuba diver, hard to tell—but between the tan and the wavy sun-streaked dirty-blond hair that fell to his shoulders, the guy talking to me was not on the job.

"Yes?"

He took a step toward me, hand outstretched, a sardonic smile twisting his lips invitingly. "I'm Bodhi Callahan from the Vegas office, and this is my partner, Josiah Redeker."

Callahan didn't look like any marshal I'd ever met. I didn't know cargo shorts and deck shoes were appropriate attire, or the T-shirt under a drug rug hoodie like I hadn't seen since college. His partner looked like maybe he ran a bar. His straight dark hair fell around his face, and I noted the mustache and heavy stubble on his chin that could have been called a beard if it was filled in along the line of his jaw. As it was, he appeared artfully unkempt, with his beat-up jump boots, faded jeans, and long-sleeved gray Henley. The two of them together did not inspire fear. But maybe they didn't need to in Las Vegas. Maybe it was low-key, though with all the drugs that moved through the state, I doubted it.

"Jed's good," Redeker told me, returning my focus to him, his hand out, ready for me to take the second I was done with Callahan. "Only my mother calls me Josiah."

They made an odd pair. Callahan's accent said California all the way, which helped the laid-back surf-rat vibe, and Redeker had a deep, rich cowboy thing happening in his voice. I wondered how they meshed together.

"How long have you been marshals?" I asked after I released Redeker's hand.

"Five years for me," he replied, "two for the kid."

"Kid?" I asked Callahan.

"I'm twenty-seven," he told me. "But apparently being eleven years older is a whole big amount of time that puts him out of reach."

His wording was odd—out of reach—and made me wonder about them right off. Why was that important to Callahan? Did he mean just as a partner, or was there more to their story?

"Were you briefed on the witness that you're picking up?" Redeker asked, taking my duffel without being asked, leaving me with my laptop bag.

I had been, so I knew that Josue Hess had run when he was supposed to stay put and enter WITSEC, thus moving him from the nice list to the naughty one. Lots of people did it, bolted instead of going into witness protection, but once the marshal service was involved, private citizens no longer got a say in the matter. The guy I was there to transfer to Chicago had left New Orleans for Vegas, but instead of disappearing as everyone had assumed he would, he simply changed locales and kept living his high-profile life.

"I read up on him on the plane." I yawned, walking between them, feeling the tension now, smack dab in the middle of whatever their deal was. "He's been working the club scene here, I understand. I watched some of his YouTube videos. He really can sing."

"Yep," Redeker agreed. "Our best guess is that he actually thinks he's not in any danger anymore since he left NOLA. He never told anyone he wouldn't testify, just said he couldn't do protective custody because of his career and what he felt he owed the rest of the band."

"So they all came out here together?"

"They did."

"Well, I hope he's not married to the idea of being a superstar." Callahan rubbed the back of his neck as we walked and then pulled his badge out and let it fall on top of the zipper on his hoodie as we passed by a guard on our way from the secured area. "Because he's got no choice. He's going into WITSEC and that's gonna kill any other kind of career for him."

Hess, front man of the rock band Decoder Ring, had witnessed a murder. He wouldn't need protection if it was simply one thug killing another, but it turned out it was Dorian Alessi killing his longtime rival in the opiate trade, Romeo Sinclair. They were both scary mean with dozens of felonies between them, and the Orleans Parish district attorney was happy to have Sinclair rotting in the morgue and Alessi in custody, remanded without bail, until his trial. Hess's appearance in court was set for February.

Hess agreed to testify and initially said no to witness protection. He moved to Las Vegas from New Orleans, certain that between changing cities and using his mother's maiden name, he'd be safe. But even though Hess was careful, the rest of his bandmates were not. They were all on Twitter and Snapchat, Facebook and Instagram, and he was the one they all took pictures of and shared, because he was the main draw... he ended up right back on Alessi's radar.

Two weeks ago, he started seeing the same faces wherever he went. It was "freaking him the fuck out"—that was actually in my report. He liked his life and wanted to keep it, but lately he was having doubts it was possible. He thought Alessi's men had made the connection and were in town to talk to him. He'd called the marshals office back in New Orleans—the Eastern District of Louisiana, because those were the men he'd started with—explained what was going on and asked if someone could come check on him. Newly alerted to his location, the marshals' office in Vegas had decided to bring him in, forcibly put him in WITSEC, and transfer him across the country. When they asked where the next available opening was, the database chugged out the Northern District Office of Illinois, our office. Kage received the transfer order and put me on a plane to take the rock star into custody. Hess was in danger, so we were responding.

Even though no one could say for certain if Hess was seeing things, the threat was considered credible since the case was ongoing.

"The band is breaking up," Callahan explained to me out of the blue. "Tonight's show at Aces and Eights is supposed to be their last."

"That's lucky."

He shrugged. "We've been watching Hess for two weeks now, and it's pretty easy to see that he's the only one with any kind of talent or work ethic. The rest of his band doesn't take their music very seriously."

"So maybe he won't be all torn up to leave them."

"Maybe."

"Aces and Eights is a club, then, or a bar?"

"It's basically a dive bar, similar to Double Down, but it's smaller and hasn't been around half as long," Redeker answered.

"I'm from Chicago," I reminded him. "I have no idea what that place is."

He snorted out a laugh. "Have you been here before?"

"Yeah, but only on the Strip."

"Then you haven't ever really been to Vegas."

"I'll take your word for it."

Callahan grunted.

"What?" Redeker snapped.

"Just because you're still drinkin' till the wee small hours doesn't mean the grownups do," Callahan said, his tone snide. "Maybe taking in a show and having a good meal is Vegas for Jones."

Redeker rolled his eyes, and I was left again feeling like I was in the middle of… if not a fight, something close.

"So Aces and Eights is on the Strip or not?" I asked Callahan.

"It's east of the Strip over on Naples Road."

I had no idea where that was, either, but they were there to take me.

We exited the terminal, got into an older-model Dodge Durango, and as he settled in on the passenger side, Redeker told me there was bottled water in the cooler behind my seat.

"You wanna eat?" Callahan asked.

"Yeah."

"Is breakfast good?"

"Always."

"Really hungry or only a little?"

"Starving," I admitted, because I was almost nauseated. That was how ravenous I was.

"Hash House A Go Go it is." Redeker yawned, rolling down his window and resting his elbow there before leaning his head back and closing his eyes. "Let's go, Cal."

"Maybe he'd like something more—"

"Just do what I said," Redeker muttered, not opening his eyes.

"You're hungover," Callahan stated, and I heard the edge in his voice.

"And you care why?"

"I *don't* care. You're just supposed to take better care of yourself. You're a grownup, after all, right? You're not supposed to do that."

"Do what?"

"Drink all fuckin' night."

Redeker grunted.

"How are you helping me if you can't aim your gun?"

"I can shoot just fine, kid."

Callahan growled.

Oh, this was fun. "So what do you guys work beyond the usual roundup stuff?" I asked, to stave off any further bickering.

"We mainly work the regular FIST Task Force," Callahan answered, looking at his partner instead of the road. "We don't normally do a lot of witness transfer anymore, but we just got a new boss and he likes to rotate everyone around."

"We do that too," I said, just to make conversation, pleased to see he started paying at least some attention to maneuvering out of the airport and getting on the freeway. "It's all interagency with us, except in our own office. We don't do undercover or stakeout unless we're in charge."

"We do a lot of crap with the DEA," Redeker rumbled, shifting to get as comfortable in his seat as he could, considering the length of his legs. He had to be at least six three, with his younger partner about my five eleven. "But that's to be expected, with all the fuckin' drugs."

I made a sound of agreement and settled in to watch the brown go by while trying Ian's phone again. I'd called from home and O'Hare, I called when I took off and called when I landed before making my way down the concourse. It went to voice mail each time, and though I wasn't surprised, it would have been nice to at least get a text with an update.

The trip to my hotel, Days Inn Las Vegas at Wild Wild West on Tropicana, was fast, being just three miles from the airport, and when we got there they waited as I checked in. It wasn't on the Strip, but I couldn't have cared less. The important part was that it was cheap and clean and, if I needed a car, the parking was free. It was perfect for me.

After I ditched my bags and the suit and tie I was wearing, we got back into the car and drove over to the Strip, to the Plaza Hotel and Casino and Hash House A Go Go inside it. It was busy, but Redeker had either called ahead or had an in with one of the managers, I wasn't sure. I didn't ask. I just followed when he told me to and took my seat in the booth across from him and Callahan.

"Don't even look at the menu," Redeker ordered. "Just have Andy's Sage Fried Chicken Benedict. You'll thank me."

"It's too big," Callahan cautioned. "Take a look at the other—"

"Starving," I reiterated, passing Redeker my menu. "I'll have that."

I had orange juice and coffee, and when my food came, what looked like ten pounds of chicken. I took a picture and was going to send it to Ian, hoping that it might spark a quick text in return, but then I realized that wasn't *me*. I'd never done it before. Even if I felt that needy on the inside, showing the ache to Ian wouldn't fly because it did nothing for either of us. I'd make him sad and then I'd feel guilty. It was useless on both sides, as was hoping for some word. When he was doing anything related to the military, there was never any word. I had to be better about reminding myself of that.

My problem was putting Ian out of my mind. It was easier said than done, especially when faced with a meal he would have found so much joy in sharing with me. Taking a breath, I pulled out the large rosemary stalk jammed into the top of my dish and dug in.

"Jesus," Callahan said a while later, staring at me. "You're actually going to finish that."

"You should see what my partner and I normally do for breakfast," I told him.

"No, I don't think I should," he teased.

Once they both relaxed, the company was as good as the meal. I got to hear about their last case, and there was much debate over who hit the windshield of the car that made the driver swerve. The conversation made me homesick for Ian, but when I went quiet, neither man noticed.

When we got back to the hotel, Callahan and Redeker checked in with their boss, Supervisory Deputy Braxton Ward, who was by all accounts a man who yelled often and hated the DEA as much as I did.

"Yeah, you could transfer out here," Callahan assured me. "You'd get along with Ward just fine."

As I worked on my laptop, pinging Ian just in case, I watched Callahan moon over his partner and wondered how Redeker was missing it when it was so transparent.

When Callahan had him look at something on his laptop, Redeker leaned in close, and even if I hadn't seen Callahan inhale, I would have heard it. He was pining… *hard*… and I was guessing from Redeker's lazy smile and "lighten up, kid" attitude that he had no clue he was inspiring such hunger. I wondered if I was ever so dense, or if Ian had been quite so oblivious.

I was probably reading way too much into their partnership.

"We need to go over the plan, Jones," Redeker said as he crossed the room and sat down beside me on the bed.

It was really very simple. We'd go to the lounge, dive bar, whatever it was, in the early evening and catch Hess between sets. If he was ready to go, we'd call for backup, follow him home, and get him into custody. If he wasn't, he'd have uniformed police officers watching him who would put a serious crimp in his freedom.

Callahan and Redeker left me about two o'clock so I could catch a nap and we could all shower and clean up. Before I crashed out for maybe a couple of hours, I called the office and Kohn and Kowalski were on desk duty, answering phones and running background checks.

"Check the news," Kohn told me after we exchanged greetings. "The interim chief apologized to Becker today."

"No shit."

He grunted.

"Did Becker go to the press conference?"

"Fuck no. You know that ain't him. Plus, a marshal that has his picture splashed all over the place is not a smart man."

"True."

"Becker did issue a statement saying that the practice of pulling people over when their only crime is driving while black must stop."

"I'm betting it was worded differently."

"It was pretty close to that."

"And how did that go over with the brass?"

"As well as can be expected."

"I'm thinking the marshals' office is not all that popular down at police headquarters at the moment."

"I'm thinking you're right."

I sighed deeply. "I'll watch the apology. I want to hear what it sounded like."

"It sounded like politics, but at least they did it. You have to keep chipping away at this shit, or it's never gonna change."

That was very true. "Vegas is boring," I told him.

"There's the whole goddamn Strip, Jones, how the hell is it boring?"

"I'm not much for gambling."

"Just the lights and the atmosphere are awesome."

I grunted.

"You're such a whiner, Jones."

I told him to go to hell.

He told me to make sure I got some sleep.

I hung up without saying good-bye.

ACES AND Eights, it turned out, was a lounge close to the intersection of Naples and Paradise Road east of the Strip. We all changed so we looked better; they dressed up and I dressed down. I went all in black: dress pants, dress shirt, and the Alexander McQueen black monk strap boots I had with me. The holster on my calf was black too, not that anyone would see it, hopefully, and my star was on my belt under the untucked shirt. I'd slicked my hair back and thought about wearing sunglasses, but I was going for scary, not douchey.

Callahan cleaned up nice in dark jeans and a white linen shirt, but really, of the three of us, it was Redeker who was going to turn heads. Between the worn cowboy boots, dark-brown khakis, and short-sleeve white cotton button-down that strained around his biceps and accentuated the heavily veined forearms, I was thinking he could get laid just standing there breathing. Callahan was having trouble moving air through his lungs, from what I could tell. I hadn't noticed him staring when we walked over together, him more or less at my back. But now, inside, under the dim lights, I could tell he was concentrating hard on the whole breathe in, breathe out thing.

When Redeker went to get us drinks, me a bottle of water and his partner a Coke, I rounded on Callahan.

"What?"

"Is Redeker gay?"

He almost swallowed his tongue. If Ian had been there, he wouldn't have let me open my big fat mouth, because it was none of my business. But me there alone, without a keeper, everyone around me was fair game.

"The fuck did you—I—Jones, do you—what?"

I snorted out a laugh. Jesus. "You should tell him you want him to fuck your brains out, and if he doesn't, find someone who will."

He looked like I'd just kneed him in the balls.

"I can see it, the pining, clear as day," I sympathized. "It's gotta be exhausting for you."

"No, you've got it all wrong."

He didn't trust me, but that was okay. He didn't know me. "I'm gay," I said levelly, meeting his gaze. "And everyone I work with knows and doesn't give a shit. If they care here and that's why you're not telling your partner, you should think about transferring. My boss is looking to bring on four more guys."

His face went from thinly veiled terror to discomfort, and I immediately understood.

"No, man, I live with someone already and he's way prettier than you."

Instant glare before he flipped me off.

I scoffed, and the smile I got in return was worth the time it took to finally see the full blazing glory of it directed at me. He was a very handsome man. If scruffy Malibu Ken dolls did it for me, I'd have been all over him.

"The hell?" Redeker was there, his hazel gaze darting between us. "You girls flirting over here?"

"Yep," Callahan assured him. "You can bring whoever you want back to the room tonight. I'll be in with Jones."

The look on Redeker's face, uncertainty mixed with something colder, deadlier, told me Callahan had much more of Redeker's interest than he thought. "Wait—" I began.

"No," Callahan snapped before he walked toward the bar.

Redeker rounded on me. "What the hell was that about?"

I weighed what to say and decided I didn't care because I didn't need to. Being careful wasn't necessary here. "I think that your partner is tired of waiting."

"What?"

"Could we not do that whole thing," I said grumpily. "I know what I'm looking at."

"And what is that?" I ignored him and he shook his head. "You're way off base there, Jones. You have no idea what you're talking about."

"Do something or don't, it doesn't affect me one bit," I clarified. "I'm outta here tomorrow either way."

Redeker studied me intently. "I could ruin his whole life, do you understand?"

I understood that he *thought* he could.

"Career, what he wants family-wise, all of it could just be gone in a moment if I forget what my responsibility is here."

With the drawl, the way his voice dropped low, husky, how rough looking he was, a little scary but with dimples at the same time, I could understand the man's allure. Everybody wanted a cowboy to call their own. "I think it's awfully shortsighted of you to think you know what he wants his whole life to be."

He shook his head like I had no idea.

"You never know until you jump."

His glare was dark. "Not all of us have the safety net you apparently enjoy up there in Chicago, with the way you're comin' at me. Everyone's all nice and out in the open, huh?"

"No, but my boss, the guys I work with—none of them give a shit about who I sleep with. They only care about how I do my job."

After a moment he nodded.

"I like having my safety net, and maybe if you don't have one here, you should think about going someplace where you will," I quipped, smiling in that way I did that pissed people off. "You guys could both put in transfer requests tomorrow, but you won't because you're scared of what that would mean for the two of you."

"You don't know anything about me or him."

"Nope," I agreed. "All I know is that your partner looks at you like you walk on water, and you like that just fine."

"Listen—"

I rode roughshod over him. "You have all the power. And he has shit because you haven't come clean and told him that the idea of taking him home with you gets you hard."

I expected him to hit me, and I was prepared if he tried. What I was not expecting was the look of absolute surprise on his face.

"Oh, come on," I said, remembering how I hid my heart from Ian and how much longer we would have been together if I had just come clean with him from the start about my feelings. "You'd have to be blind to miss what you mean to him. It's you who's playing his cards pretty damn close to his chest."

"I—"

"It was the same for me, so I get it. I swear to God, I wouldn't even be giving you shit if I hadn't been right there where you are."

"How do you know?"

I shrugged. "You were jealous when you walked up on us, and earlier today—you stand really close to him, right up in his space. I'm now familiar with that maneuver."

"Oh?"

"I live with my partner."

It took him a second. "And you're not roommates."

"No."

"Where is he now?"

"Deployed."

"Sorry."

"It's his calling."

He nodded and was quiet for a moment. "Callahan's really young."

"And you don't wanna fuck him up. I know. You told me."

"I need to keep things how they are, just friends."

I took a breath, let it go, resolved to stay out of it going forward. "Okay."

"That's it? You give me the third degree and finish with okay?"

"No, man, you're a lot stronger than I was, and if you can stand it the other way, more power to you."

"What other way?"

"Watching him fuck other people."

"The fucking don't bother me none." It was patronizing how he said it, like he was above it all.

"The falling in love with will," I volleyed.

After a long moment, he said, "I suspect you're right."

"But there's nothing to be done, right?"

He declined to answer.

The "Hey, hi, hello." came out of nowhere.

I turned, and there in front of me was five foot seven inches of Josue Hess, looking even more fragile and beautiful than he did in his pictures online. I'd noticed his eyes first because it was something I did from my days as a foster kid. Always check first to see if people had kind eyes. Hess's were dark, glittering obsidian. That and his gorgeous burnt sienna skin with undertones of ochre, a blush of antique gold under silken brown that his Jamaican-born father had gifted him with, made him traffic-stopping beautiful. But that wasn't all. From his German and Dutch mother, he received sharp elfin features: a short upturned nose, a wide expressive mouth, and long curling lashes. "Pretty" was the only word to use with such devastating genetics at work right there in front of me.

"Josue," I greeted. "May I call you Josue?"

He nodded quickly, and I noticed he was looking me over like he was examining me for flaws. It was slightly disconcerting, but the scrutiny wasn't interest, more like he was making a decision on my worth as a human being.

"How are you?" I asked.

He moved in closer and stared up into my face, studying me further. "Josue?"

"Okay," he said after a few moments of silence, nodding. "This makes more sense. Mind, body, and soul in alignment with what I expected."

"I'm sorry?"

"You actually look like I thought you would, is all."

"Pardon me?"

"You three, you're marshals," he announced, waving the pointer finger of his right hand at me and Redeker and Callahan, who'd just joined us. "But I didn't see them in my reading, only you, so clearly you're the one I'm supposed to go with."

Had he seen my badge?

"Sorry, I'm freaking you out. I apologize. I read my cards this morning, and the Knight of Swords was crossing me, and I read that as protective," he explained before grimacing and nodding to Callahan and Redeker. "These two—not so much with the inspiring faith and loyalty, but you… I get."

Cards? "I'm still not following."

He cleared his throat. "The reason I know that things are happening and that I would be okay up until this point is that I'm a medium."

Oh *no*. I looked over his head at Callahan and Redeker. "No one briefed me on the fact that he's psychic."

He tapped my chest, bringing my attention back to him. "I'm not crazy. My father had the gift, so I have the gift."

Had. Shit. Orphan trumped whatever my feelings were on psychic ability. "You're all alone, huh, kid?"

He nodded.

I could see the pain of his past written in those dark, too serious eyes, and I personally knew how it felt. My reserve melted, and I sighed as I realized what was going to happen—what I couldn't help but do. I decided right then and there. I was taking him back to Chicago whether he wanted to go or not. I was putting his life before mine; I was ready to take a bullet for him.

"Let's go pack your shit."

"Okay," he sighed, smiling at me.

"I thought I'd have to spend a lot of time convincing you."

"No. Like I said, the cards said you were coming, and I had the Tower card a few days ago, so I told the band I was done, to get ready since, yanno, my life is about to change, and fighting it is just futile."

"Uh-huh."

"That's why we let everyone know that this was our last gig. My cards are never wrong."

"Absolutely," I agreed.

He rolled his eyes. "Believe what you want, marshal, but I trust you because all the signs say I should, and the path you're leading me on promises happiness and love."

"Love, huh?"

He nodded.

"I'm taking you to your love? Is she pretty?"

"He," I was corrected, "and yes, *he* is very beautiful."

Lord. "Show me where you live, kid."

Callahan and Redeker were looking at me like I had horns growing out of my head. The whole plan of going into the lounge and scoping it out and finding an opportunity to get Hess alone was moot in ten minutes flat. Hess was ready to go, and it couldn't have been easier. No arm twisting necessary.

Since nothing was ever that simple, it made sense that as soon as we got outside and the bullets started flying—centering on Josue—that things changed quite a bit.

I heard the squeal of tires before I heard the *pop-pop-pop* of gunfire and a bullet hit the doorframe beside me. I shoved Josue up against the wall, bent over to pull my gun, shielded him with my body, and shouted for everyone to get down, wishing Ian was there with me. Not because I wanted bullets whizzing by his head too, but because he was good in life-and-death situations and always kept me grounded. Like now, I didn't return fire; I couldn't. Ian wouldn't have either. The street was too crowded, so I was hoping that between me yelling and the obvious threat, everyone would use their brains and hit the ground.

As was usual, the opposite happened, and chickens without heads would have been smarter. People never ceased to amaze me with their lack of self-preservation. They ran into the intersection instead of away from it, so I had no choice but to dart out—after warning Hess not to move—into the line of fire and direct the chaos.

"Stay there!" I roared at a woman who thought a better option than remaining crouched down behind a parked car with her daughter was to make a mad dash for a nearby restaurant.

Jesus.

When I pointed at my star, she nodded that she understood and would remain still. A young couple was going to do the same thing—dart out into the open—but I threatened to put them in jail if they moved. They looked horrified.

"He's trying to save your lives!" Josue yelled.

And of course they listened to the gorgeous aspiring rock star, lifting their hands to let him know they understood. Forget about the badge I'd tucked my shirt behind so it was visible; being law enforcement carried no weight in the face of his cult status.

"Jones!" Callahan yelled as he joined me.

"Cover him!" I ordered, waving at Josue and then bolted into the street with Redeker right on my heels. "Keep them off me!"

"Done!" Redeker thundered back.

The guys in the car shot at us, but we were flying and the distance was sprint short, not what I did in San Francisco just days ago. So the fact that I was able to get to the car and dive inside, on top of the guy sitting there, was not that big of a deal. Redeker being right there with me, launching himself through the driver's side window and wrestling for the steering wheel, was.

I felt the car lurch forward, and then we all whiplashed as it came to a bouncing stop, the sound of fists and breathing loud in the cramped space. Redeker was trying to knock the driver out and get to the ignition at the same time.

Twisted up in the back seat, my gun hit the floorboard and I went down on top of it, wedged there but just free enough to kick the guy I'd fallen over in the side of the jaw. His head swiveled hard, and he was out as I grabbed wrist of the second guy in the back seat, making it impossible for him to shoot at me but not at all impeding the man in the front passenger seat, who shot straight down at my face.

The sound of the discharge inside the small space was jarring. Hitting his arm from below made it jerk up, and the bullet went over my back and hit the seat, made a decent-sized hole, and continued on into the trunk, where I heard it hit metal as the car accelerated again.

"The fuck are you doing?" the guy I was tussling with yelled at the passenger. "You're gonna fuckin' kill me!"

"Use your goddamn knife!" the driver shrieked, still grappling with Redeker.

The Mercedes E-Class sedan we were in had lovely leg room, but after the sharp braking moments before, we were squashed together. I pinned the arm of the guy I was fighting with and hit him in the face with as much leverage as I had between the back of one seat and his lap.

There was not much power there, especially as he moved his legs and I was sinking, both of us squirming, jostling to sit up.

"Where the fuck is your knife!"

A butterfly, maybe a switchblade... that was what I expected. The *Crocodile Dundee* version that came through the seat at me, grazing over my bicep—I was not prepared for that.

"Fuck!" Redeker gasped, spotting the knife as the guy in the passenger seat yanked it out, and he hit the driver—finally—at enough of an angle to make him swerve.

My gun was under me, so no help there, and even though I was pretty flexible, I wasn't small. I carried quite a bit of muscle, and my chest and shoulders were wide enough that I was stuck, almost upside down. When the car hit whatever it hit, I thought for a second my back was broken before the knife was there again, the light sliding over the curve of the blade I could see over the console.

Adrenaline was wild. It made you able to do crazy things.

Heaving myself up, I did my best dolphin impression, contorted in a way that would have given Ian a shock—he was always surprised by the positions I could get myself into—and got my left leg between the front seats so that when the passenger lunged at Redeker, Redeker was able to grab his wrist and the blade.

"Down," Callahan yelled, there suddenly over me, gun leveled on the guy I was fighting with as he leaned in and elbowed the passenger in the face.

"Fuck," I gasped, still mostly on my head.

"We don't normally dive into cars," Redeker huffed as he clocked the driver and Callahan took guns out of the car and dropped them on the street.

"No?" I panted, righting myself before opening the back door and stumbling out of the car to stand in the street next to Callahan. "We do in Chicago. We're hardcore in the Windy City."

"Huh," Redeker groaned before he was gone from sight, out of the car and bending over to catch his breath.

"My boss is gonna eat you for this, Jones," Callahan informed me.

"But nobody got hurt but me and Redeker," I argued, gesturing around at everything. "How can he get mad at that?"

Callahan waggled his eyebrows.

"Well," I said after a moment, "he has to get in line."

Christ.

I THOUGHT the circus got crazy in Chicago. In Sin City, on this Monday night, it was insane. The police department in New Orleans wanted the men because the threat on Josue's life connected to their case, but Las Vegas PD said they were keeping the shooters because the incident occurred on their streets. The marshal service trumped both departments until the FBI said that since Alessi was wanted on racketeering and drug trafficking across several states, *they* would take the men into federal custody.

It was Barnum and Bailey.

I'd turned Josue over to the state troopers in the interim. They took him first to his apartment to collect whatever life-and-death items he needed to bring along on his adventure and then escorted him, still under heavy guard, to the hotel and my room. There the sheriff's department took over, and one man stayed outside the door and one stayed inside with him. I'd given him my number before he left, and he put it into his phone after taking a quick picture of me smiling at him as I stood there bleeding. The blood caused the EMT on-site some concern, and they wanted me to go to the hospital to see if I needed stitches, but I'd been sliced by a knife, not stabbed. I needed a Band-Aid more than anything else.

Since the only thing no one could mess with was me putting a witness into protective custody, I was cleared by the bureau "to proceed with the intake of my witness." They were such nozzles. Redeker asked if I wanted to grab a late dinner with him and Callahan, and since I knew Josue was safe—and that the troopers would be ordering him room service—I took them up on their offer.

They took me to the Peppermill, right on the Strip. It was interesting, with all the neon inside and the big round fire pit and the mirrors and all the noise. The fact that it was loud was usually not something I liked, but I appreciated it since I wasn't in the mood to talk much. I ordered a BLT with avocado and sweet potato fries and had water to drink because I really needed to hydrate. It felt like the dry heat was sucking the moisture right out of me.

Callahan got a porterhouse with sautéed mushrooms and water as well, while Redeker had wings, the pastrami burger and onion rings, and mozzarella sticks, all chased with a double screwdriver.

"You're gonna have a heart attack and die," I assured him as his food kept coming.

The portions on everything were enormous. There was no skimping on anything, including the alcohol.

"I keep telling him," Callahan said, "between what he's eating and what he's drinking, he won't make it to fifty."

I snorted out a laugh. "Man, you would love Chicago."

Redeker looked at me. "Why you say that?"

"Lots of good food there too."

He nodded.

"Chicago?" Callahan ventured, looking back and forth between us.

"Yeah," Redeker said with a cough. "Jones says his boss is looking for some more guys and thought maybe we'd like a change of climate."

Callahan nearly choked on his water. "We?" he said when he could breathe.

Redeker shrugged. "Well, yeah. Why would I go without you?"

Callahan did a slow turn to look at me.

"What?"

"Thanks for the heads-up, Jones," he said softly, like he really meant it.

I smiled at him, because I knew what it felt like to maybe have figured something out about your partner. I'd been there, after all.

THEY DROPPED me off at my hotel, and after I hugged Callahan and shook hands with Redeker, I headed toward the room. I was surprised to get a call from Josue halfway there.

"What? You're only supposed to call in case of emergency," I scolded him.

"I was worried about you."

I grunted.

"I was! You were all banged up and bleeding. For a knight in shining armor, you get hurt awfully easy."

"What are you talk—"

"The cards!" he reminded me.

"Oh yes, the cards."

"Don't use that tone about the Tarot." He was clearly horrified; it was evident in his tone.

Heaven forbid. "Okay."

"You scared me to death. I was just wondering where you are."

"I'm almost there," I said and hung up.

He called me right back.

"What?"

"You should answer the phone nicer. Like, hello, Josue darling, how are you?"

I sighed loud and long so he couldn't miss the irritation.

"So you're one of those guys who likes pain, huh?"

"What're you talking about?"

"I mean like that love of pain in a minor way… like eating spicy foods or going on a roller coaster or watching a horror movie."

"Who doesn't like all that stuff?"

"Lots of people, and you have to make sure it doesn't escalate to taking scary chances in life or on love."

Oh, he was going to be a bundle of fun to play guardian angel for. "I think when we get to Chicago that I'm gonna give you to my friends Kohn and Kowalski. They don't have any children at the moment."

"I'm not a child," he insisted petulantly.

He was a baby.

"And I refuse to be pawned off on anyone else. *You're* my marshal, my knight."

I chuckled.

"There now see, that was a yummy sound you just made. Have to love a man with a deep, warm laugh."

He was going to be such a handful.

"Guess what?"

"I don't—" I was too tired for twenty questions. "Just tell me."

"I've been playing poker with the sheriff's deputies—Kirkland, he was outside, came in—and I'm up twenty bucks!"

Cards? Why was he playing cards? Why wasn't he cowering in the corner or sitting in the bathtub rocking back and forth? "Why aren't you scared?"

"Of?" He asked like I hadn't just shielded him with my body hours before.

"Getting shot, doofus."

"But I told you already."

"No, you didn't."

"Yes I did." I could imagine the eye roll with the weight of his exhale. "You're taking me to my love. I saw that. All the signs point to me being happy and…. I'm not now, so… this is a season of change for me. I'm ready for my adventure."

And I was ready to be his guide.

"You're my marshal, but you're also my knight, Miro Jones. I know I'm safe with you."

He believed in me, and that was really kind of nice.

I stopped walking, having arrived at the door, and stood there taking a moment, letting my life settle around me. But then I heard a squeal and a hundred and thirty pounds of Josue Hess slammed into me, hard, and I almost dropped my phone in the process.

"For crissakes," I grumbled, trying to push him off me as I heard the state troopers both chuckling behind him.

"Don't you ever do that to me again!"

"What? Save your life?"

"Run into a hail of bullets!" He pulled back, frantic, eyes wide, arms flailing. It was kind of cute.

"A hail?" I questioned him. "Really?"

"Oh dear God, you're arguing word choice at a time like this?"

It was like seeing a pissed-off bunny. "Sorry, sorry."

He hurled himself back in my arms, and I patted his back as he clung to me like *he* was the one who almost died.

"The cards didn't mention that you had a death wish. Maybe we better have a reading before bed."

No. God, no. "Listen—"

"I have to read Kirkland's cards first though, I promised."

I looked over his head into the room where both troopers were shaking their heads at me. "I think they'd both be okay if you skipped that."

When he glanced over his shoulder, head shaking turned to smiles. Clearly, neither man wanted to hurt his feelings.

"Hey," I said to get his focus back on me.

Big limpid eyes returned to my face.

"Do you own a warm coat?"

He looked up. "Why?"

"Because you think this was scary, all the flying bullets, just wait until you deal with winter in Chicago."

"Does it get cold there?"

I made a mental note to get him a snowsuit.

CHAPTER 12

REALLY EARLY the next morning, I grabbed my bags and the several Josue had with him, threw them into the back of a cab, and got us to McCarran International Airport. He had plenty to say during the flight home. We were in Chicago by noon.

"How come you haven't told me to shut up?" he asked as we rode the elevator up to the office.

"You're good company," I confessed. "I wasn't going to sleep anyway, and now I've learned about Myal and Obeah and the differences between them; I know about your parents and how they met and how much they loved you and how they didn't care that you were gay, and that they believed in good food and good magic."

He was beaming at me. "You're a really good listener."

"I try."

Once we got upstairs, I dropped Josue off in the conference room with a Pepsi and a promise of a late lunch before going to my desk. I didn't even have time to sit down and search for my mouse—which was always missing because someone was forever borrowing it—before the door to Kage's office opened and he leaned out to call me in.

In his office, basically a glass fishbowl with blinds to keep out prying eyes, I found him along with four men I didn't know.

"Jones," Kage said like he was both tired and annoyed. "Have a seat."

I flopped down on the couch since the chair I usually sat in, the one right in front of his enormous cherry-and-glass-topped console of a desk, was taken.

"These men are from the FBI, and they've shared some news with me this morning that I, in turn, have to share with you."

"Yessir."

He squinted like he was in pain, and I caught my breath because I just fucking *knew*.

"The FBI moved Craig Hartley from ADX Florence two weeks ago because they needed to confirm the whereabouts of the remains of five women that one of his followers, Edward Bellamy, killed. Bellamy said that he would only give those names to Hartley face-to-face."

It was like someone walking up beside you and shoving you into a pool. One moment you were talking, laughing, the next you were drowning for a never-ending second before you got your bearings and pushed up to break the surface and breathe.

"Yessir," I croaked, my voice going out on me.

He inhaled deeply. "During the course of the transfer, when Hartley was in the custody of the FBI and no one employed by, or affiliated with, the Federal Bureau of Prisons or the Department of Justice… he escaped."

The bureau lost him, Kage was being clear on that fact. He wanted me to know that my own people—the marshals service—had not failed me.

It didn't help.

Hartley was free—again—walking around somewhere, anywhere, able to make a house call on me.

The shivering was not a surprise, and neither was the fact that as much as I tried, I couldn't stop. Just the thought of Hartley's hands on my skin, his breath, seeing his face, looking into his cat green eyes… I was going to be sick.

"Go," Kage directed me.

I flew out of his office, bolted through the office without a word to anyone, didn't see anyone on my way to the bathroom. Everything was a blur until I reached my destination, tore into a stall, and threw up bile and stale coffee because there was nothing else in my stomach.

I heaved for several minutes because every time I calmed down for a second, I thought of Hartley again and the whole cycle repeated. The tears were hot, my vision blurred, and the shivering had become all out shaking. I had no idea how long I'd been in there before I heard a voice on the other side of the stall door.

"Miro?"

No one but Ian was welcome.

"I'll be out in a minute," I called back too loud, trying to get whoever it was to leave me the fuck alone.

"Can you open the door?"

Fuck. Josue.

"Just gimme a minute, kid."

But he didn't. Instead, under the bottom of the stall came a glass of water with lemon slices in it.

"What is this?" I asked, taking it from his outstretched hand.

"Are you kidding?"

I smiled in spite of everything, because he wasn't being sassy. He was surprised. Like could I not see what it was?

"The lemons help with nausea," he informed me. "Did you know there's a huge fruit basket in your break room?"

"Yeah," I sighed. "I know."

He coughed softly. "Ginger tea would be best, but that takes a little bit of time and I didn't see any chamomile, so you got lemon water."

I sipped it slowly. Just the smell of it was soothing.

"I have peppermint oil in my bag that will help too if—"

"No, this is good. Thank you."

Then he was quiet, which was unlike him, and after a couple of minutes, I flushed the toilet and came out of the stall. I was the adult in our relationship; I had to pull myself together. I was his knight, so I had to be strong, and that responsibility calmed me.

He was biting his bottom lip as he examined my face. "Why're you crying?"

I took a breath before taking a sip of my water and turning for the sink. Placing the glass beside the next basin over, I turned on the water and splashed my face, holding on to the counter and taking shallow breaths as I let my head hang down between my shoulders.

His hand on my back, rubbing gently, was very kind.

"I'm okay," I said, opening my eyes and turning to look at him. "I just got some bad news, is all."

He stepped closer, into my space, and his hand went to the back of my neck, massaging, his fingers hitting knots of painful muscle. "You need a shower and food and to crawl into bed and sleep for a couple of days."

I nodded.

"And you need me most of all."

"Oh yeah?"

"Yes," he promised. "I will take care of you and sleep with you and hold you supertight all through the night."

It was a very sweet offer. "If my heart wasn't already spoken for, I would totally take you up on that."

His smile was warm as his hand dropped away. "I'll give it some time, but if I don't see this guy of yours in the next couple of months, I'm making the offer again."

"I have no idea how long he'll be gone," I confessed as I turned off the water and straightened up, studying my face in the mirror. "God, I look like shit."

"You look tired," Josue corrected, passing me a few paper towels from the stack beside the mirror. "And pale, and the circles under your eyes are really dark."

I took a few more sips of the water and found that my stomach was actually settling. And maybe it was the water, or maybe it was the barfing, or simply Josue's calming demeanor, but whatever it was, I felt human again.

Turning to him, I grabbed him and hugged him hard. "When my partner's not here, there's no one to watch out for me, so I appreciate it."

He gave me his weight, leaning heavily, and I knew that he was scared too. His whole life was up in the air, and I needed to remember that.

"You're gonna make someone really happy," I said.

"It could be you, marshal. Keep it in mind."

I pushed him out to arm's length. "I thought I was taking you to your love."

He squinted, clearly giving that some thought.

"Come on," I prodded, spinning him around and shoving him toward the door.

After dropping him off back in the conference room, I took my water with me and returned to Kage's office. Closing the door behind me, I walked to the couch, took a seat again, and put the glass down on the end table, making sure I used a coaster.

It was odd. No one in the room said a word. It was like they had all been frozen since I left, except Kage, who was now leaning against the edge of his desk, looking at me.

"Sorry."

"You have nothing to be sorry about," he assured me. "Let us know when you're ready."

I waited another few moments, and then when my gaze met his, Kage gave me a faint, almost imperceptible nod.

"Okay."

Everyone started talking at once until Kage raised his voice, which thundered over everyone else in the room.

"As far as the FBI has been able to piece together, he became ill on the trip from the prison to the Denver airport. They stopped at a hospital on the way, and the version of events becomes somewhat convoluted from there."

I glanced at all the suits sitting in Kage's office until one of them leaned forward after clearing his throat.

"We're unsure where the breakdown in communication was, but as you know, Hartley presents not as a violent offender, but as what he is: a meek, nonthreatening physician."

My laughter was sharp, caustic, and it happened before I even knew it was going to explode out of me.

"Marshal Jones?"

"Oh, that's such bullshit," I barked. "But begging your pardon, sir, I've never known Craig Hartley to be nonthreatening. We originally put him in prison because he killed nineteen women."

"I know that he—"

"Nineteen!" I yelled. "Dead. Murdered."

"Marshal—"

"How can a man who's killed nineteen people ever be considered *nonthreatening*?"

"We—"

"When he escaped last time, he killed a female friend of his who aided him in his flight from custody, murdered an elderly couple and FBI Special Agent Cillian Wojno, kidnapped Saxon Rice, and kidnapped and tortured me. He also murdered every man who worked for him, ten in all, who aided him in my kidnapping and torture. The words 'meek and nonthreatening' are *not* appropriate!"

No one said a word for a minute, until Kage.

"You need a minute?"

I concentrated on calming down. "No sir. I apologize."

He lifted his hand. "It's not necessary."

After a moment of regulating my breathing, I gave him a nod.

"They have confirmed sightings of Hartley crossing into Mexico one week ago, and had him flying out of the Monterrey International Airport two days after that aboard a private plane owned by Javier Aranda."

"Aranda is the head of Vicario Capital," the agent I'd yelled at told me. "He's based in Nuevo Leon, that's the front for the Salazar Cartel out of Tamaulipas."

Everyone but Kage was looking at me like I should have an opinion. "Okay," I said to get them to continue.

"When did Aranda and Hartley become friends?" Kage asked the agent. No answer from them so he turned to me. "Jones?"

I cleared my throat. "I had no idea it was Aranda, but Hartley told me that he flew to Mexico with his team a few years ago to operate on a cartel boss's mother."

"He did?" the agent asked me.

"Yeah."

"And saved her life, of course," Kage surmised.

"Yessir. He told me he'd gotten a report and she was the picture of health."

"Jesus," the lead agent let slip.

I leaned forward and put my face in my hands, not wanting to break down again, feeling the burn in my stomach and the flutter of panic in my chest. It was terrifying to be the expert on all things Hartley, to know more than anyone else since he'd shared so much on my biannual visits to him in prison because he wanted me to know him.

Everyone wanted to talk to him, all the psychiatrists and psychologists, everyone writing a book about him, every branch of law enforcement. They all yearned for insights into the deepest, darkest recesses of his mind but he was stone-silent except with me.

Only me.

I was the one he wrote to and wanted to see and begged to visit. The warden at Elgin had once told me that Hartley had to be in love with me, there was no other explanation. He was wrong, of course, they all were, and I knew that because I *knew* Hartley. He didn't love me. In fact, he wanted to kill me, but it had to be done on his timeline, at his pace. When he was in jail, without power, the only weapon he had in his arsenal to hurt me with was his memories. So he'd talked and I'd listened and learned and sadly committed it all to memory. Now Hartley had in me a living, breathing record of his life. I was the authority on him, and it had just been proven again. The FBI had no idea how Hartley and Aranda connected until I told them.

"Jones?"

I lifted my head to look at Kage.

"He knows he's going back to the supermax to rot if he ever comes back to this country," he informed me. "Interpol has his name. It's only a matter of time before he's captured."

"Yessir," I replied automatically.

"I'm sorry, Jones."

"Why're you sorry? You did everything in your power to keep me and everyone else safe. This is on the bureau. Squarely." All eyes on me. "Did he kill anyone?"

"No," the lead agent answered. "A nurse was killed by our agents when she got between them and Hartley."

"At least he stopped killing his friends," I muttered, standing up. "I need to process my witness, sir, if I may."

"Don't leave the office until I speak to you."

"Yessir," I said before I got up and left.

As soon as I closed the door behind me, the room erupted in noise. I caught enough of it to hear something about questioning me about where Hartley might have gone and Kage forbidding it absolutely and in perpetuity and he wasn't fucking around. They were never getting another shot at me.

My heart ached, and the need for Ian, in that moment, nearly drove me to my knees. I wanted to be held and to lean and to be protected, and it was stupid and needy but I couldn't help it. I wanted him more than anything.

"So?" Becker said as I began moving toward my desk.

I shoved it down—the pain, the craving for my man—and forced a smile because watching me break down, crumble, did nothing for anyone, especially me.

Looking around, I noted the whole team was there, only Ian not in attendance. "So," I announced to the room, using Becker's word. "Guess who gave the Feds the slip on his holiday from the supermax?"

"The hell you say," Sharpe gasped. "How?"

"Does the bureau not get that Hartley's a bad guy?" Dorsey wanted to know.

"That's insane," Kohn spat.

"Hartley asked for a miracle, but he doesn't need them," I teased, breaking into an exaggerated grin. "He's got the F... B... I."

"Him and Hans Gruber," Ryan groused.

I laughed but it sounded too high, too fake, and almost shrill. "Get in there and process my witness intake, monkey."

"Don't," Ryan said, getting up and crossing the room to me. "You don't have to be all how you're being. This is us."

I glanced around the room, and the looks I got back were not judgmental. Instead they were concerned.

"Let's go get the paperwork done," Dorsey offered, walking over to me and putting a hand on my shoulder. "The quicker we do, the quicker you can get home and get some rest."

"I'm fine," I said.

"You're not," Kohn argued. "I wouldn't be either. Just get your witness taken care of so we can all go get some dinner or something."

"I don't need a babysitter," I groused.

"You're arguing when you should be taking care of the mountain of paperwork," Kowalski chimed in. "You know it'll take hours."

I did know that. People thought there were a lot of documents to sign when you bought a house. A mortgage company had nothing on WITSEC. The Justice Department knew how to create a paper trail, and it started with chopping down a big-ass tree.

"Come on," Ryan prodded, hand on my bicep, tugging on me like he never did. "Let's go get your new kid processed, all right?"

I followed obediently, okay with him piloting me along. It was nice that they all cared enough to be worried. I went with him and Dorsey back to Josue, and when I took a seat beside him, Josue bumped me with his shoulder and said he'd missed me.

"I see." Dorsey yawned, nodding. "You just got two of your kids out of the house, and you're moving this one in."

I made a noise and put my head down on the table. "You know me," I whined, closing my eyes. "I'm a caregiver."

"I know," he agreed which kind of surprised me with how nice he was being.

"You need to sleep," Ryan stated.

Everyone always told me that. "I will tonight."

"See that you do."

KAGE CALLED me away from the conference room about an hour and half later, and surprisingly, instead of dragging me into his office, he took me downstairs. Not to the coffee and bagel truck always outside our building, but around the corner to one I'd never seen because I always stopped at the first one. As we got into line, I was going to ask what was good, but he started talking before I could get the question out.

"Just so you know, Carrington Adams's family really appreciated all you did in bringing them closure."

I hadn't done anything beyond report what I'd been told. "Were they happy with his award?"

"They were, and his pension is going to fund a scholarship in his name at his old high school."

"That's good."

"It is," Kage agreed, tightening the scarf around his neck. "And we have the final separation paperwork for your two witnesses."

I grunted.

"Something funny?"

"Just that, that makes it sound like Doyle and I will never see them again, when the opposite is true."

He nodded. "They're young. It makes sense that you'd stay in their lives."

Of course he understood, I would have assumed no less.

Years ago, when I'd first started working for Kage, I'd thought he was cold but fair and not sentimental at all. But over time I'd learned so much more about him. Like he was stern, but only because he worried, and when he yelled it was normally because one of us, his men, had scared him. He was loyal, dependable, and always kept his word. I hoped to someday measure up to him. He was what I wanted to be.

"Thank you, sir."

"For?"

I cleared my throat. "Understanding that not everything has to be exactly by the book."

"We get as close as we can."

"Yessir." I exhaled, feeling how down deep in my bones tired I was. "My plan is to have the new kid over for turkey as well."

"Again I have no issue with that. You and Doyle are very professional in the bulk of your dealings with witnesses. The young ones without families, the orphans…. I didn't have any of those. All the kids I dealt with had parents."

"Well, Doyle and I get all the fun stuff, sir."

"Oh yes, you do," he said snidely, stepping up to the window and smiling wide, which I never saw him do normally. "Good afternoon, Iris."

The young woman there absolutely melted, but not in the way a woman would over a handsome man. It was more like he was just too dear for words. "Uncle Sammy, your regular?"

"And one for him too."

Her eyes flicked to me and now there was interest, which was nice since lately I'd been feeling like yesterday's leftovers. "Hi there."

I smiled up at her. "Hello back."

"I'm Iris," she said, offering me her hand. "Do you work for my uncle?"

"Miro, and yeah, I do." Her hand was delicate and warm in mine.

"You must be special. He never brings anyone around."

"Enough of that," Kage grumbled.

The warm chuckle told me he didn't scare her one bit. "And are you a fan of Vietnamese coffee too?"

"Sure," I said, because I did not want to disappoint the cherub with her dark-auburn hair, great big long-lashed emerald eyes, and alabaster skin. She should have been modeling somewhere, not working on a food truck.

Kage gave her a twenty, which she shook her head over, and then his brow furrowed and she took the money. We then walked over to one of the stone benches and sat down.

It was funny, us being there together, because there I was with my boss and I couldn't remember the last time Ian and I had just taken a walk out to the food truck in the middle of the day. We were either working or he was gone. When was the last time we just hung out? Went to a quiet dinner? I also couldn't recall the last time we just sat together and watched football or soccer or went to see a baseball game. All we did was work and argue when we weren't. How had that happened? How did everything become so hard?

"Jones?"

"Sorry."

"It's fine. I just wanted to tell you that Cochran and his partner are both being loaned out to a DEA task force in Plano for the next month."

"Where is that?"

He squinted at me. "That's in Texas, Jones." The way he said it, like I was just too stupid for words, was not nice. "So do you want to be reassigned to another city due to Hartley's escape?"

I shook my head. "No thank you, sir. It didn't work that well the last time." And I didn't want to go anywhere without Ian being there to discuss it with. If he got home and I was gone…. "If he wants me, he'll find me, but maybe this time he'll actually stay away. He might be ready to get back to something other than revenge."

"Is that what you think it is?"

"Sir?"

"You do realize that Hartley has never come after you for revenge."

"I'm sorry?"

"He admires you, Jones. You caught him, and then you saved his life. He worships you."

"It's not that I doubt you, sir, but he keeps trying to kill me."

"And you keep eluding him. Again there's a lot to admire there."

"I don't think so."

"In his own sick, twisted way, he might even love you."

"Where are you getting this?"

He shrugged. "If he wanted you dead, couldn't he simply have shot you?"

That was true.

"Instead he took a rib from you. He needed something from inside your body, that's how much he needed to have a part of you."

"He's a psychopath. Nothing he does makes any sense."

"Yes, it does," he argued, straightening a bit as Iris walked over with filled paper plates and napkins and delivered one to Kage and the other to me.

"I'll grab the coffee," she said, kissing him on the cheek. "And Dad says that the lure he wants is on sale at Park, and you better get over there soon."

He cleared his throat. "You tell your father that it'll be a cold day in hell before I replace that lure."

She giggled. "Seriously. What was it, like, six bucks?"

"So not the point, little girl."

Shaking her head, she left to get us the coffee.

"That girl is your niece, sir?"

"She's my buddy Pat's oldest. She just graduated from college and already she owns four of these things. She started it with her boyfriend when they were freshmen, and they added a truck a year."

"Holy crap."

"I know. She's an entrepreneur at twenty-two."

"Can she cook?"

He tipped his head at me, and I took a bite of the messy sandwich and found out quickly that yes, God, she certainly could.

"That's amazing."

"That's her mother's hot and spicy chorizo recipe, with a fried egg and enough cheddar cheese on it to stop your heart."

It was heaven on a plate.

"Her mother must be an amazing cook."

Kage nodded as he ate, and Iris brought us two large clear cups with lids, filled with coffee mixed with milk, but it wasn't a latte. It was different.

"It's a dark-roast coffee poured on top of sweetened condensed milk," Kage explained. "That's why it tastes that way."

"It's good."

"Eat your sandwich."

"Yessir."

CHAPTER 13

I WAS exhausted. I hadn't slept more than a couple of hours in the past forty or so, but I got my second wind after I ate and even remembered to bring back a sandwich and coffee for Josue. He was very appreciative of the food but made sure Dorsey knew he was still listening attentively to all the facets of witness relocation he was going over for him.

Social Security card, driver's license, school enrollment—which Josue was certain he wanted no part of—and job placement.

"We'll be here every step of the way," Dorsey assured him.

Josue would go from being Hess to Morant, and we had new documents ready to go. It made him sad to give up his name; I could tell from the quick inhale of breath and the bite down on his bottom lip.

"It's not forever," I reminded him. "Really."

He nodded instead of crying.

"It's only for a while, and whatever you do as Morant will be reinstated to Hess as soon as you're out of the program. Or you could fall in love with Morant because it's all yours and keep it forever. It's up to you."

Another quick nod as he wiped under both eyes.

"But whatever you want."

"Okay."

Dorsey went on to explain about the furnished apartment he'd be living in until we found him a permanent one that would be his to do with as he saw fit.

"You're starting a brand new life, and that takes a fuckton of stuff," I said, interrupting for maybe the tenth time.

"Do you wanna do this?" Dorsey groused.

I shut up because reading through the titanic document, pointing out where to sign, and giving the whole spiel was not something I was up for at the moment.

It took another two hours, and then Sharpe and White went with me to show Josue where he'd be living in the interim.

The federal safe house we took him to was a suite in a high-rise downtown close to our office, in a scary security building with a guard at the door and another behind the front desk. Sharpe gave Josue the key fob that gave him access to the elevator, showed him how to use it, and White gave him the laminated instructions Josue would need once we got up to the suite. White watched him change the key code for the floor, as well as the one to get into the apartment. It was a whole ordeal of punching in digits and then using the lock on the door, which also had one of those special computer keys that couldn't be copied at Walmart or wherever. It was all state-of-the-art crap that, as far as I knew, no one had ever tried to bypass.

Josue was not a high-threat target; he was a low-risk one. High-risk assets were not kept downtown close to the federal building like he would be. They were not kept in cabins in the middle of nowhere like on TV, or in quaint little beach towns. They were kept in bunkers underground or in prison. Informing on the mob or our government or a foreign power was not at all glamorous, and that kind of security was suffocating. Regular people, like Josue, were normal everyday people who if, and only if, they were geographically accessible, would get capped. But once we moved them out of state, gave them new lives and new identities, the possibility of someone finding and killing them dwindled down to zero. As far as I knew, no one in the protective custody of the marshal service had ever been harmed.

Josue would be heavily guarded when he was being escorted to pretrial meetings or trial itself or during any other court-related appearances, but that would be the only time. The rest of his life was his own. We checked in after all court appearances had concluded and during the asset's entire time in WITSEC. Some of us even after the witness left the program. But for Josue, as it had been for Drake and Cabot, the threat was tiny, so what we were doing at the moment was overkill. Still, I watched him pick codes for the alarms and tried not to yawn.

"Won't you need a code, Miro?" He was worried about this.

"I have an override, kid," I told him.

Once he was in and his stuff was on the bed, we left again because I had to take him back to the office to fill out bank account information that could only be done after the witness was shown his domicile. Normally, because I was a little lazy, I would take the daily fund allotment out in cash and give it to the witness and tell them to go wild. The thing was that I had not placed anyone alone in years. Josue needed friends, and at the moment

I was it, so based on how I would have wanted things to work, I was getting him as set up as possible. His questions were killing me, though.

"But I don't get it. How do I get money to buy stuff? I mean—I should make something and bring it with me for dinner, right?"

"No. Don't bring anything but yourself." We were sitting at my desk forty minutes later with White, who was typing because I couldn't get my eyes to focus anymore. I needed to sleep. So did Josue. He didn't have that much more rest than I did, but I guessed newness and adrenaline were powering him.

"Hey."

Turning, I looked at Sharpe.

"Come here."

I rolled away from White's desk and over to his. "What?"

"My buddies in Jersey got back to me on that guy Ian needed checked out."

"Oh, okay. And?"

"He committed suicide like a month or so after he got back home from that tour four years ago."

It was sad and scary at the same time because Kerry Lochlyn had been dead a long time, and if he wasn't the one getting revenge on the other men in his unit, who was? "What about his family?" I asked.

"His parents were killed a year ago in a car accident," Sharpe said, reading the information on his computer screen. "There's only his sister and brother now."

"Where's the brother live?"

"That they don't know. He's estranged from the family and has been since Kerry's death."

"How estranged?"

"Like changed his name, never heard from him again estranged."

"Why?"

"According to Kramer, who talked to the sister who lives in Albuquerque now—he never forgave his folks for his brother's suicide. He thought they drove him to it."

"Jesus."

He shrugged. "Family'll make you put a gun to your head faster than anything else."

I would have to take his word for it, as I had none.

"Jones," White barked over at me, and I realized that while Sharpe and I were talking, he had Josue's total 110 percent focus on him and only him, and the questions were still coming fast and furious.

Ten minutes later, with all the information he needed for the following day—who to see at the bank, for instance, to claim bankcards—I had Josue back at my desk.

"But how do I get to see this"—he pulled the business card I'd given him and read the name off it—"Lillian Doss tomorrow if I don't have cab fare to get there?"

"That's why I said that there will be a marshal there in the morning to take you. There's a whole checklist in that packet you got, along with the laminated cards in case of emergency and the app that only works with your fingerprint on the new phone we just gave you."

"Yeah," he said in a very small voice, and then he lifted his big dark eyes to me. "Are you gonna pick me up?"

"Yes."

"Then why don't you just sleep over and we'll wake up early, have breakfast, and then you don't have to drive."

"Listen, it's—"

"Or I can go home with you, and the same plan applies."

I shook my head.

"Why?" His comical silent scream, with his head back, eyes closed, hands curled into rigor was funny, and he got a smile out of me, but we were not going to be girlfriends.

"Because with me hanging around, you're never gonna fit in."

He made a noise like I was just so irritating.

"You have to give this a try, starting now."

"No, you know, I really think I should stay with you because you're the one I trust, and trust goes a long way, and... yeah," he said, deciding something, getting worked up, nodding a lot. "Yeah... yeah, I think so. I'm sticking with you."

I took a deep breath. "Hold on, kid."

"Oh man," he whimpered. "Maybe this was a mistake."

"That's not what the cards said," I reminded him as I took hold of his shoulder, not hard, but firm, keeping him with me as I found the contact I needed on my phone. "You just need a little support."

"I think I should live with you."

He was *so* not living with me.

"Hey," I huffed, talking to one person while I concentrated on the guy in front of me having a nervous breakdown. "I need a favor."

"Anything" was the answer from the other end.

Since Drake and Cabot were now officially out of the program, I could treat them like lackeys and no one could say a word to me. And they both knew all about WITSEC, and even though it was not protocol... I did it anyway because it was in the best interest of my witness.

The boys were in my office an hour later, both with visitor badges on, smiling and ready to help. By then I'd fed Josue again, explained how things worked—again—and realized that even though he was way more together than Cabot and Drake had been, he was still very young and very alone, and when I presented myself as a life raft, I had to be prepared for people to climb on and never want to leave. Sometimes I forgot the choices weren't mine. They belonged to those I was trying to help. No one could tell you to walk; you did it when you were ready. I needed to make Josue ready, which meant the allure to jump had to be greater than the safety net I was offering.

I saw the boys come in and told Josue his new friends had just shown up.

He looked up and saw them crossing the floor, and Drake smiled and Cabot waved, and I saw Josue breathe like maybe everything was going to be all right.

"Hi," he sighed when Cabot walked right up and gave him a big hug.

"Hey," Drake greeted him happily, hugging him the second Cabot let go. "Did Miro adopt you too?"

Josue nodded, and I rolled my eyes because they were all annoying, but it was good. They started talking about the shirt Josue was wearing that was from some band they all liked.

I wasn't listening. I didn't care.

"Hey, Miro, Josue draws a webcomic, isn't that awesome?"

"Not anymore, he doesn't," I informed them, because his online presence had been deleted. He had no links to digital portfolios, no Facebook account, no Twitter, nothing. He was gone from any and all social media.

"Well, yeah, no, but Cab's working on starting one, so maybe they could do it together," Drake said, all excited.

"Great, fabulous, go away now," I commanded, using my hands to motion them toward the elevator. "I'll see all you all on Thursday."

They were talking again and I was thankfully forgotten as they walked slowly, noisily out of the bullpen and toward the hall. I went around them to go get a bottle of water out of the fridge in the break room. By the time I got back, they were gone.

When I sat down, I had a moment of bliss because it was quiet and still, and then I got a weird feeling, like something was off, hinky, and when I looked up, all eyes were on me.

Literally everyone in the room was staring at me.

"What?" I asked because it was creepy as hell.

"So," Sharpe drew out the word. "What're we having for Turkey Day?"

"I'm sorry?"

"Tell me what you want me to bring, asswipe."

"What I want you to bring?"

"Man, how tired are you?"

Was I awake?

"What?" White called over to me. "You're not just inviting the children over, are you?"

A quick glance around clarified it wasn't only the two of them asking. Everybody was interested in my answer. You could hear a pin drop in the normally noisy space. "No?"

"That's right, no," White agreed. "Me and Pam will bring some booze and her world-famous cranberry salad."

"Great," I replied woodenly, because how was this happening?

"My folks are on a cruise this year," Becker informed me as I did a slow turn in my chair to face the room. "And Olivia's family's in Portland, as you know."

I had no earthly idea that his wife's family lived in Oregon.

"What do you want us to bring?"

"I—"

"My family's going to my brother's place in Hartford," Ching explained before I could answer Becker, "but Gail has an HR training to give that Monday, so we can't go."

I nodded.

"I'll text her and see if she wants to make stuffing, and I make an ambrosia salad that'll melt your face off."

Was that a good thing?

"My mother's cooking, and she'll wanna pack a ton of it for you, so count on me for a crapton of sides," Kohn promised, giving me a nod like it was all settled.

"My folks are going to see my brother Elliot and his wife this year, Jones, so after we drop by her folks' place, Sandi and me are all yours," Dorsey said like he was doing me a favor, and with his wife, he was. I'd take Sandi Dorsey; she was kind, funny, and down-to-earth. Her asshat husband was a whole other story. "She'll wanna make this broccoli cheese casserole for you. It's real good."

I had no doubt.

"Olivia makes a pecan pie that's to die for," Becker chimed in. "She won't make it for me because I'll eat the whole thing, but I bet I could get her to make it for you."

I glanced over at him.

"She seems to like you, for whatever reason."

Jesus.

How many people were coming over for a dinner I'd bought nothing for?

"I make a killer green bean casserole," Kowalski told me, "and Theresa has this recipe for crispy roasted rosemary sweet potatoes that you'll be addicted to the minute you taste them."

"I'll bring leftovers from my mom's too. I still owe you pie, right?" Ryan yawned.

I was just slightly overwhelmed.

"I think he needs a nap," Kohn commented, and I flipped him off.

"He needs a drink," Sharpe suggested, getting up from his desk. "And it's happy hour."

And that, finally, sounded like a good idea.

I PASSED tired and hit that level sort of delirium where I was functioning outside my body and everything was brighter and funnier and more interesting than it should have been. The vodka didn't help at all. I should have just gone home, but the idea of walking into the empty house—Aruna had Chickie, as usual—of not having Ian there did scary, twisty things to my heart. So I was scared to go home and face the lonely bed, scared to sleep and face my fears, not ready to share any of that with any other soul, so eating pub food, drinking like a fish, and playing pool with the guys were the only salvation I could find.

We were loud, obnoxiously so, and Sharpe was hustling games, not in a fun, nonserious way but in a dickhead asshole way until finally White cut him off, grabbed him and his jacket, and said they were going home.

"No, no, no," Sharpe whined, reaching for me but missing my shoulder when White yanked him sideways. "Pam's gonna make me sit on the couch and share how I feel and make me watch romantic comedies while we have tea."

That was hysterical, and I couldn't stop laughing. He looked horrified as White dragged him out of the sports bar, yelling "mañana," which was funny coming out of him because it was probably the only Spanish he knew.

I was surprised that the others were ready to call it a night, all going home to their wives, which I envied, all except Kohn and Ryan, who actually wanted me to get lost because they were going bowling. Apparently Ryan had met a really nice girl who had a friend.

"Why Kohn and not Sharpe?" I asked Ryan as we left the bar.

"Sharpe's still kinda mad at his ex," he said with a shrug. "You can't be nice to someone new when you're still living in the past."

My phone rang, and I told them to go ahead without me and enjoy their night, and walked down the street a little ways where it wasn't so noisy before I even checked the display. When I did, confirmed that it wasn't, in fact, Ian calling, my heart sank. It was stupid; he was busy with God knew what. But still, I felt like a boat drifting around without an anchor, and I needed my goddamn anchor to be with me.

I needed Ian.

"Hello?" I answered, all choked up, coughing quickly, trying to play it off for whomever was on the other end. It was probably someone I knew, but I didn't recognize the number and I was too out of it to decipher the area code.

"Miro?"

Just her saying my name was enough to identify the voice. "Hey, Powell," I teased Janet. "Whatcha doin', Mom?"

She sucked in a breath.

I went from drunk to sober that fast. It always amazed me when that happened, but a sad, wet sound from one of my oldest, dearest friends did it instantly. "Oh shit," I whispered, making the only intuitive leap I could manage. "Honey, it's okay, you're gonna make a great mom."

"How do you know?"

Bingo. "'Cause you were the first person in my whole life who ever took care of me."

And that was it. She was sobbing.

"Awww shit."

Glancing around, in over my head, I noticed Ryan and Kohn still standing there.

"What?" I mouthed silently. Kohn made the sign for me to hang up. I made the sign for them to go. Ryan shook his head and I understood. No one drank alone; it was a Kage rule, a marshal rule, a federal mandate for all law enforcement that carried a firearm. It was why there were always two, why everyone had a partner, because there needed to be someone there to watch out for you and have your back at all times. Even if both marshals were drinking, unless they were at home, one drank far less. Someone always had to be, if not sober, then well under the legal limit. Neither Ryan nor Kohn would let me out of their sight until they talked to me and heard what I was doing and where I was going.

Putting my hand up for them to wait, I got back to my girl.

"Why don't you come out for turkey day and stay the rest of the weekend," I offered.

She sniffled. "Will Ian want me?"

"Ian's not here," I said, trying to keep the bitterness out of my voice. "I think he's in your city, actually, involved in an inquest about a guy he served with, or if not, he's been deployed. I've called him a million times in the last twenty-four hours and he ain't pickin' up. So if you could come keep me company and hold my hand and hug me in the middle of the night when I have bad dreams, that'd be awesome."

"You need me?" Her voice quavered.

"Yeah."

She blew her nose. "How come you're not going to Aruna's?"

"I seem to remember that she's cooking for her in-laws this year, and I didn't wanna get in the way."

"So just the two of us, then? That sounds cozy."

I snorted out a laugh. "Dude," I began—a word I only used when I was *really* tired—"I got sucked into cooking for every-fuckin'-body. You gotta help me."

I could hear her nearly swoon on the other end. "I'll be there tomorrow."

"Can I ask?"

"Of course."

"Where's Ned?"

"He said that he couldn't handle my hormones, and he went to spend the holiday with his mother."

"Fuck."

"Uh-huh."

I cleared my throat. "Not to take his side in any way," I began slowly, carefully, delicately, "but..." Oh God, it was like walking out onto new ice over a pond. "...were you maybe, possibly supposed to take the train after work on Wednesday and go over to Alexandria to spend the holidays with Ned and his family?"

Silence.

Yep, that's exactly what she was supposed to do. "So... Janet... sweetie... he didn't actually leave, right? I mean, he went up early to help his folks do all the shopping and everything." Her husband, Edward, Ned for short, was the middle child, sort of, if there was a middle of eight, so when everyone descended on his parents' home in Alexandria, Virginia, for the holidays with all the wives and husbands and kids, the parents needed help. Because Ned and Janet lived the closest, right there in Washington DC, it was normally the two of them who got there first. "He loves you and he loves the baby."

No answer.

I knew Ned Powell fairly well. We weren't as close as Catherine's husband, Eriq, and me—I was one of his ushers when they got married—or Liam and me, but Ned and I were friends. I knew if she left, he'd lose his fucking mind. He worked for the NSA, so it took a lot to fluster him, but having his wife go missing would do it.

"You wanna call him, maybe?"

"If you were straight, I would have married you."

I knew that. I felt the same. She was the one. We got along like two halves of one whole. The only place we weren't compatible was in bed. It bugged the hell out of guys I fucked and guys she dated until Ned. He didn't care one bit because we were only ever going to be friends, and he got to make her his wife. "Yeah. And?"

"It's easy with you. It always has been. I need some easy."

I sighed deeply. "Then come on, kitten. Let's snuggle."

Her whimper was adorable.

"For crissakes, you know I want you here."

"I'll be there in the morning. I'll text you the flight information and I'll call Aruna."

"No, don't call—shit," I swore when I realized she'd hung up on me.

"What's wrong?" Ryan asked as he closed in on me, Kohn right beside him.

"Nothing," I muttered, standing up. "What the hell're you guys still doing here?"

"You know," Ryan told me. "We gotta know where you're goin' and what you're doin' before we ditch you."

"Yeah, I know, sorry. Family crisis."

"Doyle?" Kohn guessed. It was a good one.

"No, my friend Janet. She's coming for Thanksgiving."

"The more the merrier," he assured me.

They were being weird, standing there, doing nothing, and it finally hit me. They had things to do, people to see, but they were waiting on me.

"I'm getting a cab and going home," I announced.

"Swear?" Ryan hedged, concerned and also, it was his job to ask, to know.

I crossed my heart for him. "I swear. No more drinking, straight home to bed. I'll see you guys tomorrow."

They both looked skeptical.

"Remember, men, if you can't be good, be careful."

That got the middle finger from both I was waiting for, but they still didn't leave until I got into a cab. It was nice that even though I'd been flipped off, I got a wave good-bye as well.

I HAD the driver dump me off a block from home so I could get some groceries, but when I got close to the store, the idea of going in under all the fluorescent lighting was daunting. I had coffee at home, and creamer, half-and-half, and ramen. I was good.

It started to rain really hard, and only then did I realize I'd left my leather jacket at work on the back of my chair and the bag I brought back from Vegas under my desk. I'd spaced on it when I left, the alcohol had warmed me in the club, and the driver had the heater going full blast in the cab. But now in the deluge of water, I could drown, but I would probably die of hypothermia first.

I was jogging toward my door when the call of my name stopped me. Barrett was standing in his doorway, letting other people in and waving at me.

Diverting since there was no one at home waiting for me anyway, I darted up his steps and stopped on his welcome mat, which burped with the water I squeezed out of it even as it absorbed more.

"You need the kind with holes in it like I have," I teased.

"Jesus, get in here," he insisted, taking hold of my bicep and dragging me inside, closing the door quickly behind me. "You're soaking."

I grunted my agreement.

He looked at me like I was nuts. "Are you all right? Your pupils are huge."

"I think I just killed my Alexander McQueens, and that's a damn shame."

He glared at me. "We're worried about a pair of shoes right now?"

"Boots," I clarified, nodding, not liking my chances of them living through all the water in them. The noise they were making when I walked, that sort of a squelchy, soggy sound, was not good.

"Take off your boots and I'll get you a towel."

I shook my head, which sent cold rivulets down the back of my neck and into my eyes. "Home is right there. I just stopped to say hi."

"You're soaked to the skin."

"I am," I agreed.

He studied my face a moment before he reached out and put a hand on my cheek. "Not that you don't look good, but what's with the all-black ensemble?"

"It's a long fuckin' story," I said, smiling at him, lifting free of his touch, roughly putting my hands through my hair, pulling out the water, squeezing the small ponytail that told me it was more than time to get it cut. Now I was surprised Kage hadn't reminded me earlier in the day.

"Do you want to stay here?" he asked softly, taking a step closer to me. "You could take a shower, and I'll run over to your place and grab some of your clothes. I'll send everybody else home and make you a real dinner."

"Real?"

"Yeah," he croaked, giving me a trace of a smile. "All I've got are burgers and hot dogs right now."

"That sounds good," I said. "How about I run home, shower, and then come back and meet your friends and eat."

His face lit up. "That would be great."

"Okay."

"Is Ian gone?"

"Yeah, he was deployed."

"Wow, that's fast. I'm sorry."

I shrugged. "It's his job."

"Yes and no," he let slip. "But go home and come back."

"If I don't it means I passed out, all right?" I said, turning for the door.

"Then don't go yet. Eat first. Let me get you a towel. I'm afraid you're going to pass out with only alcohol in you."

"How do you know I drank tonight?"

"Miro, my friend, you smell like smoke and beer."

"Gross," I said, chuckling. "I really should go home then."

He studied me. "You're not drunk, though."

"There's still a bit of a buzz left, but not much. Any food will soak up the remainder."

"Well, then let's get you fed, and after you eat, you better strip down and take a nap in my guest room. I think you need a keeper tonight."

"Ian's jealous of you," I said, because my filter was nonexistent not from alcohol but instead due to a profound lack of sleep.

He grinned slightly. "Ian should be afraid, but not of me, per se."

"Afraid?"

He put an arm around my shoulders. "Don't worry about it. Can you walk?"

"I was running," I quipped. "You just saw me."

"Yes, but I think you're fading just a bit."

I scoffed even as I felt my knees wobble ever so slightly. Eating was not the worst idea ever.

Barrett's friends were nice. They were a few guys from his gym, and some people from work who brought their husbands/wives, another partner at his firm and his husband, and a friend from college who'd come in from New Jersey and was staying with him through the weekend—like Janet would be with me—upstairs on the phone at the moment. He'd apparently been there since Monday.

"So you must be the hot guy who lives next door that Barrett's been telling us all about at work," a woman said as I inhaled my burger, far hungrier than I'd realized.

"I think he was probably talking about my boyfriend," I teased with a wink.

She smiled back. "Perhaps."

Barrett coughed, clearly uncomfortable. "You know you can have another one, right?"

I nodded as I chewed.

"Jesus, Miro, you need someone around to make sure you eat."

Not normally.

As I stood in the kitchen, damp but drying, close to the vent pumping out warm air, one of the men coming in for another beer stopped in front of me.

"I know you," the guy said.

"Wow, that's a great line," another of Barrett's friends said, smiling at me. "I think I know you too."

I shook my head, swallowing and tipping my head at the handsome man in front of me. "You don't, but he does. He was my doctor a few years back when I was in the hospital. What was your name again, Doc?"

"Dr. Sean Cooper," he offered with a smile as he got closer. "But just call me Sean, all right? And you're Miro, I heard Barrett say."

"Yeah."

"Here," Barrett said as he put a large glass of ice water down in front of me. "Drink this, let's get you hydrated."

The last of my buzz was slipping away. "I swear I'm good."

"Drink the goddamn water."

So I did as I hoovered down the burger.

"Dr. Benton is your friend," the movie-star handsome man said, returning my attention to him, as he very gently lifted my chin. "And you were shot in the line of duty."

"I was," I replied with a shrug. "And I'm sorry if she came off bossy that day. She gets that way when she's scared."

"She's a phenomenal surgeon."

"And bossy," I reiterated.

"In the line of duty?" the other man asked, having latched on to those words. "What kind of law enforcement?"

"Miro's a deputy US marshal," Barrett answered absently, tucking a piece of hair around my right ear. "You have bruises all along your jaw here."

I grunted.

"Yeah, I was noticing that," Sean admitted, trailing his fingers down the side of my neck to the collar of my Calvin Klein dress shirt and lifting it so he could see the skin underneath. "Oh, Miro, you're bleeding."

I shook my head, shoving chips in my mouth now that the burger was gone. "It's old," I said without swallowing. "I'm fine."

"You're not at all fine." Sean glowered at me. "How much have you had to drink?"

I came clean. "A lot, but it was a while ago now. I'm 90 percent sober."

He nodded. "Okay, I think we need to go to the hospital."

"I just need to go to bed."

"How about if Barrett comes with us?"

"Nope. I'm going home now anyway. I just came to eat and run."

Sean's eyes flicked to Barrett. "I think you need to insist."

"Miro," Barrett began, slipping his hand around my bicep. "Were you in a fight?"

"Deputy US marshal," I apprised him, cocking an eyebrow for his benefit. "It comes with the territory, right?"

He took a breath. "Could Sean just look you over?"

"I think he did already."

"How about you go upstairs, shower, and you can borrow a T-shirt and sweats from me, and then he can—"

"I'm just gonna go." I yawned. "I don't wanna take off my gun holster till I get home."

"You have a gun?" another friend of Barrett's asked.

I was going to say "marshal" again, but I let it go. "I do, yes."

"You're drunk," Sean said sharply. "And you're carrying a gun?"

"I'm not drunk at all, and yes, I'm carrying a gun. Not firing it."

"Maybe you should give the gun to me," Barrett offered with not quite a condescending smile, but close. It was like he thought I was simple or too stupid to understand what he was saying to me. Thing was, I followed all too clearly. I was sleep deprived, yes, but as I'd just said, not drunk.

"Miro, I think—"

"I gotta go," I informed Barrett, because now I was irritated. How dare they question me? I'd never put anyone in danger on purpose. How many other people could say that?

He caught me at the front door.

"Stop, don't leave because you're mad." He chuckled behind me.

I had it opened a crack before he banged it shut.

"Miro—"

"No," I barked, rounding on him, pointing into his face. "How dare you second-guess me or how I perform my job. You and your doctor friend don't know shit about the training that any agent of the federal government goes through because we carry a gun twenty-four seven."

"No, I—"

"I'll have you know that I was on my way home and the guys on my team made sure I was. They would never leave me alone. We all have each other as a safety net, so you questioning me is you questioning them, and I don't fuckin' like it."

This was why, beyond the four women who were more family than friends, I didn't have people in my life beyond the guys I worked with. No one else understood that you could never let yourself completely go, never let your guard all the way down, and never take off the holster until you were home.

"Miro, come on, I—"

Leaving him while he was still talking, I walked back through the living room toward the kitchen, moving fast.

Sean stepped into my path. "Hey, Miro, I really think that—"

I went around him and got to the back door, unlocked it, and went out on Barrett's back patio, down the steps to the cobblestone path that led to the small garden the last owners had put in, and then off into the lush, wet grass.

I bolted to my back steps that simply ended in the grass, went up them to the deck that was the second thing I had built when I moved in, and was fumbling for my keys, thankful for the porch light that went on automatically at dusk, when I heard Barrett yell my name.

I didn't turn. I just kept trying to get my keys out but the pants were tight anyway and now they were sticking to my sides like a second skin.

"Miro," Barrett said, arriving at my side. "Forgive me. I didn't mean to imply that you're not capable or that you would ever do anything foolish. Please, I'm just worried."

"I don't need you to worry about me," I almost snarled, finally getting the ring out of my pocket. "I have Ian for that."

"Oh? Is that right?"

"Yeah, that's right!" I flared, glancing over at his covered back porch and seeing the crowd clustered there. "And you should go back to your party."

"I don't want to go back to my party, I want to fix this with you," he insisted, grabbing my bicep and yanking hard to get me to turn to him.

"It's fine, it's fixed." And it was. He and I were done except for me to wave at him as I passed his house or saw him on the street. No one got to second-guess my job or the guys I worked with or how I conducted myself.

"No, it's not, you're mad because I questioned you and now because I'm questioning Ian's commitment."

"Don't worry about Ian," I warned him. "Ian and me are great."

"You're not great, because he's never here."

"He's here more than enough," I said, slipping the key into the bottom lock, opening it and then going to work on the dead bolt with another key.

"What do you expect?" he asked curtly. "Here you are all alone night after night, this handsome, sexy, dangerous man who needs a keeper more than anyone I've ever met in my life, and I'm just supposed to do what? Never say anything? Never put the idea in your head that you have other options, that you deserve a better one?"

"Fuck you, Barrett," I spat, disgusted. "You're supposed to be my fuckin' friend! You don't tear Ian down when he's not here, that's total shit!"

He shoved me back against the door… or tried to. I had no idea what he was thinking, but I had a lot of muscle on him and there was no way I was moving.

"Go home," I said, pushing him off me.

"Miro, just listen to—"

But the door opened, which cut him off and startled me as we were suddenly both looking at a very beautiful, very angry man standing in the doorway.

"Yes," Ian ground out, his tone dead and flat. "Go home."

Barrett's eyes were huge as he regarded the man I loved, but Ian's focus was solely on me, as evidenced by the way he fisted his hand in my wet shirt and yanked me into the house. He slammed the door so hard behind me that the glass rattled.

"You're home," I breathed out.

The way he was looking at me, predatory and hungry, should have really scared me, but a shiver of anticipation ran through me instead. "Where the hell have you been?" was the first thing out of his mouth.

It wasn't warm or loving, but it didn't matter. I didn't care. He was home.

CHAPTER 14

I STOOD there dripping in the living room, smiling like an idiot and wiping the water out of my face and eyes. "I'm so happy to see you!"

He scowled at me.

"What?"

"If you're so happy, come the fuck here."

"But I'm all wet," I said, shivering not with cold but with happiness.

"Yeah, I don't care," he murmured, lifting his arms.

I lunged at him, grabbing tight, and he hugged me back just as hard, the both of us trying to absorb the other. "I'm gonna explode I'm so happy."

His grunt was all Ian, smug and sexy. "Don't do that. I like you all in one piece."

I kissed the side of his neck, his jaw, and then took his mouth so he'd know he was missed and cherished and so very needed.

"You taste like scotch," he said, breaking the kiss, needing air, "and salt."

"Potato chips," I said, grinning, just looking at him, his face, his hair, and his eyes. God, he was pretty.

"The fuck are you wearing?"

My clothes? "Why, do I look weird?" I asked, taking several steps back, checking my wet shirt and pants, not sure what he was seeing.

"No," he said gruffly, his hot gaze traveling up and down my body before returning to my face. "'Weird' is not the word I'd use."

"Oh no? What, then?" I pried, taking a step forward, bumping into him, letting the warmth rolling off his solid muscular frame sear into me. I had expected steam to erupt when we touched before, as opposite as we were at the moment, me so cold and wet, him a simmering flame.

"Decadent," he whispered, huffing out a breath. "You walked around lookin' like that all night?"

He wanted me.

It was there in the rich, thick growl in his voice, all smoky and seductive, the dangerous glint in the depths of his eyes, and the way he wet his lips like his mouth had gone dry.

"Yeah," I purred, grinning as I knocked him back into the door, pinning him there with one hand, bracing him, making sure he couldn't move. "All yesterday, all today I had a hundred things to tell you, but right now I can't think of even one."

"How come?"

I whimpered involuntarily. "You're finally home."

His breath hitched as he lifted his hands to my face, touching my skin, skimming over bruises and contusions, smoothing over my eyebrows, tracing my cheeks as he looked with both his eyes and his fingertips. "Where were you?"

It was a loaded question, but I knew what I was really being asked. "Where do you think I was?"

"No," he growled, the muscles in his strong, square jaw cording as he continued to scrutinize me, missing nothing. "You fuckin' tell me."

"Well, first I was with the guys, and then Janet called, and then I was almost home when I stopped at Barrett's."

"Why'd you stop?" he prodded, slipping a hand inside the collar of my shirt so he could stroke over my skin before trailing his fingers first to my collarbone and then to the base of my throat. "Why didn't you come straight here?"

"I didn't know you were home. I couldn't get you on the phone."

"I know. We weren't allowed to call, and then—I just wanted to get back here."

"Oh?" My heart was pounding and my throat hurt and my mouth was dry and all of that was Ian's fault. Such simple words, that he wanted to get back to me, had me in knots of anxious, frantic happiness. I really was going to fly apart at any second.

He was silent for a moment and then said simply, "It hurt to go."

"Yeah?" I pressed, because holy fuck, Ian *never* said anything like that. There were so few confessions from his soul that when one did happen, I pounced.

"You know it did," he grumbled. "You know I hate to be away."

"From me?"

"Of course from you, who else would I—are you drunk?"

I shook my head as he began unbuttoning my sopping-wet shirt. "Not anymore. I was maybe a little tipsy a few hours ago, but now, no. Exhausted."

"Why were you tipsy?"

I shrugged as I looked at the stubble on his face, the lines in the corners of his eyes, and at his plump lower lip. My skin felt tight, flushed with heat, and I swallowed as the sensations tripped through me, sparking, sizzling, the want rising so fast I almost cried out.

"You don't know why you were drinking?"

"Missed you," I said under my breath as he eased the shirt from my shoulders.

"Jesus, you're bleeding."

"Just a bit, and it'll stop," I promised, leaning in to kiss his throat, suck the skin into my mouth and gently nibble. I'd leave marks, but he'd be able to hide them.

"Were you cut?"

"Yesterday," I got out before I lifted my head and kissed him.

He tasted so good, like toothpaste and a trace of bourbon, and his mouth was hot, and his breath coming in stuttering little gasps made me smile.

"Fuck," he panted when I stopped for a second so he could gulp air, even though all I wanted to do was kiss him senseless until he begged me to fuck him.

"I should shower and change," I said into the hollow of his throat, licking his skin, inhaling his scent, wanting it all over me, on our bed, everywhere. "I know I smell bad. I haven't slept or bathed since Sunday morning."

"You smell like rain and sweat, and your eyes are so dark and your clothes are sticking to your shoulders and your chest, and Jesus, Miro, you can't—I need to stay here to guard you so no one thinks they can be me and have what I have."

It was me. I was what he had.

The joy of being prized, wanted, coveted filled me with sweet, syrupy pride, and I reveled in it and let it fill what his absence had emptied.

"Miro," he gasped as I bumped his cheek with mine, turning into him, nuzzling, catching his jaw with my teeth before my mouth was on his and I was parting his lips with my tongue.

I took what I wanted, one kiss after another, each melting him a little more, rendering him boneless and willing, building ache and hungry, desperate, cloying need.

He bucked into my grip when I shoved my hand down the front of his sweats. He coiled his arms around my neck, clutching tight as he ground his mouth over mine, sucking, tasting, returning every bit of the delicious building heat that blazed between us.

"Jesus, I missed you," I barely managed to get out, my voice gravelly and ragged, already leaving me as I watched Ian tremble in my hands. "And I have to change that."

He pushed me back so he could see my face. "What?"

I fought to get my body under control and not jump him.

"Miro," he demanded, his temper flaring.

That was some impressive compartmentalizing, that he could simply turn off sex and turn on his logical, questioning brain. Apparently I wasn't as irresistible to him as I thought.

"What're you changing?"

Raking my fingers through my wet hair, I tried to think of what I wanted to say through my tired, and now horny, brain.

"Miro?" He husked out my name, and I heard the twitch of fear in his voice then.

I shook my head and then bent over to take off my boots and socks, picking up the wet dress shirt he'd peeled off me while we kissed.

"Talk to me."

I took a breath. "I'm missing you too much when you go, and it's making me careless with people and in situations," I said thoughtfully.

"What does that mean?" He questioned, because he had to know I was talking about the job. "Is that how you got cut? Is that why Barrett's chasing you across the lawn, talking me down?"

"It's just how it's going," I said, walking around him, heading toward the laundry room.

He got in front of me, and I had to stop or plow into him, and when I did, he grabbed everything away, let my boots and shirt fall to the floor, and took my face in his hands. "I don't want you not to miss me."

"Yeah, but you can't be everything. It's not fair to either of us."

"What in the hell are you talking about?" He slid his hands to both sides of my neck, and I fought the urge to lean into him and just breathe.

"I can't use you as a touchstone if you're not here because I end up feeling disjointed and like I don't give a shit about anything since you're not there to talk to and sleep with and laugh at me when I do something stupid." I sighed, forcing a smile. "It's not working."

"I don't understand," he said softly, coaxing, his right hand flat on my chest, pressed to my heart, the other mapping my abdomen and lower. "Make me understand."

"Somewhere along the way, I forgot how to be me without you," I said matter-of-factly. "I'm not sure when, but now I'm different, and I have to change back."

"But I don't want you to do that."

I sighed dejectedly. "Yeah, but you don't get a say, just like I don't get one with you being in the military."

"Now wait."

"It's okay," I soothed, easing free of his hands, trembling in the cold air. "I'm gonna take a shower. Can you throw my shirt in the washer and put my boots by the sink? I've gotta find some newspaper to stuff down inside of them."

"'Course," he replied before I turned and bolted upstairs.

It wasn't the best shower I ever took, but it was right up there. By the time I got out, the walls were dripping with condensation and the mirror was all steamed up. As I wiped a clear spot on it, I realized how beat up and shitty I looked before I brushed my teeth.

I had blue bruises and yellow ones, red splotches along my jaw under two days' worth of stubble, and dark black circles under my eyes. My color was off; I looked pasty, sickly, and my eyes themselves looked flat and lifeless. I had no idea what Ian or anyone else could have seen in me.

Once I was out, changed into flannel pajama bottoms and a T-shirt, and finally warm, I was surprised to find him sitting on the bed. He had a steaming cup of tea in his hand.

"Man, that looks good. I think I'm gonna go get one."

"This is yours, idiot," he groused. "I don't drink this oolong crap."

I walked over, took the cup from him, and then sat down carefully beside him so I didn't spill it. "Thank you," I said, leaning sideways to kiss his cheek.

He turned into me, catching my mouth and kissing me softly, slowly. Even the nibble he took before he pulled back was tender.

"You think it's nice to kiss me like you did downstairs and then just walk away?"

I chuckled before I took a sip of my tea.

"Hello?"

"You're the one who put a stop to it. I figured you were done."

"Done." His voice cracked. "You're making me crazy."

I put the cup of hot tea down on the nightstand and then turned back to my man, slipping my hand around his cheek and staring into those beautiful eyes of his. "I couldn't tell."

"You couldn't tell," he almost shouted at me, grabbing my hand and pressing it to his long, hard, fully erect length. "Can you fuckin' tell now?"

I squeezed him through the sweats he had on, and the mewling groan that came out of his throat made me smile. "So you're saying you want me, then," I teased.

"Yes—fuck, I want you!"

"I'm having trouble reading you," I said as I shoved him down on the bed, shucked off his sweats, curled over him, and took his cock down the back of my throat.

He roared my name, and the sound, raw, guttural, torn from his chest, ripped from deep down in his soul, washed a tight quickening of liquid heat through me that had been missing between us for a while.

I was being careful.

He was unsure.

Together we'd been loving and thoughtful, but neither of us let go, too afraid of what would happen, what we would say. A mistake might be the end, so we'd been tiptoeing around the can of snakes, neither wanting to loosen the lid.

In our hesitancy we'd created distance, because if we weren't that close, we couldn't get hurt.

I loved Ian with everything I had, but I also feared him dicing my heart up into little pieces at the same time. Meanwhile he was gambling on me, on me staying, on me being strong, and whether he knew it or not, testing at the same time. Would I stay when push came to shove? If he was gone more than he was home, would it still be worth it for me?

But now—right now—I had him at my mercy, I was driving him crazy with my mouth and hands, and there was nothing between us but ferocious, devouring need.

I sucked hard, licked him from balls to head, and then swallowed around him, showing him all the tricks in my arsenal until he was clenching my hair in a tightened fist and rocking in and out, fucking my mouth. When he pushed me off, I was surprised.

"What?" I panted, saliva dripping from my chin as I spoke.

He took hold of me, roughly wiped my lips with his thumb, and then hooked his hand around my neck and pulled me down so he could kiss me.

I ravaged him and he arched up off the bed, brushing against me as he whispered my name in endless, reverent litany.

"Ian," I ground out, shoving his T-shirt up, bending to suckle on one raised, pebbled nipple, seeing him gorgeous in his honest submission, the twisting current running between us making him jolt in my hands as I kissed him again, rougher, because my longing wasn't just reverence, but angry as well.

Why did he leave me? Why couldn't he simply stay?

The first thing I saw when I opened my eyes in the morning, the last when I closed them at night, this was what I had to have... Ian in my bed, tangled with me, breathing in tandem.

"I hate you," I snarled.

"Yes," he rasped, because he knew. He had to. "But I don't care. You love me more."

That was true too.

"Fuck me," he growled into my mouth as I delivered another punishing kiss. "I've been wanting you since I left. I just want to feel you on top of me and in me and just—fuck, Miro. How'd we get so far from us?"

He was gone, that was how.

"Nothing makes sense when I'm not here, and then I get here, and lately you're not you. Why're you being careful with me? Why are you treating me like I'm not yours?"

It was like we started and stopped. I got used to him being gone, and then he came back and I spent the whole time waiting for him to go again. I wasn't living anymore. But I loved him, so much more than was wise because how much Ian could give and how much I could take was something we couldn't answer.

Things needed to be settled between us, but not now. The only thing that mattered now was feeling Ian wrapped around me.

I sat up and rolled him to his stomach, shoved his facedown into the rumpled blankets before I dove for the nightstand to retrieve the lube.

"Do you think about me at all when I'm not here?"

"Idiot," I croaked, snapping open the tube. I slicked my cock fast and then pressed against his pale-pink hole. "You're all I think about."

"Then kiss me when I get home, and grab me and put me over the table in the kitchen and just hold me the fuck down. Please, Miro, stop pulling away. Show me."

I had to take what I wanted so he'd know he was loved. And no matter what happened between us, that was the irrevocable truth.

I pressed inside him slowly, sinuously, feeling his muscles ripple and stretch around me, the squeeze on my dick so good I nearly came. "Fuck, Ian," I rasped, my breathing choppy as I pushed his T-shirt up over his head and off so I could kiss and lick over the heavy scars that crisscrossed his back. He'd once worried I thought they were ugly, until I'd explained in lavish detail that every part of his body was a wonder to me.

"Move," he begged, pushing back, taking me in deeper. "Miro... love."

That endearment, the only one he ever used for me, and only me, never ceased to make my heart clench.

"Show me you want me."

Words only for me because I alone was trusted with his passion.

Sinking down into him, I pounded deep, hard, before easing back and repeating the motion, again and again, the rolling thrusts creating a seamless rhythm that only became hammering and relentless when Ian began stroking himself off and chanting my name.

"I swear I'm worth it," he beseeched me, his voice low, seductive, holding me as inexorably as his body. "Just stay with me."

"I know you're worth it," I gasped, slamming into him, letting go, holding nothing back, knowing my heart lived and died for him and nothing else. "Don't you think I know? Can't you tell?"

"Then don't give up. Don't ever give up."

"No," I promised, and I prayed it was one I could keep. "Now come for me."

"I want—can't—I've had to be so in control."

I had to take that discipline away from him. I was the one who annihilated his careful restraint, who allowed Ian to be completely himself in the safety of my love.

Pulling out to his howl of frustration, I fell down on the bed and lifted my arms to him. "Come ride me."

He scrambled to do my bidding, straddling my hips and impaling himself hungrily on my cock. Hands on my chest, digging his fingers into my pectorals, he rode me hard, finding the angle he needed, grinding down into me, setting a pace that was all about him and what he needed and what felt good.

His hard granite thighs clasped my sides as his ass milked my length, and I watched him jerk himself off, felt the muscles in his ass spasm and clamp around me like a vise before his climax tore through him and he spurted onto my chest.

It was so hot. Watching Ian come undone, I was seconds behind him. I just had to alter his timing enough, so I took hold of that perfect ass of his and held him tight over me so I could piston up into him, pummel him from the bottom until just that much more friction pushed me over the edge.

"Ian!" I thundered his name and he collapsed over me, his arms no longer able to hold him up, sweat and cum between us as our lips fused as tight as our bodies.

When he tilted his head, I thought he needed air, but it turned out he just needed a better angle to get his tongue farther down my throat.

CHAPTER 15

I WANTED to talk to him. It was my favorite thing in the world, lying in bed talking to Ian, but my eyes would not stay open, and when he spooned around me, his face in my hair, arm tucking me tight against him, I apologized.

"What for?" he asked, his breath in my ear.

"I'm gonna pass out and I don't want to."

"But I want you to, so go to sleep."

No more prodding was needed.

So after I slept like the dead for several hours, when I woke up, we shared a pillow and caught each other up.

He already knew about Lochlyn being dead. They'd briefed him and the others at the CID office in DC. All the active military soldiers were taken to Fort Bragg and moved on base until either they were deployed again or until the threat—now clearly not Lochlyn—could be identified and handled. As a reservist Ian was on his own, but because he was a marshal, he had more options. The main one was simply to come home and let his partner, and his team, protect him. He'd opted for that, and since his Special Forces unit was not deployed, he came home to me.

I cleared my throat. "So I have some news."

He turned his head to look at me, waiting.

It occurred to me then that maybe I should have started the conversation because, perhaps, Hartley trumped Lochlyn.

Or not. Hard to say until I opened my mouth and told him.

"M?"

I coughed softly and looked at his face, and man... he was all rumpled and sleep-tousled and a little bleary and open and trusting and I *really* didn't want that to change.

His grin curled his lip mischievously. "I think I know what it is."

I grimaced. "I don't think you do."

"I think you wanna feel me deep inside," he said gruffly, and the sound of him sent a caressing ripple through my body that made me catch my breath. "Oh yeah, you want me bad," he said, rolling over on top of me.

"Yes," I husked, eyes drifting closed as I lifted for his kiss. "And Craig Hartley is out of prison."

After a moment, I realized that he wasn't moving and the kiss was not forthcoming. Opening my eyes, I found all semblance of languor erased from my man, replaced by a glare that could have split a tree.

"Now wait."

He climbed off me and scrambled over the side of the bed.

"Ian."

"Are you kidding me?"

I groaned and grabbed the pillow, covering my face.

"*Are you fucking kidding me?*"

Oh that was loud.

"Jesus fucking Christ!"

I should have led with Hartley.

"For fuck's sake, Miro!" His roar probably rattled the house. "Craig Hartley is out of prison and you're just getting around to telling me *now*?"

I moaned into the pillow that smelled like him, and so, yes, I was in trouble, but… he was home. My heart was still dancing around, and nothing he could do would change it.

"How dare you not—Miro!" he bellowed, stealing the pillow from me only to smack me first in the abdomen with it and then in the head.

I tried really hard not to smile, but it came out anyway, which got me another smack in the face. "Owww, you shit," I griped, laughing.

"It's not funny!"

I heard it in his voice then, the fear and sadness, and saw it on his face when I looked up at him.

He was stricken with dread.

"I was so happy," I entreated, reaching for his hand, easing him close, kissing his knuckles, his fingers, rubbing them over my stubble-covered cheek. "You were home and I lost my mind, I missed you so much, and then you just showed up and… Ian… baby…."

He came down on top of me, grabbing me tight, and crushed me to his rock-hard chest, hugging me so tight I was afraid he'd compressed my lungs. But only for a second. Because in the next instant, the warmth of him engulfed me, seeped all the way down to my soul where my fear of Hartley lived, and washed calm into every dark corner.

"I should have been here," he said, the words painful as they tumbled out, suffused with regret. "Miro... forgive me."

I turned my head; my cheek wedged against his shoulder, and sighed in pleasure as I closed my eyes, more content than I could remember being in so very long. I wrapped him in my arms and squeezed, loving the feel of him, his strength and heat. "Nothing to forgive," I vowed, exhaling deeply. "You're here now."

"I am."

"Try and stay a little while, okay?"

"Wild horses and all that," he got out.

I really hoped he was right.

We stayed that way, wrapped around each other, tangled arms and legs, breathing together until I drifted off again. When my eyes fluttered open, I realized he was on the phone with someone, and after listening a moment, caught that it was Kage.

Ian patted his chest and I moved over and draped myself over him, loving the feel of his warm, sleek skin, the slight slick of faint scars, a dapple of rough on smooth that I could feel under my fingertips as I traced over his ribs.

"So they think he's where, sir?"

The steady beat of Ian's heart lulled me back to sleep so fast I didn't even realize I had passed out until I woke up under him.

"Crap, I'm sorry." I yawned, stretching.

"No more sorry. We're done with sorry," he said, his smile lazy and beautiful.

"Please don't go anywhere," I said before I thought about it.

"I hate that I'm here and all you can say is don't go."

I nodded because he was right, that was shitty. "I should get up."

"No, you shouldn't."

"Ian, I—Ian!" He tackled me when I sat up, shoving me back down on the bed, and climbed on top of me, straddling my hips so any movement was out of the question. "What're you—"

"I'm not going, I'm staying, do you understand?"

I nodded because my voice deserted me.

He bent and kissed me, and I felt it, my heart fluttering around in my chest like a caged bird ready to fly, wanting out, needing to go to Ian, always with Ian.

"I love you so much," I whispered, the hurricane inside so much like anger that I had to make sure my words didn't come out before I thought about each one. I was afraid if I vented my soul he'd find out how close to an ultimatum I truly was. Having him with me, knowing he could leave again, was almost as bad as him being gone. When they became truly equal, I wondered what would happen, and just thinking about that was terrifying.

"You're lookin' at me like I'm a ghost." He kissed my eyes and my nose and then softly, tenderly, ran his tongue across the seam of my lips, before parting them and taking what he wanted.

I opened for him, returned each kiss with all the hunger inside, and when I was squirming under him, clutching at his thighs, he pulled back and grinned down at me.

I judged him. "Evil."

His smirk was tantalizing. "Now tell me about Vegas. Who'd you bring home?"

And just with a thought of Josue, my libido died. From hot languid lover to father figure in seconds flat. "You'll see tomorrow."

"Wait," he said as I pitched him sideways before I rolled up off the bed. "Let's talk about something else."

"Too late," I announced, snorting out a laugh.

His face fell. "That was stupid."

"You're gonna like Josue," I assured him. "He's sweet. He insisted on bringing something for Turkey Day."

"Shit, we're having more company, aren't we. What is that, five of us now, or six?"

I lost it. Six. Yeah, right. In his dreams.

"Oh no."

I snickered.

"What'd you do?"

"I think we're up to like twenty." I cackled, head back, eyes closed, laughing myself silly.

"Twenty?" He sounded horrified, and that didn't help me to stop laughing at all.

The unexpected banging on the front door, combined with the incessant doorbell ringing, got me back into my discarded pajama bottoms and T-shirt and down the stairs.

"Wait," Ian cautioned sharply, his voice carrying after me. "Don't open the door—lemme get my gun."

"We both know that's not Hartley," I assured him, darting to the front door and hurling it open, ready to take someone's head off. I was startled to find Cabot, Drake, and Josue—and a very angry, very puffed-up Aruna on my doorstep, holding Chickie's leash. It was weird that they were all there at the same time since she and the boys had never met.

The werewolf got up on his back legs and licked me good morning, which scared the hell out of Josue—but not Cabot or Drake since they'd seen Chickie on a number of occasions—and then left me in a dead heat for the stairs where Ian now stood, squinting and shirtless.

"Damn, Miro," Josue breathed once he'd recovered from thinking I was wolf food. "No wonder you didn't wanna do me."

"What?" Ian called over.

I waved a dismissive hand at him and tipped my head at Aruna. "What's with you and the doorbell?" I asked because I knew the boys, even Josue, and they would have never been so insidious with the ringing. It was her.

"How dare you ask Janet to help you make dinner and not me!" She was mad, loud and shrieky.

"You told me you were cooking for your in-laws this year," I volleyed.

"I know, but they don't want me. They said I can't cook traditional."

"What? Yes, you can."

"I know," she agreed loudly. "But they don't want the Indian girl cooking."

"That's crazy," I told her.

"I know!" she almost shouted.

"You can cook anything."

"*I know*!" she yelled, fuming.

"Chickie, goddammit," Ian complained behind me.

"Wait, now," I said to Aruna. "Just stand there a second all right?"

She huffed out a breath and crossed her arms but she didn't move.

"Okay," I began, turning to the boys. "Why're you here?"

"To tell you that we're gonna go with Josue to see Lillian since we know where her office is and everything, so you don't have to."

"Oh, nice, okay," I said, my eyes slits as I regarded them. "You could've just called."

"Josue wanted to see your place."

"It's nice," he said, beaming at me, stepping in close, wrapping his arms around my waist and bumping his head against my chest. "But mostly I wanted to come over to say thank you for saving my life. I just love you."

"Hands off the marshal," Ian boomed from behind me. "Chickie, will you give it a rest!"

"You're welcome," I said, patting his back, looking to Drake for help and finding the same dopey expression on his face that Cabot, when I glanced at him, had on his. "Oh, for fuck's sake," I grumbled.

The other two boys moved in and I was the center of a group hug.

"Aww, that's nice," Aruna told me, leaning sideways to look at Ian. "You just let whoever comes in off the street hug your man?"

"I'm getting my gun," he announced, then gestured at Chickie. "Can you please call—"

"He's just happy to see you, you ungrateful piece of crap!" she snapped at him.

"Why're you mad at me?" Ian was indignant.

"Janet," she shouted. "You asked Janet to help you feed the horde, and not me?"

"I wasn't even—I didn't do—wait, what horde? There's a horde now?" Ian sounded really confused and a bit incredulous.

She made a noise of disgust and directed her attention back to me, moving forward and scattering the boys until they all let go and she stood there in front of me, hands on hips, righteous anger rolling off her.

"I didn't do it on purpose," I groused. "I thought you were with your goddamn relatives. Don't blame me 'cause you communicate for shit."

"I wanna cook."

"Why?"

"Because it calms me!"

Of course it did.

"Fine. I'd love you to cook. You know that."

"Good!"

"Fine!"

"Good!"

We were silent a minute.

"I'll pick up Janet at the airport," she squealed, excited now as she smiled, her shoulders lifting in happiness. "I can't wait to see her."

"You're insane," I assured her as she leaned up to kiss me.

I bent and offered her my cheek, and she patted it after giving me a gentle buss.

"We'll be here when you get home, so don't come in here thinking you're gonna get your kink on with your man."

"I'd pay to see that, actually," Josue piped up, looking around me, tilting his head, clearly admiring Ian's form. "That man is hot."

She put her hand on Josue's shoulder. "You ain't seen nothing yet. Wait'll you meet my husband. He's got muscles on top of muscles, and he's all burly and gorgeous—you're gonna die."

His face lit up as he looked at her.

"And"—she waggled her eyebrows at him—"he's a fireman."

"Oh girl," Josue said, fanning his face.

"I'll introduce you tomorrow, uhm...."

"Josue," he sighed, offering her his hand.

"I'm Aruna," she said, sounding all sweet and nice, which was a total lie since she was a harpy through and through. "Who are your friends?"

Somehow they all exchanged names and got to chatting, and Aruna offered to drive the boys downtown since that's the way she was going. I didn't care. They all left, so I was happy.

Closing the door, I faced a very distraught-looking Ian, whose hair was all standing up on one side.

"What'd you do?"

Apparently Chickie had licked it up that way.

"Your hair is full of dog drool," I said, laughing.

"Horde?" he repeated, sounding a bit unhinged.

"Group," I amended helpfully.

He left me for the kitchen in search of coffee.

LATER THAT morning, in the office, Kage wanted to see Ian alone, and while he was in with the boss, I got a call from downstairs that I had visitors at the security checkpoint. As I got closer to the front doors, I heard my name.

I was halfway expecting Janet, even though Aruna said she was picking her up, and Josue and the boys would not have been a surprise, though with Josue being a present witness, he could have come through security. So it was a surprise to see Colin Doyle, Ian's estranged father, standing there with his wife, Linda, Ian's stepmother.

After walking out through the checkpoint, I offered him my hand as soon as I was close enough.

"Hello, sir," I greeted him, and then Linda, who I was surprised reached for me as well. "How are you?"

"Good," he said quickly, looking uncomfortable. "But we're having a problem with Lorcan, our youngest."

"And what's that?"

"His friends told us that he was picked up by the police, but we've been calling since last night and can't find him anywhere," Linda said frantically, looking sheepish for having blurted all that out.

"What was he arrested for?"

"We don't know," Colin told me.

"Okay, let's go upstairs." I moved them both in front of me, and the three of us went through the express line reserved for officers of the court. I put lanyards on both of them once we were through and signed them in to the visitor log.

As we got off the elevator, I looked toward my desk, and in that instant when Ian saw me, his face lit up, and then he saw his father, and his face fell.

"He hates me," Colin mumbled.

"No, sir," I corrected him. "Begging your pardon, but no, Ian hasn't reached out, but neither have you."

"That's what I told him," Linda explained, and I took a moment to look at her. Even though I would never like her after what she pulled on Colin's 60th birthday party—excluding Ian, and his dead mother, from a slideshow of his father's life—she was, empirically, a very beautiful woman. She had grace and a delicate voice, was immaculately dressed, and her makeup and jewelry were elegant and understated. What she was doing with Colin, I had no idea. He was a bull; she was a ballerina. I didn't really get it, but I didn't have to. "I said that if he wants a relationship with Ian, he has to call him and stop waiting for him to need a dog sitter."

"Yes," I said, leading them into one of the smaller conference rooms and sitting them down. After I checked to see if they were thirsty, I left them there to go back to my desk and get on my computer.

"What're they doing here?" Ian asked, rolling around his desk and coming to a stop beside me. He crowded close, as he'd always done. I'd missed seeing that the first three years of our partnership, before we got together.

"He's here looking for Lorcan. It doesn't have anything to do with you."

"But he didn't want my help?"

"I think he's hedging his bet, right? He comes here asking for me, and if you get involved, then he has his in. If you don't… well… he still needs help finding his kid."

"His kid," Ian repeated.

"Which you are too," I pointed out.

"Not really," Ian said quietly. "I haven't really been his since he left my mom and me."

I turned to look at him. "Does being the most important thing in my life help at all?"

He leaned so his lips brushed my right ear. "It's everything now, M. You know that."

I shivered, feeling the goose bumps erupt down my arm. "Knock it off, I'm working. Giving me wood at my desk is not helpful."

His low chuckle made me think of sex, which was bad when I was in marshal mode.

"Can you go back to your desk?"

He bumped me with his shoulder before looking at my screen and squinting.

"Why're you doing that?"

"Doing what?"

"Can you see that screen?"

"What?" His voice rose almost to a squeak.

"Holy shit, you need glasses."

"I do not."

"You need reading glasses."

"I do not."

"For fuck's sake, Ian, ya do too."

"Could you get back to finding Lorcan, please, so they can get the fuck outta here?"

Giving up for the moment, I went back to hunting the NCIC database.

"So what happened exactly?"

"Your dad says that Lorcan got picked up by CPD, but that they can't find him."

"So you're thinking what, he's sitting in a holding cell somewhere?"

"Could be, but I'll bet you it has more to do with whatever he was picked up for. Maybe they're squeezing him to get to somebody else."

"So we're assuming it's drugs."

I shrugged.

"Who has drugs?" Kohn asked from his desk.

"Shuddup," Ian snapped.

"Oh, by the way," Kohn added. "My mother wants to meet you guys, so she's coming with me when I visit. Prepare yourselves."

I stared at him. "Your mother?"

"My mother."

I glanced at Ian.

"What? I'm sure she's lovely."

Kohn cackled. "Oh, she's the best, but in your business she will be."

"She always wants to know when me and Theresa are gonna have kids," Kowalski chimed in. "And she thinks Theresa doesn't feed me enough."

Kowalski was a mountain. How could Kohn's mother say he wasn't eating enough?

"I don't see anything here at all," Ian said, having commandeered my mouse so he could scroll around. "I think you're gonna have to call."

"Call who?" I asked. Considering the US Justice Department investigating the Chicago Police Department's use of force, deadly or otherwise, we were not at the top of their want-to-help-them-out list. I would have had better luck if I was a fed.

"Call Cochran," Ian suggested.

"Are you nuts?" I asked, my voice going up way too high, but seriously, was he insane? "He fuckin' hates me, and it goes both ways. And he might've gone to Plano already."

"Maybe."

I eyed him. "Do you know where Plano is?"

His scowl was instant. "Of course, it's in Texas. Everybody knows that."

I grunted.

"Just try and call him," Ian went on. "From what the boss man said, you helped him out, didn't let them do anything but the minimum for what he did to you. I'm thinking he owes you."

Even though Ian's logic was faulty, I called over to the Fourth District, Central, and asked to be transferred upstairs to Violent Crimes and Detective Cochran's desk.

"Cochran," he answered on the fifth ring, sounding as surly as ever.

"I need help."

"Fuck you, Miro, you just ruined my life," he retorted and hung up.

"Well, that was great," I groused. "Now we're never going to find him."

"Find who?"

We both looked up to find Kage looming over my desk. He passed me the final paperwork on Cabot and Drake as he waited for an answer.

"Ian's dad and stepmother say that his half brother got picked up by CPD, but he's not in their system. At least, there's nothing on their server."

Kage nodded. "Come with me."

In his office he used his speakerphone and called over to the Eighteenth District, Near North, and did the same thing I did, except he didn't ask for a detective. He asked to be connected to the new acting commander, Duncan Stiel.

"It's terrifying who they'll promote these days," Kage said jovially once Stiel came on the line. I'd never heard that particular tone from him. It was strange.

"Yeah, well, when a department on the whole looks quite this shitty, the good PR of furthering the career of an openly gay officer sounded pretty good to the brass."

"You havin' any trouble?"

"A little pushback but nothing major." He sighed. "I've been on the job too long, too many guys know me, and at this point, saying anything about me or to me just shines the light back on them."

"Good, I'm glad."

"Hey, while I've got you, remember the ballet is tonight, and Hannah needs to be ready to go by six. Aaron will be by to pick her up then."

"Are you going?"

"No, man, I work for a living."

Kage grunted.

"Why are you calling me at work?"

"I have two of my marshals here with me, Jones and Doyle, and they're looking for Doyle's stepbrother—" He tipped his head toward us.

"Lorcan Doyle," Ian supplied.

"His folks say he was picked up, but there's no record," Kage continued.

Deep sigh from Stiel. "Hold on."

It was silent a few moments, and then we heard keyboard tapping.

"Hey, weren't Doyle and Jones the ones who found Hannah right before Thanksgiving last year? Am I remembering that right?"

"Yes," Kage said irritably, probably not wanting to be reminded that his daughter was kidnapped for a good half an hour the year before. She got away because she was very smart and very brave. With Kage as her father, it hadn't been a surprise.

"Doyle's first name is Ian, right?"

"It is."

"Ian's a good name," Stiel said wistfully, and I had to wonder what that was about. "Okay, here we go. Lorcan Colin Doyle, twenty-five, of Marynook.... oh, he's out."

"Out?"

"Yeah, looks like the sister posted bail, and he's being charged with drug possession with intent to sell."

"Which was?"

"Uh... oh, pot."

"Pot?"

"I'm just reading, don't judge me. Marijuana is still illegal here."

Kage groaned.

"And it looks like he was carrying an unlicensed firearm as well," Stiel added. "If he doesn't do any time, I'd be surprised."

"But like you said, at the moment, he's free."

"Yep."

"Thank you."

"I'd say it was my pleasure," he said, chuckling, "but I'd be lying."

"Glad to see your promotion hasn't gone to your head."

He chuckled. "Oh, so you know, we'll be there tomorrow around one, all right? You need us to bring anything?"

"No," Kage said adamantly. "Please, no."

"You said bring dessert last time."

"There was a catering van in my driveway just to unload plates and napkins. Just… no."

Stiel laughed and hung up, and Kage hit the button on his phone, killing the line.

"Okay, so go tell them he's out."

"I wonder why the processing isn't in our system."

"Probably because the judge accepted a plea and that's public record, but I doubt CPD's system will update until after the holiday. You would have found it if you'd known he was bailed out already. You were just looking in the wrong place."

"Thank you."

"Yep. Have a good weekend, gentlemen. I'll see you Monday."

He was taking the day after the holiday off. The rest of us were all in on Friday.

I prodded Ian to go talk to his father and stepmother alone, which gave me time to check in on Aruna.

"Do you have the package?" I teased.

"I do." Aruna giggled. "And the package is in deep shit."

"What?"

I heard sounds of a struggle: smacking, slapping, and then Janet was calling Aruna a narc, and Aruna called Janet fat—which drew a gasp of outrage—before the phone got dropped.

"I'm not fat, you witch, I'm pregnant!"

"You're three months pregnant," Aruna said in her superior tone. "If you keep eating like you are, you'll be as big as a house."

Second gasp of profound outrage.

"Hello!" I yelled into my phone. "Why are you in deep shit, Powell?"

"I'm sorry, what?"

Oh crap, I thought. "Oh crap," I said. "You didn't tell Ned you came here."

"I think we have a bad connection," she said, and then she was gone.

I was so dead. Janet's husband was going to think I kidnapped her, or worse, was in on her plan from the start.

"Hey."

I turned to Kohn, and he tipped his head. I looked where he was directing to see Ian standing with Colin and Linda, and he was motioning me to him.

Crossing the room quickly, I was surprised to see Linda holding Ian's hand. It was just as odd when she reached for me.

"Thank you." She was adamant.

"We didn't do anything," I told her with a shrug. "Your daughter bailed him out."

"But we had no idea where he was, and now we don't have to wait to hear from either of them. We can call and find out what's going on."

"We can help," Colin said.

Linda turned to me. "Ian says that you have plans tomorrow, but if anything changes, please come by and—"

"You should come by our place," I said before my brain kicked in. "We have tons of friends coming by, so please feel free. We're gonna have people in and out all day—it's like a Thanksgiving open house." I smiled at them. "We'd love to have you."

"I'll be stuck home cooking all day, but—"

"I'll be by," Colin said, taking hold of Ian's shoulder. "I wouldn't miss it."

Linda inhaled sharply. "What am I thinking? Things are going to be strange this year and—I'll be by as well," she finished, putting a hand on Ian's cheek and patting it gently.

If looks could kill, the one Ian shot me should have dropped me dead where I stood.

"HAVE YOU lost your fuckin' mind?" he railed as we walked downstairs to the garage together.

"It was the right thing to do."

"My father?" He was incredulous. "Are you serious?"

"Lighten up, Doyle," I taunted, leading him toward the car.

When we got closer, his eyes widened, and he stopped moving like he'd stepped in front of a firing squad. He lifted his hand and gestured wildly.

I snickered because, God, it was just too good.

"The fuck is that?" He asked, clearly horrified.

I spread my arms wide. "That, my friend, is a 1988 Volkswagen Cabriolet convertible. In carnation pink."

"The hell you say!" he roared.

There was no way not to laugh. "You're gonna look badass driving this, man."

"The hell I will!"

"It's either this or the 1966 Dodge Rambler, and at least the Cabriolet will hit eighty."

"No, no, no, no," he lamented. "How the hell did this happen?"

"Well, you know how normally one of us runs a diversion upstairs and the other one comes down and picks the best car?"

"Yeah?"

"I had no partner, so you get what you get."

"So you're saying this is my fault?"

"You wanna drive?" I said instead of answering.

"Shit."

He had to drive. He was compelled. He was a control freak, and letting me navigate us around Chicago was never going to be possible.

"There's no iPod jack in here," he complained loudly from the interior before I got in.

I was *really* so glad he was home.

CHAPTER 16

IAN AND I met Aruna and Janet at Lou Malnati's over on State because it was close to work and Janet was craving it so bad she told me she was going to die.

When we got there, I saw Janet's smile quiver just a bit when she saw Ian, but she recovered quickly. Apparently Aruna neglected to tell her Ian was home.

When I hugged her, she burst into tears and clung tight.

"We'll stay up all night and snuggle on the couch, pet, I promise."

She squeezed me tighter, burying her face in the side of my neck, and I simply held on and rubbed her back and told her how much I loved and adored her. It was easy to say nice things to my girl since they were all true.

In the booth she did a really sweet thing and reached out for Ian. He took her hand quickly and then kissed it before holding on. She went a little melty right there.

"So where's Ned?" Ian asked.

Her gaze shifted to the ceiling. "It's so cute in here, don't you think?"

Ian glanced at me. I shrugged.

Aruna mouthed "MIA" and pointed at Janet.

"He's gonna kill me," I assured her.

"Oh, he will not, and geez, Miro, don't be so dramatic. Ned just hates that," she said irritably, letting me know exactly how Ned had sounded when he was talking to her. "I mean, heaven fucking forbid his pregnant wife gets a bit emotional!"

"He's just learning to navigate the hormones," Aruna commented. "Liam had a learning curve too."

Janet passed judgment. "Liam's a saint. My husband is an ass who cares more about being with his family for the holidays than being with me."

I sighed deeply as I carded my fingers through my hair. "Tell me he's not expecting you to show up in Alexandria tonight."

"He's not expecting me to show up in Alexandria tonight." The dazzling smile I got made it even worse.

"He's gonna murder me."

"We're talking about Ned," Janet said with a contentious sneer.

"You're not being nice."

"Like I—"

"Shut up," Aruna commanded as she read something on her phone.

"That's not very nice," I said, trying playfully to swipe it out of her hands.

"Stop—oh my God," she snapped, her hands shaking as she shoved the phone at Ian. "Did you know?"

I leaned sideways to see what had her all in a twist, and there was Craig Hartley grinning back at me. The words "escaped from federal custody" and "manhunt" were especially noticeable in the headline.

"Yeah, I know," Ian told her, reaching for her hand and reclaiming Janet's at the same time. "And I promise you both that it's gonna be okay."

Neither woman was looking at me. Ian had them riveted as they each grabbed a hand tight and caught their breath.

"Everything's fine," he promised, nodding as he spoke, and after a second, Aruna was nodding too, along with Janet, mirroring Ian. "The office is on it, every law enforcement agency you can think of is involved, and Miro will not get hurt."

They were bespelled, neither of them could look away.

"I love him, yeah?"

More nodding in agreement.

"You guys know I do."

And again.

"I couldn't—I mean, he's my life, so… what would I do without him?"

My chest hurt with all the honesty. He loved me and he was telling my friends, the people closest to me in the world. I was stunned that he would be so open with them and even more overwhelmed that he didn't seem to care in the least where we were. For a man who so hated any public display of affection, he was being awfully touchy-feely at the moment.

"You have to know I'd protect him with my life."

Both sets of dear sweet eyes welled up with tears at the same time. I figured Janet would, she was hormonal after all, but Aruna was a tough cookie.

"I've got this, all right?"

The final round of nodding and he gave both hands a final squeeze before turning to me.

"I knew you loved me," I sighed.

"You're such an ass."

Not what I was expecting. "But you just said you—"

"Shut up."

I turned to my friends.

"How dare you not let me know about Hartley," Aruna admonished.

"That's terrible to make us worry," Janet joined in.

"I—"

"Thank God Ian is here," Aruna said, smiling at him.

"Yes, thank goodness," Janet agreed, also lavishing him with a huge smile.

I threw up my hands in defeat.

IAN CALLED Kage after we finished lunch, having gorged on deep-dish pizza—spinach for me and Aruna, sausage for Ian and Janet—and asked if there were uniformed patrolman in front of our house in Lincoln Park. I was surprised when Kage answered that there were FBI agents there actually because Hartley had "gotten lost" on their watch and they were taking it as a personal affront. If Hartley didn't make a move on me in a few weeks, priorities would be reevaluated. But at the moment, that's who was guarding our Greystone.

I knew Ian's glare was supposed to be scary, was supposed to shame me into being careful, not taking any chances, and staying inside, but all it managed to do was make me hot. All that bristling, simmering anger furrowing his brows, darkening his eyes, and making him growl and snap needed an outlet, and I was ready to provide.

Once we got home at the end of the day, I followed Ian upstairs and shoved him down on the bed.

"No, I'm pissed at you," he snarled, rolling over fast but not quite making it before I came down on top of him. "Get off me."

"Oh, come on," I entreated, kissing him softly, chastely, before sucking his bottom lip into my mouth. "You don't want me?"

I wiggled on top of him, pressing my ass to the rise in his dress pants before I rubbed my groin over the washboard abs I could feel the bumps of through his shirt.

"What if Hartley shows up? What if he takes you again?"

"He'd never come for me in a million years," I stated, absolutely certain I was right. I loved the feel of his thickening cock under me and him tightening his hands on my ass. "But I'll come for you."

"It's not funny."

"No," I agreed, moving back and forth, writhing, needing him before we were invaded by some of my favorite people on the planet. "Not funny."

"Stand up."

I did as ordered, and he turned over like he was boneless, found the lube in the riot of blankets since we hadn't made the bed that morning, and then sat up and got his belt open and shoved his briefs and pants to his ankles. He snapped open the cap, dribbled lube on the flared head of his cock, and then ordered me to get naked.

"Shouldn't I leave my shirt and tie on in case someone shows up at the door?" I asked playfully, baiting him.

"No. I wanna see you," he said. His voice was flat and hard and left no room for argument. "Do what I say. Take off your clothes and get in my lap."

Oh... God.

It was like a switch had been flipped and I had a different man on my hands, one who wanted to claim what was his.

"Did you hear me?"

I huffed out a breath as pure liquid need washed through me.

"Miro?"

"Yes," I rasped because Ian all possessive and dominant was enough to bring my cock to full, drooling attention in moments. I liked to be the one to hold him down and give directions, but it was a big fat turn-on to hear him issuing demands.

"Yes, what?"

"Yes, sir."

"Good."

Moving quickly, I toed off my dark-brown Prada wingtips and then tore everything else off as fast as I could. Once I was stripped bare, I stood there a moment, taking in the decadent sight of him just sitting there, stroking his own length.

"I will take care of you, do you understand?"

"Yes."

"In every way."

I couldn't speak. My words deserted me in the face of his obvious need to protect and reassure himself that I was there and whole.

"Come here."

I lunged at him, but he stopped me, slowed me with a gentle hand on my hip, and carefully guided me down into his lap so I was straddling his hips.

"Take me in."

The words, his words, swept everything else from my mind. Gone was worry or fear, gone was Hartley and the military, babies and any other plans. There was only me sinking down over him, the slide and the burn, feeling every inch as he filled and stretched me, riding the wave of arousal as it crested and receded, loving his hands sliding over my back, up my sides and down, touching, smoothing, before he took my face in them and pulled me close for a kiss.

He made love to me with his mouth, with his tongue, and I in turn rode him, lifting and lowering, impaling myself over and over, rocking into him until he was buried to the hilt one second and almost free the next.

"Oh God, you feel good," he said thickly, sounding drunk as I grabbed hold of his shoulders so I could lever down harder, deeper, and faster. "Fuck yourself on my dick."

In minutes I no longer cared who saw us or who came in. There was only Ian moving inside of me and working my cock with one hand as he anchored me to him with the other. He'd leave bruises, as tight as he was holding on, and between what I could feel in my heart and the erotic counterpoint of my muscles greedily fisting around him, I climaxed seconds later in a rush of euphoria that for a split second was blinding.

He cupped my face in his hands again and kissed me like I was food, air, all of it, voracious in his attention, sucking on my tongue so I couldn't pull away. He reached for my legs and wrapped them around his hips, toppling me onto my back fast and easy.

He rolled forward, draped my legs over his arms, and pounded down into me, the pumping lasting only seconds before his body tightened and he came.

"I'll take care of you," he promised as he released my legs and found my mouth, kissing me deeply, at the same time shoving both hands under my ass, kneading, squeezing, not ready to let me go. "Always."

I stared up at him, at the man I loved.

"Do you understand?"

"Yes."

"Good," he whispered before he kissed me and then hugged me. Tight.

Ian was a good hugger, the best, because he always gave me his whole heart when he did it. I could always feel his body settle, and breathe.

"What was that?" he asked abruptly, breaking the spell.

"I don't hear—" But there was suddenly the jingle of keys in the lock on the front door. "Oh crap!"

Ian slid gently from my body and kissed me one last time.

"Are you guys here?" Liam bellowed as he came through the door. He'd been watching Chickie all day, and by the sound of it, had brought him back.

I dived down on the side of the bed as Ian popped up and leaned over the railing.

"You guys need to learn to knock," he yelled down from the loft.

"And your boyfriend needs to learn not to take what isn't his."

"I'm sorry?" I said, offended as I stood, wrapped up in a sheet from the bed, and moved over next to Ian so I could stare down at him.

Unfortunately, Janet was there, too, as was Aruna, carrying Sajani, and both women were looking up at me with wide eyes, judgment all over their faces.

"What?" I barked at them. "This is *my* house."

"And you're allowed to get your freak on whenever you like," Aruna assured me as Sajani called my name and waved. "But how pervy do you feel right now?" she asked as Sajani started waving at Ian too.

I groaned.

"I feel like a god," Ian announced, as Janet snickered, Liam rolled his eyes and went to put groceries down in the kitchen, and Chickie tore up the stairs to us.

Aruna nodded. "Good for you, Irish," she said, giving him the thumbs-up.

He gave her his killer grin, and I left to change as Chickie darted by me on his way to Ian.

"Get off the bed!" The all-powerful god ordered his dog to absolutely no avail.

I TRIED to give Aruna cash for the groceries, but she fought me, as usual, and even when I shoved the money in Liam's back pocket, she took it out.

"I feel like a stripper," he said.

"I could see that," I told him.

"Over my dead body," Aruna assured me.

"Take the money," I ordered her.

One eyebrow lifted and I gave up. "I'm putting it in Sajani's college fund."

"Now that is a good idea," she conceded as she began doing the prep, issuing orders to Liam and Ian as I helped with the chopping and cutting, and Janet sat on a bar stool in the kitchen and ate ranch dip and veggies.

Every time Liam got close to me, Aruna gave him another task.

"But I have something to say to Miro," he growled.

"*After* you go through their fridge and make room for everything I'm going to be putting in there, as well as figuring out the best place to put the cooler for the drinks, you can."

He wasn't happy and nearly yanked the fridge's door off the hinges when he opened it. I glanced at Aruna, who rolled her eyes and shrugged. Clearly whatever it was, was not life or death.

Ian eventually took Sajani and Chickie for a walk, and as soon as the door closed, Liam, who was pacing back and forth in the living room, started in on me.

"You can't just keep them. They're not yours anymore!"

I glanced over at Aruna. "What is he talking about?"

"I have no earthly idea," she said, feeding me a spoonful of the green curry she made a few days ago and brought for us to eat.

"They all love you—Aruna, Janet, Min, Catherine—and come at a moment's notice when you call. Do you have any idea what I had to threaten Aruna with when you were in that hospital in Phoenix? She was buying herself a plane ticket when I told her that I'd tie her to the bed if she tried to leave."

"Kinky," I teased.

"Bowchickabowmow," Aruna said, turning to give Liam an exaggerated wink.

He threw up his hands, which looked funny on the huge mountain of muscle that he was. "You need to cut the cord, Miro! These women are your family, yes, but they have other families now too!"

Janet slid off the stool and walked over to me, leaning in and wrapping her arms around my waist. "I'm so glad I can come move in with you and Ian once the baby's born."

I looked down at her, completely lost. "I'm sorry, what?"

"I asked Ian. He said I could. He loves Sajani, and he said he'd love another little one around here as long as I was part of the package."

It was really sweet of the love of my life to say that to Janet. He obviously loved me and so would make room in his life for my dearest friends. Yes, it was really very sweet, but no way in hell was that actually going to happen.

"Awww," Aruna cooed, making a face at me. "He loves my little muffin."

I hugged Janet tight and looked over at Liam, who muttered, "I hate you."

I smirked at him as his phone rang and he answered.

"What kind of cranberry salad should I make?" Aruna asked me.

"Don't you just open a can?"

"Heathen," she labeled me.

"Oh," Liam said loudly, dramatically, walking into the kitchen with his phone to his ear, "actually, why, yes, yes she is, Ned. Let me put you on speaker." He held it in his hand, smiling triumphantly as he stepped into the center of all of us. "Go ahead."

"Janet Eugenia Powell, how dare you go out of town and not tell me!"

"Eugenia?" Liam asked.

"She doesn't like it," I told him.

"She kinda hates it," Aruna echoed me.

Janet shot him a look that was meant to kill.

"Miro, you selfish piece of crap!" Ned shouted on the other end of the line.

"What?" I retorted, surprised that he actually sounded mad. "I didn't do anything."

"Yes you did! You always do!"

Everyone was crazy except me and Ian.

"Did you even think for one second of telling her not to get on the plane? Did you think, oh, she's pregnant; this Thanksgiving she'll be pregnant, and won't that be awesome for her to spend time with her family on—"

"I'm with my family!" she shrieked, pulling free of me as she went to stand over Liam's phone so she could scream directly into it even as the big man began slowly leaning away. "And that's the part you never get! We always do everything with *your* family, every goddamn holiday we're with *them*, but what about *my* family? When do I get to come here and see them? When is it my year?"

"Janet—"

"Just because they're not related to me by blood doesn't make them any less important to me or vital to be around, and that's the part you refuse to understand!"

"Janet—"

"You think when my mother died that I became an orphan, but just because Miro and I don't have any blood relatives doesn't mean we don't belong to a motherfucking family!"

We were all silent and nobody moved.

"So yes, I know you don't get it, and neither do Liam or Eriq or that new guy Min's dating—" She turned to look at Aruna. "What does he do, again?"

"Some kind of performance art where he drinks coffee and looks at you," Aruna explained. "And draws at the same time."

"How is that different from college?" I asked Aruna.

She shrugged.

"Janet," Ned tried again. "I just—"

"I'll be home on Sunday, and we can talk and figure out what to do for Christmas and New Year's this year. If you want to stay there, then—"

"No!" he yelled. "I love you, and I'm sorry I was a dick about your hormones. I was an insensitive asshole because I've never been through this, either. We're both just finding our way. But in my defense, I'm used to number-cruncher girl, and emotional passion girl threw me for a loop."

We could all hear the kitchen clock ticking on the wall. It was a good clock, I liked it. I'd picked it out when the old one died. It was stainless steel, very retro 1950s chic.

"You thought I was passionate?" she asked tentatively, and by the way her voice dipped, got silvery and sweet, it was more than clear that she loved the rest of us, but Ned was her endgame.

"Yes, darling, very."

"Do you miss me?"

"Terribly."

Her sigh was loud.

"I'll be there tomorrow," he told her. "And we're staying with Aruna and Liam; they at least have a guest room."

"Hey," I growled.

"And I'm going to kick the crap out of you when I see you," he warned me.

"If you can get through the Green Beret to me, more power to you."

There was a moment of silence.

"Ian's a Green Beret?"

I grunted.

"Huh."

"Yeah, huh."

"Well, Liam will help me."

"Have you met Ian?" Liam asked.

Ned cleared his throat. "I'll be there in the morning, and God help you if my flight's delayed."

I really hoped he'd have clear skies. "I'll see ya tomorrow."

"I need you all to go away so I can speak to my wife."

Liam took it off speaker, and Janet took his phone and walked into the living room, curling up on one end of my couch.

"He loves her," Aruna said, hand over her heart. "It's sweet."

"Do I get to eat any curry?" Liam asked her as she made me a plate and added the dill rice I loved that she'd made special.

"I don't know, are you sure you want it?" she asked sharply. "Your mother didn't."

"For crissakes, woman, that's not what she said."

"Oh?"

I wanted to hear the explanation as well.

He huffed out a breath in exasperation. "She said since you were going to make the Indian dishes, that she would make the traditional ones so you didn't have so much to do."

She nodded slowly. "Because I can't do both. Because it was finally my year to host, and now she's going to horn in and cook."

"No, she was just trying to help because you work, plus you take care of Sajani."

"She didn't ask Karrie if she needed help last year, and Karrie has two kids, Liam, *two*, plus she's a full-time graphic artist, so…. Where's the disconnect here?"

"Maybe Karrie wanted help too."

"She did, and she asked me, not your mother! When it's finally your turn to have the whole Duffy clan over, you don't want to mess it up! But your mother is just waiting for us to crash and burn because then this experiment will be over, and she'll go back to hosting all the holidays at her house."

"Well, sweetie, she is the matriarch of the fam—"

"Who complained every year for years that it was so much work, and so we all agreed to the rotating holidays, and now this year, when it's finally my turn, she needs to help me because my dishes are too ethnic?"

He made a noise of pure disgust. "That's not what she said!"

"She hates me."

"Oh, she does not."

"The acid that drips from her voice when she speaks to me could etch diamonds," she said flatly.

I lost it.

"Oh God," her husband lamented.

"You know what, you can go over there and eat with your family, but Sajani stays with me. We'll be here eating with *my* family."

"We went to see your family in Dallas last year."

"Well, I'm lucky I have family there too. I have you, Sajani, Miro, and Ian here, and that way I'm never alone, even if I never lay eyes on your mother again."

His smile was defeated and gentle at the same time. "You realize you counted me in with our kid and the boys, right?"

She glared at him. "Of course I did. You belong to me. Why wouldn't I include you?"

He moved then, fast, and grabbed her, scooping her up off her feet in the princess carry, and she wrapped her arms around his neck and leaned in and kissed him.

It was not a PG kiss, and when she leaned back to smile at him, I saw that he was flushed.

"I'm still not going over there, even if you sex me up."

I choked on my curry.

Liam groaned.

And Aruna looked very pleased with herself.

When Ian and Sajani and Chickie came home right before the sky opened up and dumped down rain, Ian asked what he'd missed.

"Not too much," Aruna assured him, swapping him a plate of food for her daughter. "Eat something. You're too thin."

He glanced at me.

"Just eat."

After I fed Chickie, I got a call from Barrett. I let it go to voice mail, as well as the other four.

"Oh shit," Aruna announced. "I need marshmallows. Crap!"

Sometimes it was a domino effect. Ian needed beer, and Liam was more than ready to go with him to get that. Janet wanted some things from the store because now Ned was coming, and there was a grape salad that was his favorite thing in the world. But Chickie had eaten, so he had to take his constitutional.

"I'll stay here," I told everyone.

No one moved.

"Oh, for fuck's sake, you know I'll be fine."

But no one was moving, especially Ian, who crossed his arms as he looked at me.

"Oh come on."

He didn't move an iota.

"May I remind you that there are two FBI agents on our front curb."

"Aren't they the ones that lost Hartley to begin with?" Aruna asked.

Ian tipped his head at her like yeah, that.

It was stupid, but the idea of Ian and Liam walking around together, choosing beer, made me very happy. I wanted the man I loved to bond with the man Aruna loved because, clearly, as evidenced earlier, he was getting close to the girls, and I wanted the same with their significant others. So Ian doing something without me or Aruna, with just Liam, I wanted that. I wanted to build a network of friends, and I could be honest: the more Ian liked everyone, the more rock solid the foundation of our life became.

But at the moment, he wasn't going anywhere.

"I'll be fine," I assured him.

He shook his head.

And then my hip was bumped as a loud dog yawn caught my attention. There was Chickie beside me, sitting, his head coming to my waist.

I motioned to the dog, because, really, there was no arguing with 150 pounds of werewolf. Chickie's protective instincts had been proven time and time again.

Ian gave in because it made sense. "Yeah, all right." No one was stupid enough to try to get past Chickie into the house. That was simply suicidal, and Hartley had never been labeled that.

As I herded everyone out, Ian charged over and gave me a scorching kiss good-bye. When I had to grab for the counter, I got a world-class smirk. He was so proud of himself and of his power over me. I liked seeing him like that—smugly confident. It was very sexy.

Once I was alone, I let Chickie out, got the towel ready for him when he came back in, and started washing dishes. When I heard a soft knock on the back door, I turned and saw Barrett there, and with the lighting in the background, he was bright, outlined for a moment, and then he was in shadow again. I trotted over and opened up slowly.

"Hey," he greeted me softly. "Can I talk to you?"

I shook my head. "I don't know that we have that much to say."

"No, I think we do."

"Listen, Barrett, I—"

"Miro, I want you to meet my old friend from New Jersey."

I began to say no when another man came up behind him, wet like Barrett was, about his same height, but nowhere near as handsome. He was thicker, with lots of muscle on him. What riveted me, though, was not his countenance, but the Walther P22 he had in his hand that was pointed right at me.

"I need a word," the man said coldly.

"Who the fuck are you, and what're you doing here?"

"I'm Eamon Lochlyn, Kerry's older brother."

Of course he was.

CHAPTER 17

WHEN HAD I become such a crappy judge of character?

"Don't blame yourself, Miro," Barrett said kindly. "There was no way for you to know about us. Nobody did."

"What do you want?" I asked Lochlyn.

He looked at me oddly. "I would think by now, after the others, that that would be self-explanatory. Clearly, I want to kill Ian Doyle for what he did to my brother."

"And what was that?"

"He and the others drove him out of the Army, and my parents drove him to suicide because they told him he was a failure and not a real man because he couldn't be a soldier."

"Your parents are dead, I understand."

"Well, they are now."

When you're an orphan, you dream of having parents. I always had. To imagine anyone hurting theirs was beyond me and made my heart hurt. "You killed your own parents?"

He cleared his throat. "No. Barrett did the honors there."

I glanced over at the man who I thought had been my friend. We'd been to hockey games together, had dinners and bowled. And all that time, I missed who he really was. "You killed people?"

He nodded.

Lochlyn snapped his fingers to get my attention.

"So as I said, I want to kill Ian Doyle, but he's better trained then the others—the man's Special Forces, after all—so getting the drop on him is damn near impossible."

I would have agreed, but I was listening, not talking.

"So when he comes back, I'm going to point the gun at you, have him follow us outside, and then I'm going to shoot him dead."

My stomach threatened to empty, but I took several deep breaths in rapid succession.

"And I know what you're thinking right about now," he informed me. "Those men who are supposed to be watching the house will protect me. But unfortunately they've both died very recently."

"Those were FBI agents; you'll get the needle for that."

"I don't think you have to worry about what's going to happen to me," Lochlyn said with a smile. "Because about a second after I put a bullet in Ian Doyle's head, I'm going to shoot you and everyone else who walks through the door with him."

I would put money on Ian not getting shot, and he was trained to not negotiate for hostages because nine times out of ten, the hostage died too.

Ian would be all right.

It was the girls.

It was Liam and Sajani.

They would panic, and Lochlyn would start with shooting Liam and work his way down to that beautiful little baby girl.

I could never allow that.

Charging forward, I plowed into Lochlyn, catching him off balance, spinning him around and slamming him down onto my reclaimed barn wood floor. It was solid, I knew it was, and as hard as his head hit, he wasn't getting back up.

The gun went skittering across the floor, and I scrambled off Lochlyn's prone body to grab for the grip, but Barrett wasn't tangled up, and he ran.

He reached the gun first and aimed it at me. "The hell was that?" he shouted, furious and scared at the same time.

"People never expect you to rush them from a fixed position, so they let their guard down," I informed him. "It's a thing they teach you."

"It's a gamble."

"It is, but it was worth it."

"How so?"

"There's only one of you now, and I can yell out for Ian before anyone else gets in here. I may die, but Ian's safe."

"Eamon!" he yelled.

"He's out," I informed him. "He ain't getting up any time soon."

"Shit," he said angrily, pointing the gun center mass on me. "What the hell was he thinking? He had no respect for the fact that you're a marshal."

"And you do?"

"Of course I do," he admitted. "Jesus, Miro, I'm completely enamored of you."

"And yet"—I tipped my head, indicating Lochlyn—"you're in love with a crazy man."

"What? No, you've got it all wrong. I loved Kerry. Kerry was the one I wanted, but he came back from Afghanistan all messed up, and then he said he couldn't be with me anymore because he was no longer a soldier."

"That makes no sense."

"I know, but he believed that being a soldier made the gay all right, but without the military… it wasn't enough. He wasn't a real man, then."

As horrible as that was, I had a terrible fear that Ian thought the same thing. If he wasn't a Green Beret anymore, if the Army was no longer part of his life, was he still a man? Was Ian figuring out who he was going to be?

"Everyone turned their back on Kerry, and I tried to be everything to him, I wanted to be, but his parents hurt him too deeply, and so I made sure they paid, and Eamon promised me he'd make sure all the soldiers did too."

"It was a division of priorities."

"Yes," he agreed. "And now you—oh *shit*."

Turning, I saw what Barrett did.

I'd forgotten all about him, too caught up in the life-and-death struggle in the kitchen. But Chickie had come in through his doggie door, dripping water after he'd been outside running around like a dork because I wasn't there to call him in.

"Keep him still, Miro," he warned.

Chickie was unsure, I could tell. His head was down, his ears were laid back, and that was because of me. I was acting weird; I wasn't moving or yelling at him or reaching for the towel to dry him. None of that was normal, so he looked from me to Barrett and back again, deciding, checking, waiting for a sign from me that wasn't forthcoming.

"I'm not kidding. He needs to stay still."

"Stay, Chick," I commanded, terrified he wasn't going to listen to me. It was touch and go at best on most days. Chickie was better at following Aruna's orders than mine.

Hard to say what it was that gave the dog pause. It could have been the timbre of my voice, the breathiness or the quaver of fear. Perhaps it was the fact that I didn't call him to me, but whatever it was, he took a step forward.

"I'll kill him."

"No, please," I begged, and I heard the catch then, the pleading in the air between the words.

"Then send him out."

"Chickie, out," I commanded, my voice rising in fear for him, not me, swallowing because my mouth was dry.

He took another step toward me.

"Out," I shouted, and that was it.

He turned and rushed Barrett, snarling, all killing stroke, ready to defend me.

I heard the shot, saw Chickie get thrown left and slam into the bookshelf between the back door and the tiny hallway. There wasn't a lot of blood, but what there was, on his head below his right ear, told me he was dead by the time he hit the ground in a crumpled heap.

The sound that came out of me, one of agony and regret, was loud in my head.

I never thought when Ian first decided to adopt Chickie after the raid we'd been on that day, that I would ever feel like I did at this moment. I couldn't breathe, and I thought, *I was going to take him with me to do this and this*, and it all rushed through my mind, and then boom…. Heart stopped. How did people ever live through losing someone they loved, if the stupid dog could make everything hurt this much?

I took one shuffling step forward.

"Don't fuckin' move."

Lifting my gaze to Barrett, I realized I could barely see him through my swimming eyes.

"I'm going to kill you now, Miro, and put you right here on the floor next to the dog."

I shivered, but not for me. It was for Chickie Baby, who I would miss even in these last few seconds.

"It's a shame about the dog. I really liked him."

I couldn't tell that from how lifeless he'd left him.

"Now Ian will suffer like Kerry did."

What was I supposed to say? He already knew Ian loved me, loved Chickie too. That was the whole point of him and Lochlyn doing all this.

"I really wanted to fuck you."

Like anybody cheated on the love of their life.

"I'll make sure to comfort Ian when I blame all this on Eamon and say I got here too late to save you or Chickie."

"Go to hell," I spat out.

"You first," he said, lifting the gun.

"Well, now, this is embarrassing."

We both froze, and then I looked toward the back door for the second time that night, and there, with a gun in his hand, was the last person on the planet I thought I'd see.

"Who the hell are you?" Barrett barked at the intruder.

"Oh, I'm Dr. Craig Hartley," he said in the velvety tone people always mentioned whenever they spoke of him. It was always on the Internet or in the paper about how refined he sounded, how rich and silky his voice was. "And you have something of mine."

I honestly had never had reason to use the saying, "out of the frying pan and into the fire"—until now. It was like when you woke up from a nightmare only to find yourself in another, and then when you came to the second time, only then did you realize how fucked up dreams could be.

I was about to be killed in cold blood, only to have it stopped by a man who wanted to torture and maim me before *he* too ended my life. It was a mindfuck.

Barrett glanced at me and then back at the immaculately dressed doctor—in his three-piece herringbone tweed suit under a chocolate-brown wool overcoat, five layers in all with a pocket square—who was at the moment a wanted fugitive.

"And what's that?"

"Well, Marshal Jones here, of course," Hartley replied drolly. "He most assuredly belongs to me, and before you even have time to turn that gun on me, I'll shoot you with mine."

Barrett stared wide-eyed at him.

"You don't believe me, and us without the time for you to google me," Hartley mused, brows furrowing in consternation before he lifted them and his face brightened. "Oh, I know."

Without a flicker of hesitation, he put four bullets in Eamon Lochlyn, ending his war on the men left in Ian's old unit.

Barrett screamed, and Hartley lifted his hand to quiet him.

"Now," he exhaled, "let me tell you a little about my gun."

I saw the fear and horror cross Barrett's features then as he regarded Hartley, who'd just killed someone but was preternaturally calm. Really, it was unnerving.

"What I have here is a .50-caliber Titanium Gold self-loading Desert Eagle that has a six-inch barrel and holds seven rounds. It is, I'm told, one of, if not *the* most powerful handguns in the world, and, as you can see, makes quite a mess."

With a .50 caliber bullet, no way it wouldn't.

"It was a gift."

"From Aranda?" I offered because Hartley I knew, Barrett I certainly didn't. Of the two of them—and it was crazy, but *still*—I'd rather the doctor have the power. Hartley didn't give a damn about Ian or the girls or anyone else but me. Barrett was the only one in the room who would hurt people I loved.

"Oh, you heard about that?"

I nodded, swallowing quickly, not wanting to retch, so afraid that I would and then Hartley would know how terrified I was. It wasn't that he would kill me—that wasn't my fear—the horror came from imagining that he'd make me leave with him and then we'd be alone. I never wanted to be alone with him again. "I did," I managed to get out.

"It's always good to have friends."

"It is," I agreed.

We were just talking like we always did, and it would probably have been weird to other people, I was sure, but I was used to the rambling. Barrett was not, and he was very frightened. It was all over his face.

"I don't care who the hell you—"

"I'm not to be trifled with," Hartley instructed icily. "I'll shoot you dead where you stand if you don't drop the gun into the sink on the count of three, and take five steps back."

"No, I—"

"One."

"I can't just let—"

"Two."

Barrett let the gun slip from his right hand into the stainless-steel sink and took the requisite steps away.

"Oh, you're lovely, bravo," Hartley praised before he walked over to me, reached out, and put a hand on my cheek. The muzzle of his gun was pointed directly at my heart. "Why are you crying?"

I almost threw up right there. My stomach twisted, lurched, but I inhaled through my nose sharply, and when I noticed he was wearing leather gloves, I fixated on that and the fact that his skin wasn't on mine, and calmed.

"Miro?"

I dared a glance at Chickie.

"Oh dear," he tsked, walking over quickly, kneeling down, and touching Chickie's neck. His eyebrows lifted, and then he touched Chickie's head. After a moment he put his glove in his mouth, bit down on the tip of his index finger gently—didn't want to crease the leather—so he could slide his hand out of it before examining my dog's skull with his fingers again. It was nuts that I even noticed all that, but I did, with *him*. Always. It was like I studied him so I'd know what he'd do in every situation, and so I never looked away when he was in front of me. Ever. "All right, so he's unconscious, the poor lamb, but not dead."

I gasped and he gave me a smile. "Grab a few dishtowels and tie a tourniquet to stem the bleeding. It's clotting already, but there should be pressure."

"You're sure he's not dead?"

"I'm sorry, when did you become a doctor?" he inquired gently.

"He shot him," I stated, rushing to the towel drawer to do exactly as he told me.

"Well, I didn't think you did it, dear."

"He'll be all right, you think?" And of course it was beyond insane that I was asking Hartley and praying he was right at the same time.

"Have I ever, in our association, even once, lied to you?"

No, he hadn't.

The look on his face, patronizing, even bored, as he awaited my reply, made the truth even more obvious.

I shook my head.

"Well, there, you see? Your dog has a bullet wedged in his skull that will need to be extracted, and the piece where the bone is cracked might have to be replaced by a metal plate."

"But for sure he'll live?"

"It's going to be expensive. Are you prepared to do all that for a dog?"

"Oh yes."

"Well, then," he sighed, smiling at me. "Hurry and wrap up his head."

I moved fast and used three towels, one folded over Chickie's wound, and the other two tied around his head like someone with a toothache in those old cartoons.

"Why do you give a crap about a dog," Barrett choked out, furious. "You'll kill me, but not a fuckin' pet?"

He glared at Barrett. "I don't kill children or pets. My God, what do you think I am?" Hartley asked, horrified.

"Well, you're clearly insane."

Hartley exhaled sharply. "Listen, when I used to watch television, I loved anything about crime, but I could never bring myself to watch things like *Law and Order*, the SVU one, if it was about kids. That kind of thing makes me ill. I know everyone is someone's little boy or little girl, but once you're over twenty-five, the choices you make are your own. If you wind up in the wrong place at the wrong time, it's on you. But children and animals, that's ridiculous. Hurting them is obscene."

Barrett looked at me. "And him?"

"Miro belongs to me," he explained to Barrett. "He saved my life, and—oh my God," he said, turning to me. "I think we're even now, aren't we?"

I nodded, scared and relieved at the same time. "We are."

"And now I can kill you," he said happily, his voice full of relief and glee as he looked back at Barrett. "How fortuitous that you came to be here."

"So you're going to shoot him?"

Hartley nearly choked, and it took a couple of moments for him to recover. "Shoot him? I'm sorry; did you just ask me if I was going to shoot him?"

"Yes."

"Never."

"You're going to let him go?"

"Oh heavens, no. I came to pick him up and take him with me to Paris, where I plan to torture him at my leisure until he dies from his injuries."

And even though I had a moment of shock, of cold deep-down fear, at least I knew his plan. He was not, as I always assumed, about to walk up behind me on the street and shoot me in the head. It wasn't what he wanted. His heart's desire was me bleeding out slowly so he could watch every drop of life leave my body. Was it sick? Hell yes. But it would not be quick, so at the moment, I was far safer than Barrett.

"How are you getting him on a plane?"

"I have help."

Hartley normally did.

"I don't understand."

"I want to bite him until he bleeds and chew his flesh in my mouth."

Barrett's face, the terror on it, was sort of comical considering he himself had planned to kill me. "You're a cannibal."

"No, no, no. I'm not some fictional character who eats livers with beans. I'm not going to cook him and use him in lasagna or such. I just want to eat some of his flesh, drive knives and perhaps skewers of some kind into his back, and I think… suck his cock."

Barrett's mouth fell open.

I inhaled through my nose again. "Since when?"

He regarded me coolly, tipping his head to the side. "The cocksucking, you mean?"

"Yeah."

"It happened during my stay at the supermax. There was nothing to do all day but think, and as you know, you're the only thing that can fully occupy my thoughts from morning to night."

I concentrated on breathing because I really didn't want to hyperventilate.

"And you look terrible, by the way," he commented, "but it's not surprising."

"Why's that?"

"Well, I've been dreaming about you, as usual, and everyone knows that when you can't sleep at night, it's because you're awake in someone else's dream."

Everything he said was always so matter-of-fact that sometimes I wondered if he was the sane one and maybe I was crazy.

"Or nightmare," he amended.

I nodded.

"I'll try and stop so you can get some rest."

"Thank you," I said weakly.

The two of us were quiet.

"That's nuts," Barrett chimed in, shattering the silence.

Hartley turned to him, his thick short blond hair, perfectly styled in a polished fade, catching the light when he turned. He looked like he belonged in a romance novel. "What is?"

"The ego on you. To think that you influence Miro's sleep in any way is just insane."

Hartley's lips pursed and I saw the condescending look he gave Barrett. "I think we all know who's ill here, don't we?"

"Me?"

"Well, yes, clearly you and your dead accomplice there."

"You're in his kitchen with a fancy handgun."

Hartley tsked again. "It's a Titanium Gold Desert Eagle, as I mentioned before, and you're the one who shot his dog." He opened his eyes wide and gave his head a quick shake, the "duh" totally implied. "I think it might have been Gandhi who said that the greatness of a nation and its moral progress can be judged by the way its animals are treated."

"Which has what to do with—"

"You just tried to kill a dog," Hartley reminded him, scowling in judgement. "You're a complete and utter barbarian."

"He was going to attack me!"

"Because you're in Miro's house," Hartley said implacably. "Of course he's going to attack you. That's only logical. It's like getting upset with a shark because it tries to eat you when you're swimming around in *its* ocean. That's madness to take personally."

Barrett glanced at me.

"Miro will agree with me. You'll get no support from that quarter."

"No, you won't," I said to Barrett as Hartley moved the gun so the muzzle bumped my abdomen, at the same time sliding his hand around the back of my neck.

"Are you aghast at being in agreement with me on anything?" he asked me.

"I am." I sighed, wondering if I was actually awake or if this was a really scary, really powerful, really vivid dream.

"Do tell me, what are your thoughts on me wanting to taste your cock?"

I coughed softly. "Don't you think that's more homicidal than sexual?"

"How so?"

"I think it's the idea of hurting me that's doing it for you."

"Yes, that's what I thought, but now, at night, in my bed, when I imagine you bleeding, with your back open, and me taking out your rib… I get an erection."

My stomach clenched but my voice remained steady. "I think you're mixing up your bloodlust with sex."

"Which is quite possible," Hartley admitted. "But I also think of you naked on that bare cot that I had you on last, and imagine lifting you to your knees and driving my penis into your ass."

I knew when he was talking, when we were communicating, that he was being thoughtful and so wouldn't act. The trick was to keep his mind working on things other than homicide. "With lube?" I asked, repulsed but knowing I had to give him more things to consider. "Or without?"

He lifted one eyebrow. "Oh, now, that's interesting, isn't it? Because that, too, penetration without any kind of lubrication, would cause bleeding, would it not?"

"It would."

"Oh, so you're probably right, then. The desires aren't really sexual, but are, in fact, a pathway to pain, which in the end would cause death."

"There you go," I said quietly, working to sound sedate, to regulate my breathing, in and out, trying to not make a mistake, instead remaining calm.

He tipped his head, smiling at me fondly. "You always see things so clearly."

"I try."

"*The fuck*?" Barrett roared. "Are you going to kill him or not?"

That was a mistake.

When he yelled, he startled Hartley, and because he did, because Hartley never, ever liked to be jolted or surprised, he let out a huff of air and then shot out Barrett's right kneecap.

Barrett's scream was deafening, as were the others after that.

"Do stop, or I'll do the same to your head," Hartley said, clearly exasperated. "I have several more rounds for the gun in my coat."

Not that he was out of bullets yet. I knew that, I was counting.

Barrett quit with difficulty, having to shove his fist in his mouth and bite down.

"Miro, do you have any more towels?"

"Upstairs in the linen closet," I answered, waiting for what he'd allow.

He bit his bottom lip. "Do be truthful now; is there a gun up there?"

"There are three: two of mine, one of Marshal Doyle's. But they're all in a gun safe."

"I really don't like the idea of the stairs. You could turn and push me, and you're stronger and better trained…. No, I'm sorry, I can't risk it. Use the man's belt, put it around his leg above the injury on his thigh, and tighten it until you see an ebb in the bleeding."

Diving toward Barrett, I pulled off my T-shirt, wadded it up, and shoved it against what was left of his knee, at the same time working open his belt and yanking it off him before winching it hard enough to make him cry out.

"Oh, there, see, that's excellent work," Hartley commended even as Barrett passed out. "We'll call the police on our way out, and people will be here shortly to save him and your dog."

"Are you sure?"

"Pardon?"

"I'm worried," I began, swallowing to steady my nerves, "that whoever comes will take care of Barrett but not Chickie, and then my dog'll die after you saved him."

He thought a moment. "It is possible. People might look at them both and make the wrong choice about who is the more important of the two."

"Yes."

"A quandary, yes." He slowly lowered the gun as he gave my words some thought, as we both heard sirens in the distance. Someone was on their way, probably from when Barrett fired the first round at Chickie.

"Do you hear that?" I asked.

"I do."

"That changes things, doesn't it?"

"A bit."

I stood up from where I was kneeling beside Barrett. "Tell me something."

"Anything."

"What'd you do with my rib?"

"What do you think I did with it?" he asked playfully.

"Did you eat it?"

He made a face. "Only to void it later, and have it parted from me? Are you mad?"

It hit me then, like I'd always known the answer. "You replaced your floating rib with mine."

His gaze was kind, almost loving, or what amounted to that, since it was him.

"Didn't you." I phrased it as a question, but it was a statement and we both knew it.

"I did," he said, grinning in that mad way of his. "Lovely gesture, don't you think? It hurt me too."

Which, to him, made us even.

The sirens were getting closer, but there was still a lot of time.

"So?" I prodded.

"I want you to come with me, but your dog…." He sighed.

He kidnapped me without a second thought the year before, but he had help. At the moment his help was elsewhere.

"You'll never get out of the city," I promised.

"Stop," he said dismissively. "We both know that's not true."

"I—"

"Oh, I forgot to ask after Detective Cochran. Do you happen to know where he is?"

"Why? Did you go see him?"

"I did, but only his wife and kids were home, so I didn't stay."

I didn't need to ask. I knew he left them as he found them. He only ever kidnapped one little girl, and that was only to force her mother to intercept me. He didn't hurt her; she'd been scared but rebounded well, as her mother had told me when she came by the office to thank me for her and her daughter's lives. She still checked in from time to time, and I was betting I would hear from her in the next couple of days now that the news had broken that Hartley was on the loose again. She'd be worried about me and I'd get a phone call.

"So?" Hartley prompted.

"Sorry, he and I got in a fight and it was his fault, so he was assigned to a task force somewhere in the southwest. If he wasn't home, I'm guessing he left already."

"I see. Well, I left him a note, anyway."

"Somewhere he could see it?"

"Oh, he can't miss it. I used his daughter's oil paint."

I was betting his wife would want to move to Japan.

"Miro," he whispered, taking a step closer, pressing the muzzle of the gun up against the inside of my thigh. "Come here and kiss me and let me see if I like it."

I had two thoughts in quick succession: One, he might kill me if I didn't. And two, he saved me and my dog from a guy I actually hated much more than him—Barrett had been my friend, I had trusted him. I'd never had such a bond with Hartley. He couldn't hurt me like Barrett had.

I grabbed at Hartley, took his face in my hands, leaned in and covered his mouth hard and fast, inhaling deeply, not wanting to breathe with him, done before he even responded. I tilted my head, exhaled sharply, and would have stepped back, but the gun muzzle bumped my hip as he turned it on me and slipped a hand around the back of my neck to pull me close.

"You should go," I said, refusing to meet his eyes, even as close as we were. That intimacy was reserved solely for Ian. "They'll shoot you on sight."

"Such care for my well-being," he mused before he leaned in and kissed me.

His tongue slipped between my lips, rubbing gently over mine as his hand fisted in my hair, holding me tight and still as his mouth took possession of me, fitting us together like long-lost puzzle pieces.

When I was a police detective, I'd once questioned a high-end call girl in a murder investigation, and because we were there late, I went out and got her good coffee and we'd talked about other things besides her dead drug-dealer boyfriend/pimp. She had told me that, much like in the movie *Pretty Woman*, kissing was actually much more intimate than fucking.

"You can fake intercourse," she told me. "You can fake an orgasm and everything else in bed, but with kissing... you can't. With kissing, you're right there, eye to eye, cheek to cheek, and if you don't feel anything, your hands don't automatically reach out to grab and hold. The opposite is true and you want to push away—get away."

I had listened and she'd smiled.

"You can't fake a kiss. If you don't want it, it's a dead thing, and there's only cold and that terrible awful fear in the pit of your stomach that the other person will know and feel your disregard." She had slipped her bird-boned hand around my wrist. "A kiss from a man you don't want is a disgusting press of flesh and spit and his taste on your tongue chills you to the bone. Never do it, darling. Only kiss men you love or at least want in your bed."

"Okay," I agreed. "I swear."

I'd kept my promise to that woman I'd never seen again. Kept it until now.

It was exactly as she said it would be. It was like kissing a corpse, and my heart hurt with the horror of the act.

But things were a jumble in my head.

I was terrified of Hartley, but he'd just saved me. Thoughts of him near me, holding me, woke me nightly from a dead sleep in a cold sweat. The only thing that kept memories of him away was sleeping with Ian, but Ian was gone more than he was around lately, which wasn't his fault, and I had to learn to live with that and not blame him, but....

Hartley was here. He was the dreaded *thing*. He was the monster in all my nightmares and was responsible for me getting no amount of meaningful sleep and my half-ass functioning zombie state, but... he was here.

The gun gave me my out. The gun said I had no choice but to comply with his wishes. I'd bury this feeling that I was going to show the psychopath only because he was really good at keeping secrets.

I cupped his face again, my warm breath puffing over his skin before I kissed him, hard, grinding my mouth over his, sucking on his tongue, giving him more of me in that moment than I ever had, showing him the dark places that I was normally so careful to hide.

I'd been abandoned my whole life, and trust came *so* hard. Lately I'd fooled myself that the guy on the outside, the happy-go-lucky guy, was me. I'd pulled the girls into my life in college on a fluke. Janet was first and I'd acted without thinking, and there she was, firmly planted in my life before I even realized the friendship had taken root. I'd changed, not so mercenary with my attention and affection until finally I realized it was love. Each of them I loved, but not romantically, never the drowning, devouring, soul-mate kind of love that was supposedly waiting for everyone on the planet that, combined with sex, was like heaven on earth.

Until Ian.

I could actually feel my heart beating sometimes when Ian walked with me. I could feel the reverberation of his footsteps inside me because he was mine, *my* love.

I'd thought if I was in love, everything else was easy and fixable and good.

The reality was that I needed Ian where I could see him. The idea of him was not enough, and instead of hiding from that, I had to face it head-on. It would hurt if we parted, but it was better than taking what I needed from a psychotic madman who would kill me if he could.

Wrenching away from Hartley, I wiped my mouth with the back of my hand, horrified and ashamed.

He took a step forward and I braced for a fight without thought.

"You're ravenous inside."

I was, and he saw it, felt it. There was no lying.

He licked his lips. "I've changed my mind."

I couldn't speak yet, too shaken, too guilty.

"I don't want to kill you."

I nodded.

"Hurt, yes; kill, no."

The sirens were wailing now, so close.

"Go," I whispered.

He lifted his hand, motioned at me with his fingers. "Come with me."

"We're not… you know we're not."

"It tasted like we were."

"Mistakes were made," I grimaced.

"Or not," he concluded. He gave me a sad smile before he turned and bolted out the back door, running out into the dark night, the rain swallowing him up like he was never there.

CHAPTER 18

I DIDN'T go to the hospital with Barrett. I went with Chickie because he needed me. The guy who tried to kill me had his own voice. My dog did not.

My phone rang as Dr. Alchureiqi came out of his surgery room, so I let it go to voice mail and stood to talk to him instead. "I'm so sorry to call you with an emergency on Thanksgiving eve."

"But this is the very definition of an emergency, is it not?"

I was too tired to think. "I just appreciate it so much."

"Of course," he replied, his voice gentle like it always was, even when he was criticizing me for not brushing Chickie's teeth or trimming his nails.

I girded myself for bad news. "So is he—"

"Mr. Wolf is resting comfortably at the moment, and I'm quite confident that he will make a full and speedy recovery."

I finally breathed. "And will he need a metal plate in his head?"

He squinted at me. "No, no. The bullet wedged in his skull, yes, but it was a simple extraction and we were able to remove it, mend the hairline fractures and smooth the edges easily. We've completed all necessary procedures."

"So he's all closed up and bandaged and stuff?"

"Yes."

"And he'll just wake up when the anesthesia wears off?"

"Precisely."

My knees were wobbly, so I sat back down hard.

"The tourniquet saved him from bleeding to death—that was very good of you—and Chickie is a powerful dog with a strong heart, so really, stop worrying. He'll recover well."

I nodded.

"You can see him first thing in the morning. He's sleeping now, and we'll be with him for the rest of the night and then tomorrow as well. You should go home and go to bed."

"Yeah."

"You look terrible," he added.

I grinned. "Thanks, Doc."

"No, I'm serious. I think you need a sedative too."

He wasn't wrong.

"And put on a shirt and coat, for goodness sakes. It's freezing outside."

I'D DRIVEN Chickie to the vet in my truck, laid him in the front seat with his head in my lap, so I had blood on my jeans. I didn't take the time to put on a shirt when I left the house, too caught up in the swarm of people there. They tried to argue with me about going to the hospital, wanting to take a statement, but I shouted about my dog and they made a hole for me to get through.

Of course, I'd stopped to kiss Hartley, so maybe Chickie wasn't such a priority for me if I wasn't concerned for him then.

But Hartley was a doctor, a real one, was one of the best in the United States before he got caught killing people, so when he told me Chickie would live, I believed him.

Yes, he needed to see the vet, but I wasn't scared until Dr. Alchureiqi was. When he saw Chickie, his face fell, and fear and remorse slammed into me. I'd held my breath, waiting, panicking in the hallway, terrified that Ian's werewolf would die after all.

But then he was okay and the adrenaline drained out of me all at once. Now, in the front seat of my truck with blood- and rain-soaked jeans, shivering, zapped of energy, I wasn't really sure what to do.

Leaning back in the seat, I finally answered my phone.

"Miro."

He never called me by my first name. "Eli," I sighed, using Kohn's. "How ya doin'?"

"Where the fuck are you?" he shouted.

"I'm outside the vet's," I murmured. "Where are you?"

"I'm at your place because the Feds alerted us when two of their agents didn't report in."

"Eamon Lochlyn killed them."

"I see. And how do you know that?"

"He told me."

"Okay."

"So you're at my house?"

"I am."

"Kowalski too?"

"Of course."

"Is Ian home yet?"

"No. I've been trying to call him, but he's not picking up."

"Okay."

"Your place is covered in bullets and blood, and the crime scene guys just pulled Hartley's prints from in here."

"Yeah, I know he was there. I just saw him."

"You saw him?"

"Well, we talked, yeah. He killed Lochlyn. He's got a new gun he's sort of loving."

"Miro!"

He was shrieking, which was weird. "What?"

"Miro!"

Again with my name. "Jesus, what?"

"Are you hurt?"

"No."

"You sound hurt."

"Huh."

"Miro?"

"I'm not hurt."

"Out of it, then."

"Maybe."

"No maybe about it."

"It's raining."

"Yes, it is. Are you in the rain?"

"No."

"Are you cold?"

"Yeah," I agreed fast.

"You might be in shock."

"From what?"

"Oh, I dunno? Your friend trying to kill you, Hartley, take your pick."

"That makes me sound kinda weak, huh?"

"*No.* You've been through more than most people I know."

"Really?"

"Do you know that most people don't get kidnapped in their lifetimes?"

"That's probably true."

"Where are you?"

"I told you, at the vet."

"Why?"

"Barrett shot my dog."

"He shot Chickie?"

"Didn't anybody at my house tell you that?"

"I just got here! Ryan and Dorsey went to the hospital because that's where we thought you were going to be."

"Oh." That made sense.

"Miro!"

"God, stop yelling," I groaned, lying down sideways across the seat. "Fuck, it's cold. I think I need a shirt."

"Why don't you have a shirt?"

"I had to use it to help save Barrett."

"And you forgot to put on another one?"

"Chickie had to go to the vet."

"Okay."

"I don't think the truck's on."

"Fuck," he moaned. "Tell me the address of the vet."

I told him, and then I hung up and closed my eyes. When my phone rang a few minutes later, I answered but didn't open them.

"Hey," he said softly, gently, just the sound of him utterly thrilling. I'd miss him when he was gone.

"Ian," I almost moaned.

"What'd you do, fall asleep?"

"No."

"You sound like you're in bed."

I exhaled. "We need to break up."

Silence. It went on for so long I almost drifted off.

"*What*?" He sounded angry and frantic.

I took a breath so I wouldn't need to take another for a bit. "I miss you too much, and I know it's shitty and needy and whiney and everything 'cause hundreds and thousands of people wait on soldiers every year, and they're so strong and awesome, and I'm weak. So weak. You deserve better. You deserve the kind of person who can be strong for years on end if need be, and that ain't me."

"Love—"

"And I don't just wantcha 'cause you keep the demons away, because I don't need you to do that anymore. I mean, if I can kiss Hartley, I think the fear factor is kinda gone, right?"

"I'm not—I don't—*what?*"

"And you were jealous of Barrett, but you shouldn't have been, because he was never my friend. He was in love with Kerry Lochlyn, and his brother Eamon—Kerry's brother—he was the one who killed the other guys on your team. He's dead now, though. Eamon. And Barrett's in the hospital. So you don't have to worry anymore, and you should tell the other guys so they can leave Fort Bragg."

"*What?*" he asked breathlessly.

"Call Kohn. I gotta take a quick nap," I said and hung up because I really needed the rest.

The rain bouncing off the truck's roof was soothing, and I tried to imagine my life without Ian. It would be hard to stay in Chicago, and maybe this was a signal to move. Ian could get the Greystone and Drake and Cabot, and now Josue too. I wondered if he'd let me have Chickie. I couldn't lose everything all at once. It would be too much.

I was having a dream that I was fishing with an alarm clock, which made no sense until I woke up enough to answer my phone.

"Miro."

"You have the best-sounding voice," I told him. "Has anybody ever told you that?"

"Yeah, you. All the time," Ian assured me, and it occurred to me he was breathing strangely, fast, and I could hear the crackling in his tone.

"So Barrett shot Chickie, but Hartley saved me, and he had a gun and I kissed him, and when I was kissing him, I thought—Ian would be pissed 'cause if you kissed anybody else, I'd fuckin' kill you, and then I thought that's sorta hypocritical of me since I went all needy on Hartley, and even though that was bad, I realized that I'm not being fair to you. I'm lying and saying that it's okay that you're gone, but it's not. I'd rather be by myself than miss you all the time, and if I kiss anybody else, then I won't have to feel guilty about it."

"You're at the vet, you said?"

"Are you listening to me?"

"Every word, yes."

"It's not fair of me to ask you to change," I said, opening my eyes and watching the rain pelt my window. "And it's not fair of you to ask me to need you less."

"Neither of those is fair, I agree."

"I'll sell the Greystone and give you half."

"Just wait."

"We gotta clean it though, since there's blood in the kitchen right now."

"We'll clean it."

"Chickie tried to save me."

"But he got hurt and you got hurt, and Craig Hartley had to save you both from a man who wanted to kill me."

"Yeah, that's true," I said, my eyes fluttering shut. "How funny."

"Miro—"

"I didn't get hurt," I corrected.

"Oh, I think you did."

"I'll never be clean again, you know."

"What?"

"I kissed Hartley. I'll never get that off."

He hung up then, which was a little rude since we were breaking up and everything, but I understood. Maybe it wasn't that important to him.

When my phone rang again, I answered.

"Miro, honey, is the heater on in the truck?"

Ian calling me honey made me sigh like an ingenue in a really bad movie on the Lifetime channel. "What?"

"The truck. Is the heater on in the truck?"

"Nuh-uh."

"Could you turn it on for me?"

"But the truck's not on."

"Miro—"

"I'm so sorry, Ian." I gulped down a sob. "You deserve someone who—"

"Shut up!" he yelled. "You're the one who deserves fuckin' better, but fuck you, M, that ain't gonna happen! You're stuck with me, and that's it, that's the end of it, do you understand? Do you get it? You don't get to make a decision alone. Neither do I. We're in this together, and we're staying together. Period."

"I can't," I said hoarsely. "I break when you go."

"So do I, you stupid shit!"

He did? "You do?"

"Fuck, Miro, yes."

"Then why do you go?" I asked, trying not to sound as forlorn as I felt.

"Because I think I had an idea in my head about being a man and what a man does and how a man is, and because I'm with you, I felt like I had to do even more, be even more."

"You didn't want anyone to think that being with me made you soft."

"Yes," he rasped.

"But that's really stupid. Being gay, or bi, or whatever doesn't make you weak."

"Yes, I know."

"Then?"

"It's one thing to know it and one thing to think it about yourself sometimes."

"Yeah, I get that." I did. Logically you knew things but it didn't always help, and it didn't always translate to the real world.

"Not only do I leave the man I love when I go, but I leave my work partner, too, and you get hurt when I go because there's no one here to watch your back."

"That's not true," I said in deference to my friends. "The guys watch out for me just like they would for you."

"But you're not a priority for anyone but me."

"'Cause you love me," I whispered, wanting him so bad that my skin ached with the need. "Right? Ian? You love me?"

"I've never loved anyone more. Ever."

My breath hitched. "I'm sorry I kissed Hartley."

"I forgive you since he had a gun."

"Yeah, but it wasn't just the threat of death."

"No, it could be the loneliness and gratitude, and probably a healthy dose of shock."

"Shock?"

"Barrett shot Chickie. He told you he was going to kill you, right?"

"Yeah."

"Didn't expect that, didja?"

"No," I said, my teeth chattering.

"Oh God, love, please turn on the truck and get the heater going."

"I will."

"Never mind, I'll do it. I see you."

"What?" But I understood when there was pounding on the window and I checked and found Ian standing in the pouring rain.

"Open the door!" he yelled, but it was muffled through glass and sheets of water.

Sitting up, I unlocked and shoved over quickly so he didn't drown.

He immediately snatched the keys from me and started the truck. Once hot air was blowing through the cab, he turned to me. "So even though the timing is shitty because you're completely out of it right now, I'm still going to tell you that I made the decision to go ahead and leave the military."

I was hallucinating.

"Miro?"

"I think I might be in a coma or something."

"I assure you you're not."

"I'm in shock."

"That I will agree with."

"You're really quitting?"

"Yes."

"Why?"

"Because it doesn't make sense anymore," he said flatly.

"What do you mean?"

"It used to be right for me—it's who I was—but now I'm more invested here, at home, with you."

I was afraid to let his words sink into me because they were exactly what I'd been hoping for and really, seemed too good to be true.

"I think if I wasn't a marshal that I'd have trouble walking away from the military because the service—military or law enforcement—defines me."

It did, I would agree. Ian was the guy who volunteered to put his life second to someone else, for someone else, because it was how he was made, how his heart was made. "It's because you're a good man, Ian Doyle."

He shook his head. I knew there were things he'd done in his life that he knew were the opposite of good, and those haunted him. "I'm not leaving the military because I think I can't be an asset to them anymore, I'm leaving because I think I can do better things here with you, at home, being a marshal, and being your partner both at work and at home."

I shivered because his words were exciting and scary at the same time.

"You're a big part of the reason that I'm going to retire, but you're not all of it, and I'd think that would be comforting in a way."

It was. The decision wasn't all on me, then. It wasn't just because of me. His own thinking had changed as well, and I couldn't ask for better.

"I truly believe that I can do more good here instead of halfway around the world."

I wanted to take him at his word and start his life, but that wasn't fair. It wasn't what he would do if the shoe was on the other foot. "Are you sure?"

"I'm sure."

"Yeah, but—"

"I thought this was what you wanted."

"It is. You know it is."

"Then be happy."

"Not if you're sad. Not if you'll be missing who you are. I'd rather us break up than have that happen."

He took my face in his hands. "I'm not sad. I get to stay home with you now, and believe me, that's exciting."

"I want you to be sure."

"Oh, I am. I know you're the adventure."

"No, that's not what I—"

He laughed and then tried to ease me forward to kiss me.

I pulled back, away, or tried to, but he tightened his hold so I couldn't move.

"The hell are you doing?"

The tears were not a surprise. "I have to go home and brush my teeth and shower and be dipped in lye or something. I'm covered in filth."

"You're covered in our dog's blood and Barrett's, who tried to kill you and who you still saved, but more than anything, you're still you and you still love me, right?"

I couldn't even see him through the tears.

"It's a mess, all of it, but you need to kiss me now to remind yourself what kissing and being kissed by the man who loves you feels like."

"How can you even want to?"

"Don't be an idiot," he scolded softly. "You belong one place, and that's with me."

I took a stuttering breath.

"Isn't that right?"

"Yes," I husked.

"Then don't pull away from me, not *ever*."

I exhaled the shame and fear as Ian leaned me forward and kissed me. And it was probably my imagination, but the way he took, the kiss felt different. It was possessive and languorous, like he had all the time in the world.

"Ian?"

"I'm really, truly home now. You're never getting rid of me."

"Swear."

"Oh, I do, trust me. You promised to marry me, remember?"

I had to close my eyes with the swell of emotions that rolled through me. "Yes."

"We should do that very soon."

I was overwrought. That was the only reason for the tears that came hot and blurring.

"Come on, gimme 'nother kiss. Let's seal the deal."

I had to take him at his word and jump with him, so I kissed him with every bit of hope and happiness and trust that was in me.

He was home and he was staying. It was officially the best Thanksgiving ever.

"And now we're going to the hospital to check you out," he announced as soon as our lips parted.

"What? No. I'm fine, I swear to God. I was out of it, probably still am, but I just need sleep. Lots and lots of sleep, and lots and lots of sex," I begged him. "Please, Ian, it's a waste of time. I wasn't the one hurt, I swear."

He studied me for a second and then nodded and passed me his phone. "Call Kohn. Tell him we're coming home, and tell him to get the crime scene—otherwise known as our kitchen—released right fuckin' now."

I groaned as I put on my seat belt and we flew away from the curb. "Those guys are federal. They're never going to—you're just gonna leave the Cabriolet there?" I asked, noticing the car parked a few spaces down from where we were.

"Yeah, maybe we'll get lucky and it'll get stolen."

I had to smile. Fucking Ian. "That's not nice."

"Cabriolet or an ancient Dodge, the hell," he grumbled.

"But as I was saying, federal crime scenes can take days to process."

"Normally, yeah, but you're a witness and Barrett's a witness—and by the way, you don't get to pick out your own friends anymore," he mandated with a look that dared me to say a word.

"Yeah, okay."

He grunted.

"But so you're thinking, because I'm a witness and can say what happened, and Barrett's story will probably corroborate most of mine—"

"He might change motivation in his version, but blood spatter and bullets, fingerprints, and everything else will tell the tale."

"Kohn won't be able to rush them. A good crime scene investigator will never be rushed. They can hold the scene for as long as they want."

"Yeah, but they've got direct evidence in this instance. They have you."

I groaned. "I will be explaining what happened for days. I'll be lucky if I'm out of interrogation to even eat anything tomorrow, let alone play host."

"We have a lot of people to help us. Anything can happen. Have a little faith."

I could do anything now. Ian was staying home.

CHAPTER 19

THERE WAS good news and bad news, and the good was that my kitchen, as crime scenes went, was pretty cut-and-dried.

All the bullets Hartley fired were in Lochlyn, aside from the one that blew out Barrett's knee. He didn't fire any others, and all the blood in the kitchen belonged to either Lochlyn or Barrett. The Walther in my sink had only been fired once in the house, and that bullet was with Chickie at the vet and would be collected from there.

All the blood by the bookcase was Chickie's.

I thought the federal forensics team would take a hundred times longer than the regular police, but the exact opposite was true. They had double the personnel, were hyperefficient, and took enough pictures to recreate the entire room in single photos, if abstract art was their goal. As it was, the sheer number of people processing the room put them at done in record time.

By the time Ian and I got home, they had been there for three hours already. I would have thought I'd lost time, but as Ian reminded me, Chickie had been in surgery for a while and I'd been sick with worry, so the time sped by.

"Where's Aruna and Janet and—"

"They're all at home. She and Liam took Janet with them."

"Okay."

"Let's get you a T-shirt and sweater and some tea, all right?"

I nodded and Kohn bolted over and hugged me like he never did, full body, all up in my space, and squeezing tight.

"Jones," Kowalski said as he joined us. "I already called a service to get this place cleaned up, they should be here in an hour and—"

I eased out of Kohn's hold, and he grabbed Ian next. "How did you manage that? Tomorrow's Thanksgiving?"

"Tomorrow's in like an hour already, but anybody works whenever as long as you pay them," he reminded me.

"It'll cost a mint."

"Do you care?"

I didn't, actually. "Thanks, Jer."

"My pleasure," he said, smiling at me, which was a new and different experience. "And now the fun starts," he groused as in through the front door the suits walked.

The FBI was leading the investigation, but CPD was there, too, along with Kage—which was nice, that he would come when he was technically off for the holiday, but it was also technically his job—the OPR guy again, McAllister, who was there to listen to what I said and prepare a statement and was also a lawyer and could advise Kage, if needed. Everyone looked crisp and polished, which was impressive for them all coming though the rain and the lateness of the hour the night before a holiday. Kage looked especially good in a navy-checked suit, a black cotton long-sleeved shirt, and monk strap shoes I was fairly sure were Ralph Lauren. He was dressed to go out.

"Were you on a date?" I asked him, ballsier than normal because of the night I was having. Big highs and horrific lows.

He did a slow pan to me. "I was, yes."

"Sorry."

"People trying to kill my marshals take precedence over my love life, Jones, but I warn you now—there had better be no shenanigans tomorrow. Do you understand?"

"It's not—this is not my fault."

His dismissive grunt told me that maybe he didn't so much believe me.

We all sat down in our living room: me, Ian, Kohn, Kowalski, Kage, McAllister, the parade of suits, and Special Agent Tilden Adair, who turned on his phone to record me. He asked me to please explain, as carefully as possible, what had transpired.

"First, I'm so sorry about your agents. Eamon Lochlyn said he killed them both. I hope they didn't suffer."

"Thank you, and no, it doesn't appear that they did. We were surprised that Hartley wasn't the one who killed them."

"No, it was Lochlyn. Did he shoot them?"

"They were both shot, yes."

"With the Walther?"

"The bullets would seem to be a match, yes, but we're still waiting on ballistics to confirm."

"Okay."

"What gun was Hartley carrying?"

So I explained about the fancy Desert Eagle and why he shot Lochlyn, and how Barrett startled him, which was how he got shot. Then I started over, and I left nothing out. I made them all squirm a bit—except Ian and Kage, and, interestingly enough, Adair—as I recounted kissing Hartley, at gunpoint, and how he wanted to hurt me and fuck me in equal measure. I included why and for what reason Lochlyn had decided on his revenge killings and why Barrett Van Allen assisted him.

"Hartley saved your life," Adair commented, and I realized I'd never actually met anyone with jet-black hair and matching eyes before. He was a very striking man, though "handsome" might not be the word I'd choose.

"Yes, he did."

"My understanding was that Hartley wanted to kill you in Phoenix."

"Yeah, but he doesn't want to be rushed when he does it. He wants to kill me on his timetable, no one else's."

Adair nodded. "Are you in fear for your life, marshal?"

"Not anymore."

"Do you think that if Lochlyn and Van Allen had not killed the agents, that they would have, in fact, been killed?"

"No."

"And what leads you to that supposition?"

"Hartley thinks everything out. He never just *does* anything. The agents would have fired on Hartley as soon as they saw him, but they didn't do that with Lochlyn or Van Allen, which is probably the reason they were killed. They let them get too close because they didn't realize Lochlyn and Van Allen posed a significant threat."

He nodded. "I would agree. They were both highly trained. They just didn't expect to be blindsided."

"No, how could they have."

The question-and-answer session lasted a couple of hours, and I was surprised Adair allowed the crime-scene cleaning team to come in while he was still talking to me until I realized they were all wearing noise-cancelling headphones like tarmac workers at the airport. Kowalski, who had foresight most people didn't give him credit for, apprised them of the possibility and they'd come prepared.

"We will keep your name out of the news, of course, but I'm sure that there will be reporters who put events together."

"We can deal with that, Agent," McAllister assured him. "We take care of our own."

"Special Agent," Adair corrected him.

"Chief Deputy," Kage said, and since clearly he had the biggest dick in the room, everyone else shut up. "Is that all, Special Agent?"

"For now, yes."

Why it took another half an hour for the Feds to go, I had no idea, but when they finally left, McAllister whirled around and said he would personally contact CPD and have uniformed officers there, watching the house round the clock going forward.

I shook my head. "If Hartley wants me, he's gonna get me. But I have to be honest and say that I really do think he's going to go to Paris like he said he was and be some underground sensation there."

"He said he'd have a following?"

"No, he'd think that was pretentious. But I think he's got other plans at the moment that don't include me, if they ever do again."

"Why would you think that?"

"I just… our dynamic just changed. And I'm not saying that we're friends, because that would be insane… but he said it himself. He doesn't want to kill me anymore. Hurt, yes—if he got the chance—but kill, no. So now I'm not like a prop he can move around anymore. He would have to talk to me in a way that wouldn't include coercion. It's a problem he has to work out, and it'll take him a while—maybe even forever—to solve."

"So if I'm hearing you correctly, you believe that he'll stay clear of you until he figures out a way to get you to go with him willingly."

"Yes, exactly."

"I'm not sure that you're qualified to make this call, marshal."

"Sadly, no one knows Hartley better than me," I told him. "So please, don't waste people here I don't need."

He looked to Kage for help.

"I agree with McAllister," Kage said, which was surprising. "Every night there will be men stationed outside this house, but we'll do that internally. I've already contacted Judicial Security, and the assistant director promised me protective personnel starting Monday."

"And from now until then?" McAllister wanted to know.

"Marshal Jones is on house arrest and he'll be checked in on every four hours, and as you know, he lives with Marshal Doyle, and as an ex-Green Beret, he's more than qualified to provide protection."

"Ex?" I whispered.

"Lives with?" McAllister asked.

Ian grinned smugly. "Yeah. We're getting married."

It took several moments, and I was worried for a few of them because McAllister looked so stricken, I thought he was going to either burst into tears or let loose a volley of hateful words. But neither happened. He smiled instead. Huge, wide, which was a surprise because I didn't think he did that.

"I didn't know, but that's wonderful. Congratulations."

"Yes," Kage said, getting up, which signaled McAllister and the other four lawyers—who Kage hadn't introduced—to get up as well. I'd found out that if he didn't like you, he didn't tell anyone your name. So clearly he found them bothersome and was showing his disdain. It also meant, whoever they were, that they were up there on the food chain. Kage never treated any underling poorly; it wasn't his way to take out irritation on the messenger.

"You're a PR dream, Marshal Jones."

"I'm just a marshal on Sam Kage's team, sir."

He nodded. "I must say that after meeting Marshals Becker and Ching, then you, that I suspect the chief deputy of building quite the team."

"As fun as this is…." Kage griped before grabbing my bicep and walking me with him to the front door. He opened it and looked out at the rain a moment before directing my gaze to the porch. "You step one foot out here before Monday morning when you come to work, and I will strip you of your investigator status and loan you, permanently, to Finance or Management Support or"—and I knew before he even said it, because yeah, he was evil like that—"Asset Forfeiture."

I shivered.

"Either way, I'd have to find Doyle a new partner, just like I was going to have to find a new one for you."

"For me, sir?"

"He was deployed too often. I would have had to replace him as your partner. I would have kept him on the team, but you need someone here. That's the whole purpose of a partner."

I cleared my throat because I had a horrible sinking feeling. "Is that what you talked to him in your office about yesterday, sir?" Ian being my partner was most of what I loved about my job. Without him there, at my side, the best part of my day would be gone. I couldn't even imagine what that loss would be like.

"No," he said, almost irritably. "I wanted to talk to him about the Lochlyn investigation, but since he couldn't tell me much, we weren't in there long. And of course I brought him up to date on the Cochran situation, in case there was any retaliation from other cops Cochran knows. Turns out I shouldn't have bothered."

"Yeah, nobody likes him."

"Nobody likes him, that's right."

"Sir, why didn't you tell Ian—Doyle—about Hartley?"

"Because I assumed you already would have. I won't ever make assumptions where you're concerned again, Jones."

For some reason that gave me a warm feeling, and I might even have bumped him with my shoulder, but he chose that moment to threaten me again.

"Not one step outside this house, Jones, unless the house is on fire, and I mean heavily engulfed in flames, so much so that your friend Aruna's husband the lieutenant has to come and put it out."

"How do you know Aruna, sir?"

"We met at the hospital after you were shot protecting Nina Tolliver. I met them both."

And he remembered. "Yessir."

"Not one, Jones," he said, flipping up his collar and dashing down the steps.

As no one followed him immediately, I turned around, and the other four people were clustered a few feet away.

"Did you need to talk to me?"

"No," one of the men told me. "We were just waiting for your insufferable boss to be on his way."

"Scary boss," another man amended. "I think 'scary' is what you meant to say."

The first guy tipped his head like, *maybe*.

Once they were gone, Ian shut the door, locked it, kissed me, and then told me to get upstairs to take a shower.

"Yeah, Jones, you stink," Kowalski said as he pulled some of the curry Aruna had made out of the refrigerator.

As I headed for the stairs, I realized the cleaning crew had done an amazing job and that they too were gone.

"When did they leave?" I asked Kohn.

He shot me a look.

"What?"

"They say that the power of observation is one of the first things to go when someone is overly tired."

"What?"

He turned to Kowalski. "I know I'm speaking English."

Kohn groaned before focusing on me. "Listen, you really do need to take a shower and go to bed. We'll be down here with Doyle, so don't worry."

But I wasn't worried about Hartley. "Do you think anyone will want to still come over with the threat of Prince Charming here?" I asked, using the name the media had coined for Hartley when he was first discovered to be a killer.

"I already called my mother, and she's really worried about you. She's making you some of her special matzoh ball soup to bring with us. And she can't wait to tell all her friends that she's spending time in a house where Craig Hartley was."

"Great."

"He's big news; you gotta be ready to have people all over you again like they were when you and Cochran first brought him in."

"I hope everyone else will still want to come to dinner."

"I don't think you have to worry."

I DIDN'T have to worry.

From what I could tell and hear when I woke up, the house was already full. I wanted to go downstairs and say hi, but when I got out of the shower, I was dizzy, and Ian made me lie down again right away. It had been dark when I first fell asleep, and it was overcast when I woke up, and then, of course, because it was Chicago, it snowed. I actually loved being inside on snowy days, and since I could see it falling outside the windows and accumulating on the skylight Ian and I had installed sort of off-center above the bed, it was nice, soothing, and I passed out.

When I woke up again, Ian said it was early afternoon. Kohn brought his mother upstairs, and when I smiled at her, she walked over in her big, fluffy mink coat and hugged me and petted me and told me what a good boy I was. A chair was brought for her so she could sit and watch me eat the soup while we talked.

It was nice. I liked mothers. I was crazy about Janet's before she'd passed away, liked Ryan's since she made me my own peach pie and sent it with him, and of course, loved Aruna, who had always mothered me.

I got sleepy again after the soup but woke up when Ian told me he'd been to the vet to see Chickie. He was still doped up, but Dr. Alchureiqi— who met Ian there to give him an update, having left several of his minions to babysit all the patients—said he looked really good and that he could come home the following morning, on Friday.

"That's great news," I whispered, smiling up at him.

He bent and kissed me once, then again, and finally stretched himself out on top of me and kissed me long and deep. I wrapped my arms around his neck so he couldn't move.

"I love you so much, and thank you for retiring and planning to marry me, and I just don't want you to have any regrets, okay? Not any."

"No," he whispered, kissing along my jaw. "No, baby, no regrets."

Man… "honey" and "baby" added to "love." I was really crazy about the new, solid, confident Ian Doyle I had in my arms. His demeanor, everything was different. Like he felt good in his skin, not worried about what anyone else thought, just grounded and secure. He'd decided who he was going to be, and the happiness was simply rolling off him.

"You look so good."

"Well, I feel good," he rumbled before he kissed me again.

I managed to roll him to his back right before Aruna and Janet came up the stairs.

"And people wonder how gay porn could be hot."

"Who wonders if gay porn is hot?" Janet asked her seriously.

Ian got up—to much whining from all of us—and explained to the girls that we were not there to entertain them and told me he'd be back.

They got in bed with me, on each side, and we cuddled as I promised I was fine, just exhausted. I really wanted to go downstairs as soon as I could stand and not get dizzy. I could sit up, but that was as far as I could get.

Ned showed up around three, came pounding up the stairs like a pissed-off rooster, found me propped up on pillows talking to Liam, and got on the bed and hugged me.

"You're in bed with him," Liam remarked as he himself was sitting in the chair that had come up with Kohn's mother and never moved.

"I'm a man confident in his own heterosexuality," Ned told him. "And besides, it's really comfy, and I had a long flight."

We ended up taking a nap together as Liam kept vigil while watching a football game on my iPad.

Margo Cochran, Norris's wife, whom I hadn't seen since he and I stopped being partners, came over about four and brought me her special carrot cake that I'd always loved. It was my favorite, not too sweet, moist, and the frosting was thin on the top.

"Why?" I asked as I sat up in bed and looked at her. Becker's wife, Olivia, had taken it from her when she came upstairs. Olivia was there thanking me for backing up Becker the night of the traffic stop, and I said of course; he was my brother. We were hugging when Margo was allowed up by Aruna, who had made herself guardian of the stairs.

"Because if you hadn't made Nor pay for what he did to you, he would've been home, and my kids would have no father and me no husband."

I nodded because there was no doubt in my mind. Hartley had stopped first for Cochran, to end things with him.

"We're moving to Boston when he gets back. I didn't give him no choice."

It wouldn't matter. If Hartley wanted Cochran, he'd get him eventually. But I would put money on the fact that with Hartley changing his mind about killing me, his desire to gut Cochran might also have fallen by the wayside.

"So, uhm, can I…." She lifted her arms in question.

"Yeah, come on, let's go."

She dived onto the bed and hugged the hell out of me.

"Oh, he looks like a good hugger," Olivia commented and she was next—after passing the carrot cake back to Margo—which was how Becker found us a few minutes later.

"I'm not even gonna ask," he sighed, and then pointed at the baking dish Margo was back in possession of. "Is that carrot?"

She beamed up at him. "It is."

"Carrot's my favorite."

"Well, let me cut you a piece." She sighed, turning for the stairs. "Come with me."

"I think another woman tempted your husband away with food," I informed Olivia as I watched them go.

"They all do try, but I have a secret weapon."

"Which is?"

She arched a sinful eyebrow for me.

"No, no, no, don't tell me."

Her cackle was just the right amount of evil and fun.

Ian led his father and stepmother up the stairs to the loft sometime around six. She took a seat in the chair and Colin stood next to his son. It was awkward, but they talked about Chickie and what a good dog he was, and then about Lorcan and when his trial was and how much they'd love it if Ian and I could come for a Sunday dinner sometime soon. Ian promised that we would, without committing to a specific date, and then led them back downstairs so they could eat. He was back a few minutes later.

"Are you okay?" I asked.

"Yes, baby, I'm good," he promised, bending down to kiss me before disappearing again.

Cabot, Drake, and Josue had been there for hours, apparently, helping Aruna—Cabot was her favorite—serving food, washing dishes, and in Josue's case, reading tarot cards in the laundry room, where he was laying the cards out on top of the dryer. They were finally allowed upstairs to see me, and of course all three of them flopped down on the bed, never mind the chair sitting right there.

Josue put his hand on my head. "You don't have a fever. Do you feel all right?"

"I'm okay," I yawned. "I'm just wiped out."

He nodded. "Well, you never sleep, and you don't take care of yourself at all. I could move in here and do that for you."

"That's me," Ian said as he came up the stairs with an enormous plate of food for me and a huge glass of apple juice. "I take care of him."

"But you're never home," Cabot said, looking sheepish. "I mean, shouldn't we start taking care of Miro since—"

"I'll be home all the time now. I'm done with the Army, so you'll see a lot more of me."

He was baffled, I could tell from his squint, when they all clapped, even Josue.

"Oh, I'm so glad," Drake sighed. "I mean, if I missed you a little, I can only imagine how tore up Miro was."

Ian nodded and sent them all downstairs. Josue stopped at the top and looked back at me.

"What?"

He bit his bottom lip. "I met a guy at the record store in Oak Park, where I'll be working. His name's Marcello McKenna. Isn't that awesome?"

"It is. You think he might be special?"

"Miro, he was looking at me all weird, and he finally said that he'd dreamed about me coming into the store."

"And?"

"He blurted out that he didn't believe in any woo-woo stuff."

"But?"

"But he dreamed about me."

I nodded. "Maybe just be his friend before you hit him with the whole you-saw-him-in-your-cards thing, huh?"

He nodded, bolted back to me, bent and kissed my cheek, and then pounded down the stairs, announcing to Aruna that he was ready to read her cards.

When I turned to Ian, he was chuckling.

"What?"

"You have the strangest effect on people."

His on me was sort of self-explanatory. "Would you please put the plate down, take off all your clothes, and let me have you under the covers?"

"Oh, baby, it's gonna be days before you see me naked again. White brought his Xbox over with him, and Sharpe is doing laundry. It's gonna be an endless loop of guys through here until Sunday night."

I groaned. "His Xbox? Do you know how annoying he is with all those shooter games?"

"As if he can beat me."

"Oh no. Please don't go into hypercompetitive mode."

"What?" he balked. "I am so not competitive."

"Do me a favor and go stand on the other side of the room so the bolt of lightning doesn't hit me too."

He scoffed. "I'm sure God has better things to do."

Perhaps.

"What?"

I couldn't stop staring at him.

"Speak."

"You just got here. I want to kiss you and hug you and fuck you and…. Jesus, Ian, I need you so bad."

He leaned in and kissed my cheek. "Here, have a little nosh. You'll feel better."

"Don't you care at all?"

"Yes, baby, and don't you worry, you can have me any time you want from now on."

I perked up.

"After Sunday."

It was going to be the longest three days of my life.

ARUNA BROUGHT me pumpkin pie with a mound of Cool Whip on it, and I wondered what she was doing there since she loved hosting and it made no sense that she wasn't.

"Liam's mother is downstairs," she said quickly, flipping through Netflix to find something she wanted to watch.

"And?"

"And nothing. I'm staying up here with you."

I cleared my throat.

"What?" she said without turning.

"Hey."

"I don't want to talk about it."

"She hurt your feelings," I said, because I knew my friend and knew it had.

"Well, we both know I'm a lot of things, but a diva is not one of them. I know what she said and I know what she meant. She honestly didn't think I could cook anything traditional, and that's why she wanted to help me."

"Sure," I agreed. "But she's down there, right?"

"Yes."

"So she came."

She rolled her head on the pillow so she could look at me. "Your point?"

I shrugged. "She made an effort and she's eating your food now, right?"

"Begrudgingly, I'm sure."

I raised my eyes to the sky.

"We both know she never liked me."

"Oh, gimme a break," I muttered, bumping her with my elbow. "That woman adores you. Liam was wild and took way too many chances before you came along. But because he fell so hard, he grew up, and now that he's a husband and a dad, he's ridiculously grounded."

She huffed out a breath.

"You don't think she knows that?"

She made her eyes flutter like I was giving her fits.

"Just go down there and be the bigger person."

"And if I don't want to?"

"But you do want to, 'cause you actually really like her too."

She waited another moment, but she got up, kissed me on the forehead, and left to go confront her mother-in-law.

Feeling better, I got out of bed and went to change out of the pajama bottoms and T-shirt I'd had on all day. My plan was to go downstairs, but once I was in jeans and a heather gray sweater, I lost steam. I was sitting on the bed debating socks when Ian appeared at the top of the stairs.

"What're you doing?"

"Gearing up to be sociable," I said, chuckling.

He walked over to the bed and sat down beside me. "It's breaking up soon, anyway. Just gonna be us and the guys."

I sighed. "Not that I'm not thankful, but everybody's not coming up here to say good-bye, are they?"

"No," he murmured, leaning sideways to nuzzle my cheek before he planted a kiss there.

I made a noise he must have liked because he slipped a hand around the side of my neck and turned my head with gentle pressure from his thumb on my jaw. When I was staring at him, he leaned in and kissed me.

I wanted to soak up every drop of his attention, so happy with him, with his choices, with how things could be now that he'd really given us a chance. I could feel my stomach that had been in knots for so long finally begin to unclench as I parted my lips and let him in.

I felt it, instantly, the spike of raw pleasure driving to my core, heating me from the inside out, filling me with the familiar need to have his naked skin all over mine.

"Ian," I panted, driving him down under me on the bed. "Take off your clothes."

"Oh, I would love to," he said, threading his fingers through my hair and pushing it back from my face. "But like I said before, it ain't happening until Monday."

I grunted and sat up, straddling his thighs, content to sit there and look at him beneath me, all beautiful and mine.

"I'll make you a deal."

"I'm listening."

"You get all rested, and next month we'll go somewhere, just us."

"A vacation?" I said drolly. "You're saying you'll take me on a vacation."

"Yeah."

"How?"

"We both have a crapton of time saved up."

"Yeah, but—" And then it hit me, that I *had* him, he wasn't leaving me anymore because he was, in fact, leaving the Army instead.

I took a quick breath.

"You'll get used to it."

"What's that?" I said, trying to keep it together. It wasn't every day your whole life started. The overwhelming feeling of joy was swelling inside my chest and it was hard not to scream or cry or just lose it all over the man I loved.

"Me being around."

I coughed. "I'm good with it now."

He laughed softly at me, hands on my thighs, squeezing tight.

"So, a vacation?" I rasped.

"Yeah. Wherever you want."

I nodded. "I'm holding you to it."

"Good."

I rolled off him and lay down close, still touching. "So tell me, how does it feel to be ex-Special Forces?"

He was quiet for a few seconds. "I'm not really sure yet. It's so new. Not even official yet."

"Yeah, but—"

"I wanna tell you," he insisted, "I do. But it's just an us thing, no one else."

"Okay."

He got to his side to face me and trailed his fingers along my jaw. "I mean it. I want to talk to you and bore you with every little detail, but there are way too many people here, and once I get started, I won't want to stop, much like when we're screwing."

I laughed. "That's so romantic."

His smile was arrogant. "I knew you'd think so."

"Ian—"

"I know you wanna know everything, M, and I promise to tell you."

"It's important."

"I know," he agreed, tracing over my eyebrow with his thumb.

"Will you at least tell me why the inquiry into Lochlyn ended so abruptly?"

"There was nothing new for them to find out from the past. Clearly Lochlyn was unstable, and that was pretty evident from all the reports. Keeping us there was not gonna shed any new light on anything, so they let us go."

I was very thankful. "I missed you more than normal the last time."

"Me too. I felt the times between me going getting shorter and shorter, and when leaving makes you physically ill—something's gotta give."

His words were guaranteed to make my heart stop.

"You know it's gonna be different for us."

"What's that?"

"Me being around all the time," he explained as he pushed my hair out of my face again. "I know guys who got divorced after they quit 'cause they drove their wives nuts."

I slid a hand over his chest. "Yeah, you don't hafta worry about that."

"You sure?" he teased.

"Yeah, baby, I'm sure," I sighed, and then I took a breath. "So can I ask how long it takes for your retirement to go into effect?"

His lazy smile accompanied a rumbling sigh.

"What?"

"You said that like you weren't dying for my answer."

I growled at him. "Just tell me."

"Well," he began, his voice velvet and deep as he slid his fingers into the hair at the back of my neck, cupping my head, "it'll take about nine months to a year to process my packet once I drop it."

"Drop it?"

"Turn it in," he clarified, easing me forward into a kiss of blatant ownership, languid and insistent at the same time.

I needed to know things, had to, but this—him treating me like I was utterly his, I just wanted more.

My shiver made him smile and ease back.

"No—"

"So once I turn in the packet," he said, which silenced my pleading, "I won't be sent out on missions anymore."

My breath caught. "You won't?"

He shook his head. "I'll just have to do my one weekend a month drills and two weeks AT in the summer."

I knew what that was, annual training, so I didn't have to ask. "Will they have to schedule that ahead of time or can they just call you up and make you do that whenever?"

"They schedule it," he assured me, leaning in to kiss me again, just a quick one, before he continued. "There's no more of the no-notice missions for weeks or months on end, and they aren't allowed to transfer me, either."

It was too good to be true, and when I saw the slight furrow of brows, I tensed. "What?"

He squinted at me. "One thing that could happen is that my CO, or someone else, could ask me to withdraw my packet because they really need me and can't find a replacement."

I kept the fear out of my voice, but it still cracked just a little when I spoke. "Would you do that? Withdraw your packet?"

"If it meant the difference between men living or dying," he said softly, "what would you want me to do?"

"That's not fair."

"Who told you life was fair?"

I nodded.

He folded me into his arms and tucked my face into the crook of his neck. "I'm really not worried about that possibility, M."

"Okay," I said, trying to be supportive when all I wanted to do was tie him to the bed.

"I promise you."

"You promise what?"

"That I'll get out. I will."

I'd been holding my breath for a long time; it was only for a bit longer. I could wait it out. I could. I would. He was worth everything.

"You trust me?"

"Of course," I said honestly and then realized I had things to say as well. "So...we should talk about Hartley, right?"

"Later," he whispered. "We've got time now."

I closed my eyes and relaxed against him.

"We should make the vacation a honeymoon."

It took me a second and then I popped my head up in time to see his wild, wicked grin. "I'm sorry, what?"

He was laughing at me, and it only got louder when I shoved him to his back and climbed on top of him.

"Ian?"

"You heard me," he said, still chuckling.

I took hold of his hands, keeping them over his head, pinned to the bed. "Could you maybe elaborate?"

"Why, yes, Miro," he baited, rolling his hips provocatively under me. "We should go to a justice of the peace next week, get married, and go on a honeymoon. Doesn't that sound good?"

It sounded *perfect*, and I would have told him so if every bit of air had not rushed from my body and my heart had not stopped beating.

"Love?" he said quickly, and I saw the playfulness leach from his face, replaced instantly with worry.

"Yes?" I answered with a voice that sounded like crushed leaves,

"You *do* still wanna marry me?"

"I do," I managed to get out with a trembling breath. "More than anything."

He exhaled sharply. "Jesus, you made my heart stop for a second."

I knew the feeling.

His flashing grin was back fast. "So, yeah, next week?"

"Next week," I echoed, feeling the happiness bubbling up to the surface.

"You're all mine now."

I had always been his, from the moment we met.

"Gimme kiss."

Like he ever needed to ask.

MARY CALMES lives in Lexington, Kentucky, with her husband and two children and loves all the seasons except summer. She graduated from the University of the Pacific in Stockton, California, with a bachelor's degree in English literature. Due to the fact that it is English lit and not English grammar, do not ask her to point out a clause for you, as it will so not happen. She loves writing, becoming immersed in the process, and believes without question in happily ever afters, and writes those for each and every one of her characters.

ALL KINDS
OF TIED DOWN

Mary Calmes

Marshals: Book One

Deputy US Marshal Miro Jones has a reputation for being calm and collected under fire. These traits serve him well with his hotshot partner, Ian Doyle, the kind of guy who can start a fight in an empty room. In the past three years of their life-and-death job, they've gone from strangers to professional coworkers to devoted teammates and best friends. Miro's cultivated blind faith in the man who has his back… faith and something more.

As a marshal and a soldier, Ian's expected to lead. But the power and control that brings Ian success and fulfillment in the field isn't working anywhere else. Ian's always resisted all kinds of tied down, but having no home—and no one to come home to—is slowly eating him up inside. Over time, Ian has grudgingly accepted that going anywhere without his partner simply doesn't work. Now Miro just has to convince him that getting tangled up in heartstrings isn't being tied down at all.

www.dreamspinnerpress.com

FIT TO BE TIED

Mary Calmes

Marshals: Book Two

Deputy US Marshals Miro Jones and Ian Doyle are now partners on *and* off the job: Miro's calm professionalism provides an ideal balance to Ian's passion and quick temper. In a job where one misstep can be the difference between life and death, trust means everything. But every relationship has growing pains, and sometimes Miro stews about where he stands with his fiery lover. Could the heartstrings that so recently tied them together be in danger of unraveling?

Those new bonds are constantly challenged by family intrusions, well-intentioned friends, their personal insecurities, and their dangerous careers—including a trial by fire when an old case of Miro's comes back to haunt them. It might just be enough to make Ian rethink his decision to let himself be tied down, and Miro can only hope the links they've forged will be strong enough to hold.

www.dreamspinnerpress.com

LAY IT
DOWN

Mary Calmes

Paradise can be hell.

Most people would say being stranded in the villa of Spanish shipping magnate Miguel García Arquero on the beautiful isle of Ibiza wasn't such a bad deal. But Hudson Barber isn't one of them. To him, being stuck without a passport in a foreign country far from home is a nightmare, made worse by the fact that the person who did the stranding was his flighty twin brother.

Unwilling to turn Dalvon in for identity theft, Hudson is forced to wait, but meanwhile he discovers the chance to rehabilitate Miguel's failing local businesses—enterprises left to Dalvon's inexperienced care. The flagging ventures are a badly wrapped gift from heaven, and if Hudson can turn them around, he might be able to leverage the experience to finish his MBA.

Then Miguel returns to Ibiza, and instead of finding a boy toy, he discovers Hudson has turned his cold villa into a warm, welcoming home. Miguel's path is clear: convince Hudson to lay down his defenses and let love in.

www.dreamspinnerpress.com

ROMANUS
Mary Calmes

Stopping to offer help one sultry summer night, Mason James is unprepared for the change that this simple act of kindness will bring. After giving an old man a ride home, Mason discovers a new, magical, and even dangerous world he cannot hope to understand. But he also finds Luc Toussaint and is intoxicated at first sight… and even the secret Luc protects won't be enough to keep Mason away from the truth of his heritage and their love.

www.dreamspinnerpress.com

SLEEPING 'TIL SUNRISE

Mary Calmes

MANGROVE
Stories

Mangrove Stories

Everyone in Mangrove, Florida, knows Fire Chief Essien Dodd is a saint. He took care of his ex-wife until she died, is raising his teenage daughter alone, and is the kind of man who pulls kittens from trees. All in all, the man's a catch. But Roark Hammond has sworn off getting involved with a man who's been hurt before because he can't guarantee he won't hurt his prospective love again. If only he could get Essien out of his mind long enough to focus on anyone, or anything, else.

Strong emotions are in play. Essien is lonely but determined to focus on Ivy; Ivy wants her father to have a new life so much that, to his horror, she's trying to find him a man; and Roark is so scared of the present and past, he won't allow himself to commit. To have any chance of sleeping 'til sunrise and greeting each new day together, Essien and Roark will have to rethink how they're living their lives and focus on what's most important.

www.dreamspinnerpress.com